I0592200

Elias Nasan

The Life and Public Services of Henry Wilson, Late Vice-President of the United States

Elias Nasan

The Life and Public Services of Henry Wilson, Late Vice-President of the United States

ISBN/EAN: 9783337402860

Printed in Europe, USA, Canada, Australia, Japan

Cover: Foto ©Raphael Reischuk / pixelio.de

More available books at **www.hansebooks.com**

THE

LIFE AND PUBLIC SERVICES

OF

HENRY WILSON,

LATE VICE-PRESIDENT OF THE UNITED STATES.

BY

Rev. ELIAS NASON,

AUTHOR OF "LIFE OF CHARLES SUMNER," "GAZETTEER OF MASSA-
CHUSETTS," ETC., ETC.

AND

Hon. THOMAS RUSSELL,

LATE COLLECTOR PORT OF BOSTON.

"I have striven ever to be true to my country in peace and war; to maintain the cause of equal, impartial, and universal liberty; to maintain a
policy that tended to enlighten our countrymen, lift burdens from the toiling
millions, and make our country what we wish it should be, — a grand democratic republic, the admiration of all the world." HENRY WILSON.

BOSTON:

PUBLISHED BY B. B. RUSSELL, 55 CORNHILL.

PHILADELPHIA: QUAKER CITY PUBLISHING HOUSE.
SAN FRANCISCO: A. L. BANCROFT.
PORTLAND: JOHN RUSSELL.

1876.

Entered according to Act of Congress, in the year 1875,

BY B. B. RUSSELL,

In the Office of the Librarian of Congress at Washington.

Boston :
Rand, Avery, & Co., Stereotypers and Printers.

TO

THE WORKING-MEN OF AMERICA

This

LIFE OF A WORKING-MAN

IS

RESPECTFULLY DEDICATED.

PREFACE.

A STATESMAN eminent for patriotism and integrity is a national instructor. The record of his life, his services, and his opinions, is, to some extent, an exposition of the spirit and progress of the people whom he represents; and the people have the right to claim it, not only as a memorial of the past, but as an inspiration for the present, and a light for times to come.

Pre-eminently may this be asserted in regard to the distinguished man whose biography we now purpose to write.

Holding himself steady to his noble purposes, he was so prominent an actor in the remarkable events of the last twenty years, he was so identified with the life of the republic, that an account of his official career becomes, in some respects, the key to the history of the country for that period; while in the development of the principles of freedom which he made, in the consistent life he led, and in the counsel he imparted, we have our hopes in the permanency of popular government brightened, and our steps directed as we rise to national strength and grandeur.

1*

In making a register of his life, the authors have had access to original sources of information, and have availed themselves of every aid within their reach for the verification of their statements as to matters of fact. They have endeavored to present opinions frankly and fairly, and to render this biography as complete as the allotted time and space would permit.

If this book, in spite of any errors, tends to do justice to the character and course of one of the representative men of the present times, to give dignity to labor, to inspire working-men with confidence in themselves, and stronger love for our country, the end for which it is written will be attained.

CONTENTS.

7

CHAPTER VIII.

CHAPTER IX.

CHAPTER X.

CHAPTER XI.

CHAPTER XII.

CHAPTER XVII.

CHAPTER XVIII.

CHAPTER XIX.

LIFE OF HENRY WILSON.

CHAPTER I.

INTRODUCTION. — MR. WILSON'S FAMILY, BIRTH, BOYHOOD, APPRENTICESHIP, AND EDUCATION.

The Colbaths. — Farmington People in 1812. — Mr. Winthrop Colbath and Wife. — Introduction of Son to Mrs. Guy's School. — School-Books of those Days. — Change of Residence. — Visit to Mrs. Eastman. — Testament. — Hard Times in the Family. — Young Colbath goes to live with Mr. William Knights. — His Labors on the Farm. — Kindness of Mrs. Eastman. — Young Colbath's Love of Books. — His Reading. — Faithfulness to his Employer. — His Frugality. — Freedom. — Compensation. — Change of Name. — Character. — Search for Labor. — Resolves to go to Natick and become a Shoemaker.

ONE of the essential benefits of liberal institutions is the opportunity afforded by them for developing the mental energies of the masses of the population. Freedom is the fostering mother of the intellect and intelligence of the entire people.

The voice of civil liberty, like that of Christianity, is, "Ho! every one that thirsteth, come ye to the waters; and he that hath no money; and whosoever will, let him come." Hence America is the best country in the world for men to make themselves.

"Sometimes," remarked an intelligent Japanese, "we express our feelings in Japan: opinions we have none."

Here we entertain opinions ; we express them freely ; and, through the clashing of opinions, make advancement. Our destiny is placed in our own hands ; and every man is rated, as he ought to be, according to his worth. There is the goal, the prize : the track is clear, and the best champion wins.

Thus from the bosom of the people came up Washington, Jackson, Clay, and Lincoln ; and thus arose the legislator whose career we now attempt to trace.

Henry Wilson is the son of Winthrop and Abigail Colbath ; and was born in Farmington, N.H., on the sixteenth day of February, 1812. His father was the son of Winthrop Colbath ; and was born in that town on the seventh day of April, 1787 ; and died in Natick, Mass., on the tenth day of February, 1860. His mother was born on the twenty-first day of March, 1785 ; and died on the eighth day of August, 1866. They rest side by side in the cemetery at Natick, where the son has erected marble headstones to their memory.

The Colbath family, originally, as supposed, from Argyleshire in Scotland, emigrated to the north of Ireland in the troublesome times of James the First ; thence to America, and settled at Newington, N.H., early in the eighteenth century.

At the time of Mr. Wilson's birth, his parents were living in a small cottage on the right bank of the Cocheco River, about one mile south of the " Dock," as the village of Farmington was then called. The site of the cottage is on a gentle eminence commanding a pleasant prospect of the river and surrounding country.

Farmington, which is in Strafford County, and about thirty-five miles north-east from Concord, and seventeen north-west from Dover, contained, at this period, about twelve hundred inhabitants; and they were mostly engaged in agricultural pursuits. They earned their livelihood by the sweat of the brow. They had but slender educational advantages; and their style of speech, of dress, of building, and of life in general, was plain and unpretending. They generally spun and wove their own garments from wool of their own raising. They stored their barns with hay in summer, their cellars with apples and cider in the autumn. They spent the long winter evenings around the ample fireplace in shelling corn, making brooms, cracking nuts, singing songs, and telling stories of the times gone by.

Mr. Winthrop Colbath was a poor day-laborer, engaged for many years in running a saw-mill on the river below his house. He was rather tall, good-looking, agile, brave, and quick at repartee. His wife was handsome, fond of reading, sensible, and industrious. Her eyes were very keen and piercing. For his father and mother Mr. Wilson ever entertained and cherished the most affectionate and kind regard.

Like other indigent and hard-working people of New England, Mr. Wilson's parents saw the value of the public school, and early introduced their bright-eyed son to the tuition of Mistress Guy, who quickly taught him how to read and spell, from Perry's "Spelling-Book" and "The Primer," in the old wooden schoolhouse.

He was a studious and obedient pupil, improving well the opportunities he had for learning in his boyhood.

The school-books at that time in Farmington were Welch's and Adams's "Arithmetics," "The English Reader," "The American Preceptor," and "The Columbian Orator." Over these this boy spent many an hour in the long seats of the unpainted district schoolhouse;

and whatever entered his retentive memory remained as in a vice, — fixed and unchangeable.

When he was about seven years old, his father built a small house in front of an old grove of pines, just where the Cocheco River makes a beautiful bend to the right, and to this place removed his little family. Nothing now remains to indicate the spot except the cellar, and some peach and cherry trees growing in the enclosure.

When he was eight years old (1820), a little incident took place which had some influence upon his future course of life. Mrs. Anstress (Woodbury) Eastman, wife of the Hon. Nehemiah Eastman, and sister of the Hon. Levi Woodbury, seeing him pass her house, called him to her, gave him some clothes of which he was in need, and inquired if he knew how to read. " Yes, pretty well," he answered her. " Come, then, and see me at my house to-morrow," she replied with kindness. Early the next morning he presented himself before the lady ; when she said to him, " I had intended to give a Testament to some good boy that would be likely to make a proper use of it. You tell me you can read : now take this book, and let me hear you." He read a chapter in the Testament. " Now carry the book home with you," said she, " read it entirely through, and you shall have it."

Gladly he accepted the condition ; for a book he had never owned, and to him it was a golden treasure. He hurried home to read it. After seven days he called again at Mrs. Eastman's house, and said to her that he had read the book from beginning to end.

" It cannot be ! " said Mrs. Eastman with surprise. " But let me try you." So, calling him to her side, she carefully examined him till she was fully satisfied that he had read the Testament entirely through, and fairly won the prize he coveted.

Mr. Wilson has publicly declared that the reading of this Testament, which he still keeps, together with the subsequent examination, was the starting-point in his intellectual life.

The times, especially for the working-men, were very gloomy at this period. The war with England had impoverished the country. Money was scarce ; wages were low. Want and sickness entered the Colbath family. Three of the little children died, and were buried in the field opposite the house. In reference to these days of trial, Mr. Wilson once, in public, said, " I was born in poverty : Want sat by my cradle. I know what it is to ask a mother for bread when she has none to give."

So, in his reply to Mr. Hammond, who had characterized working-men as " the mud-sills of society," he thus touchingly alluded to these early days of trial : —

" Poverty cast her dark and chilling shadow over the home of my childhood, and Want was there sometimes an unbidden guest. At the age of ten years, to aid him who gave me being in keeping the gaunt spectre from the hearth of the mother who bore me, I left the home of my boyhood, and went to earn my bread by ' daily labor.' "

This active boy, nurtured in adversity, had a vigorous constitution : above all, he had an inspiration ; and a boy with an inspiration is far better than a boy with a great fortune.

In the summer of 1822 he was bound by indenture to a hard-working farmer of the neighborhood to serve him on his farm until the age of twenty-one. By the terms of the indenture, he was to have one month's schooling in the winter, food and raiment, with six sheep and a yoke of oxen to be delivered to him at the expiration of his time of service. He went to live with Mr. Knight upon the

2*

seventh day of August, being then a little more than ten years old, and began at once the hard work of the farm. As he increased in age, his toil became more steady and severe. In summer he swung the scythe, or handled the sickle, till the evening stars appeared: in winter he cut timber in the forest.

But while thus laboring uncomplainingly, and developing by incessant toil his physical system, he was also turning every moment he could save from house and farm work to the improvement of his mind. He read with intense avidity whatever books came in his way; and he remembered what he read.

"I believe," says Walter Scott, "one reason why such numerous instances of erudition occur among the lower ranks is, that, with the same powers of mind, the poor student is limited to a narrow circle for indulging his passion for books, and must necessarily make himself master of the few he possesses ere he can acquire more."

This poor boy had, at first, no books except his Testament and the text-books of the district school. He read them over and over again, committed many parts of them to memory, and longed for more. Mrs. Eastman, as a kind of guardian angel, still watched over him. She noticed his regard for books: she kindly made selections for him from her husband's library, and lent him volume after volume. This was a godsend to him. Every moment he could now steal from toil was spent in reading. This was his pastime and his recreation. Some of the happiest moments of his life were spent in running, when work was over, to the dwelling of his benefactress for another book. By the light of the kitchen-fire — for he had no money to purchase oil — he went through volume after volume; sometimes reading on, unconscious of the flight of time, until the morning broke. In this way he perused the leading works of the British and American statesmen and historians, the fascinating pages of Irving, Cooper, and Scott, all the then published numbers of " The North-American Review," and many other current publications of the day.

Judge Whitehouse of Farmington also lent him many books, and directed him in his course of reading. It was fortunate that he met with such intelligent guides, and that the best works in English and American literature thus fell into his hands; for it is the quality rather than the quantity of the material received into the mind that yields valuable increase.

So industriously had this hard-working boy availed himself of these means of culture, that, at the expiration of his time of service (February, 1833), he had read, and then held in mind, nearly a thousand volumes of history, biography, philosophy, and general literature. Thus he bore away from that hard farm more solid information, and a heart better prepared to toil and to achieve, than many bear away with the diploma from the university.

To the interests of his employer he was ever faithful. His eye was quick, his judgment clear; his health was good; his habits were correct; and hence his services were valuable.

On closing them he received the promised compensation, — six sheep and a yoke of oxen, all of which he sold immediately for the sum of eighty-four dollars cash. So poor had he been up to this period, that he had never possessed two dollars; and a single dollar would cover every penny he had ever spent.

Having now arrived at the age of twenty-one, he, by an act of the legislature, had his name changed from Jeremiah

Jones Colbath to Henry Wilson. This was done by the advice of the family he had lived with, and with the approval of his parents.

The question now before Mr. Wilson was, " How shall I obtain a livelihood, and assist my father and his family ? " He set himself at once to seek employment ; and the struggles which it cost him to obtain it will forever keep alive his sympathies for the working-people.

He hired himself for several months in Farmington ; but the compensation was so trivial, that he soon resolved to leave his native town, and find work elsewhere. He packed up his clothes and visited several places, seeking for it, but in vain. He himself shall tell the story. Addressing the citizens of Great Falls last February, he said, —

" I know what it is to travel weary miles, and ask my fellow-men to give me leave to toil. I remember, that, in 1833, I walked into your village from my native town, and went through your mills, seeking employment. If anybody had offered me eight or nine dollars a month, I should have accepted it gladly. I went down to Salmon Falls, I went to Dover, I went to Newmarket, and tried to get work, without success ; and I returned home weary, but not discouraged, and put my pack on my back, walked to the town where I now live, and learned a mechanic's trade. I know the hard lot that toiling men have to endure in this world ; and every pulsation of my heart, every conviction of my judgment, puts me on the side of the toiling men of my country, — ay, of all countries. I am glad the working-men in Europe are getting discontented and want better wages. I thank God that a man in the United States to-day can earn from three to four dollars in ten hours' work easier than he could, forty years ago, earn one dollar, working from twelve to fifteen hours. The first month I worked after I was twenty-one years of age, I went into the woods, drove team, cut mill-logs, rose in the morning before daylight, and worked hard until after dark at night; and I received for it the magnificent sum of six dollars! — and, when I got the money, those dollars looked as large to me as the moon looks to-night."

Unsuccessful in obtaining employment in New Hampshire, Mr. Wilson finally determined to seek his fortune in the State of Massachusetts. He had heard of the prices paid for making shoes in the enterprising town of Natick: hence he resolved to go there, and to try a new vocation. He had learned to endure hardship without murmuring. His hand and eye were well trained; his head was clear; his heart was honest; his store of knowledge large; he had a sound mind in a sound body. His purpose was to work: what, then, could be expected of him but success?

CHAPTER II.

IN December, 1833, Mr. Wilson packed up his slender
wardrobe, bade his friends farewell, and set out on
foot for the town of Natick. He had but little money in
his pocket; and he resolved to make the journey with as
little expense as possible. On the first day he travelled as
far as Durham, where he obtained lodging with a farmer; the
next night he reached Salisbury, on the Merrimack River;
and in the morning following visited Newburyport, where, to
ease his blistered feet, he purchased for twenty-five cents a
pair of slippers, in which he more comfortably pursued his
way. Arriving at night at Saugus, he found entertainment in

22

a private family ; and his waking dreams were of the famous
city of Boston, which he was to see, for the first time, on
the morrow.   The two points of special interest to him
were Bunker Hill, whose story had so often thrilled his
imagination ; and the office of "The North-American
Review," which had sent forth so many learned articles to
instruct him, and to lighten the burden of his toil at
Farmington.

Rising early, and paying twenty-five cents for his lodging, he recommenced his journey, and in a few hours stood
upon the celebrated spot where Warren fell.   His quick
eye swept over the whole scene ; his imagination pictured
forth the first grand action on behalf of freedom in America.   It was to him an inspiration.

On leaving this memorable spot, he inquired the way to
the office of "The North-American Review," which he
found to be at 141 Washington Street, and something less
than he anticipated.   "Can so much good," thought he,
"come out of Nazareth ?" and so, having seen what he
considered worthy of consideration in the city, he inquired
the way to Natick.   Some one misdirected him, and sent
him by a *détour* of several miles, through the town of
Dedham.   On arriving about midnight at his point of
destination, he stopped at the old tavern on the turn-
pike in the western part of the village, and found, on examining his exchequer, that he had spent just a dollar
and five cents in travelling the whole distance of about a
hundred miles from Farmington to Natick.   Such Spartan-
like endurance and economy were no mean elements in
the training of the future statesman.

Natick, which in the Nipmuck language signifies "a
place of hills," is seventeen miles south-west of Boston,
and, as the name would indicate, has its full share of

scenic beauty. From the summits of Fiske and Pegan Hills the eye enjoys enchanting prospects, sweeping from Fiske Hill over the waters of Cochituate Lake and the handsome buildings of the village; while from Pegan it follows the meanderings of Charles River through the valleys of Needham and of Dedham, and rests upon the distant spires of Boston and the monument on Bunker Hill.

In passing through the southern section of the town, Washington once remarked, " Nature seems to have been lavish of her beauties here." It was at the point where the celebrated John Eliot had an Indian church, and taught, beneath the shade of an outspreading oak, the principles of the gospel to the aborigines.

At the time of Mr. Wilson's arrival, the town contained about a thousand people, mostly farmers; and at the central village there was a Congregational church, of which the Rev. Erasmus D. Moore, who became an earnest friend and counsellor of Mr. Wilson, was the pastor. There was then no lawyer in the place, nor any need of one. There was but little culture, enterprise, or aspiration. Less than eight hundred dollars annually were appropriated to the support of public schools; and the buildings in which they were taught were rude and comfortless.

But that branch of industry for which this town has since become so celebrated had already gained a foothold here. A few enterprising men had begun to manufacture shoes, yet on a very limited scale and capital, for the Southern market. Division of labor, machinery, and those various arts and appliances which render this business at the present day so lucrative, had found no entrance into the workshop.

Then, instead of working on a single part, each work-

man made the entire shoe. It was called a "brogan,"
and was sold by wholesale at the rate of about a dollar
per pair.   The process of making was slow; the teaming
to Boston was expensive; and hence the business was not
specially remunerative nor inviting.   Mr. Wilson was,
however, glad to find employment.   Any thing was better
than the exhausting drudgery of the farm he left, which
afforded him very little leisure either for recreation of
the body, or cultivation of the mind.   He hired himself
at once to Mr. William P. Legro, who agreed, for the
consideration of five months' labor, to teach him the art
of making shoes.   With his knife and hammer he set
to work with several laborers in a little shop in the
western part of the town to learn his trade; but, ere
many days had passed, perceived that he had bargained
away his time incautiously; and therefore he agreed
with his employer, for the consideration of the sum of
fifteen dollars, to release him from his obligation.   At
the end of seven weeks, he began working for himself.
Anxious to obtain money for an education, he now applied
himself to shoemaking with unflinching assiduity.   The
very first day after leaving Mr. Legro, he made eight
pairs of shoes; and very soon outsped the fastest workman in rapidity of execution, making sometimes two
shoes to his one.   He used to labor sixteen hours a
day; and "not unfrequently," says one of his companions, "he worked all night and two days in succession
without sleep."

   "He is a very good young man; we like him much,"
said Mrs. William Perry, with whom he boarded: "but he
keeps us all awake by his continual pounding through the
night."

   Once he determined to make fifty pairs of shoes without

taking any sleep. This usually required the labor of a week; but his hand and eye, as we have said, are quick, and therefore he attempted this surprising feat. Forty-seven pairs and a half he actually made without reposing; when he found, in spite of his resistance, sleep at length would overpower him in the interim between the raising and striking of the hammer on the shoe in hand; and so, reluctantly, he yielded to its influence.

There is something touching in this scene, — the youth, smitten " by the wild delight of knowing," sunk in sleep over that last shoe. Was it not an earnest of that indomitable energy he has since exhibited in the halls of Congress?

On the 19th of April, 1835, Mr. Wilson heard for the first time the eloquence of Edward Everett in his masterly oration on the battle of Lexington, and was inspired by it with fresh ardor to obtain an education : he also went on foot to Boston to hear Daniel Webster on the presentation of the vase at the Odeon, and listened with admiration to the voice of that distinguished statesman. His aspirations were awakened; but what hopes had he — an unknown, friendless shoemaker — any right to entertain? He returned to his hard toil, to think and to work on even to the very limit of his power.

In the summer of 1835 the Boston and Worcester Railroad was opened through the central village of Natick. The coming of the locomotive engine gradually broke up the old modes of thinking and of manufacturing. It brought in life, light, enterprise. New firms were soon established, new buildings erected, and new societies organized Among these was one, which, although limited as to the number of its members, had, nevertheless, a lasting influence over the intellectual character of the community.

It bore the name of "The Natick Debating Society." It was formed in the winter of 1835, and originally had but thirteen members. Prominent among these were Henry Wilson, Alexander W. Thayer (now United-States consul at Trieste), George M. Herring, J. B. Mann, Dr. James Whitney, and Willard A. Wight. The design of the association was to discuss, either in speaking or in writing, the current literary, scientific, or political questions of the day. The meetings were held in the old schoolhouse in the village, generally once, and sometimes twice, a week. They were continued until 1840, when the society was merged in the Natick Lyceum.

To this little assembly of disputants Mr. Wilson resorted when the arduous toils of the day were ended; and here he engaged most heartily in discussing the various questions of the times, especially that of slavery, which was then, through mobs, and acts of violence, to some extent, receiving the attention of the public. Here, in this debating society, he learned to "think upon his feet;" to arrange his thoughts in logical order; to detect and expose the sophistry of an opponent; to settle questions by solid argument based on fact instead of theory. Here he acquired skill in parliamentary practice, and in a measure qualified himself for a seat in the deliberative assemblies of the state and nation. This debating club was his political training-field: in it he went through the drill for coming conflict; to it he owes, in some degree, that cleverness and that steadiness in debate for which he is distinguished. His associates were not unfrequently surprised to see him exhibit such familiarity with the history of his country; and although he trembled when he spoke, and sometimes deviated from the principles of Lindley Murray's Grammar, they felt and said that he had power to command the attention of his fellow-men on a broader field, and to render signal service to his state and nation.

On one evening he had spoken but indifferently on a certain question, and incurred the ridicule of his opponents. This aroused him; and, rising again, he broke into a strain of eloquence which electrified his hearers. They proposed that the question should be taken up again at the next meeting; and he then discussed it in a style so masterly, that his opponents ever afterwards made their attacks with more consideration, and admitted that " the fire and the force " to do great things were slumbering in his soul.

As to himself, so to the other members, this society proved to be of signal service. Almost every person who belonged to it has attained distinction in his chosen sphere of life, and now exercises healthful influence over the destinies of his fellow-men. Some have been senators; some have written useful books; some adorn the liberal professions: all are intelligent, honorable, and progressive men. May not this debating club be cited as an example deserving the attention of the working-people of our country?

On coming to live at Natick, Mr. Wilson felt at once the need of books. There were no libraries in the place like those he left at Farmington, whereby he might gratify his appetite for reading; and he had not the means to purchase what he wanted.

There was, however, an old town-library of about two hundred volumes, then in the keeping of Deacon William Coolidge, a man of great simplicity of manner, heart, and doctrine. His wife was of the same spirit, pious, kind, obliging. Of the old Puritanic style of people they were models; rigorous in opinion, yet indulgent in respect to those who disagreed with them, and ever ready to encourage such as had an aspiration for improvement. In order, then, to gain access to the books in this old library, and to enjoy the society of these good people, Mr. Wilson prevailed on them to receive him as a boarder in their family. Here he found generous sympathy, wise religious counsel, and a happy home. With them he attended church and social meetings; by them he was treated as a son. Amongst his firmest friends at this period Mr. Wilson doubtless reckons Deacon William Coolidge and the Rev. E. D. Moore, who ever took the liveliest interest in his welfare; who clearly saw, that, though he was the son of toil, he was the son of genius also; and, by kind advice, encouraged him to bring out the manhood of his nature.

By his incessant labor in the workshop, supplemented by his literary toil at night, Mr. Wilson's health became so much impaired, that it seemed to him imperative that he should take some relaxation. The laws of health were not well understood by him, and he had continued working on unseasonably, until his strength gave out, his color fled, and hemorrhage of the lungs commenced. He had laid by several hundred dollars, with which he hoped to acquire such an education as would enable him to enter on the practice of the law. But, his health continuing to decline, his medical adviser recommended, that, before commencing on his studies, he should make a journey to the South. He therefore, in the month of May, 1836, set out for Washington. The changing scenes, the rest from toil, the thought that he was soon to look upon the Capitol and the lawmakers of the nation, was the very medicine which he needed.

Passing through Maryland, he for the first time saw slaves of both sexes toiling half-naked in the fields, and expressed his opinion to a gentleman in the cars that slavery was an evil. The gentleman replied to him with some severity, that " he could not be permitted to express such sentiments in the State of Maryland."

The thought was startling, that, in a land of freedom, his own tongue was fettered as was the bondman's body.

On arriving at Washington, May 15, he entered the Capitol, listened to the stormy debates in Congress, and saw the petitions of the philanthropic men and women of the country against the traffic in human flesh and sinews laid upon the table. He saw Mr. Pinckney's infamous resolution against the right of petition forced through the House of Representatives under the pressure of the previous question, and Mr. Calhoun's Incendiary Publication Bill pass one of its stages in the Senate by the casting vote of Mr. Van Buren, the vice-president. He saw the subserviency of Northern politicians to the domination of the South. He grasped at once the commanding question of America. Mr. Wilson remained at Washington until about the middle of June, boarding on Capitol Hill, and sitting at table with Senator Morris of Ohio, who fearlessly opposed the advocates of human servitude.

He visited Williams's notorious slave-pen on the corner of Seventh and B Streets; he saw the poor people sold, manacled, separated, and marched away to toil and suffering beneath the whip of unfeeling taskmasters at the South. His sympathies for the bondmen, his indignation against the cruel system of human traffic carried on hard by the Capitol of a nation boastful of its freedom, were re-awakened, so that he then and there determined, that, come weal or woe, the powers which God had given him should thenceforth be devoted to the destruction of an institution so revolting to every instinct of humanity, so inconsistent with the declaration of our national independence, and so antagonistic to the whole teaching and spirit of the gospel.

This is the key to Mr. Wilson's political career; and by it his public acts must be interpreted. To this principle of human freedom, deeply embedded in his heart and running through every fibre of his intellectual character, he has held, through all the political changes in the state and nation, with unflinching steadiness: so that, as one has truly said, " He floated into power upon the wave of principle; while others timorously declined to take that wave, and now lie strewn as wrecks along the barren strands of compromise and expediency."

Alluding to this memorable visit to Washington, the scenes then witnessed, and the resolution formed, Mr. Wilson, in an address at Philadelphia, 1863, observes, —

" I saw slavery beneath the shadow of the flag that waved over the Capitol. I saw the slave-pen, and men, women, and children herded for the markets of the far South; and at the table at which sat Senator Morris of Ohio, then the only avowed champion of freedom in the Senate of the United States, I expressed my abhorrence of slavery and the slave-traffic in the capital of this democratic and Christian republic. I was promptly told that ' Senator Morris might be protected in speaking against slavery in the Senate; but that I would not be protected in uttering such sentiments.' I left the capital of my country with the unalterable resolution to give all that I had, and all that I hoped to have, of power, to the cause of emancipation in America; and I have tried to make that resolution a living faith from that day to this [applause]. My political associates from that hour to the present have always been guided by my opposition to slavery in every form, and they always will be so guided.   In twenty years of political life I may have committed errors of judgment; but I have ever striven ' to write my name,' in the words of William Leggett, ' in ineffaceable letters on the abolition record.' Standing here to night in the presence of veteran anti-slavery men, I can say in all the sincerity of conviction, that I would rather have it written upon the humble stone that shall mark the spot where I shall repose when life's labors are done, ' He did what he could to break the fetters of the slave,' than to have it recorded that he filled the highest stations of honor in the gift of his countrymen."

On returning home from Washington, Mr. Wilson, hav-ing then about seven hundred dollars in cash, went to Strafford in New Hampshire, and, on the first day of July, began upon a course of study in the academy at that place, then under the tuition of Mr. Dickey.   He was induced to go to Strafford because it was near his early home, and also because one of his early friends, W. W. Roberts, a young man of remarkable ability, was then a student there.   These two scholars were of congenial tastes and aspirations ; and the death of Mr. Roberts in his first year at Dartmouth College was an event of which Mr. Wilson speaks to this day with sorrow and regret.

In delightful sympathy with this fine scholar, Mr. Wilson made the most of his time and privileges at this academy, pursuing such a course of study as would enable him to engage in teaching school in the coming winter.   At the close of the scholastic term, he, at the public exhibition, spoke in the affirmative on the question, " Ought slavery to be abolished in the District of Columbia ? "

It demanded courage in New England even then to ex-press such views on slavery as he was known to entertain.

To be called an abolitionist was a reproach which few could bear. The antislavery student met the question boldly, presenting cogent arguments for the immediate emancipation of the bondmen at the seat of government.

" That man," said some of the good people who then heard the speaker, " will make a minister."

It is remarkable that he himself, after a struggle of a quarter of a century, should have introduced the measure into Congress which realized the aspirations he expressed in his first effort on the stage of the academy, in the first public speech he ever made. In February, 1872, it so happened that Mr. Wilson addressed the citizens of Strafford assembled on the very same spot where he made his maiden speech in 1836; and some were present who remembered it, and congratulated him on the fruition of his hopes.

Anxious to avail himself of the instruction of Miss Eastman, daughter of his benefactress at Farmington, Mr. Wilson entered, in the autumn, the academy at Wolfsborough, on Winnipiseogee Lake ; and, pursuing his studies here one term with unabated zeal, he engaged and taught in the winter one of the district schools in that delightful town. The schoolhouse was situated on Mink Brook, and was about a mile and a half from the village. This term of teaching served to bring his literary acquisitions into practice, and to fix the rudiments of learning indelibly in memory. His leisure moments were devoted to the prosecution of his studies. The Rev. Thomas P. Beach, afterwards imprisoned at Newburyport for disturbing a religious meeting, was of signal service to him while a resident of this town. In the spring following (1837), Mr. Wilson commenced study at the academy in Concord, then under charge of the Rev. T. P. D. Stone, a gentleman of

ability, who had given much attention to the art of elocu-
tion. Here Mr. Wilson's principal recitations were in
Euclid's "Geometry," Newman's "Rhetoric," "Mental
Philosophy," Butler's "Analogy," and "The Geography
of the Heavens." These and kindred branches he pursued with the same untiring assiduity he had manifested
in the workshop when toiling for money for his education.
Study with him meant business; and, with his quick per-
ceptions and retentive memory, he soon left his fellow-
students far behind. His special forte was extemporane-
ous speaking and debate; and here he found in Mr. Stone
an excellent instructor. When in debate, he seemed to
hold the whole history of the country in his memory; and
woe to his opponent who had not power to wield the same
effective weapon!

The principles advocated in "The Liberator" were now
slowly gaining favor with the young men of New Hampshire, and a State antislavery convention was held by
them this year at Concord. Mr. Wilson was chosen a
delegate to this body; and here he made an earnest and
able speech on behalf of human freedom, characterizing
slavery as an infraction of the laws of God and man, a
national dishonor, and an impediment to the peace and
progress of the people.

While pursuing his studies at Concord in the summer
term of 1837, a gentleman in Farmington, to whom he
had loaned the money he had earned by such incessant
toil at Natick for the expenses of an education, failed, and
left him penniless. This was a bitter disappointment
He must give up his cherished plans; the workshop must
again be his academy, and hard toil his teacher.

At this crisis in his affairs he found a sincere friend in
Mr. Samuel Avery of Wolfsborough, who kindly offered

to board him on credit just as long as he might wish to attend the academy in that town. Accepting his friend's proposal, he returned to the academy at Wolfsborough, where he spent the autumn of 1837, closing in with study just as if his final opportunity for it had come. At the expiration of the term he started once more for the town of Natick, and, on his arrival, had less money than when first he came to it on foot four years before. His integrity and ability had, however, gained him many friends; and he was at once appointed teacher of the centre district school for the ensuing winter. He taught successfully; for he had tact to govern, information to impart, and glowing words to render it acceptable. To inspire is to instruct; and this he could not fail to do. The meetings of the debating club he faithfully attended, and as faithfully employed the evenings not so spent in study. On finishing his school, and paying off his debts, he had twelve dollars left; and on this capital he began to manufacture shoes for the Southern market. In this business he continued steadily employed, except when public duties drew him away, for ten consecutive years. At first he occupied Mr. David Whitney's shop; but afterwards removed to one on Central Street, where his dwelling-house now stands.

During the ten years which cover Mr. Wilson's business-life, the town of Natick made remarkable advancement in respect to population, wealth, and enterprise. Division of labor, and machinery to some extent, were introduced into the manufactories, and goods of a better quality and finish were sent forth. In these improvements, as well as in the general prosperity of the village, Mr. Wilson took an active part. He attended the social gatherings of the people, identified himself with them in their joys and sorrows, and lent a helping hand, as well as word, to every scheme for the promotion of the public good.

As a business-man he was upright, courteous, fair, and manly, ever taking sides and sympathizing with the working-people. He paid his laborers promptly; he encouraged them with friendly words, and made them feel that they, as well as he himself, had rights to be respected. He had their confidence and esteem; for every one of them knew that Mr. Wilson would share with him his very last dollar before seeing him come to real want. In one year (1847) Mr. Wilson manufactured a hundred and twenty-two thousand pairs of shoes, employing a hundred and nine workmen; and the whole number of pairs of shoes made by him while engaged in business was six hundred and sixty-four thousand. In general, he sold these shoes to Southern dealers, who sometimes visited him at Natick to make their purchases. One of them once wrote to him, that, having failed in trade, he was unable to pay him more than fifty cents on a dollar. On looking over his creditor's assets, and seeing that they included several slaves that would be put into the market, the honest manufacturer immediately sent him word that he could not consistently take any money coming from the sale of his fellow-men; and thus, by his adherence to his principles, he lost seven or eight hundred dollars in this failure.

Generous and obliging to a fault, Mr. Wilson never stooped to questionable means for making money; nor was he, either by his taste or temperament, well adapted to the turns and tricks of trade. He had no wish, no faculty, to hoard up gold. He went into the shoe-business by necessity: his thought was running along another plane. His aspiration was to transact business on a broader scale; to grapple with questions that bore upon the vital interests of the working-men throughout the country. Hence he closed the manufacture of shoes without much gain or much regret, and entered on that broader sphere of action, for which Nature, by her liberal gifts, had evidently intended him.

CHAPTER III.

BY the dismissal of Rev. E. D. Moore from his pasto-
ral office at Natick, and by his consequent departure
from that town, Mr. Wilson lost the daily counsel and encouragement of a sincere and valuable friend, who sympathized with him in his political views, and had confidence
in his ultimate success. The kindest social relations still
subsist between these two gentlemen ; and it is doubtless
gratifying in a high degree to Mr. Wilson's earliest living
pastor to see his expectations in regard to one of his society
in Natick so fully realized.

88

The Rev. Samuel Hunt, an able minister and a steady advocate of human freedom, succeeded Mr. Moore in July, 1839, and continued as Mr. Wilson's pastor until 1850. He also felt a profound regard for the spiritual welfare of his distinguished parishioner, and aided him in his researches. He rejoiced in the noble stand which his friend took against the aggressions of proslavery power, and labored with the clergy and the churches of his association to sustain him. He was well aware of Mr. Wilson's intellectual energy and growth, of his integrity, of his sincere devotion to the cause of freedom; and he predicted his political success. He endeavored so to guide him as to make it sure.

Under the faithful ministry of Mr. Hunt, the mind of Mr. Wilson became seriously impressed with the momentous relations between himself and his Maker, so that he not only listened with profound attention to the instructions of the sacred desk, but sometimes took an active part in religious meetings. He taught for several years a Bible-class in the sabbath school with great acceptance; and the members of that class are now, for the most part, intelligent and progressive members of the church.

On his part, Mr. Wilson encouraged and supported Mr. Hunt in the arduous labors of his ministry: he sympathized with him both in joy and sorrow; and the tie that early bound their hearts together still remains unbroken. On the presentation of a watch to Mr. Hunt at his retirement from his pastorate at Natick, Mr. Wilson made the following beautiful and affectionate address: —

"RESPECTED FRIEND, — The relations which have existed between us for eleven years having now been dissolved, we have assembled here to-night to express our high appreciation of your services as a pastor, our profound re-

spect for your character as a man, and our personal regard
for you as a friend. We are here also to pass a few fleeting
moments in your society; to exchange with you a few
parting words; to take you once more by the hand; and,
with hearts overflowing with emotion, to bid you farewell.

"Could these friends have controlled events, the chain
that bound us together in the relation of pastor and people
would have remained unbroken: you would have continued with us and of us. Having passed your days with us
in the performance of your duties, participating in our joys
and sharing in our sorrows, when your ' race of existence
was run,' we would have you repose in the bosom of our
mother-earth with the people of your early choice, — in
yonder spot, hallowed and consecrated as the last resting-
place of this people and their children.

"But it has been ordered otherwise. We must acquiesce in an event we could not avert. You are to leave us
to seek other fields of labor, to form new relations, to
gather around you other friends. But, sir, wherever you
may go, be assured that you will bear with you our warmest wishes that Heaven will shower upon your pathway its
choicest blessings. Wherever in the providence of God you
may be summoned to labor, may friends — true-hearted,
steadfast friends — cluster around you to cheer you onward
in every beneficent effort to advance the cause of religion
and humanity!

"You will leave behind you, sir, in retiring from the place
you have so long filled, many evidences of your deep and
abiding interest in our present prosperity and future welfare.
The recollection of your many acts of kindness will be cherished by us with unabated affection until the hearts upon
which these acts are engraved shall cease to beat forever.

"Desirous that you should carry with you some parting

token of our friendship, your friends have purchased the watch I hold in my hand, and have commissioned me to present it to you. In their behalf I beg you to accept it. Take it, sir; cherish it, not for its intrinsic worth (for it is of slight value), but as a trifling tribute to your worth, and a memento of the respect, esteem, and affection of its donors. As a memorial of our friendship, I trust you will not consider it altogether valueless. It will not beat more accurately the passing moments than will the pulsations of our hearts ever beat responsive to the friendship we entertain for you.

"We fondly indulge the hope, sir, that in after-life, amid its pressing cares and duties, it will sometimes remind you of the friends of those

> ' Earlier days and calmer hours,
> When heart with heart delights to blend.'

In the calm and quiet of your study, where the world and its cares are shut out, as the ear shall hear it beat the fleeting seconds, or the eye see it mark the passing hours, may it recall to mind reminiscences of the past!—recollections of these scenes; of this place, where were passed the first years of your ministry; where were spent so many years of your early manhood,—that portion of existence when impressions are most indelibly engraved upon the mind and heart; where your children were born; and where your home was blessed and made joyous by the grace, love, and piety of the wife of your bosom,—the pure and gentle being, the loved and lost one, who now sleeps far away amid the scenes of her youth, but whose memory will ever be fondly cherished by this people; for

> ' None knew her but to love her,
> Nor named her but to praise.' "

4*

On the twenty-eighth day of October, 1840, Mr. Wilson was united in marriage, by the Rev. Mr. Hunt, with Miss Harriet Malvina Howe of Natick. She was the daughter of Mr. Amasa and Mrs. Mary (Toombs) Howe, and was descended on her mother's side from Mr. Daniel Toombs, an early settler of the town of Hopkinton. She was a lady of good education, refined in sentiment, gentle in manner, and remarkable for the sweetness of her disposition. By her unostentatious way of doing good, she made religion lovely. Her thoughts were noble; and her influence upon the society in which she moved was like the fragrance of flowers. She could not but make her home happy; and her husband had a just appreciation of her excellence. To him, in his toils and trials, her clear voice was an inspiration. In her he beheld a pattern of true womanhood, and for her sake he longed to deserve well of his country. To her sweet influence over him may be in part attributed that delicate and profound respect which he entertains for woman, that sincere regard which he manifests for her intellectual and social elevation. His ideal of womanly virtue and devotion was realized in her pure and lovely life of trust and duty.

Three or four years subsequent to his marriage, Mr. Wilson built on Central Street, in Natick, the neat and commodious dwelling-house which he has since occupied. It is furnished with republican simplicity, yet with elegance and taste. To its hospitalities his friends and neighbors always find a cordial welcome; and the absence of luxury and parade is more than compensated by smiles of cheerfulness, and words of good will. On the eleventh day of November, 1846, the hearts of the parents were gladdened by the birth of a son, whom they named Henry Hamilton. He was their only child.

RESIDENCE OF HON. HENRY WILSON NATICK, MASS.

In principle and in practice, Mr. Wilson has always been opposed to the use of intoxicating liquors as a beverage; and to his strictly temperate habits may in part be ascribed that robust health and physical strength which he now so eminently possesses. As early as 1831 he joined a temperance society in Farmington; and in public and in private he has ever exerted his influence to dissuade his fellow-men from the use of stimulating drink.

In a speech in Tremont Temple, Boston, April, 1857, he said, —

" I shall strive ever and always to promote and advance that great cause of our common humanity. It is no merit in me that has made me a life-long friend of temperance. God in his providence gave me no taste, no desire, for intoxicating liquors; and every day of my life, as I grow older and see the measureless evils of drunkenness, I thank my God that he gave me no desire for that which degrades and levels down our common humanity.

" From my cradle to this hour I have seen, felt, realized the curse of intemperance. When my eyes first saw the light, when I came to recognize any thing, I saw and felt some of the evils of intemperance; and all my life long to this hour, and now, my heart has been burdened with anxieties for those of my kith and kin that I loved dearly. With no desire for the intoxicating cup, with the evils of intemperance about and around me, and with a life burdened with anxieties for dear and loved ones, it is no wonder, ladies and gentlemen, that I have abhorred drunkenness, while I have loved and pitied its victims."

Aware of his regard for temperance, and having confidence in his ability as a thinker, his friends in Natick, advocating what was known as the " Fifteen-gallon Law," presented his name in 1839 as a candidate for the General

Court. He failed by a very few votes of an election, and continued quietly manufacturing shoes, and studying the condition of his country. No representative was sent that year from Natick; and the party in opposition to that law placed Marcus Morton in the executive chair of the State.

In 1840 occurred the celebrated presidential campaign, in which William Henry Harrison, "the hero of the Thames and the Tippecanoe," was brought forward by the Whigs in opposition to Mr. Van Buren, then president. The experiments of the government upon the currency had embarrassed the financial operations of the country; had seriously affected the industrial interests of the North, and reduced the wages of the working-people. Hard times came on. The laboring-classes murmured against the measures of the government, and keenly criticised the course of the president and his cabinet. Mr. Wilson, ever on the side of the working-men, felt the pressure, and saw the ruinous tendency of Mr. Van Buren's financial policy; and, although he had hitherto sympathized with the Democratic party, now came prominently forward with the Whigs, and espoused the cause of Mr. Harrison. "Having entered life on the working-man's side," says the author of "Men of our Times," "and having known by his experience the working-man's trials, temptations, and hard struggles, he felt the sacredness of a poor man's labor, and entered public life with a heart to take the part of the toiling and the oppressed."

Up to that period, no political campaign in this country had so aroused the enthusiasm of the people. Mass-meetings were held in churches, halls, and groves; log-cabins were erected, and sometimes mounted on wheels, and drawn from town to town; banners with mottoes were unfolded, and immense processions of all ranks and classes bearing torchlights were formed. The ablest speakers took the stand; and eloquence and patriotic songs set forth the virtues and exploits of " the hero of North Bend " before the people.

" Tippecanoe and Tyler too " rang as a war-cry through the Union. Mr. Wilson shared in the enthusiasm. He studied well the course of legislation as presented in " The Washington Globe," and made his first campaign-speech in the Methodist meeting-house at Natick in opposition to Mr. Amasa Walker, who was an advocate of a specie currency and of the general policy of the national administration. The ability of Mr. Wilson as a public speaker was at once acknowledged. He was invited to discuss the questions of the day in many other places; and, during the campaign, made more than sixty speeches in the neighboring towns and cities. In Charlestown, Cambridge, Roxbury, Lowell, Lynn, Taunton, and other towns and cities, he addressed large and enthusiastic audiences with telling effect; so that the general exclamation was, " How came this Natick shoemaker to know so much more than we do on national questions? "

The answer might have been, " This Natick shoemaker was studying ' The Federalist ' and the proceedings of Congress while you were asleep.

In some instances, attempts were made to interrupt him in his speaking; but holding himself steadily to the point in question, and to his good nature, of which the fund seemed inexhaustible, he manfully maintained his ground, and carried his audiences with him. He spoke extemporaneously, but never without careful preparation. He read the best models of American eloquence, — such as Adams, Everett, Otis, Channing, Webster; and, after committing parts of his speeches to memory, he would sometimes retire to Deacon Coolidge's old oak-grove, and there rehearse them to himself alone. He is remembered by those who heard him in this campaign as a young man of lithe and agile form, of an intellectual cast of countenance, clear complexion, earnest, searching voice, and sparkling eyes. He usually bent over the desk in speaking, as if to come as closely in contact with his audience as he could. His object seemed to be to reveal the thought of his hearer to himself; and herein lies one secret of a speaker's power. · He also defended his positions by a very frequent appeal to facts; and one who well remembers him at that time avers, "He had a very winning way in presenting them."

At the close of the campaign, he had the pleasure of seeing Mr. Harrison, for whom he had spoken so many times, elected to the presidential chair by a large majority, — two hundred and thirty-four to Mr. Van Buren's sixty electoral votes, — while he himself was chosen a representative from the town of Natick to the General Court of Massachusetts. The legislative hall is now his academy; the constitution is his text-book, and liberty his teacher.

When he entered the House of Representatives, he observed that an honest farmer, twenty years his senior, had drawn one of the most eligible seats in the hall; and he at once offered him three dollars for an exchange. The farmer gladly took the money; for one seat to him who never spoke was just as good as another. But, some time afterwards, he referred to the circumstance as revealing the pride of the young member. "No," said one who better knew his spirit: "it reveals his foresight. He gave you three dollars for your seat in order that he might be in the best position to hear the arguments of other members, and also to present his own with most effect. **This style of doing things, if carried on, will give him influence here.**"

It was carried on. He entered upon his legislative career with the determination of bestowing his whole time and attention upon the business coming before him. With sleepless vigilance he watched every transaction, listened to every speaker, and followed every question. He was a working-man; he entered the legislative hall to work; he did not fail to work; and workers win.

It is noticeable that his first legislative speech was in favor of the working-man. It was delivered Jan. 25, 1841, on a bill to exempt laborers' wages from attachment in certain cases. He said the honest poor of the State would deprecate the passage of such a law: it would protect dishonesty. The class of men who lived upon the earnings of others were daily increasing. There were many men, too, who judged of morality by law alone. Such a law would impair the credit of the poor man. He hoped this bill would be considered on its merits alone, with no intermixture of party-spirit. He sympathized with the poor men with whom he had been reared, and with whom he now was. He moved to strike out the enacting clause.

Inured as he had been to hard and unremitting labor, and with sympathies alive to human suffering, it was natural that Mr. Wilson should be opposed to the whole system of domestic servitude. His mind revolted at the wrongs the bondman bore in a boasted land of liberty: he keenly felt the cruelty of that code of laws that held him subject, and without redress, to the caprice of an insolent and hard-hearted master. The instincts of a noble nature, the teachings of the gospel, the training he himself had undergone, the philanthropic spirit of the age, the opinions of the founders of the Constitution, all conspired to lead him to abominate the traffic in human blood, and the **tyranny of subjecting innocent men and women to servile**

labor.   The more he thought upon it, the more iniquitous
appeared the system: it despoiled the slave of his just
rights; it demoralized the master; it impoverished his
country.   At the same time, he saw that the slave-power,
ever intolerant and exacting, had long held ascendency in
Congress; had by the craftiest plans extended its territory
so as to maintain that ascendency; and, while menacing
the North, had contaminated the source of political power,
and brought the free States, to a great extent, into subserviency to its schemes of aggression.

Such, it is believed, were Mr. Wilson's views and sentiments at this period; and, if he did not enter the abolition
ranks, it was not because he was opposed to their leading
principles, but because he hoped to exert a stronger influence towards the ultimate redemption of the slave by acting with the progressive men in the Whig party.   In the
legislature his voice was ever heard, his vote was ever cast,
on behalf of the rights of those in bondage.   In the House
of Representatives, in 1841, he advocated the repeal of the
law, which has been termed the last of the slave code in
this State, forbidding the intermarriage of blacks and
whites; and, in the next session, made another strong
speech in opposition to the law, maintaining that it was
founded on inequality and caste.   He declared "that the
bill was not inspired by political, but by humane motives;
and, though it might be defeated then, it would ultimately
be enacted.   It was only a question of time."   This
obnoxious law was repealed at the next session of the
legislature.   In November, 1842, Mr. Wilson was a candidate for the State Senate; but the Whig party was that
year defeated in his county, as it was in the State.   There
being no election of governor by the people, the legislature, in January, 1843, elected Marcus Morton for a second

term.   In 1844 Mr. Wilson obtained a senatorial seat, and took an active part in the deliberations of that body, ever ranging himself upon the side of progress and reform.   He made an elaborate report on military affairs, and carried it through the Senate.

He was again a member of the same body in 1845, where he again labored successfully for the improvement of the military system of the State, and also to improve the condition of the colored people.   He strenuously advocated the right of negroes to seats in the railroad-car, from which they had in several cases been insolently ejected; and also their right to admission to our public schools, from which prejudice had excluded them.

A bill reported to the Senate, providing that any child unlawfully excluded from the public schools should be entitled to recover damages, had been rejected.   Moving the next day a reconsideration of this vote, Mr. Wilson made an able speech in behalf of the bill, in which he said that he considered it the most important one which had come up that session.   "It concerned," said he, "the rights and feelings of a large but humble portion of our people, whose interests should be watched over and cared for by the legislature; whose imperative duty it was, when complaints were made of the invasion of the rights of the poorest and the humblest, to provide a remedy that should be full and ample to secure and guard all his rights."   He said the common-school system, the pride and glory of Massachusetts, was based upon the principle of perfect equality, and that the distinction set up at Nantucket aimed a blow at its very existence.   The colored people said, and rightly, that their feelings were trifled with, and their rights disregarded.   Denouncing the spirit that excluded colored children from the full and equal benefits of com-

5

mon schools, he said, "It is the same which has drenched
the world with blood for six thousand years, made a slaveholder in South Carolina, and a slave-pirate on the coast of
Africa." He said that those whose rights he wished to
guard and secure had but little influence or power; while
those who opposed them had both, and were only too willing to use them for their own aggrandizement. It was
more popular to keep along with the current of prejudice,
than, by resisting it, to be denounced as a "radical or abolitionist." "In retiring from the legislature," he said, "I
am sustained by the consciousness that I have never uttered
a word or given a vote against the rights of any human
being. I had far rather have the warm and generous
thanks of one poor orphan-boy down on the Island of Nantucket, that I may never see, nor even know, than to have
the approbation of every man in the Commonwealth, whether in this chamber or out of it, who would deny to any
child the full and equal benefits of our public schools."

Such sentiments are creditable to the senator's heart.
They had their effect on the Senate. Mr. Wilson's
motion was adopted by a large majority: the bill was committed to the judiciary committee, which reported a similar bill that became the law of the State. Thus slowly,
through the influence of the friends of freedom, Massachusetts came to see and to acknowledge the rights of a
long-abused and shamefully-neglected race of people.
Between the lofty and the lowly there was need of a medi-
ator, who by his intellect could reach the one, and by his
hand of toil the other; and such was Henry Wilson.

> "Then on! for this we live, —
> To smite the oppressor with the words of power;
> To bid the tyrant give
> Back to his brother Heaven's allotted hour."

CHAPTER IV.

MILITARY SERVICES. — ADDRESS ON TEMPERANCE, 1845. — INFLUENCE AT HOME.

His Military Turn of Mind. — Reading. — Views of War. — Views of the Militia System. — Election as Major, 1843. — Colonel and Brigadier-General, 1846. — Regard for Discipline. — Popularity with Soldiers. — Speech in the Senate. — Peace and War. — Preparations for more Important Duties. — His Regard for Temperance. — Speech at Natick, 1845. — A Citizen at Home. — Appreciated by his Townsmen.

BY nature Mr. Wilson possesses the endowments requisite to success, not only as a political, but also as a military leader. Rapid in his combinations, quick to discover the weak point in an opponent, fertile in expedients, fearless and far-seeing, he has elements both of mind and body for a commander. His thoughts were early turned towards military life; and, during his minority, he took delight in reading the history of the campaigns of Marlborough, Wolfe, Washington, Wellington, Napoleon, and other eminent generals. He drew in his mind the plans of celebrated battles, and criticised, as he could, the movements of distinguished leaders in the field. He first appeared upon the training-field in Farmington, where he was appointed to an inferior military office. On coming to Natick, he continued to take a lively interest in military affairs. He abominated war, viewed simply as a means of attaining personal glory; but he felt

51

that it was sometimes indispensable to self-protection, and that the military system of Massachusetts needed revision and support.

This opinion he privately and publicly expressed as opportunity occurred. In the State Senate, 1844, he was appointed chairman of the Military Committee, and made a strong speech on the 14th of February of that year in favor of increasing the pay of soldiers doing military duty.

In 1843, without his knowledge or consent, he was elected major of the first regiment of artillery, of which William Schouler was then colonel. He knew nothing of his election until he saw the announcement of it in the public papers. His duties as a major he faithfully discharged, and thereby won the confidence and respect of the soldiers under him. In June, 1846, he was elected as colonel of the same regiment; and, six weeks later, brigadier-general of the third brigade of the Massachusetts volunteer militia, in which office he continued for the next five years. During this period he studied military tactics carefully, and by his skill and industry brought his brigade up to an admirable state of discipline. His soldiers loved him and obeyed him, carrying out his orders with alacrity, and priding themselves upon the bearing and ability of their commander. He had the reputation of drilling his brigade with greater thoroughness than any other officer in the State, and of being, at the same time, highly popular with his men. By his strenuous exertions in the legislature, much was done to revive the military spirit in Massachusetts, and to put her into position for a struggle which some prophetic eyes discovered even then to be impending. In a defence of the integrity of **the soldiers at the polls**, Mr. Wilson, referring to his own connection with the militia of the State, said in the Convention of 1853, —

"I may speak from some little experience, having been a member of the volunteer militia of Massachusetts for nine years, and having during these years held the offices of major, lieutenant-colonel, colonel, and brigadier-general. I held the command of a brigade of more than eight hundred men for five years; and during these nine years I made many acquaintances and formed many friendships I shall ever fondly cherish. Not one unkind word ever passed between me and any officer or private of the brigade during my nine years of connection with it. I received from many of my comrades many acts of kindness I hope never to forget. During these years I was five times a candidate for senator of Middlesex, the county where the members of my brigade resided; and I can truly say that I do not know or think that I ever received a single vote owing to my connection with the brigade. Four of the five gentlemen who were members of my staff were of a different political faith from mine; and I have no reason to think they ever sacrificed their opinions on account of our personal relations as members of a military family. The members of the volunteer militia of Massachusetts are generally men of intelligence and character, who are not won from their political allegiance by the plume and epaulet."

So in the same speech he thus eloquently expresses his views of peace and war: —

"I am not one of those men who cry peace when there is no peace without slavery, injustice, and wrong. I may be in error; but I have sometimes thought that the song which the peace-movement has hymned into the ear of Europe during the past five years has made far easier the march of the legions of Russia and Austria upon Hungary and Italy, and the march of the legions of France — of apostate republican France — upon Rome. While the people have listened with softened hearts to the songs of peace, their masters have disarmed them, and sent forth their increasing standing armies to crush every manifestation of freedom, progress, and popular rights. When tyranny is overthrown, and freedom established; when standing armies are disbanded, and the people armed for their own protection against arbitrary power, — then I would write ' Peace ' on the banners of the people, and send them forth to make the tour of the world. My motto is, ' LIBERTY first; PEACE afterwards.' "

By these faithful military services in his own State, Mr. Wilson was unconsciously making preparation for the intelligent performance of the important duties which devolved on him as chairman of the Military Committee of the United-States Senate during the Rebellion. For that post, not only comprehensive views, and industry that fears no task, but large experience and information gained by actual practice, were demanded; and these Mr. Wilson had.

In regard to temperance Mr. Wilson's record has ever been clear, decided, and consistent. With profound sorrow he early saw the havoc produced among his fellow-men by the use of stimulating drink; and with unwavering steadiness he has ever used his tongue, his pen, and his vote, to dissuade and to restrain them from the sale and from the use of any thing which intoxicates the brain. Next to slavery, he has considered intemperance as the tremendous evil of this nation; and therefore, as a friend of humanity and a lover of his country, he has ever striven most earnestly to arrest its progress. His views on this question in 1845 appear in an animated address delivered on behalf of the Young Men's Temperance Society in Natick on the presentation by a lady of a beautiful banner to that body. It will be read with interest: —

"MADAM, — In receiving at your hands this beautiful banner from the ladies of the Martha Washington Society, permit me, in return, in behalf of my associates, to tender to you, and the ladies whose organ you are, our sincere and grateful acknowledgments for this expression of your favor. For this evidence of zeal in our cause, and regard for our success, you have the thanks of many warm and generous hearts, that will ever throb with grateful recollection of your kindness till they shall cease to beat forever. We receive, madam, with the deepest and liveliest sensibility, the kind sentiments you have expressed in behalf of our society. Be assured that these sentiments are appreciated and reciprocated by us.

"You have this day, ladies, consecrated and devoted this banner to the great moral movement of the age. We accept its guardianship with mingled feelings of pride, hope, and joy. It is indeed a fit and noble tribute, an offering worthy of the cause and of you. May its fair folds never be stained or dishonored by any act of ours! Tasteful and expressive in design and execution, we prize it highly for its intrinsic worth; but we prize it still higher as a manifest and enduring memorial of your devotion to principle and duty. Ever proud shall we be to unroll its gorgeous folds to the sunshine and the breeze; to gather round it, and rally under it, and guard and defend it, as we would defend from every danger its fair and generous donors. It was not intended that the eye should feast alone on its splendor, but that, so often as the eye should

gaze upon it, a quick and lively appreciation of the transcendent magnitude of the cause to which you have
devoted it should live in our understanding, and affect our
hearts.

"Ours is a peaceful reform, a moral warfare. We are
not called upon to leave our homes and the loved ones
that cluster around our domestic altars to go to the field
of bloody strife on an errand of wrath and hatred. Our
battles are bloodless; our victories are tearless.

"Yet the contest in which we are engaged is a fearful
one; for it is a struggle with the vitiated and depraved
appetites and passions of our fallen race, — foes that have
triumphed over earth's brightest and fairest, over all that
is noble in man and lovely in woman. These foes have
gathered their victims from every clime and every age.
No age, sex, or condition, has escaped. Heroes who have
led their mailed legions over a hundred fields of glory and
renown, and planted their victorious eagles on the capitals
of conquered nations; statesmen who have wielded the
destinies of mighty empires, setting up and pulling down
thrones and dynasties, and stamping the impress of their
genius upon the institutions of their age; orators who have
held listening senates in mute and rapt admiration, and
whose eloquence has thrown a halo of imperishable light
and unfading glory over their age and nation; scholars
who have laid under contribution the vast domains of
matter and mind, grasping and mastering the mighty
problems of moral, intellectual, and physical science, and
left behind them monuments of toil and wisdom for the
study and admiration of all ages, — have been the victims,
the slaves, of these foes, — foes which we have pledged
ourselves to conquer. In this fearful contest we will bear
aloft this banner; and when the conflict thickens, when

trials, doubts, and temptations come around us like the floods, may it glitter through the gloom like a beacon-light over the dark and troubled waste of waters, a sign of hope and promise, to which may come, in the hour of loneliness, sorrow, and penitence, some erring and fallen brother! You can sustain us by your prayers, and cheer us by your approving smiles. You can visit, as you have done, the drunkard's home of poverty, destitution, and misery, and by offices of kindness and charity do something to dry up the tears and alleviate the wants of its neglected and sorrowing inmates.

"Every great struggle for humanity has been blessed by woman's prayers, and aided by her generous toil. The history of our country, of our own renowned commonwealth, is full of the noblest instances of her constancy and devotion. She trod with our fathers the deck of 'The Mayflower.' She sat beside them in unrepining and uncomplaining constancy as they gathered in council, houseless and homeless in mid-winter, to lay in prayers and tears the foundations of a free Christian commonwealth. In the long, perilous struggles with the wild sons of the forest, she shared without complaint their privations and dangers; and, in the great struggle for independence, she counselled the wise, infused courage into the brave, armed fathers, husbands, sons, and brothers, and sent them to the field where freedom was to be won by blood. In the great struggle in which we are engaged to free our native land from the blighting, withering, soul-destroying curse of intemperance, our fair country-women have shown that they inherit the virtues of our patriotic mothers.

"Ladies, you have this day given us substantial evidence of your friendship, sympathy, and co-operation.

May we not, then, indulge the hope that our societies will move along in union and harmony, each in its appropriate sphere of duty, laboring to hasten on the day when every drunkard shall be redeemed, and restored to his manhood and to society?

"Friends and associates, we shall doubtless, in the changes and mutations of life, be called to separate. Wherever we may go, on the land or on the sea, in our own or other climes, may a deep and abiding sense of duty go with us! May the influences of this hour be ever upon us! May this banner, the gift of those near and dear to us, ever float in our mind's eye, inciting us to duty, and guarding us in the hour of temptation! And when life's labors are done, its trials over, and its honors won, may each of us have the proud consciousness that we have kept the pledge inviolate; that we have done something in our day and generation for our race, — something that shall cause our names and memories to be mentioned with respect and gratitude when '*the golden bowl shall be broken and the silver cord loosed*,' when our '*bodies*' shall have mouldered and mingled with the dust, and '*our spirits have returned to God who gave them*'"!

Thus at home, among his own immediate friends and acquaintances, Mr. Wilson's words and example were from the outset unchangeably on the side of sobriety, civil order, social progress, and reform. If any thing beneficent was to be attempted, his friends knew where to find him. His hand and heart were ready. On the young people of the village his influence was ever salutary and inspiring. His friendly counsel was ever given for a higher, nobler course of life. In the social circle, in the shop, the lecture-room, or in the street, he was always on the right side. Very many of his companions can trace their success in life mainly to the elevating influence he exerted over them. The steady vote of Natick in his favor, and the public demonstrations of joy which that town has made on his advancement to political power, evince the estimation in which he is held as a townsman, friend, and neighbor at home. Those who know him best appreciate him most highly as a citizen and as a man.

CHAPTER V.

Southern Efforts to annex Texas to the United States. — Mr. Wilson's Amendment to Resolutions against Annexation in the Senate adopted. — Call for a Convention. — Opposed by Whigs. — Held in Faneuil Hall, Jan. 27. — Address to the People. — The True Reformer. — Meeting at Waltham. — Mr. Wilson's Views. — Convention at Concord, 1845. — Mr. Hunt. — Meeting at Cambridge, Oct. 21. — Address of Mr. Wilson. — Persistent Efforts. — Carries Petitions to Washington. — Refuses to take Wine with Mr. Adams. — State Representative in 1846. — Introduces Resolution on Slavery. — Eloquent Speech thereon. — Mr. Garrison's View of it. — Regard for the Constitution.

ON the death of Mr. Harrison, April 4, 1841, the slave-power found in Mr. Tyler, his successor, a willing advocate of its extension; and then brought forward with unblushing front the gigantic scheme of annexing Texas to the Union. This, said Gen. Hamilton, would "give a Gibraltar to the South." "The Madisonian," the organ of the administration, declared that it would have the most salutary influence upon slavery, and that "it must be done soon, or not at all;" and Mr. Upshur asserted in January, 1844, that, "if Texas should not be attached to the United States, she cannot maintain that institution [slavery] ten years, and probably not half that time." Stormy debates occurred in Congress on the

60

question; the Whigs, in general, opposing the annexation, while " Texas, or disunion!" became the watchword of the South. The question was carried into the presidential election of 1844; and James K. Polk thus came into the chief executive chair.

In the State Senate Mr. Wilson took an active part against the Texan scheme. He moved an amendment to the resolutions against annexation, " requesting Massachusetts senators in Congress to prevent, if possible, the consummation of that slaveholding scheme." The resolution implied a rebuke for their timid action; and he commented freely on what he characterized as their want of spirit. He wished to call their attention to the fact, that, upon the question of slavery, the legislature was in sober earnest; that it wished " them to feel, to think, and to act as Massachusetts men, who have been reared under the institutions of the Pilgrim Fathers, should think, feel, and act." His amendment was unanimously adopted by the Senate; and, though amended in the House by the insertion of the words " representatives in Congress," it had the desired effect upon our senators in that body. Mr. Wilson spoke eloquently and earnestly in the Senate-chamber against annexation, maintaining that, " if Texas should be admitted by a legislative act, that act could and ought to be repealed at the earliest possible moment." In order to develop and concentrate public sentiment on this question, he drew up a paper calling a convention of the State. Many eminent men of the Whig party in the General Court declined to sign the paper. This was the entering wedge in the division of the Whig party of Massachusetts in respect to slavery, which resulted in open rupture three years afterwards, and, finally, in complete extinction. Glory-ing in its past record, and intimidated by the effrontery."

6

the South, that party failed to see the "logic of events," and wore away until it received from its distinguished leader, Daniel Webster, in his speech on the seventh day of March, 1850, its final death-blow. The world was moving : not to move with it was to perish.

The State convention was held in Faneuil Hall upon the 29th of January ; and its discussions were characterized by earnestness, vigor, and determination. An address, in part drawn up by Mr. Webster, and declaring that " Massachusetts denounces the iniquitous project [of annexation] in its inception, and in every stage of its progress, its means, and its ends, and all the purposes and pretences of its authors," was unanimously adopted, and widely circulated. " Thoughtful men," says Mr. Wilson, "filled the hall; speakers and hearers partook of a common sentiment : they realized as never before the imminence of the impending calamity, the gravity of the occasion, and the pregnant issues of the hour."

" The true reformer," says some writer, " is the man upon whose mind the light of great truths has fallen before it has reached the mass of his fellow-men, and who feels called of God to shed it abroad in the darkness." The declarations of Mr. Wilson at this period show that he distinctly saw the " impending crisis," the upheaving of the moral power of the nation, and the downfall of the deep-rooted institution of human servitude.

Although a treaty of annexation had been signed by the president, and Texas had accepted the conditions, she was not yet a State of the Union. Efforts were therefore strenuously made by antislavery men against her admission as a State. On the anniversary (Aug. 1, 1845) of the West-India emancipation, a large meeting was held at Waltham, Mass., where eloquent speeches were made by

William Henry Channing, Ralph Waldo Emerson, John Weiss, and Henry Wilson, in which the usurpations and iniquities of the slaveholding power were forcibly set forth.

"The calamity and disgrace of annexation," said Mr. Wilson, "had come upon the country through the treachery of Northern men: even the representative of Concord and Lexington had proved recreant." To the question, "What should be done?" he said, "Act. Hold meetings in every district, town, and county in the State. Oppose the admission of Texas into the Union as a slaveholding State, and appeal to the people of the free States to arrest the consummation of the great iniquity. Say to the men of the South, ' You are warring against civilization, against humanity, against the noblest feelings of the heart, the holiest impulses of the human soul, and the providence of God; and the conflict must ultimately end in your defeat.' "

Mr. Wilson soon after obtained the signatures of a large number of influential men for a convention to be held at Concord on the twenty-second day of September, 1845, which, as set forth in the call, was to "take into consideration the encroachments of the slave-power, and recommend such action as justice and patriotism shall dictate to resist those encroachments, and arrest the progress of events so rapidly tending to that fearful consummation when slavery shall have complete control over the policy of the government and the destinies of the country." Men of all parties, sects, and pursuits, were invoked to "devote one day to the country and the oppressed." "Let old age," he said, "with its garnered treasures of wisdom and experience, be there, let manhood in its maturity and vigor be there, let youth with its high hopes and aspirations be there, to devise such measures and awaken such a spirit as shall free the country from the dominion, curse, and shame of slavery."

Mr. Wilson had the pleasure of seeing a large, enthusiastic convention, and of reporting a preamble and resolutions ; the former of which had been prepared by his pastor, the Rev. Samuel Hunt, who, he observes, " had always, in the pulpit, in religious and political organizations, and at the ballot-box, acted for the slave, and against the domination of his master."

" We solemnly announce our purpose to the South," said the resolutions ; " and to the execution of that purpose we pledge ourselves to the country and before Heaven, that, rejecting all compromise, without restraint or hesitation, in our private relations and in our political organizations, by our voices and our votes, in Congress or out, we will use all practicable means for the extinction of slavery on the American continent."   Letters were received from Charles Francis Adams, and John G. Whittier the poet ; and eloquent speeches were made by William Lloyd Garrison, Stephen C. Phillips, and other antislavery men.   The resolutions were unanimously adopted.

At an adjourned meeting of the convention, held in Cambridge on the 21st of October, Mr. Wilson presided, and, on taking the chair, made an earnest appeal for prompt and fearless action ; in which he said, " Let us at once take an advanced step against the slave-power.   Let us act, and, as far as we have the constitutional right, go in favor of emancipation.   Let us make it the cardinal doctrine of our creed, the sun of our system.   Let us inscribe, in letters of light, emancipation on the banners under which we rally.   Let us go to the country on that issue.   We shall reach the heart and conscience of the people.   They will come to the rescue, and we shall lay the foundations of an enduring triumph."

A committee appointed at this convention prepared an

address to the people, and received in response petitions, signed by sixty-five thousand names, against the admission of Texas as a State into the Union. Mr. Wilson and John G. Whittier were chosen to present this remonstrance of the people of this State to Congress. On the tenth day of December, Mr. Adams laid these petitions before the House of Representatives, and moved that they be referred to a select committee ; but the House by a large majority laid them on the table, and Texas soon became a State of the Union. But, though the Southern power was thus augmented, there were forces rising and combining which portended " irrepressible conflict."

While at Washington, Mr. Wilson was invited to dine with John Q. Adams ; and, when wine was urged upon him at table, held himself, as did Daniel at the court of Babylon, to his principles of temperance, and declined to taste it. Surrounded by fashion, and moved by the example of the great and gifted, as he was, he has since spoken of this as one of the strongest temptations, in respect to total abstinence, of his life. Mr. Adams afterwards heartily commended him for his consistency.

In 1846, Mr. Wilson, who had declined being a candidate for the State Senate, held a seat in the House of Representatives, and, as usual, took a leading part in the deliberations of the session ; ever casting the weight of his influence upon the side of humanity and progress. He introduced a resolution on the third day of February, declaring " the unalterable hostility of Massachusetts to the further extension and longer existence of slavery in America, and her fixed determination to use all constitutional and legal means for its extinction." This resolution he supported in a speech of signal power, evincing profound

research and a complete mastery of his subject. He met
with stern opposition from some leading men of the
Whig party, with which he was still acting; though none
could answer his strong and lucid argument. Of this
speech "The Liberator" said, "This is unquestionably
the best antislavery speech that has ever been delivered in
any legislative assembly in this country, — more direct,
more comprehensive, more important;" and "The Boston
Courier" truly averred that "the spirit of independence
is manifest in every paragraph." Inasmuch as Mr. Wilson, in this appeal for freedom, fearlessly discloses his
opinions as a legislative champion of antislavery, clearly
states the issues between the parties, ably answers the
objections to his own position, marks out his future course,
and prophetically announces coming events, we introduce
it, with few omissions, to the reader : —

SPEECH ON SLAVERY IN THE MASSACHUSETTS HOUSE
OF REPRESENTATIVES, 1846.

"I am not, sir, a political abolitionist; or, rather, I am
not a Liberty-party man. I have no connection whatever
with that party as a party. I am an abolitionist. and have
been a member of an abolition society for nearly ten years.
I am proud of the name of 'abolitionist:' I glory in it. I am
willing to bear my full share of the odium that may now
or hereafter be heaped upon it. I had far rather be one
of the humblest in that little band which rallies around the
glorious standard of emancipation than to have been the
favorite marshal of Napoleon, and have led the Old Guard
over a hundred fields of glory and renown. I have, here
and in the other branch, always advocated and supported
all measures that tend to the freedom and elevation of the

colored portion of our countrymen. At all times and on all occasions, in public and in private, I have endeavored, according to the convictions of my judgment, to advance the cause of emancipation. I have been a candidate for seven years in succession for this House or the Senate, and have never, to my knowledge, received the vote of a solitary political abolitionist; and, should I ever again be a candidate for public office (which I do not anticipate), never expect to receive from one a vote. I hope, therefore, that no more insinuations will be thrown out that I only wish to court and please a ' *a little knot of political abolitionists.*' At any rate, I shall not shrink from the performance of duty from any such insinuations here or elsewhere. I have said that I have no connection with the Liberty party; yet I am free to say that I am ready to forget the past, to let bygones be bygones, and to act with any set of men — Whigs, Democrats, Liberty men, or old organizationists — in all lawful and constitutional measures that shall tend to arrest the extension, and overthrow the entire system, of slavery in America. It is time for the friends of freedom to bury minor differences of opinion, and march shoulder to shoulder, with lock-step, against the slave-power. How stands Massachusetts at this time? What is her position in reference to slavery? As long ago as 1838, during the presidency of Mr. Van Buren, an effort was made to bring Texas into the Union. The subject was brought before the legislature; and the late lamented James C. Alvord of Greenfield, then a member of the Senate, made a very able report on the subject, concluding with resolutions against the admission of Texas, which were unanimously adopted as the sense of the people of the Commonwealth. And in 1843, when the Democratic party had the control of the State government, a resolution was likewise unanimously passed, setting forth the evils of annexation, and declaring that under ' no circumstances whatever would Massachusetts consent to it.' In 1844, when rumors were rife that the administration of John Tyler, — which has been aptly called a ' gigantic joke,' — casting about for popular themes which should give it a chance for a renewed term, had pitched upon this project of annexation, the legislature, by nearly a unanimous vote, passed resolutions that such annexation would be a ' palpable violation of the Constitution, a deliberate assault upon its compromises.' I know very well, and everybody knows very well, that the Democracy have abandoned the position we all then assumed. . . . But the deed has been done. The last act in this great drama of national guilt and infamy has been performed. Texas has been admitted. She is now a sister State. She has been admitted in violation of the Constitution, and under circumstances which leave but little doubt that the measure was carried by corruption, — by a free use of the patronage of the executive. Men who had committed themselves against it, and whose constituents were strongly opposed to it, also voted for it, and have since received their reward by appointment to places of honor and emolument.

" We must now act. We are in a position where we cannot stand still with honor and dignity. We can adopt three courses of action, — say and do nothing; stand just where we now are, and win, as win we should, the unenviable reputation of talking loud beforehand ; and, when the act is finally accomplished, shutting our mouths in silence, and submitting to the wrong without a murmur. Such a position is one of shame and humiliation, unworthy of old Massachusetts.

" We may declare that this gross outrage of the General

Government is an entire revolution, which will justify Massachusetts in dissolving all connection with the government. We may declare our independence, withdraw our delegation from Congress, exercise exclusive jurisdiction over our territory, and maintain it by force. Very few will recommend such a course of action. Such a step would doubtless lead to bloodshed, which few can contemplate without horror. Were the people ready and prepared for it, the circumstances would not, could not, justify such action. What, then, can we do? We can pledge all the moral, social, and political power of the Commonwealth against slavery, and for freedom. We will remain in the Union; but we remain there to fight the battles of freedom. We will stand by the Constitution: but we stand by it to rescue and defend it from the slave-power; to exercise all its just powers for the overthrow of slavery. We can dedicate ourselves to freedom, and wage eternal hostility to slavery and its power. This is, in my judgment, the only true course for Massachusetts to take. Her duty to the country, and her own honor and dignity, demand that she should take that position, and maintain it with unfaltering devotion."

Having forcibly discussed the allegations of the preamble to the resolution, he continued: —

"Sir, this republic was based upon the grand idea of the freedom and equality of all men; and yet now, in the middle part of the nineteenth century, — in this age of light and knowledge illuminating our pathway, — it has committed itself against freedom, and for slavery. And so it stands committed before all nations, and before Him who has declared that ' *righteousness exalteth a nation, and sin is a reproach to any people.*' Our position before the world is now one of disgrace and shame; and there is no true American, who cares any thing for the fame and glory of his country, that does not blush for his native land. We are drawing upon ourselves the scorn and derision of the universe. With the friends of freedom abroad we are fast losing sympathy and character. It is the universal sentiment all over the civilized world, that we are false and recreant to the principles of our own Constitution. Even the great and good Lafayette declared, a short time before his death, to Clarkson, that *he never would have drawn his sword for America if he had known he was aiding to found a slaveholding republic.*

"At the present time, Mr. Speaker, slavery governs the country: it holds possession of the government, and its vast power is everywhere seen and felt. Its eye is fixed upon California, and turned towards Cuba; and Mr. Calhoun has even gone so far as to send a secret and special agent to Hayti to stir up a rebellion for the purpose of crushing the negro republic. Slavery has its sleepless eye upon the rich provinces of the Mexican republic. Our own gifted Prescott may yet live to write again ' The Conquest of Mexico,' not by the Spanish, but by the Anglo-Saxon race; and for what? Simply, solely, and singly, for the extension of negro slavery over those fair and rich fields.

"The effects of slavery upon the whites and the blacks, upon the moral, social, and intellectual condition of the people, are visible to the most casual observer. It has left its impress upon man, upon institutions and society, and upon the face of Nature. Like the fabled upas-tree, it blasts, withers, and consumes all of life that comes within the circle of its influence. Of the five millions of white population in the slave States, only about three hundred thousand are slaveholders; the great mass of the population being poor, ignorant, and degraded, many of them but little, if any, above the slaves : and slavery has reduced them to that condition.   The soil is cut up into vast estates, owned by a few aristocrats who disdain labor, and despise the laborer. Common schools, the glory of New England, hardly exist ; and education is almost unknown by the mass of the people.   It is our boast in New England that our soil is divided into small estates ; that its cultivators stand upon their own acres, which they till ; and that education is accessible to all our people.   These are the main supports of our republican institutions.   What are the results of the two systems ? One system has, for example, made Massachusetts the pattern State of the Union : the other has made old Virginia, the mother of States and of statesmen, a poor and drivelling commonwealth, with a broken-down and proud aristocracy (mere pensioners upon the government for menial and petty offices), and a helpless and dissipated people. Such is the legitimate result of slavery everywhere ; and nothing can be more preposterous than the idea of sustaining republican institutions in a land of slavery.   It has ever been the bane of empires.   It corrupted and destroyed the ancient republics.   It has retarded the progress of the race.   It destroyed the Roman republic ; it corrupted her aristocracy ; it annihilated the democracy, impoverished the masses, and converted them into paupers that were fed from the public crib.   We talk of Cæsar's crossing the Rubicon, and prostrating the liberties of his country : Roman liberty had perished forever before Cæsar returned from his Northern conquests.   When Tiberius Gracchus, seeing and comprehending the tendencies of slavery, attempting to arrest its corrupting influence by dividing the public domain into small estates, — thus creating an independent yeomanry that should preserve and perpetuate the liberties of the commonwealth, — fell with three hundred of his followers in the Forum beneath the blows of the slaveholding aristocracy, and his body was thrown into the Tiber, that day the liberties of Rome went down, to rise no more forever. We talk of the Northern barbarians despoiling Italy. Before the Scythians left their rude huts in the North, and crossed the Alps, the rich fields of Italy had been converted into barrenness and desolation by the barbarism of slavery, so that those once fertile fields would only yield one-third as much as our own cold, sterile soil of New England. Look at the once proud monarchy of Spain. For three centuries the gold and the silver of the New World were poured into her coffers. It seems now that the hand of God was upon her, avenging the wrongs of the black and red man.

"The issue is now clearly made up. Slavery assumes to direct and control the nation. The friends of freedom must meet the issue. Freedom and slavery are now arrayed against each other. We must destroy slavery, or it will destroy liberty. The path of duty is plain. We are bound to exert our utmost efforts to restore our government to its original and pristine purity. The contest is a glorious one ; and let us be cheered by the fact that the bold and daring efforts of the slave-power to arrest the progress of free principles have awakened and aroused the country. True, that power has won a brilliant victory in the acquisition of Texas ; yet it is only one victory in her series of victories over the constitution and liberties of the country. Other fields are to be fought ; and if we are true to the country, to freedom, and to man, the future *has yet a Waterloo in store for the supporters of this unholy system.* The tendencies of the age we live in are all against slavery ; the progress of literature and science is against it ;

every thing that is beautiful and holy in the works of God is against it ; God himself is against it ; and, sooner or later, fall it must. Let us not be the last to engage in the good work.

"Sir, I wish for the adoption of this resolution, because thereby Massachusetts would take an entirely new and noble position. It is clear, distinct, and plain in its terms, and is based upon the aggressions of slavery itself upon freedom, the liberties, the rights, of the people of the country. It pledges Massachusetts to resist to the utmost all extension of the accursed institution, and to use all her just powers for the entire extinction of the whole system. Let her adopt this sentiment, and act in accordance with it. I wish that it could be written, in the words of Daniel Webster, 'in letters of light on the blue arch of heaven, between Orion and the Pleiades,' so that every one might see and read it, and ponder upon it. But I am not one to believe that our whole duty will have been discharged by the adoption of a resolution of this character. We must make its principles a living faith. We must sustain it at any cost and at any sacrifice. We must send to the halls of Congress men ready and willing at all times to support it. We must carry it into every department of our government, and bring the whole moral force and power of the State to bear in favor of it ; and in doing this we shall at last inevitably succeed.

"It is asked what we of the North can do. Sir, we can prevent slavery from ever gaining a foothold in the vast Territories of the republic ; and we can abolish it in the District of Columbia. And, in regard to this point, we of Massachusetts are just as responsible for the existence of slavery there as are the people of any State in the Union : and are more guilty than some ; for we sin against

7

our own convictions.   In that District the prisons of our
own government are converted into slave-pens; and side
by side with our national public edifices are private prisons,
where our fellow-beings are immured, and kept for sale like
cattle.   I have visited one, and have seen crowds of slaves
awaiting purchasers, thence to be sent to the cotton-fields
and sugar-plantations of the far South-west.   One of our
own representatives told me that he saw at the railroad
dépôt a poor negro woman torn away from her children,
shrieking in the bitterness of her agony, and reproaching
her owner for the violation of his promise that she should
not be separated from her offspring.   A distinguished member of Congress from South Carolina was his companion at
the time, and exclaimed, ' Great God ! what a sight is here !
no wonder that you of the North are abolitionists !'   We
can stop this in the District of Columbia, and abolish
throughout the country this vile inter-state slave-traffic;
and the world and God will hold us to a fearful responsibility until we do it.

    " Then the revenue force of the government is now
used to prevent the escape of fugitive slaves; the garrisons
are used for prisons, and the army is the mere body-guard
of slavery; the navy, if not created, is used almost wholly
(at least the home squadron), for the protection of the domestic slave-trade.   The General Government can correct
all this; and, were that government to exercise its constitutional right and power, slavery would die.   The free
States, and Massachusetts among them, are responsible for
this; for they have the power to do it, and do not exercise
it.   They can bring the whole force and power of the government to bear in favor of liberty.   They can change the
provisions of the Constitution and the laws which now protect slave-property.   As the Constitution now stands, a

slave escaping here has no refuge, no protection; and the soil of our own State has long been the slaveholder's hunting-ground. The panting and fleeing fugitive, with bloodhounds at his heels, may enter Faneuil Hall, and he is still a slave. He may cast himself down under the shadow of yonder monument, and he is still a slave. He may come into this very chamber, or penetrate to the council-chamber of the executive for protection, and he is still a slave, and his master can drag him away into bondage. The law and the Constitution that allow this can be changed, as well, also, as that provision which allows a representative of slave-property in the national councils. This subject was once acted upon by this legislature; and, though then unsuccessful, repeated and constant effort will enable us to accomplish the end. But we are met with the assertion that the slaveholders have rights under the Constitution, and that the existence of their property was guaranteed by that instrument. Now, *I* undertake to say that the Constitution was made for a free people. The whole history of the country from 1774 to the adoption of the Constitution proves this. The first Congress which met in 1774 declared, —

" ' That they would not import or purchase any slaves; that they would not be concerned in the trade themselves; and that they would neither purchase slaves, use ships in the slave-trade, or sell their commodities and manufactures to those engaged in that traffic.'

" The Congress of 1774 declared, ' God never intended a part of the human race to hold an absolute property in, and an unbounded power over, others.'

" The ordinance of 1787 for the government of the North-west Territory, drawn up by a distinguished son of Massachusetts, expressly and forever prohibited slavery throughout that vast region. From 1775 to 1789, six of the States abolished slavery within their limits. If we look at the Madison papers, and into the debates of the several State conventions for the adoption of the Constitution, we shall find it established as clear as noonday light, that the framers of the Constitution never entertained the idea of the long continuance, far less the spread, of this great wrong; but the universal opinion was that slavery would soon die out, and be forever extinguished. Such was the opinion of the Washingtons, Jeffersons, Madisons, Henrys, Masons, and Martins of the South; of the Jays, Gerrys, Hancocks, Rushes, Adamses, Franklins, and Hamiltons of the North. They thought that everywhere the institution would soon pass away under the influence of our higher civilization and larger liberty. The whole concurrent testimony of all these great men, some of whom were among the purest and best characters the world has ever produced, proves that they all held this opinion and held this belief. We had no statesmen then who believed that 'slavery was the corner-stone of the republican edifice.'

"But, say some, the abolition of slavery and the agitation of the subject will lead to dissolution of the Union. Now, sir, I profess to be, and am, as strongly attached as any man to the union of these States. From boyhood I have been taught to regard disunion — in the words of Daniel Webster — as plunging the country into 'the gulf of fire and blackness.' I wish to see the whole country, from North to South, from the shores of the Atlantic to those of the Pacific, one country, great, glorious, and free, — an example for all the nations. I am for 'liberty and union;" but it must be 'liberty and union.' At all events, I am for liberty; and if dissolution of the Union must be the result of the abolition of slavery, or of lawful and constitutional action, why, then, let that dissolution come. Let the Union go; the sooner, the better. Better have liberty without union than union without liberty. But let me ask of these grave and conservative gentlemen who deprecate the agitation of this question, who would keep the subject of slavery out of sight forever, lest its discussion should hazard the perpetuity of the Union, or change or modify existing institutions, would they, if living at the time, have been found among the small flock gathered around Brewster and Robinson on the wild, barren heaths of Lincolnshire? Would they have been on board ' The Mayflower '? Would they have gathered with them in council to lay in prayers the foundation of a Christian commonwealth? Would they have been among the choice spirits rallying around and supporting Adams and Hancock? Would they have followed Warren to Bunker Hill? No, sir; no! They would have preached *moderation*. They would have kept aloof from the contests, if possible; have left the country rather than meet the crisis; and, if compelled to take a decisive part, would probably have been found arrayed against liberty, and on the side of the stronger power. They worship the past, gild their fathers' sepulchres, but crucify all that is noble of the present. Such men as these now call themselves conservators of our institutions, and oppose all attempts to agitate the momentous question of the abolition of slavery. Away with such stuff! I am sick of it. He alone is the true conservative who takes his stand on the foundation of justice and right, and maintains that position to the last.

" Our opponents seek to portray in vivid colors the terrible dangers that would attend the abolition of slavery.

7*

But look at this a moment. Eight of our States have emancipated all the slaves within their borders, and no difficulty whatever has followed. None of these dreadful evils have occurred; but, on the contrary, every thing has worked well, and to the greatly-increased prosperity of such States. And we have a more recent example in the British West-India islands, where circumstances were infinitely more unfavorable to the success of emancipation than they are with us; where the planters to a man were deadly opponents of the scheme; where the blacks and slaves were as nearly ten to one of the whites free. Yet the project was carried out, and no harm has been the result: so far from it, indeed, that, whereas nearly all the planters were bankrupt before the abolition, their condition is now vastly more prosperous; and whereas the slaves were then dying off at the rate of five thousand per year, under the pressure of the lash, to save the island from bankruptcy, the health and condition, moral, social, and intellectual, of the colored race, now free, has greatly, almost wonderfully, improved. All this is established by irrefragable testimony; and it far outweighs all the arguments and fears, real or pretended, of the opponents of emancipation.

"This emancipation of the West-India slaves was conceived and carried out, not by the planters and owners of the slaves, but by England. This very act is the brightest gem in her diadem of glory. It will live forever in the remembrance of mankind, even if the memory of her arms, literature, and arts, the achievements of her Nelson and Wellington, the works of her Shakspeare and Milton, should pass away into oblivion. If her power should be broken forever, and if she should to-morrow sink beneath the ocean, and the waves of the

Atlantic roll over the place where she now stands, still the renown of this great work, by which she taxed her own people a hundred millions of dollars, and gave liberty to eight hundred thousand men three thousand miles away sunk in the lowest depths of degradation, will endure through all time, and be quoted and commended by the lovers of freedom. Sir, it was the saying of a famous Athenian that the glory of his rival would not permit him to sleep. I trust that the glory England has acquired by this measure will not suffer us of America to slumber till we have emulated her example. I love not England; I am not dazzled by her power: but I envy her the glory of that great achievement.

" But we are again met with the argument that we are a commercial people, and cannot afford to disturb our relations with the rest of the country. Now, it is a notorious fact that the slave States do not pay dollar for dollar what they purchase from us. I know what I say; for I have examined the subject. There are many manufacturing towns and villages in our State that have lost hundreds of thousands of dollars by their dealings with the South: my own town has large business-connections there, and has been one of the sufferers. Our prosperity, so universally diffused among us, is the result of ceaseless and untiring industry. Slavery, sir, cannot support itself. The slave-holding power draws its living from the heart's blood of the slave, and the toil and the sweat of the hard-handed free laborer of the North. Our mariners brave the dangers and endure the tempests of the deep; our farmers till a hard and barren soil for a scanty subsistence; our mechanics and artisans labor all their days at their forges and in their work-shops; and a great part of the fruit of their honest toil is drawn from them to support the slave aristocracy of the Southern States. What they cannot whip out of their negroes they cheat out of us. I would rather that our noble ships that now whiten every sea should go down to their graves beneath the dark rolling billows of the deep, and our manufacturing villages be levelled with the dust, so that a squadron of cavalry could gallop over them unimpeded as the wild steeds sweep over the ruined cities of the desert, than that Massachusetts should forget her duty, forsake her principles, and bow down and crawl and grovel at the feet of the slave-power. Better, far better, that her sons should till her cold and barren soil, and cast their nets into the deep for a poor subsistence, than that her coffers should be filled with gold soiled and dimmed by the blood and tears of the bondman.

"We are often told, sir, that this agitation of slavery can do no good ; that it has thrown back emancipation for half a century. This is all sheer nonsense. Emancipation is not only nearer in point of time, but it is nearer in point of preparation. We often hear the same sage and profound observations upon the great and kindred cause of temperance, and with just as much reason. The press, at least in the free States, now often utters its voice for the slave ; faint and feeble, it is true. Ten years ago it was dumb, or sided with the oppressor. Religious societies and associations are discussing and deciding upon it. The cause of the slave is now advocated in most of our Northern pulpits : the religious sentiment of the land is setting in favor of the poor bondman, recognizing him as a man and a brother. The friends of freedom can utter their sentiments now without being beaten down by mobs of . 'gentlemen of property and standing.' A great change has also taken place in the slave States. Ten years ago it was dangerous to utter a word against slavery in the capital of the nation: now one can speak of slavery out of the halls of Congress with freedom. It can be established by the records and reports of the religious societies of the Southern States that more has been accomplished for the improvement of the slave than at any similar time in our history. We are told that we shall stand alone. I have no objection to that if we stand in the right. Massachusetts is used to standing alone. The gentleman from Stockbridge (Mr. Byington), upon another question the other day, said that Massachusetts exerted a vast influence on the new States of the confederacy, and that many of her sons went forth to mould and fashion her institutions. It is all true: and yet, notwithstanding she has long been the pattern State of the Union, she is under the ban of the empire; she is regarded with a jealous eye, and as little better than a conquered province. Her people are almost ostracized by the government. An occasional sop is now and then thrown out to some of them if they are false to her, and true to the *peculiar institution;* and, for one, I wish that not a single individual of her people could be found willing to take office under the National Government while wedded to slavery. Let us have one of Cromwell's self-denying ordinances while the government remains as it now is. If it be her destiny to stand alone in support of the right, alone let her stand, — alone, sir, in the language of one of her sons who now sleeps by the banks of the Connecticut, — ALONE LET HER STAND IN SOLITARY GRANDEUR. When the passions of the hour shall be hushed, I desire that the historic pen that shall record in letters of light for the study of after-ages the acts of this great struggle shall record the glorious fact, that there was one State, one free Commonwealth, that was faithful among the faithless to the teachings of the founders of the republic.

"But she will not stand alone if she does her duty. Look at the present condition of affairs in the former Gibraltar of the slave-power of the North, and behold a proof of this. Not Georgia, nor even South Carolina herself, has ever been more subservient and obsequious to the will of the slaveholding portion of the country than has New Hampshire; yet her granite hills are shaking and trembling to-day to the earthquake-voice of her citizens, aroused at last to a conviction of their duties and their rights. So will it be elsewhere.

"Let Massachusetts but do her duty, and other States will rally round her, and she will lead them on to the rescue of the constitution and the government from the slave-power. Her high and lofty principles, her stern and lofty purposes, may be sneered at and derided; timid friends may chide her: but the stout-hearted and true all over the land will gather round her. Standing on the broad and elevated platform of equal rights, living out and illustrating her own great principles, she will speak to her sister States with a thousand tongues. She will come to the rescue. She will be the standard-bearer in the contest. She led the van in the great struggle for independence: then the post of danger was hers. She has a right to lead now. Her descent from the sturdy old Puritan stock, her free labor and her free schools, all point her out as the leader in the great struggle between freedom and slavery. South Carolina has placed herself in advance as the leader of the cohorts of slavery. Let the descendants of the old Cavaliers and Puritans meet once more, not as their fathers met on the fields of Naseby and Worcester, but in the stern conflict of opinion. I have no fears for the issue. Every thing will be with us: the free impulses of the age will be with us; civilization will be with us; the wild and generous impulses of the human heart will be with us; and God will be with us.   Cassius M. Clays will arise in all the slave States, pointing them to our example.

"Our country was the child of hope and expectation When our fathers launched our government upon the tide, the prayers, hopes, and sympathies of the friends of liberal institutions throughout the globe were with us.   The oppressed began to hope for self-government; and they looked hither with trembling anxiety to see how we should carry out in practice our sublime declaration of the equality and freedom of all men.   We have not, perhaps, lived in vain.   Had America been true to herself, to her own sublime principles, the friends of religious, social, and civil liberty everywhere would have taken courage from her example, and the oppressors of our race would have loosed their hold upon unjust power: there is hardly a throne upon the globe but would now be tottering to its fall.   Ours is the duty, be ours the glory, to rescue our country from the 'dominion, curse, and shame of slavery, and make her great and glorious among the nations.' The past with its crowded memories of the tears and labors of the martyrs of truth who have perished on the field, the scaffold, and in the dungeon, the present with its warm and generous sympathies, and the future with its high hopes and brilliant expectations, all cheer us onward in the path of duty and of glory.

"I do not wish to 'allude to parties;' and yet I cannot well avoid it.   I have recommended that the State should take a bold stand against slavery; and I am willing that the majority here shall be held responsible for it, as they will surely be.   It is alike undeniable and notorious, that, during the struggles of the last ten years, the party now in the majority here has generally been arrayed on the side of liberty on all the incidental questions that have arisen. It has gone just far enough to lose the confidence and sympathy of the South, and to encounter defeat in almost every thing; but it has not gone far enough to gain the entire confidence and obtain the support of the free impulses of the North. On the other hand, our opponents, the party here in the minority, it is equally notorious and undeniable, have usually sided with the slave-power on all the questions connected with the interests of slavery; and they stand in that posture to-day, committed — fully and entirely committed — to slavery and the slave-power.

"Thus far they have reaped all the advantages of such subserviency; but hereafter, when, in the contests of the future, a day of retribution shall come, — as come it surely will, — they will find themselves by their own folly placed in a position of shame, defeat, and disgrace, as opponents of the progress of liberty, enlightenment, and civilization.

"Sir, I wish to have 'Emancipation' inscribed on the banners under which we rally, in characters of living light, and also that we go for 'the protection of man.' We go for the protection of his labor: let us give security, first to himself, and afterwards to his labor. That is the true ground we must take; and, if it be taken boldly and manfully, I am willing to risk myself, and all that I have or hope for, on the issue, confident that in five years our cause will sweep through the country like a tornado. We shall carry every free State with a whirlwind: it will go like the fire over the prairies of the West. If not, we are accustomed to defeat; and it is far better to be in the right than to hold the reins of government, and roll in wealth and power. I say without hesitation, that the stand I have spoken of we must take. We cannot resist so doing if we would. It is our 'manifest destiny.' Even were we base enough to desire it, we could not regain our influence with the slaveholding South by any means; no, not by the veriest servile and wretched truckling to all her arrogant demands. I would not regain it if we could. Then, in Heaven's name, let us go on in the right. If victory come, let us hail and improve it: if, on the contrary, defeat be our lot, it will be a glorious defeat; for we shall have been right, and shall have deserved success. At any rate, we shall do something for our race, something for liberty, which will secure for us the confidence and the respect of the good and the true. A single word, Mr. Speaker, of a personal character, and I shall have done. I have ever been and am a party man; and I shall always go with my party in what I think right and best: but I am determined never to be either driven or kicked out of any party with which I may choose to act; and it is my pride to believe that four-fifths of the party now in the majority in this State concur in the view I take of this subject, and are anxious that we should commit Massachusetts against slavery. It is so especially with regard to the young men, — those who are shortly to hold the reins of power. The city influence is, I know, the other way; but, sir, 'the gods of the valleys are not the gods of the hills.'

"For one, I am ready to stand with any man, or set of men, —Whig, Democrat, Abolitionist, Christian, or Infidel, — who will go with me in the cause of emancipation.

"It is unpleasant to me to say what I have now said; it is painful to differ from esteemed and respected friends whose good opinion we value. I know the feelings of many who hear me. All sorts of unworthy motives will be ascribed to me, and my judgment and discretion questioned. Sir, I have no personal motive: I see nothing to be gained, and something to be lost. At any rate, I know I shall lose the good opinion of some friends, who will doubtless regard me as a fanatic. But I have made up my mind, after some little reflection, that we must either destroy slavery, or slavery will destroy our government and our liberties; and I had far rather act according to the dictates of duty and of patriotism than to receive the approving smiles of friends. I shall go for the abolition of slavery at all times and on all occasions, now and hereafter. I loathe, detest, and abhor it. It is at war with Nature and Nature's God.

"I have no apologies to make for it; and no hope of political reward, no fear of ridicule or reproach, shall ever deter me from using all the moral and political influence I possess, in such a manner as my judgment shall approve, to accomplish the entire extinction of slavery, and to make my native land, which I love with the affection of a son, what it should be, — glorious and free, and an example to all nations."

This resolution, so ably advocated, was, after much discussion and excitement, adopted in the House by ninety-three majority: in the Senate, which was more conservative, it was lost by four votes. In the minds of the people it lived, inspiring noble hearts, and calling to the rescue of the bondman.

Mr. Wilson was no revolutionist, except through constitutional and legal means. He loved the Union: he had no desire in any event, as an aggressor, to appeal to arms. He believed, that, under the Constitution, Southern men had no right to extend slavery over our territorial domains; and on that ground he would meet the question. When, on the 3d of March, he presented to the House a

memorial from Francis Jackson for the withdrawal from
Congress of the Massachusetts delegation, and the consequent dissolution of the Union, he declared that he held
the right of petition sacred; that he was for the abolition
of slavery: but, continued he, " it must be accomplished
under, by, and through the Constitution ; " not by violence,
but by " sovereign law," the " collected will " of the people, which

> " O'er thrones and globes elate,
> Sits empress, crowning good, repressing ill."

CHAPTER VI.

IN the autumn of 1847 Mr. Wilson declined being a
candidate for the legislature ; but through his generous
sympathies, temperate habits, and uprightness as a man,
his intelligence and sagacity as a legislator, and his steady
adherence to the principles of human freedom and the
interests of the working-classes, he was still gaining the
respect and confidence of the people. Even those who
looked contemptuously upon him as rising from the workshop of a shoemaker were obliged to admit his eminent
ability as a speaker and leader. His bold, direct, and
logical speech, in the House of the last year, on slavery,

88

had turned the thoughts of the abolitionists to him as their legislative champion.

The laboring-people, from whom he had sprung, and of whose opinions he was, perhaps, the best exponent in the State, were proud of his success, and entertained for him increasing admiration and esteem. They held even then — for in this country they have always had the clearest vision of impending crises — that we were on the eve of great political events, and that he would be the man for the occasion.

On the death of John Quincy Adams in February, 1848, and the consequent vacancy in the House of Representatives, a Whig convention was held in Dedham to select a candidate to supply his place. The three leading men for whom that body had a preference were Henry Wilson, William Jackson, and Horace Mann. After the third balloting, Mr. Wilson withdrew his name in favor of Mr. Mann, who was nominated. The convention then, by an almost unanimous vote, appointed Mr. Wilson delegate to the Whig National Convention to be held in Philadelphia in the ensuing month of June. He supported Mr. Webster for president in that convention on account of his principles in favor of liberty; yet he had misgivings in regard to this statesman's position on this question, which were sadly realized in 1850. He had previously declared in public and in private, that if Gen. Taylor should receive the vote of the Whig party in that convention, unpledged to the Wilmot Proviso, he not only would not support him, but would do all in his power to defeat him. The convention nominated Gen. Taylor for the presidency. Mr. Wilson, and his colleague Mr. Charles Allen, denounced the action of the convention, and, retiring from it, held a meeting of a few Northern

8*

men, and appointed a committee, who, with others, called the Buffalo Convention, where Mr. Van Buren received the nomination.

Returning home, Mr. Wilson and his associates held a convention in the city of Worcester on the 28th of June. It was large and enthusiastic. The subserviency of the Whig party to the interests of the South was fully discussed, and its inadequacy and unwillingness to meet the demands of freedom and the progressive spirit of the age were most eloquently set forth. For the vindication of free labor, for the maintenance of freedom in the Territories, for resistance to the aggressive policy of the South, which bo'h Northern Whigs and Democrats, though to some extent in words opposing, still accepted in acts, the organization of the Free-soil party was begun. " A few days after," Mr. Wilson said, " I called on Mr. Webster at his own request; and, he expressed his cordial assent to the principles of the convention." Untiring in his endeavors to arouse the North to a sense of the nation's injustice towards the slave, Mr. Wilson in September purchased " The Boston Republican," which he edited with signal ability from the autumn of 1848 to January, 1851, defending steadily the principles of freedom, and holding an advanced position in civil, social, and political reform. It was the chief organ of the Free-soil party, of which he was the acknowledged leader ; and it was continued one year as a daily paper. The articles of agreement between Mr. Wilson and the publishers of the paper are dated Boston, Nov. 11, 1848: " The subscribers, Henry Wilson of the first part, William S. Damrell of the second part, and Curtis C. Nichols of the third part, have this day formed a copartnership, to be known as the firm of Wilson, Damrell, and Co., for the purpose of publishing ' The Daily Republican,' ' Semi-weekly Republican,' and ' Weekly Emancipator and Republican.' " The political creed of the paper was, " No extension of slavery over the Territories; no more slave territory to be added to the Union; no more slave States to be admitted into the Union; no compromise with slavery must be made." Mr. Wilson wrote most of the original articles, including the book-notices, for the paper; but was sometimes assisted by Mr. William S. Robinson and other political and literary friends. On retiring from the paper, he found that he had lost something like seven thousand dollars in the enterprise; yet it had been of essential service to the Free-soil party, and he cheerfully submitted to the pecuniary damage. It was an effective educator of the people in respect to the cardinal doctrines involved in that irresistible conflict between free and slave labor which is now forever settled on this continent.

Appointed chairman of the Free-soil State Committee in 1849, he most industriously labored, by the circulation of pamphlets and by delivering addresses in various sections of the State, as well as through the columns of " The Republican," for the advancement of the party. Four years he spent in this capacity; and they were years of ceaseless vigilance and toil: yet by these exertions he was not only deepening the antislavery sentiment of the State, but also gaining wisdom and experience for sterner effort and severer conflict. When Heaven has something great and good for any man to do, it prepares and proves him for the occasion.

In 1850 Mr. Wilson was again a member of the lower branch of the State Legislature, where he labored with his accustomed zeal and energy. The Free-soil members gave him their votes for the speakership; but he was not elected. He had been urged by his own party and the Democrats in union to become a candidate for the Senate; but he preferred a seat in the more popular body, as having broader influence.

It was during the session of this legislature that Mr. Webster made his 7th-of-March speech on Mr. Clay's resolutions in the Senate of the United States. The sentiment of the North was deeply wounded by it. Mr. Wilson fearlessly declared to the House that the people would repudiate that speech and those who should indorse it; and that, at the next election, the deserters from the cause of freedom would surely find themselves deserted. His words, though meeting the defiance of many of the leading Whigs, proved true. By the famous coalition of the Free-soil and the Democratic parties, the Whig party of Massachusetts, once so strong and so triumphant, was defeated. This coalition, Mr. Wilson, for the most part, organized. Calling together the State Committee and about seventy members of his own party at the Adams House in Boston in the summer of 1850, he declared to them that Mr. Webster's speech and Mr. Fillmore's timid administration could be condemned; that a member of the Free-soil party could be sent to the United-States Senate to take the place of Mr. Webster (made secretary of state) for the long term, and a member of the Democratic party for the short term; and that thus antislavery men could be brought to control the policy of the State. After a long and animated discussion, the meeting refused to form the coalition: but Mr. Wilson and his friends laid the scheme before the people, who accepted it, and, through the legislature, elected George S. Boutwell as governor; and the General Court, after a long and bitter contest and many ballotings, in 1851, sent Charles Sumner to the United-States Senate for the long term, choosing also Robert Rantoul, a Democrat, for the other term.

Many causes — such as the persistent labors of antislavery men through public addresses and the press, the general awakening of the people to the insolent aggressions of the Southern demagogues, and the course of Mr. Webster — conspired to aid this triumph of the friends of freedom; but all admitted that it was largely due to the sagacity, the organizing power, and the unremitting activity, of Mr. Wilson. Perhaps no political movement had ever so aroused the people of Massachusetts, or had been so significant of her advance in liberal ideas. Hard and insulting names were freely bestowed upon the leader; but he had no time nor wish to strike " back-blows."

The agency which he had in the election of Mr. Sumner to the Senate is recognized in the following frank avowal: —

CRAGIE HOUSE, CAMBRIDGE, April 25, 1851.

MY DEAR WILSON, — I have this moment read your remarks of last night, which I think peculiarly happy. You touched the right chord. I hope not to seem cold or churlish in thus withdrawing from all the public manifestations of triumph to which our friends are prompted. In doing so, I follow the line of reserve which you know I have kept to throughout the contest; and my best judgment at this moment satisfies me that I am right.

You who have seen me familiarly and daily from the beginning to the end will understand me, and, if need be, can satisfy those, who, taking counsel of their exultation, would have me mingle in the display. But I shrink from imposing any thing more upon you.

To your ability, energy, determination, and fidelity our cause owes its present success. For weal or woe, you must take the responsibility of having placed me in the Senate of the United States.

I am prompted also to add, that, while you have done al this, I have never heard from you a single suggestion of a selfish character, looking in any way to any good to yourself: your labors have been as disinterested as they have been effective. This consideration increases my personal esteem and gratitude. I trust that you will see that Mr. B.'s resolves are passed at once *as they are,* and the bill as soon as possible. Delay will be the tactics of the enemy.

Sincerely yours,

CHARLES SUMNER.

The Hon. HENRY WILSON.

This coalition sent Mr. Wilson to the State Senate for the session of 1851 by a majority of twenty-one hundred votes; and he was then made president of that body. On taking the chair the first day of January, he made the following appropriate address: "Senators, I tender to you my sincere and grateful thanks for this expression of your confidence. In return, I promise to bring to the chair an earnest determination to perform its duties with fidelity and impartiality. Conscious of a want of experience, I solicit your indulgence. I feel that. I occupy this place under the disadvantage of having been preceded by some of the most eminent men who have illustrated the legislative history of the Commonwealth. Relying, however, on your friendly co-operation, I enter upon the performance of the task to which your partiality has called me. My hope is, that we shall so conduct our deliberations as not only to secure harmony among ourselves, but also to sustain those great principles which are conducive to the glory and the prosperity of the Commonwealth.

Having done this, we shall give back to the people the power they delegated to us, with the proud consciousness of having done something to advance the ideas of freedom and progress, — something to promote the renown of the republic, and to cement that union which makes us one people."

Eighteen years before, he was a friendless youth, homeless and penniless, seeking the privilege to toil for his daily bread ; but through untiring industry, undeviating steadiness to principle, through an unshaken confidence in human progress, and self-denying sacrifice for the relief of the oppressed, he raised himself, against persistent opposition, to this honorable post. It is the fortune of but few men to make such advancement in so brief a period ; yet his success, so nobly merited and won, may serve as an encouragement to those, who, under adverse circumstances, are aspiring PER VIRTUTEM AD GLORIAM.

On the 21st of January, 1851, the anniversary of the twentieth year of the existence of " The Liberator" was held in Cochituate Hall ; when Mr. Wilson thus again expressed his views and hopes upon " the irrepressible conflict : " —

" Sir, allusion has been made to-night to the small beginning of the great antislavery movement twenty years ago, when ' The Liberator ' was launched upon the tide. These years have been years of devotion and of struggles unsurpassed in any age or in any cause. But, notwithstanding the treachery of public men, I venture to say that the cause of liberty is spreading throughout the whole land, and that the day is not far distant when brilliant victories for freedom will be won. We shall arrest the extension of slavery, and rescue the government from the grasp of the slave-power ; we shall blot out slavery in the national capital; we shall surround the slave States with a cordon of free States; we shall then appeal to the hearts and consciences of men; and in a few years, notwithstanding the immense interests combined in the cause of oppression, we shall give liberty to the millions in bondage. (Hear, hear.) I trust that many of us will live to see the chain stricken from the limbs of the last bondman in the republic; but, sir, whenever that day shall come, living or dead, no name connected with the antislavery movement will be dearer to the enfranchised millions than the name of your guest, William Lloyd Garrison." (Prolonged applause.)

During this session of the Senate, Mr. Wilson took a leading part in obtaining an act for a third convention for revising the Constitution of the State; in carrying the Homestead Exemption Bill, which reserved to the family of the insolvent debtor five hundred dollars from the hands of creditors; in the fiercely-contested election of Mr. Sumner, carried in April over Mr. Winthrop; and in securing the act for the re-organization of the board of overseers of Harvard University, by which they were to be chosen by joint ballot of both branches of the legislature, so that all sects and parties might be represented by their most competent men.

On the 15th of May he vigorously defended the principles of the Free-soil party, claiming it to be a Union constitutional organization, and in forcible terms rebuked the course of Mr. Webster.

At the close of the session (May 23, 1851), it was ordered that the "thanks of the Senate be presented to the Hon. Henry Wilson for the able, impartial, and satisfactory manner in which he has discharged the duties of the chair."

In reply, he said, —

"Senators, this expression of your approbation excites in my bosom the liveliest emotions of gratitude. The uniform courtesy and kindness you have all, individually and collectively, extended to me through this protracted session, and the kind words now spoken, give me the most ample assurance that this vote is no formal or unmeaning compliment. Be assured, gentlemen, be assured, I shall ever fondly cherish the recollections of your many acts of kindness, until the heart upon which they are indelibly engraved ceases to beat forever."

"Knowledge of human nature," said one of the daily journals of this season, "and the art of winning the confidence of men, are among the chief elements of political efficiency; and, in addition to these, Gen. Wilson possesses a more powerful element of success in the whole-souled devotion with which he supports the cause of freedom."

He was this year chosen vice-president of the Legislative Temperance Society, and industriously availed himself of every occasion to promote the temperance cause.

Appointed delegate to the National Convention of the Free-soil party, held at Pittsburg, Penn., in 1852, he was elevated to the chair of that body, when he made an eloquent address: he was also made chairman of the National Free-soil Committee, in which capacity he served with fidelity and acceptance. During this year he was supported by the Free-soil men of the Eighth District for a seat in Congress, but failed of an election by less than a hundred votes, although there was a heavy majority against his party in that district. He was also urged by his political associates and by many Democrats to become candidate for the gubernatorial chair; but, in a public letter, he peremptorily declined a nomination.

Again he was a member (1852), and was again elected president of the Massachusetts Senate by sixteen out of twenty-seven votes. During the session, he assisted vigorously in obtaining the act for a constitutional convention, and for a law prohibiting the sale of intoxicating liquors; on behalf of which he made a strong speech in February, wherein he said, " Heretofore we have tried to regulate the sale of ardent spirits. This bill will stop it."

He was appointed chairman of the legislative committee to welcome President Fillmore to Massachusetts, and also to extend a reception to Gov. Louis Kossuth, the distinguished Hungarian exile to our State. In company with twenty-one senators, he met this noble advocate of freedom and humanity on his arrival at Springfield, April 26, 1852, and, in the presence of a vast multitude of people who had gathered to greet the heroic opponent of Austrian despotism, gave him a cordial welcome to the hospitalities of Massachusetts in the following eloquent and appropriate words : —

" Gov. Kossuth, in the name and in behalf of the government, I bid you welcome to the Commonwealth of Massachusetts, to the hospitalities of the authorities, and the sincere and enthusiastic greetings of the people. I welcome you, sir, to a Commonwealth which recognizes the unity of mankind, the brotherhood of men and of nations, — a Commonwealth where the equality of all men before the law is fully established ; where ' personal freedom is secured in its completest individuality, and common consent recognized as the only just origin of fundamental laws.'

" Welcome, sir, to the soil consecrated to the tears and prayers of the Pilgrim exiles, and by the first blood of the Revolution. Welcome to the halls of council, where Otis and Hancock and the Adamses breathed into the nation the breath of life; to the field of battle, where Warren and his comrades fell fighting for freedom and the rights of man, and where the peerless chieftain to whose tomb you have just made a pilgrimage first marshalled the armies of the republic.   Welcome to the native State of Franklin, who pleaded the cause of his country to willing and unwilling ears in the Old World as you are pleading the cause of your country in the New World.   Welcome to the acquaintance of a people who cherish your cause in their hearts, and who pronounce your name with affection and admiration. Welcome to their free institutions, — institutions of religion and of learning and of charity, reared by the free choice of the people for the culture of all and the relief of all, — institutions which are the fruits of freedom such as you strove to give to your fatherland, for which crime you are this day a homeless and persecuted exile.

"To-day you are the guest of Massachusetts.   Sir, the people of Massachusetts are not man-worshippers.   They will pay you no unmeaning compliments, no empty honors. But they know your history by heart.   Your early consecration to freedom; your years of persecution and imprisonment; your sublime devotion to the nationality and elevation of your country; the matchless eloquence and untiring industry with which at home you combated the Austrian despotism, with which in exile you have pleaded the cause of Hungarian liberty, the cause of universal democratic freedom and of national right; the lofty steadiness of your purpose, and the stainless purity of your life, — these have won their sympathy, and command their profoundest admiration.   Descendants of Pilgrim exiles, we greet you warmly.   Sons of Revolutionary patriots, we hail **you as the exiled leader of a noble struggle for ancient** rights and national independence. We receive you as the representative of Hungary, as the champion of republicanism in Europe. We welcome you as we would welcome your gallant people into the sisterhood of republics, into the family of nations.

"The people of this Commonwealth, sir, watched the noble struggle of your nation with admiration and with hope. They felt that the armies which you organized and sent into the field were fighting the battles, not of Hungary alone, but of the world, because they were fought for freedom and for progress. Your victories were our victories; and when, by the treachery of Görgey, Hungary fell before the armed intervention of Russia, they felt, and still feel, that the czar had not only violated the rights of Hungary, but had outraged the law of nations and the sentiment of the civilized world. On this subject the message of his Excellency the governor, and the resolutions pending before the legislature, utter the sentiments of the people of Massachusetts.

"The wave of re-action has swept over Europe. The high hopes excited by the revolutions of 1848 are buried in the graves and in the dungeons of the martyrs of freedom; are quenched in the blood of the subjugated people. The iron heel of absolutism presses the beating hearts of the nations. The voice of freedom is heard only in the threatening murmurs of the down-trodden masses, or in the sad accents of their exiled leaders. But all is not lost. God lives and reigns. The purest, the noblest, the most powerful impulses of the great heart of humanity are for right and liberty. Glorious actions and noble aims are never wholly lost. The

'Seed of generous sacrifice,
Though seeming on the desert cast,
Shall rise with flower and fruit at last.'

" When you quit the shores of the republic you will
carry with you the prayers of Massachusetts that the days
of your exile may be few, and the subjugation of your
people brief; that your country may speedily assume her
proper high position among the nations ; and that you may
give to her counsels in the future, as you have given in the
past, the weight of your character and the power of your
intellect to guide her onward in the career of progress and
of democratic freedom.

" Again, sir, in the name of the government and people
of Massachusetts, I welcome you to our hearts and to our
homes. I welcome you to such a reception as it becomes
a free and democratic people to give to the most illustrious
living leader and champion of freedom and democracy." *

Mr. Wilson afterwards in an appropriate manner welcomed the illustrious exile to the Senate, and was highly
gratified with the brief interviews which he held with
him ; for their opinions on the great questions of civil liberty were in harmony, and their experience in endeavoring
to maintain it brought them into immediate personal
sympathy. Mr. Wilson presided over the deliberations of
the Senate with dignity, impartiality, and acceptance. But
once only was a question raised on his decision during the
time he occupied the chair, and then but five voted against
him. At the close of his State senatorial career in the
spring of 1852, he took leave of his associates in an appro-

---

* In a letter of Mr. Sumner to Mr. Wilson, dated Senate-chamber, April 29,
1852, he says, " Seward has just come to my desk; and his first words were. ' What
a magnificent speech Wilson made to Kossuth ! I have read nothing for months
which took such hold of me.' I cannot resist telling you of this, and adding the
expression of my sincere delight in what you said. It was eloquent, wise, and
apt. I am glad of this grand reception. Massachusetts does honor to herself in
thus honoring a representative of freedom."

priate address; and a gold watch was presented to him by his friends in token of his faithfulness and courtesy as the presiding officer.

It bears this inscription : —

" HON. HENRY WILSON, FROM MEMBERS OF THE MASSACHUSETTS SENATE, 1852."

During the sessions of the legislature in 1850–1–2, he was absent from his seat but one day, and that was to attend the funeral of a friend. As was said of Mr. Adams, one might as soon expect to see a pillar of the Capitol absent from its place as Mr. Wilson from his seat.

CHAPTER VII.

MR. WILSON AT HOME. — THE STATE CONSTITUTIONAL
CONVENTION. — HIS PART IN IT. — SPEECHES. —
RESULT OF THE CONVENTION.

A Friend of his Pastor. — Hard Study. — Temperance. — Books and Authors. —
The Source of Civil Liberty. — No "Back-Blows." — Cheerful Spirit. —
Home. — Gift to his Minister. — Revision of the State Constitution. — Elected
by Natick and Berlin. — Punctuality. — His Course. — How he looked at a
Legal Question. — Chairman *pro tem.* — Speech in Favor of Colored Troops.
— On the Death of Mr. Gourgas of Concord. — On the Course of Harvard
College in Respect to Prof. Bowen. — Address to his Constituents. — Reason
for Defeat of the Amendments. — Cost and Influence of the Convention.

IN May, 1852, the Rev. Elias Nason was settled as pastor of the Congregational church at Natick, where he continued until the autumn of 1858. During his pastorate at Natick he found in Mr. Wilson a firm and cordial friend, ever prompt and liberal in the support of the institutions of religion and of benevolence, and ever aiding with heart and hand in the promotion of the welfare of the community. On the sabbath he was usually in his seat in church, and an attentive listener. He was always frank and open in the expression of his opinions upon every subject, whether political, social, or religious; and he loved to have other people speak with the same freedom. Plain and unaffected in his manner and his dress, he associated freely with the working-people; and the very humblest found a welcome

103

at his open door. In the social circle the sight of his fresh and smiling countenance was indeed a benediction.

He pursued his studies with untiring energy, sometimes reading or writing — as he had once labored in the shop — fifteen or sixteen hours in succession. When he commenced upon a theme, he loved to finish his investigations ere he left it; and this often carried his labors far into the night: yet still he came forth as bright the following day as if he had spent the night in repose. His physical as well as mental system always seemed to be in splendid working-order. By looking at his clear complexion and his vigorous frame, one had an argument for temperance more eloquent than any orator could present. In his reading he was rapid and select. He chose the best, — of foreign writers, Macaulay, Hallam, Carlyle, De Tocqueville; of American, Sparks, Bancroft, Prescott, Everett. History was his favorite reading; yet now and then he spent an hour with Emerson's "Essays," Hawthorne's "Scarlet Letter," "Uncle Tom's Cabin," "Jane Eyre," and "David Copperfield."

In his interviews with his pastor he often expressed his profound sympathy for the slave and for the working-people, and said that his brightest hope was that he might do something in his life towards breaking the fetters of the bondman. Constitutional and civil liberty, he frequently asserted, came from the principles of the New Testament: by those principles every human being ought to be a freeman, and on those principles aggression against the slaveholding system must be made. His forecast as to the turn of the impending contest seems surprising; and, on being asked in 1867 how he came to be so "good for guessing," he replied, "By looking, not at one point only, but over the whole field of action."

Though not then a communicant of the church, he held the church in high regard; complaining only now and then that the clergy moved too tardily in matters of reform.

"Men misunderstand my motives, and malign my character," he often said; "but I have no time nor wish to strike back-blows. I desire to advance upon the line of right and duty, and to make every one as happy as I can along the way."

This course of action gave him a cheerful spirit, and made others cheerful in his presence. His home, enlivened by the smile of an amiable wife and sprightly boy, was happy; and surrounded by affectionate friends and neighbors, who well knew his worth, and were proud of his advancement, he was considered as one of the most useful and most enviable men in that community.

When his pastor left Natick, Mr. Wilson, with a tear in his eye, came up to him, and said, "I am a poor man; but take this in remembrance, and I wish it were a hundred times as much."

On the fourth day of May, 1853, the convention for the revision and amendment of the Constitution of the State assembled in the State House, Boston. This instrument, framed in 1780, was revised in 1820; and through successive changes in legislation, and the progress of liberal ideas among the people, evidently needed reexamination, and, in respect to some of its articles, improvement. The act of the legislature for holding this convention was obtained by a hard struggle on the part of the progressive members; and, to form it, some of the ablest legislators in the State — as Rufus Choate, George S. Boutwell, Benjamin F. Butler, George S. Hillard, N. P. Banks, and Benjamin F. Hallett — were elected. Mr.

Wilson was chosen by the town of Natick, and also by the town of Berlin. "On Monday last," he pleasantly said in the convention, "I visited the people of that town for the first time in my life (perhaps, if they had known me better, they would not have elected me); and I told the people that I would serve them to the best of my ability, if they desired it; but, under the circumstances, I should be under great obligations to them if they would allow me to resign as delegate from their town: and I obtained their unanimous vote to that effect." He was appointed chairman of the committee for the best mode of proceeding in the business of the convention, and also chairman of the committee on that part of the Constitution relating to the Senate. He set himself at work in this body with his usual zeal and industry: he took a leading part in its debates, and made many able and effective speeches. During the whole session, running through ninety days, he was not absent from his seat more than thirty minutes; and every paper, every motion, every speech, received the attention of his observant eye or ear. True to the sentiments he had so frequently expressed, his voice was always heard in the defence of equal rights, of the cause of human freedom, and of the working-people. He met the conservative element in the convention courteously, but fearlessly; and by standing firmly to his point, and supporting himself by quick appeals to the principles of equity, to present need or past experience, he often gained the victory.

On being asked one day why he ventured, ignorant as he was of law, to meet on certain legal questions gentlemen eminent for their knowledge of the law, his characteristic answer was, "Such men mystify things by their abstractions and their technicalities: whereas by using common sense, and looking at things fairly, fearlessly in the face, we generally come out right."

During the illness of Mr. Banks, the speaker of the convention, he was appointed to the chair, and presided ably over the deliberations.   Among his speeches in this body, that in favor of election by the majority instead of the plurality vote, that against an elective judiciary, that against the limitation of the State credit, as also that in opposition to the tax qualification of the voter, may be cited as evincing marked ability.   In regard to the admission of colored persons into the military service of the State, he nobly said, "The first victim of the Boston massacre, on the 5th of March, 1770, which made the fires of resistance burn more intensely, was a colored man. Hundreds of colored men entered the ranks, and fought bravely on all the fields of the Revolution.   Graydon of Pennsylvania, in his Memoirs, informs us that many of the Southern officers disliked the New-England regiments because so many colored men were in their ranks.   At Red Bank they received the commendation of their commander for their gallant conduct.   A colored battalion was organized for the defence of New Orleans, and Gen. Jackson publicly thanked them for their courage and conduct.   When the country has required their blood in days of trial and conflict, they have given it freely, and we have accepted it ; but in times of peace, when their blood is not needed, we spurn and trample them under foot.   I have no part in this great wrong to a race.   Whenever and wherever we have the power to do it, I would give to all men of every clime and race, of every faith and creed, freedom and equality before the law.   My voice and my vote shall ever be given for the equality of all the children of men before the laws of the Commonwealth of Massachusetts and the United States."

His remarks on the death of his friend Francis R. Gourgas, which occurred on the twelfth day of July, are beautiful as they are just: " The death of a member of this convention," said he, " could not but be received with mournful sadness by us all. But, sir, he who has fallen was a friend of many years. In 1842, eleven years ago, it was my privilege to meet him upon the floor of this House. Then I formed a personal acquaintance with him, — an acquaintance which ripened into a personal friendship which has been continued from that day to this. I have ever found him a man

> ' Of soul sincere,
> In action faithful, and in honor clear.'

" During the last five years, it has been my peculiar fortune to meet him on many occasions connected with public affairs ; and, sir, I can truly say, that, among all my acquaintances and friends, I know of no one among the living who excelled him in ripe and sound judgment, in discretion and prudence. He was a man of inflexible purpose, of integrity undoubted. He entertained his own opinions with the tenacity of sincere conviction ; and at the same time, in carrying out those opinions, he always exercised the greatest prudence, discretion, and wisdom. It was his fortune, years ago, to enter upon the duties of editor of a leading political journal in the town of Concord. In the severe political conflicts of those times, he doubtless had many strong opponents ; but in his own town of Concord he enjoyed the confidence, the respect, and the affection of men of all parties. His townsmen and neighbors loved and honored him ; for they knew his worth.

" Having a family of three children, an accomplished, intelligent, and faithful wife, he has, during the past few years, devoted himself, when not engaged in the duties of public life, to the welfare of his family, and to the cultivation of his beautiful garden. His library, for which he had recently fitted up an appropriate room, reflected the refinement of his taste and the cultivation of his mind. He was surrounded by every thing to make life agreeable and desirable. But, sir, he has fallen, — fallen in the vigor and maturity of his manhood, — mourned by all his neighbors, and deeply regretted by all his associates and friends in political life. In him I have lost an associate and friend whose name and memory I shall ever cherish with affection until my heart shall cease to beat.

"A comrade has fallen. We may pause for a moment, and drop a tear of affection to his memory; but duty compels us to close up the ranks, and hurry on in the performance of life's labors."

His speech on the course pursued by the friends of Harvard College in respect to Prof. Francis Bowen, who had been set aside from his professorship, as Mr. Wilson stated, for "misquoting, misstating, and garbling historical authorities," is marked with manly force.

"I do not, sir, mean to charge it" [the restoration of Mr. Bowen], "directly or indirectly, to the corporators of that institution. I charge it upon a certain class of individuals, who seem to think that they own the institution, president, corporators, overseers, and all, — a class of individuals who assume it to be their mission to keep Harvard College from the influences of the outside barbarians. I would not, if I could, take Harvard College from one sect of religionists, and place it under the control of another sect. I would not take it from the control of one political party, and place it under the control of another political party. I would introduce into its government men of all religious sects and of all political parties ; men of genius and knowledge ; men devoted to the cause of sound learning and literature ; men of liberal ideas ; men who would bring that institution, founded by our fathers in their days of weakness, abreast of the progressive march of the age, and within the circle of popular sympathy.

"Mr. President, in 1850, Francis Bowen, editor of 'The North-American Review,' was nominated professor of history by the corporators of Harvard College. On the sixth day of February, 1851, his nomination came up for confirmation before the board of overseers in the Senate-chamber. A majority of the board of overseers of that year believed that he entertained sentiments and opinions which unfitted him to be a teacher of history in that university, or anywhere else in America ; and he was rejected, ignominiously rejected, — rejected for sentiments and opinions that disqualified him to be the teacher of American youth ; and rejected, also, for the historical ignorance he had shown ; for the perversions, misquotations, and blunders he had made in defending his obnoxious sentiments and opinions.

"Sir, I ask the gentleman from Boston (Mr. Lothrop) if the nomination of Francis Bowen to the professorship of history by the corporation of Harvard College, in 1850, was an evidence of the desire of the men who control that institution to keep it along with the wants of the people and the spirit of the age. Are such sentiments and opinions as Bowen has expressed for years through 'The North-American Review' such sentiments and opinions as fit him to teach the young men of Massachusetts and of the country ? Are such historical mistakes, blunders, and perversions, as he has exhibited in his Hungarian controversy, evidences of qualifications to teach the young men of Harvard? Is such dishonesty as he has shown in garbling historical authorities an evidence of fitness for the chair of the professorship of history in the oldest university of the country? Is such a temper as he has manifested in the controversies growing out of his historical discussions an evidence of his fitness, of his impartiality? His sentiments, opinions, historical ignorance, mistakes, perversions, blunders, plagiarisms, and garbling of authorities, were not unknown to the corporators when his name, in January, 1851, was submitted to the board of overseers. When, on the 6th of February, his nomination came up for confirmation, they were there, not to withdraw the nomination in obedience to the almost united voice of the American press and the American people, who loathed and abhorred his sentiments; but they, and the peculiar friends of the college, were there to sustain the man whom the voice of the people had pronounced unfit to be the teacher of American youth. And, sir, when the majority of the board of overseers had rejected their nomination, that board of corporators, sustained by the self-constituted friends of the college, seized the first accidental opportunity which turned up to place that man in the chair of the professorship of moral philosophy.

" These men knew Bowen's sentiments; they knew he had been proved ignorant of the subjects he professed to understand; they knew he had been convicted of dishonesty in garbling, perverting, and misquoting historical authorities; they knew that the public, with a voice approaching unanimity, demanded his rejection: yet they pressed his nomination; and, when that nomination was rejected, they seized the first opportunity to obtain a snap-judgment for him, and placed him in a professor's chair. Does the member from Boston (Mr. Lothrop) think this an evidence of liberality, of a desire to keep along with popular opinion ?

" Mr. President, the men who have thus, in defiance of the popular voice, sustained Francis Bowen, cannot plead ignorance of his sentiments and opinions. For several years he has edited ' The North-American Review,' — a journal which claims to be the leading literary organ of the country, but which, in comparison with the English reviews, in ability, learning, and scholarship, is like a Cape-Cod fishing-smack compared to a line-of-battle ship. Through the columns of this journal, for years, he has avowed sentiments and opinions which show that whatever passes through his mind is perverted; that it is impossible for him to give a truthful and philosophic view of the events of history in the Old World or in the New, — of the events of the past, or of the events of the present day. Narrow, bigoted, intolerant, he, and the class of which he is the head, have converted ' The North-American Review,' — once graced by the genius and learning of Edward Everett, and the ripe scholarship and comprehensive views of Alexander H. Everett; a journal once presided over by that liberal and true-hearted scholar, John G. Palfrey; by Jared Sparks, who has done more for American history than any other man in the country; and by other eminent men, who made ' The Review ' worthy of the country and of its rising literature, — he, and the class of which he is the head, have converted that Review into a narrow, intolerant, bigoted organ of that conservatism which shrinks from every thing progressive at home or abroad. Could the spirit of William Gifford — who battled with such ferocious vigor and ability through ' The London Quarterly Review ' against the spirit of progress, against the rights of the many, and for the exclusive privileges of the few — come back to earth, he would be delighted with its tone of fanatical conservatism, if he did not feel utter contempt for its want of power, vigor, learning, and ability. Through the columns of that journal, Francis Bowen has poured out his slanders and libels upon the great leaders of European republicanism. Men illustrious for genius, ability, learning, eloquence, and self-sacrificing patriotism; men who have perilled all for the cause of republicanism; men who have been driven into exile for their devotion to popular rights, — are sneered at, libelled, and slandered by this professor of history, this teacher of moral philosophy, through the pages of his journal.

"When the re-action of 1850 overran Europe; when the high hopes excited by the popular revolutions of 1848 were buried in the graves and dungeons of the martyrs of freedom, quenched in the blood of the people; when the voice of freedom was heard only in the murmurs of the down-trodden masses, or in the sad accents of their exiled leaders; when Hungary went down before the armed intervention of Russia; when the hopes of Italy fell before the soldiers of Louis Napoleon; when the hopes of the friends of republicanism in France, Italy, Germany, Hungary, and on all the continent, had failed; when the prisons were crowded with patriots; when banishment was the sad fate of some of the noblest men of the age; when Kossuth was languishing in his Turkish exile, — Francis Bowen placed 'The North-American Review' on the side of the oppressor, and falsified and garbled even the oppressor's historical authorities, in order to blast the names of the champions of freedom. When Kossuth was in a Turkish prison, Francis Bowen sneeringly called him 'a renegade,' 'a fanatic and ultraist,' 'a demagogue and radical of the lowest stamp.' Such were the epithets

applied to one whom so many now here have welcomed
to this Commonwealth, where he won all hearts by his
noble qualities of mind and character.   Mazzini, Gari-
baldi, and the Italian patriots, are denounced as ' conspirators ' and ' brigands.'   And, sir, this man, this libeller
of European republicanism, this narrow, bigoted advocate
of a conservatism that shrinks from all change, is the man
selected by the corporators of Harvard College to teach
the young men of that university history and moral
philosophy ! "

After the close of the convention Mr. Wilson published
an address to his constituents, in which he explains with
remarkable clearness the nature, and recommends the
adoption, of the proposed amendments.   The State, however, refused to sanction them by its vote ; and the reason
for it appears in the concluding part of his remarks : —

" Ardent friends of constitutional reform may have felt
a degree of disappointment at the action of the convention upon some questions deemed by them of the first
importance.   These friends of reform should remember .
that Massachusetts is an old Commonwealth ; that she has
a history, a glorious past, full of recollections and memories.   They should remember that her people cherish with
affectionate regard the works and memories of their
glorious ancestry : they will not touch with irreverent
hand the works achieved by their fathers.   They should
remember that the people of Massachusetts instinctively
shrink from all untried experiments.   They should also
remember that the first proposition for a convention to
revise the Constitution was lost in 1851, and that in 1852
it was carried by immense efforts.   Recalling to mind
these facts, they cannot fail to realize the profound wisdom

of that policy by which the convention was guided, — a policy which refused to peril wise and beneficent measures of reform by the adoption of untried and hazardous experiments, or radical changes which the people were not prepared to sustain. The men of the majority of the convention, the men whose untiring efforts had carried the convention before the people against powerful combinations and great interests, the men whose efforts had secured more than a hundred majority of reformers in the convention, clearly saw that the hope, the last and only hope, of the leaders of the opposition, who had denied the constitutionality of the act calling the convention, who had voted against it two years in the legislature, opposed it before the people, and demanded its repeal by the legislature of 1853, depended solely upon the adoption of untried experiments and radical changes. When the chiefs of the opposition saw that the men who had proposed and carried the convention, and were a controlling majority in it, were masters of their work, they showed unmistakable signs that the last hope to which they clung had forever vanished, and that the battle was lost.

" The organs of that conservatism which has, to use the words of Rufus Choate, ' *a morbid, unreasoning, and regretful passion for the past*,' are now making unwonted efforts to rally, steady, and marshal the reeling columns and oscillating ranks of the opposition."

CHAPTER VIII.

ALTHOUGH Mr. Wilson received in September of
this year (1853) all but three of the six hundred
votes of the Free Democratic Convention as their candidate for governor, he failed of an election. This was
owing mainly to a letter of Mr. Caleb Cushing, denouncing, on behalf of the administration, the union of the
Democrats with the Reform party, and to the animosity
of the Whigs, arising from the active part Mr. Wilson took
in support of liberal principles in the Constitutional Convention. In spite of this combination, however, over
thirty thousand votes were thrown for him; and neither

116

he himself, nor his supporters, wavered in their purpose or
their hopes. Defeat was, to them, the signal for renewed
vigilance and exertion. The Southern Congress-men
were pressing their proslavery measures with more and
more audacity; while the Northern members, Charles
Sumner and his few compeers excepted, anxious for
personal power, and intimidated by the constant threatening of a dissolution of the Union, presented but a feeble
opposition. It was not the time for the friends of the
slave, though defeated, to fall back, or to be disheartened.
" The principles of civil freedom," said Mr. Wilson,
" spring from the New Testament; and the word of the
Lord will stand. Let us, then, go forward."

In the following year (1854) the attempt to abrogate
the Missouri Compromise (carried into effect May 31),
and thus extend the blight of slavery over the vast
domains of Kansas and Nebraska, threw the country into
intense excitement. Mr. Wilson went to Washington in
May, and held a consultation with the opponents of the
Kansas and Nebraska Bill, then pending, in the hope
of uniting men opposed to slavery into one solid organization against its further extension over the States and
Territories of the Union. His grand idea was free
labor for the whole continent of America. For party,
or for name or men, he had but little care, provided he
could in any way arrest the encroachments of the slave-
power, and make advancement towards the consummation
of his purpose. His thought was one, — it was earnest and
sincere, — and that was, " death to human servitude."
He would not, unless compelled, resort to force, but was
ready to unite with any organization for the overthrow of
a system which he deemed indefensible either by the laws
of God, of nature, or humanity, opposed to civil progress,

barbarous and cruel, and a dishonor and disgrace to the American name. He was called an agitator: he had no time to answer, but moved onward. Finding that the Free-soil party had not strength to meet the exigency, he avowed, in a convention of this body held in Boston on the last day of the month (May), that they were ready to abandon every thing but principle, and unite with men of any political standard for the sake of union in resisting the aggressive policy of the South. They were willing to place any men in power who would stand faithful to the cause of freedom and of human right. "They were ready," he declared, "to go to the rear. If a forlorn hope was to be led, they would lead it. They would toil: others might take the lead, hold the offices, and win the honors. The hour had come to form one great Republican party, which should hereafter guide the policy and control the destinies of the republic."

For the purpose of uniting political parties on the slave-question, a convention was held in Worcester on the tenth day of August, 1854; and there, again, Mr. Wilson and his associates urged with great force and ability the fusion of the different organizations into one grand body for the effectual resistance of the aggressive policy of the South. "The Free-soil party would concede every thing but principle: all they demanded was the acceptance of their doctrines of perpetual hostility to the slave-power." These overtures were steadily rejected by the Whig element in the convention; yet, with unabated energy, Mr. Wilson continued to press the importance of merging every political creed in one. In his desire to combine the antislavery elements in the State, he accepted the nomination of the Republicans for governor, and was again defeated at the election. For entering into the American organization this year, his course was criticised by many: but the people, finding union under the Whig leadership impossible, went into that party; and he, *believing* that it might be so liberalized and broadened in its principles as to advance the cause of freedom, decided (March, 1854) to cast in his influence with them.   Personally he is, and ever was, a friend to the foreigner, and ever bids him welcome to the rights and privileges of this free country: but then the slave-power was triumphant in the passage of the repeal of the Missouri Compromise; and he deemed it advisable to array, as far as possible, the powerful American organization against the proslavery propagandists.   In his expectations he was not disappointed; for this union resulted in the election of several liberal men as representatives to Congress, and "of the most radical antislavery State legislature ever chosen in America."

In a letter dated April 20, 1859, he thus presents the course of policy which he has undeviatingly pursued; and in it we may discover the reason of his union with the American party: —

"For more than twenty years I have believed the antislavery cause to be the great cause of our age in America, — a cause which overshadowed all other issues, state or national, foreign or domestic.   In my political action I have ever endeavored to make it the paramount question, and to subordinate all minor issues to this one grand and comprehensive idea.   It seems to me that the friends of a cause so vast, so sacred, should ever strive to save it from being burdened by the pressure of temporary interests and local and comparatively immaterial questions.   With the issues involved in the solution of the slavery question in America, with the lights I have to guide my action, I should feel, if I put a burden on the antislavery cause by pressing the adoption of measures of minor importance, that I was committing a crime against millions of hapless bondmen, and should deserve their lasting reproaches and the rebuke of all true men who were toiling to dethrone that gigantic power which perverts the National Government to the interest of oppression."

Mr. Wilson, as an acknowledged leader, evinced the skill of a practised engineer in so blending and combining political parties as to form a legislature of an anti-slavery character.   But it will be remembered that the sentiment of the State against the aggressions and the insolence of the South had for several years been steadily gaining strength.   The passage of the Fugitive-slave Act, 1850, by which the North became a vast slave-hunting field; the trial and rendition of Anthony Burns in 1854; the passage of the Kansas-Nebraska Bill, by which the Missouri Compromise was virtually repealed; the border-ruffianism and the reign of terror in Kansas, in which many people from Massachusetts lost their property or their lives, — these with other acts and outrages of the slaveholding party, whose policy was to select for leaders Northern men with Southern principles, awakened more and more the indignation of this State.   The pulpit began to speak upon the theme; the press proclaimed the iniquity; the workman in his workshop talked of the Missourian barbarities in Kansas; and the statesman showed the suicidal policy of the South: so that the anti-servile legislature of 1855 was but an exponent of the spirit of the State; and Mr. Wilson, as he himself declared, "instead of controlling circumstances, was, by the force of circumstances," led into success.

While the heart of the Commonwealth was throbbing under the arrogant assumption of the slavocracy, now

triumphing in the reclamation of the fugitive, in the atrocities of the Missourians in Kansas, and the subserviency
of a Northern president, Mr. Edward Everett, on account
of failing health, sent in his resignation to the Senate. Mr.
Sumner was making great efforts to resist Southern influence, and dealing gallant blows in defence of freedom.
Now, who shall be sent to stand by him? Who shall take
the place of the accomplished orator, four years of whose
term were unexpired, and face with an unfaltering front
the issues on the floor of Congress? Who has the historical
knowledge, the legislative skill, the statesmanship, the honesty, the unconquerable will, the force, and the backbone,
to meet the exigency? Who can best represent the principles, the spirit, and the fire of Massachusetts in the Senate-chamber? The answer of the State was, " Henry
Wilson." On the first ballot in the caucus he was nominated, notwithstanding strenuous opposition, by a majority
of more than a hundred votes. Pending the election,
several gentlemen in favor of nationalizing the American
party solicited him to write a letter modifying his avowed
opinions on the slavery question, that they might, consistently with their political principles, give him their support.
They might as easily have moved the granite hills from
which he came. He assured them that his opinions on the
slavery question were the matured convictions of his life,
and that he would not qualify them to win the highest
position on earth ; that he had not travelled one mile * nor
uttered one word to secure his nomination ; that, if elected,
he should carry his opinions with him into the Senate ; and,
if the party with which he acted proved recreant to freedom,
he would shiver it, if he possessed the power, to atoms.

* In a letter to Hon. Gilbert Pillsbury, dated Natick, March 10, 1855, he says,
"You also know that I never travelled a single mile to secure a vote, or asked a
single member of the House or Senate to vote for me."

He was elected by two hundred and thirty-four to a hundred and thirty votes in the House, and twenty-one to nineteen votes in the Senate;* and took his seat in the Senate of the United States on the tenth day of February, 1855. It was a time of wild and stormy debate in Congress on great questions between the friends and foes of slavery. The Southern men were combining with a section of the American party of the North, and presenting an unbroken front against the advocates of freedom. They seemed to menace and to fight, as if the crisis and the doom of their inhuman domination had arrived. The great "Northern hammer," wielded by the stalwart arm of Giddings, Hale, or Sumner, was descending with effect; and the cry of "No more slave States" was pealing through the land.

The halls of Congress rang with fierce invective, threats of violence, and oaths of condign punishment. "To me," said Mr. Giddings, "it is a severer trial of human nerve than the facing of cannon and bullets on the battle-field."

Mr. Wilson was now forty-three years old: † he had arrived at the full vigor of manhood; his health was perfect; his principles were fixed, his plans matured; his heart and hand were ready for the contest; and, on entering that tumultuous assembly, he took position at once, and stood firm as a rock for truth and liberty. Though he had not the grace or rhetoric of his predecessor, he had the knowledge, the tact, the working-power, the dauntless

---

* N. F. Bryant of Barre and J. A. Rockwell were the principal opposing candidates in the House, and E. M. Wright in the Senate.

† The following description of Mr. Wilson's personal appearance was written at the time: "The senator from Massachusetts is about five feet ten inches high; and weighs, I should think, about a hundred and sixty-five pounds. He has a small hand and foot, and seems built for agility. His complexion is florid, his hair brown, and his eye blue. His ample brow indicates ideality and causation; his voice is strong and clear. He is, on the whole, decidedly good-looking; and seems fearless and good-natured in the performance of his senatorial duties."

heroism, which come to the front when mighty interests are at stake.

In his first speech in the Senate he announced his determination fearlessly to stand with his antislavery friends in the defence of the rights of the colored race. It was upon the bill of Mr. Toucey of Connecticut, " to protect persons executing the Fugitive-slave Act from prosecution by State courts." " Now, sir," said Mr. Wilson, " I assure senators from the South that we of the free States mean to change our policy. I tell you frankly just how we feel, and just what we propose to do. We mean to withdraw from these halls that class of public men who have betrayed us and deceived you, — men who have misrepresented us, and not dealt frankly with you ; and we intend to send men into these halls who will truly represent us, and deal justly with you. We mean, sir, to place in the councils of the nation men who, in the words of Jefferson, ' have sworn on the altar of God eternal hostility to every kind of oppression of the mind and body of man.' Yes, sir, we mean to place in the national councils men who cannot be seduced by the blandishments, or deterred by the threats, of power, — men who will fearlessly maintain our principles. I assure senators from the South that the people of the North entertain for them and their people no feelings of hostility ; but they will no longer consent to be misrepresented by their own representatives, nor proscribed for their fidelity to freedom. This determination of the people of the North has manifested itself during the past few months in acts not to be misread by the country. The stern rebuke administered to faithless Northern representatives, and the annihilation of old and powerful political organizations, should teach senators that the days of waning power are upon them. This action of the people teaches the lesson, which I hope will be heeded, that political combinations can no longer be successfully made to suppress the sentiments of the people. We believe we have the power to abolish slavery in all the Territories of the Union ; that, if slavery exists there, it exists by the permission and sanction of the Federal Government, and we are responsible for it. We are in favor of its abolition wherever we are morally or legally responsible for its existence.

" I believe conscientiously, that if slavery should be abolished by the National Government in the District of Columbia and in the Territories, the Fugitive-slave Act repealed, the Federal Government relieved from all connection with or responsibility for the existence of slavery, these angry debates banished from the halls of Congress, and slavery left to the people of the States, the men of the South who are opposed to the existence of that institution would get rid of it in their own States at no distant day. I believe, that, if slavery is ever peacefully abolished in this country, — and I certainly believe it will be, — it must be abolished in this way.

" The senator from Indiana (Mr. Pettit) has made a long argument to-night to prove the inferiority of the African race. Well, sir, I have no contest with the senator upon that question ; but I say to the senator from Indiana, that I know men of that race who are quite equal in mental power to either the senator from Indiana or myself, — men who are scarcely inferior, in that respect, to any senators upon this floor. But, sir, suppose the senator from Indiana succeeds in establishing the inferiority of that despised race : is mental inferiority a valid reason for the perpetual oppression of a race? Is the mental, moral, or physical inferiority of a man a just cause of oppression in republican and Christian America? Sir, is this democracy? Is it

Christianity ? Democracy cares for the poor, the lowly, the humble. Democracy demands that the panoply of just and equal laws shall shield and protect the weakest of the sons of men. Sir, these are strange doctrines to hear uttered in the Senate of republican America, whose political institutions are based upon the fundamental idea that ' all men are created equal.' If the African race is inferior, this proud race of ours should educate and elevate it, and not deny to those who belong to it the rights of our common humanity.

" The senator from Indiana boasts that his State imposes a fine upon the white man who gives employment to the free black man. I am not surprised at the degradation of the colored people of Indiana, who are compelled to live under such inhuman laws, and oppressed by the public sentiment that enacts and sustains them. I thank God, sir, Massachusetts is not dishonored by such laws! In Massachusetts we have about seven thousand colored people. They have the same rights that we have ; they go to our free schools ; they enter all the business and professional relations of life ; they vote in our elections ; and, in intelligence and character, are scarcely inferior to the citizens of this proud and peerless race whose superiority we have heard so vauntingly proclaimed to-night by the senators from Tennessee and Indiana."

Mr. Wilson's uncompromising attitude in the Senate drew forth many expressions of admiration, even from his political opponents at home. The following frank letter from the late Hon. George Ashmun indicates the spirit with which many, who then disagreed with him, regarded his consistent action : —

11*

SPRINGFIELD, Feb. 28, 1855.

DEAR SIR, — This world has many seemingly queer changes. It seems queer to see you in the United-States Senate, and perhaps more queer for me to say to you an approving word. But I have a short memory for wrongs which are merely personal to myself, and am quite ready to do justice in spite of some needless abusive things which the newspapers have formerly reported from you. I therefore sit down for a moment to say that your letter to " The Organ," and some brief speeches in the Senate, have given me entire satisfaction. It is not very important for me to say it, nor for you to hear it: but, having myself cut loose from all party alliances for the present and the future, I can afford to do what a party man cannot; i.e., tell the truth of friend or foe.

Your demonstrations thus far show two things: 1st, That, when a man of sense finds himself in a national position, he is quite sure to throw off the slough of provincialism ; and, 2d, That, whatever your antecedents may have been, you have the courage to take ground which men of sense at home will sustain you in.

I mean to see in you nothing else than a Massachusetts senator, and hope to see in your course nothing else than a vindication of Massachusetts honor. You have, by the present confusion of all old parties, a clear field, and ample room to conquer all the prejudices which the low and miserable strife of factions at home may have given life to ; and you will find but feeble and fickle support in the mere appliances of party. You cannot conform to the narrow and exacting spirit of a local party ; but you can deserve and command the respect and confidence of those whose eyes look beyond a village or a provincial horizon.

It is and has been too much the habit of our people to

abuse their senators and representatives at Washington for any nonconformity to every article in their several and individual creeds. Your predecessors have been shamefully treated in this respect ; and the consequence has been that their hands have been weakened, and Massachusetts has lost nearly all its ancient influence.

I hold to a different doctrine, and feel that a liberal confidence in advance is due alike to ourselves and our servants. Therefore, while I should not by my vote have placed you in the Senate, and while I cannot agree to some of your heresies, I feel moved to send you this expression of my sincere gratification at the ground on which you have placed yourself at the outset of your career.

Very respectfully,

Geo. Ashmun.

Mr. Wilson.

In a sermon delivered July 1, 1855, the Rev. Theodore Parker thus, in his plain way, refers to Mr. Wilson's advancement and his brave defence of freedom : —

" When a noble man rises in the State, how much we honor him ! when a mean man, how we despise him ! Massachusetts, within a few months, has taken a man from a shoemaker's bench, and placed him in the Senate, in the very chair left vacant by the most scholarly man, who had fallen from it, and rolled wallowing in the dust at his feet ; and, when the senatorial shoemaker speaks brave words of right and justice (and in these times he speaks no other), the people, not only of Massachusetts, but of all the North, rise up, and say, ' Well done ! here are our hands for you.' "

The following letter also shows Mr. Parker's estimation of his senatorial course : —

BOSTON, July 7, 185?

MY DEAR WILSON, — I cannot let another day pass by without sending you a line — all I have time for — to thank you for the noble service you have done for the cause of freedom. You stand up most manfully and heroically, and do battle for the right. I do not know how to thank you enough. You do nobly at all places, all times. If the rest of your senatorial term be like this part, we shall see times such as we only wished for, but dared not hope as yet. There is a North, a real North, quite visible now. God bless you for your services, and keep you ready for more !

Heartily yours,

THEODORE PARKER.

CHAPTER IX.

THE AMERICAN PARTY. — SPEECHES. — PHILADELPHIA CONVENTION, 1855. — CONTEST. — SPEECH AT SPRINGFIELD.

Defection of the American Party. — Southern Influence. — Wilson's Resolution. — Interesting Letter. — Address in New York. — Antislavery Cause in Peril. — Brattleborough, Vt. — Delegate to American National Council, June, 1855. — Stand for Freedom. — Protest. — Defiant Speech. — Letter from Amasa Walker. — Remarks of "The Tribune." — Activity in forming a New Party. — Speech at Springfield. — Twenty-one-Years Amendment. — Opposes it. — Friendly to Foreigners. — Letter to Francis Gillette. — Catholic Spirit.

THE favorable attitude toward slavery which the National American party assumed in the council assembled at Cincinnati in November, 1854, led Mr. Wilson to fear that the Southern element might soon obtain entire control of it; and his experience at Washington during the ensuing spring served to convince him that his fear was far from being groundless.

Indeed, strong efforts were made by leading men immediately on his arrival as senator in that city to secure his aid and influence in the organization of a great American party which should ignore the slavery issue, and sanction the assumptions of the South. His honest heart rebelled against such recreancy to principle; and he unhesitatingly avowed his determination to maintain the stand ' he had already made for freedom during his entire political career.

Speaking of this Southern influence in a speech before the State Council at Springfield, Mass., he said, —

" On my arrival at Washington, I saw at a glance that the politicians of the South, men who had deserted their Northern associates upon the Nebraska issue, were resolved to impose upon the American party, by the aid of dough-faces from New York and Pennsylvania, as the test of nationality, fidelity to the slave-power. Flattering words from veteran statesmen were poured into my ears ; flattering appeals were made to me to aid in the work of nationalizing the party whose victories in the South were to be as brilliant as they had been in the North. But I resolved that upon my soul the sin and shame of silence or submission should never rest. I returned home, and determined to baffle, if I could, the meditated treason to freedom and to the North."

Again, in a noble reply to a letter from a friend, he most frankly speaks of his course at Washington, and prophetically announces the character of the coming session of Congress : —

NATICK, July 23, 1855.

DEAR SIR, — On my return from a trip to the West, I found your very kind note ; and I need not tell you that I read it with grateful emotions. Your approbation — the approbation of men like yourself, whose lives are devoted to the rights of human nature — cannot but be dear to me. I only regret that I have been able to perform so little for the advancement of the cause our hearts love and our judgments approve ; that I have not ability to do all that my heart prompts. I hope, however, my dear sir, to be able to do my duty in every position I may be in, if not with the ability the occasion demands, at least with an honest heart that shrinks not from any danger.

Sometimes I read over the letter you were so kind as to send to me when I first took my seat in the Senate. You dealt frankly with me in that letter, and I thank you for it; and I hope to be the better and wiser for it. I shall endeavor while in the Senate to act up to my convictions of duty, — to do what I feel to be right. If I can so labor as to advance the cause of universal and impartial liberty in the country, I shall be content, whether my action meets the approbation of the politicians or not. I never have sacrificed, and I never will sacrifice, that cause to secure the interests of any party or body of men on earth. The applause of political friends is grateful to the feelings of any man in public life, especially if he is bitterly assailed by political enemies; but the approbation of our own consciences is far dearer to us.

Last year, after the attempt was made to repeal the prohibition of slavery in Kansas and Nebraska, the people of the North began to move; and, from March to November, the friends of freedom won a series of victories. The moment the elections were over in the North, I saw that an effort was to be made to assist the antislavery movement by the American movement. When I arrived at Washington, I was courted and flattered by the politicians; even told that I might look to any position if I would aid in forming a national party. I saw that men who had been elected to Congress by the friends of freedom were ready to go into such a movement. I was alarmed. I saw that one of three things must happen, — that the antislavery men must ignore their principles to make a national party; or they must fight for the supremacy of their principles, and impose them upon the organization, which

would drive off the Southern men ; or they must break up
the party. I came home with the resolution to carry the
convention if I could ; to have it take a moderate but
positive antislavery position : if not, I determined that it
should be broken at the June council, so that the friends
of freedom might have time to rally the people. Since my
return in March, I have travelled more than nine thousand miles, written hundreds of letters, and done all I
could to bring about what has taken place. But the work
is hardly begun. Our antislavery friends have a mighty
conflict on hand for the next sixteen months. It will demand unwavering resolution, dauntless courage, and ceaseless labor, joined with kindness, moderation, and patience.
The next Congress will be the most violent one in our
history : it will try our firmness. I hope our friends will
meet the issues bravely ; and, if violence and bloodshed
come, let us not falter, but do our duty, even if we fall on
the floors of Congress. At Philadelphia, for eight days, I
met the armed delegates of the black power without shrinking ; and I hope to do so at the next session of Congress if
it is necessary to do so. We must let the South understand that threats of dissolving the Union, of civil war, and
personal violence, will not deter us from doing our whole
duty.　　　　　Yours truly,

H. WILSON.

In an address before a large audience in the Metropoli-
tan Theatre, New York, delivered on the 8th of May,
1855, and repeated in many towns and cities in New
England, he traced the growth of the antislavery sentiment in America for the last twenty years, and warned
his hearers that any party ignoring this rising power
would be overthrown by an indignant people.

"He owed it to truth," he said, "to speak what he knew, — that the antislavery cause was in extreme peril; that a demand was made upon us of the North to ignore the slavery-question, to keep quiet, and to go into power in 1856. If there were men in the free States who hoped to triumph in 1856 by ignoring the slavery-issues now forced upon the nation by the slave propagandists, he would say to them that the antislavery men cannot be reduced or driven into the organization of a party that ignores the question of slavery in Christian and republican America. Let such men read and ponder the history of the republic. Let them contrast antislavery in 1835 and antislavery in 1855. Those periods are the grand epochs in the antislavery movement; and the contrast between them cannot fail to give us some faint conception of the mighty changes that twenty years of antislavery agitation have wrought in America. Antislavery in 1835 was in the nadir of its weakness: antislavery in 1855 is in the zenith of its power. Then a few unknown, nameless men were its apostles and leaders: now the most profound and accomplished intellects of America are its chiefs and champions. Then a few proscribed and humble followers rallied around its banner: now it has laid its grasp upon the conscience of the people, and hundreds of thousands rally under the folds of its flag. Then not a single statesman in all America accepted its doctrines or defended its measures: now it has a decisive majority in the national House of Representatives, and is rapidly changing the complexion of the American Senate. Then every State in the Union was arrayed against it: now it controls fifteen sovereign States by more than three hundred thousand popular majority. Then the public press covered it with ridicule and contempt: now the most powerful journals in America are its instruments. Then the benevolent, religious, and literary institutions of the land repulsed its advances, rebuked its doctrines, and persecuted its advocates : now it shapes, moulds, and fashions them at its pleasure, compelling the most powerful benevolent organizations of the Western World, upon whose mission-stations the sun never sets, to execute its decrees, and the oldest literary institution in America to cast from its bosom a professor who had surrendered a man to the slave-hunters. Then the political organizations trampled disdainfully upon it : now it looks down with the pride of conscious power upon the wrecked political fragments that float at its feet. Then it was impotent and powerless : now it holds every political organization in the hollow of its right hand. Then the public voice sneered at and defied it : now it is the master of America, and has only to be true to itself to grasp the helm and guide the ship of state hereafter in her course.

"This brief contrast," continued he, "would show the men who hoped to win power by ignoring the *transcendent issue* of our age in America how impotent would be the efforts of any class of men to withdraw the mighty questions involved in the existence and expansion of slavery on this continent from the consideration of the people.

" . . . Now, gentlemen, I say to you frankly, I am the last man to object to going into power (laughter), and especially to going into power over the present dynasty that is fastened upon the country. But I am the last man that will consent to go into power by ignoring or sacrificing the slavery question. If my voice could be heard by the whole country to-night, by the antislavery men of the country to-night of all parties, I would say to them, Resolve it, write it over your door-posts, engrave it on the lids of your Bibles, proclaim it at the rising of the sun and the going-down of the same, and in the broad light of noon, that any party in America, be that party Whig, Democratic, or American, that lifts its finger to arrest the antislavery movement, to repress the antislavery sentiment, or proscribe the antislavery men, it surely shall begin to die (loud applause) ; it would deserve to die; it will die ; and, by the blessing of God, I shall do what little I can to make it die."

In an address on the " Position and Duty of the American Party," delivered at Brattleborough, Vt., on the 16th of the same month, he still points out in stirring words the only course by which it can escape destruction.

" He had," he said, " no sympathy with that narrow, bigoted, intolerant spirit that would make war upon a race of men because they happen to be born in other lands, — a dastardly spirit that would repel from our shores the men who sought homes here under our free institutions. Such a spirit was anti-American, devilish : he loathed it from the bottom of his heart. He knew there were men who called themselves Americans who would abolish the naturalization laws altogether, who would forever deny the right of suffrage to men for the fault of being born out of America. He had no sympathy with that class of men whose opinions were at war with the spirit of American institutions and the laws of humanity. Such anti-American sentiments had brought dishonor upon the American movement ; and, unless they received the rebuke of the American party, they would defeat the real reforms contemplated, and cover the movement with dishonor.

" He regretted to say that there were some members of the American party in favor of excluding by constitutional amendments all adopted citizens from office. He deeply deplored the action of the legislature of Massachusetts in proposing an amendment to the Constitution embodying this doctrine. He hoped the gentlemen who had given their votes for this proposition — a proposition that would not permit Prof. Agassiz, one of the first living scientific men of the age, to fill, under State appointment, an office even of a scientific character — would see their error, and retreat at once from a position which justice, reason, and religion condemned. What little influence he possessed would be given with a hearty good-will to defeat the proposition. He had no sympathy whatever with the spirit that would send out of the country the sons and daughters of misfortune, who, by the storms of life, were thrown upon us for support. Whenever the authorities of the Old World sent their poor here to be relieved themselves of their support, he would promptly redress the imposition; such an abuse ought to be immediately corrected: but when a poor man lands upon our soil, and by the misfortunes of life is thrown upon the public charity for support, he would as soon send a poor fleeing bondman back to the land

> ' Where the cant of democracy dwells on the lips
> Of the forgers of fetters, and wielders of whips,'

as to banish such a man from the land he has sought. There is a kind of native Americanism far more alien to America than are the adopted sons of the Old World it would degrade into servile races. True genuine Americanism rebukes bigotry, intolerance, and proscription; reforms abuses; adopts a wise, humane, and Christian policy towards all men, — a policy consistent with the idea that all men are created equal.

"If the American party is to achieve any thing for good, it must adopt a wise and humane policy consistent with our democratic ideas, — a policy which will reform existing abuses, and guard against future ones ; which shall combine in one harmonious organization moderate and patriotic men who love freedom and hate oppression.

"Upon the grand and overshadowing question of American slavery the American party must take its position. If it wishes a speedy death and a dishonored grave, let it adopt the policy of neutrality upon that question, or the policy of ignoring that question. If that party wishes to live, and to impress its policy upon the nation, it must repudiate the sectional policy of slavery, and stand boldly upon the broad and national basis of freedom. It must accept the position that ' freedom is national, and slavery is sectional.' It must stand upon the national idea embodied in the Declaration of Independence, that ' all men are created equal, and have an inalienable right to life, liberty, and the pursuit of happiness.' It must accept these words as embracing the great central national idea of America, fidelity to which is national in New England and in South Carolina. It must recognize the doctrine that the Constitution of the United States was made ' to secure the blessing of liberty ; ' that Congress has no right to make a slave or allow slavery to exist outside of the slave States ; and that the Federal Government must be relieved from all connection with and responsibility for slavery.

"In their own good time the Americans of Massachusetts have spoken for themselves. They have placed that old Commonwealth face to face to the slave oligarchy and its allies. Upon their banner they have written in letters of living light the words, ' No exclusion from the public schools on account of race or color ; ' ' No slave

12*

commissioners on the judicial bench;' 'No slave States to be carved out of Kansas and Nebraska;' 'The repeal of the unconstitutional Fugitive-slave Act of 1850;' 'An Act to protect Personal Liberty.' The men who have inscribed these glowing words upon their banner will go into the conflicts of the future like the Zouaves at Inkermann, 'with the light of battle on their faces;' and, if defeat comes, they will fall with their 'backs to the field, and their feet to the foe.' "

When Mr. Wilson saw the national American party hopelessly committed to slavery, he abandoned it. In the American National Council, assembled in Philadelphia in June, 1855, he manfully held his ground, and nobly repelled the assaults upon freedom and the State he represented. "When Massachusetts," said he in reply to an attack, "pleads to any arraignment before the nation, she will demand that her accusers are competent to draw the bill."

An attempt was made, for sentiments he had expressed, to deprive him of a seat in the council; but the delegation from his State stood firmly by him, and he was admitted. In the exciting debates of that council, which sat for many days, he came to the front as the unterrified champion of the friends of freedom, and defiantly repelled the charges made against them. To a delegate from Virginia, who, approaching with a pistol, denounced him as the leader of the antislavery party, he replied, that his threats had no terrors for freemen; that he was then and there ready to meet argument with argument, scorn with scorn, and, if need be, blow with blow; for God had given him an arm ready and able to protect his head. It was time that champions of slavery in the South should realize the fact, that the past was theirs, the future ours."

Here was the fire of the dauntless Mirabeau in the French National Assembly when he said, "Go tell your king we are here by the will of the people; and nothing but the point of the bayonet shall expel us."

His speech on the 12th of June is characterized by masculine vigor. In regard to the proslavery platform he defiantly declared, "The adoption of this platform commits the American party unconditionally to the policy of slavery, to the iron dominion of the black power. I tell you, sir, I tell this convention, that we cannot stand upon this platform in a single free State in the North. The people of the North will repudiate it, spurn it, spit upon it. For myself, sir, I here and now tell you to your faces, that I will trample with disdain on your platform. I will not support it. I will support no man that stands upon it. Adopt that platform, and you carry against you every thing that is pure and holy, every thing that has the elements of permanency in it, the noblest pulsations of the human heart, the holiest convictions of the human soul, the profoundest ideas of the human intellect, and the attributes of Almighty God. Your party will be withered and consumed by the blasting breath of the people's wrath. There is an old Spanish proverb which says that 'the feet of the avenging deities are shod with wool.' Softly and silently these avenging deities are advancing upon you. You will find that 'the mills of God grind slowly;' but they grind to powder.

"When I united with the American organization in March, 1854, in its hour of weakness, I told the men with whom I acted that my antislavery opinions were the matured convictions of years, and that I would not modify or qualify my opinions, or suppress my sentiments, for any consideration on earth. From that hour to this, in

public and in private, I have freely uttered my antislavery
sentiments, and labored to promote the antislavery cause ;
and I tell you now that I will continue to do so.   You
shall not proscribe antislavery principles, measures, or men,
without receiving from me the most determined and unrelenting hostility.   It is a painful thing to differ from our
associates and friends ; but, when duty — a stern sense of
duty — demands it, I shall do so.   Reject this majority platform, adopt the proposition to restore freedom to Kansas
and Nebraska, and to protect the actual settlers from
violence and outrage, simplify your rules, make an open
organization, banish all bigotry and intolerance from your
ranks, place your movement in harmony with the humane,
progressive spirit of the age, and you may win and retain
power, and elevate and improve the political character
of the country ; adopt this majority platform, commit
the American movement to the slave perpetualists and the
slave propagandists, and you will go down before the burning indignation and withering scorn of American freemen."   These words had the flaming spirit of James Otis
and of Patrick Henry.   They were the death-knell of the
American party.   On the adoption of the platform, Mr.
Wilson and his associates uttered their protest against the
proceedings of the council, and formally withdrew from the
American organization.

One of Mr. Wilson's early political opponents thus addresses him on the manly stand he took in the convention : —

N. Brookfield, June 22, 1858.

Dear Sir, — I have just read your speech at Philadelphia.   You had a splendid opportunity to annihilate the
Northern dough-faces and hurl defiance at the Southern
slave propagandists, and you availed yourself of it fully and

handsomely. I thank you for what you have done so bravely and well. You met the crisis nobly, and have placed yourself at *the head* of the political antislavery movement: that is a settled matter. I am glad you had health and strength and courage to do the work which so many Northern men have shrunk from in times past.

You have nothing to do now but to go ahead. *The North* looks to *you.* A great responsibility rests on your shoulders; but I have the utmost confidence that you will meet it, and can assure you that every true man of all parties in the free States will rally around the standard of freedom.

I have no advice to give: you need none. My only object is to thank you for what you have done, and assure you of my confidence in the future.

Ever and truly yours,
Amasa Walker.

Hon. Henry Wilson, U. S. senator, Natick, Mass.

Referring to Mr. Wilson's bold and independent course, "The New-York Tribune" truly said, "The antecedents of Mr. Wilson naturally made him the particular object of hostility to the slave-drivers in the convention; and one of the earliest displays after the body was organized was a grossly personal attack upon him by a delegate from Virginia. But the assailants had now met with an antagonist who was not to be cowed or silenced; and the response they received was of a character to induce them not to repeat their experiment. We have the unanimous testimony of many Northern members to the signal gallantry and effect of Mr. Wilson's bearing, and to the bold, virile, and telling eloquence of his speeches. While all have done so well in bringing about results so gratifying, it

may be invidious to particularize; but a few names among
the Northern members, who were devoted from the start
to the work of creating a unity and a strength of Northern backbone, should justly be exposed to the public
appreciation and honor that they deserve. First stands
Henry Wilson of Massachusetts, pre-eminent as the leader
in the whole movement. He was handsomely sustained
by all his associates; and the numerous insidious efforts
of the enemy to separate them from him only attached
them the more closely to his side. He has the highest
honor in this contest, exhibited the greatest political ability,
and broke down many strong prejudices against him, both
among Massachusetts men who were witnesses to his conduct, and among the delegates of the other States North
and South. No man went into that council with more
elements of distrust and opposition combined against him :
no one goes out of it with such an enviable fame, or such
an aggregation to his honor. He is worthy of Massachusetts, and worthy to lead the new movement of the people
of that State which the result here so fitly inaugurates."

Returning home from this council, Mr. Wilson spent
the summer and autumn in strenuous efforts to effect a
fusion of the parties into one grand organization, which
might bear the standard of progress and freedom, and control the councils of the nation. He travelled thousands
of miles, visited thirteen different States, conversed with
many leading men, and addressed immense audiences in
towns and cities East and West.

On the 7th of August he made a strong speech in the
State Council of the American party, at Springfield, " On
the Necessity of the Fusion of Parties," in which he
urged the members to unite with other organizations in
forming a great Republican party, with strength to meet
the important issues of the day.

"The gathering hosts of Northern freemen of every party," said he, "are banding together to resist the aggressive policy of the black power. Freedom, patriotism, and humanity demand the union of the freemen of the republic for the sake of liberty now perilled. Religion sanctions and blesses it. How and where stands Massachusetts? Shall she range herself in the line, front to the black power, with her sister States? or shall she maintain the fatal position of isolation? Here and now, we, the chosen representatives of the American party of this Commonwealth, are to meet that issue, to solve that problem.

"The American party of Massachusetts, dashing other organizations into powerless fragments, had grasped the reins of power, placed an unbroken delegation in Congress pledged to the policy of freedom, ranged this ancient Commonwealth front to front with the slave-power, and written with the iron pen of history upon her statutes declarations of principles, and pledges of acts, hostile to the aggressive policy of the slaveholding power. When the black power of the imperious South, aided by the servile power of the faltering North, imposed upon the national American organization its principles, measures, and policy, the representatives of the American party of this Commonwealth spurned the unhallowed decrees, and turned their backs forever upon that prostituted organization; and their action received the approving sanction of this State Council by a vote approaching unanimity. The American party, as a national organization, is broken, and shivered to atoms. By its own act the American party of Massachusetts has severed itself from all connection with that product of Southern domination and Northern submission.

" The American party of Massachusetts has, during its
brief existence, uttered true words and performed noble
deeds for freedom. The past, at least, is secure. Whatever may have been its errors of omission or commission,
the slave and the slave's friends will never reproach it.
Holding as it does the reins of power, it has now a glorious opportunity to give to the country the magnanimous
example of a great and dominant party in the full possession of consummated power, freely yielding up that
power for the holy cause of freedom to the equal possession of other parties who are willing to co-operate with it
upon a common platform.   Here and now, we, its representatives, are to show by our acts whether we can rise
above the demands of partisan policy to the full comprehension of the condition of public affairs, to the full
realization of the obligations which fidelity to freedom
now imposes upon us.

" If the representatives of the American party reject
this proposition for fusion, I shall go home once more
with a sad heart.   But I shall not go home to sulk in
my tent ; to rail and fret at the folly of men : I shall
go home, sir, with a resolved spirit and iron will, determined to hope on and to struggle on until I see the lovers
of universal and impartial freedom banded together in
one organization, moved by one impulse.   For seven
years I have labored to break up old organizations and
to make new combinations, all tending to the organization of that great party of the future which is to relieve
the government from the iron dominion of the black
power.

" Sir, gentlemen may defeat this proposed fusion here
to-day ; but they cannot control the action of the people.
A fusion movement will be made, under the lead of gen-

tlemen of the Whig, Democratic, and Free-soil parties, of
talents and character. The movement will be in harmony with the people's movements in the North. Sir,
such a movement will put a majority of the men who
voted with you last autumn in a false position before the
country, or drive them from your ranks. I cannot speak
for others: but I tell you frankly that I cannot be placed
in a false position; I cannot, even for one moment, consent
to stand arrayed against the hosts of freedom now preparing for the contest of 1856. I tell you frankly, that, whenever I see a formation in position to strike effective blows
for freedom, I shall be with it in the conflict; whenever I
see an organization in position antagonistic to freedom,
my arm shall aid in smiting it down."

On the proposed amendment of the Constitution, requiring foreigners to reside here twenty-one years before
being allowed to vote, he said, —

"Sir, the American movement is not based upon bigotry, intolerance, or proscription. If there is any thing
of bigotry, intolerance, or proscription, in the American
movement, if there is any disposition to oppress or
degrade the Briton, the Scot, the Celt, the German, or
any one of another clime or race, or to deny to them the
fullest protection of just and equal laws, it is time such
criminal fanaticism was sternly rebuked by the intelligent
patriotism of the state and country. I deeply deplore,
sir, the adoption of the twenty-one-years amendment.
It will weaken the American movement at home and in
other States, especially in the West, and tend to defeat
any modification whatever of the naturalization laws. I
warn gentlemen who desire the correction of the evils
growing out of the abuses of the naturalization laws
against the adoption of extreme opinions. I tell you,

13

gentlemen of the council, that this intense nativism kills; yes, sir, it kills, and is killing, us; and, unless it is speedily abandoned, will defeat all the needed reforms the movement was inaugurated to secure, and overwhelm us all in dishonor. Every attempt, by whomsoever made, to interpolate with the American movement any thing inconsistent with the theory of our democratic institutions, any thing inconsistent with the idea that 'all men are created equal,' any thing contrary to the command of God's holy Word, that 'the stranger that dwelleth with you shall be unto you as one born among you, and thou shalt love him as thyself,' is doing that which will baffle the wise policy which strives to reform existing evils and to guard against future abuses."

With such strong, liberal, and statesman-like views, ever holding the question of slavery paramount, he labored to enlighten public sentiment, and prepare it for the day of universal freedom. Towards the foreigner he entertained fraternal feelings; and his only aim in going into the American party was to turn its power to the extinction of a system which was coming rapidly to undermine the liberties of the Northern people.

"I loathe," said he in a speech at Indianapolis in July, 1855, "the idea of opposition to foreigners as foreigners;" and in a letter on the two-years amendment, written to Mr. Gillette in 1859, he says, —

"I have ever declared that I would support no measure, even to reform these abuses, which would in the slightest degrade any man, or class of men; that I would give to every human being equal rights, — the same equality I would claim for myself or my own son.

"No power on earth could force me to vote for any proposition which fair-minded and intelligent men felt to

be unequal or personally degrading. Never have I supported any measure inconsistent with the equal rights of
man ; but, if I had ever unintentionally made such a mistake, I have nothing of that pride of consistency in regard
to mere measures which would induce me to continue in
the wrong because I had been wrong once. Better be
right in the lights of to-day than be consistent with the
errors of yesterday."

The following characteristic letter clearly states his position on this question : —

Natick, Mass., July 29, 1872.

J. O. Culver, Esq., State Journal, Madison, Wisconsin.

My dear Sir, — The mail has just brought me your
note, and extracts clipped from newspapers, purporting to
be speeches made by me. In answer to your queries, I
Lave to say, that they, and all thoughts and words of like
character which have appeared in the papers, are pure inventions, wicked forgeries, and absolute falsehoods. Never
have I thought, spoken, or written those words, nor
any thing resembling those words, nor any thing that
the most malignant sophistry could torture into those
words. I could not have done so ; for they are abhorrent to every conviction of my judgment, every throb
of my heart, every aspiration of my soul. Born in
extreme poverty, having endured the hard lot the sons of
poverty are too often forced to endure, I came to manhood passionately devoted to the creed of human equality.
All my life I have cherished as a bright hope, and avowed
as a living faith, the doctrine, that all men, without distinction of color, race, or nationality, should have complete
liberty and exact equality, — all the rights I asked for myself. My thoughts, my words, my pen, my votes, have
been consecrated for more than thirty-six years to human

rights. In the Constitutional Convention of Massachusetts, in eight years' service in her legislature, in more than seventeen years' service in the Senate of the United States, in thirteen hundred public addresses, in the press, in speeches and writings that would fill many columns and make thousands of pages, I have iterated and reiterated the doctrines of equal rights for all conditions of men. Is it not, my dear sir, passing strange, then, that partisanship should so blind men to a sense of truth, justice, and fair play, that they will forge and print abhorrent sentiments insulting to God and man, and charge them upon one whose life has been given to the cause of equal rights at home, and whose profound sympathies were ever given to the friends of liberty of all races and nationalities abroad?

Yours truly,

HENRY WILSON.

CHAPTER X.

AFFAIRS IN KANSAS. — ASSAULT ON MR. SUMNER. — RE-
PLY TO MR. BUTLER, AND RESULT. — NO SUP-
PLIES FOR SUBJUGATING KANSAS.

Troubles in Kansas. — Slave and Free Labor Antagonistic. — Reply to Mr.
Toucey. — Mr. Douglas. — Assault on Mr. Sumner. — Aided by Mr. Wilson.
— Scene in the Senate-Chamber. — Challenge of P. S. Brooks. — Reply. —
How received. — Letter of Mr. Harte. — Reply to Mr. Butler of South Caro-
lina. — Letter from Whittier. — Labors in the Senate. — Views on Slavery.
— Speech July 9. — Musket-Ball. — Speech against sending Military Sup-
plies to subjugate Freemen in Kansas.

THE collisions between the free people and the slaveholders in Kansas, consequent on the passage of the
Kansas-Nebraska Act in May, 1854, were becoming more
and more violent and sanguinary. On that broad and distant field the defenders of slavery were committing the
most barbarous atrocities upon the settlers from the North,
and substantiating practically the truth, that free and slave
labor cannot harmoniously co-exist in the same State.
Antagonist in their nature, the success of one is the destruction of the other. The outrages of the border ruffians,
who were murdering unoffending men and carrying the
polls by force for slavery, roused the Northern people to
great excitement; and they demanded speedy and decisive
action on the part of the national executive. Instead of
extending protection to the injured party, the adminis-

tration fanned the fire of the aggressors. Mr. Wilson
now came grandly up to the occasion.

A message from the president to the Senate, enclosing
an iniquitous report of the secretary of state on the existing state of affairs in Kansas, drew forth from him in the
Senate, Feb. 18 and 19, 1856, one of the boldest defences
of the outraged people, one of the sternest rebukes of
border violence, which had yet been made. " Mr. President," said he, " the senator from Connecticut (Mr.
Toucey) closes his speech with the assumption that there
may be those in the country who do not wish the president to preserve order; and he is pleased to say, that, if
the executive does so, their ' vocation ' will be gone.
Let me say to the senator from Connecticut, that the
' vocation' of those to whom he alludes is not fawning,
abject servility to power. No, sir : they do not

'Bend to power, and lap its milk.'

" If the senator from Connecticut alludes to those who
have opposed the uncalled-for and wanton repeal of the
Missouri prohibition ; if he alludes to those who condemn
the policy of the administration in Kansas ; if he intends
to charge the intelligent, patriotic men who sympathize
with the wronged and outraged people of Kansas, bravely
struggling to preserve their firesides and altars, their property and lives, against the armed aggressions of lawless
invasions from Missouri, with a disposition to violate or
resist the laws of the country, or to cherish sectional animosity and strife, — he makes a charge unsupported by even
the shadow of truth ; and here and now, to his face, and
before the Senate and the country, I pronounce the charge
utterly unfounded. If he intends to insinuate a charge of
that character against me, I promptly meet it ; and before
the Senate I brand it as it deserves.

"The senator from Connecticut, with an air of confident assurance, calls for facts. Evidently possessed with the vast knowledge embodied in these documents sent here by the executive, the senator assumes the air and tone of one entitled to speak by authority; and he invites us to deal in facts. Sir, he shall have facts; for it so happens that the friends of those who are struggling in Kansas to protect their lives, their property, their all, against unauthorized power and lawless violence, know something of the facts which have transpired there. All knowledge, sir, of affairs in Kansas, is not in the keeping of the executive and his senator from Connecticut. The tree of knowledge, sir, was not planted in the executive garden; and I sometimes think, if it had been, its forbidden fruit would have been more secure than were the fruits of that tree plucked by our first parents.

"The senator from Connecticut commends us to the consideration of this correspondence; and the senator from California (Mr. Weller) asks us to print ten thousand extra copies of it to be scattered broadcast over the land. I now say — and I can establish what I say before any committee of investigation, so that no man can question the declaration — that this correspondence utterly and totally misstates and misrepresents the state of affairs in Kansas. These documents, sir, are made up of telegraphic despatches, of letters, of statements, of orders, written by Gov. Shannon and others, on the rumors of the hour, in a large territory, at a time when the people were deeply agitated by all sorts of reports that flew over the land in rapid succession. We are called upon now to publish these rumors, — rumors that turned out to be exaggerated or false, — rumors recognized and admitted to be false by the governor of the Territory in his conversation and in his treaty with the citizens of Lawrence. Yes, sir, the Senate is now called upon to print and send over the country, as official documents, these stupendous misrepresentations of facts. They will carry a gigantic falsehood to the American people. He who reads only these documents has no accurate knowledge, no true conception, of the actual condition of affairs in Kansas at the time covered by them.

"The year 1854 opened upon a vast territory lying in the heart of the continent, extending from thirty-six degrees thirty minutes on the south to the possessions of the British queen on the north; from the borders of Missouri, Iowa, and Minnesota, on the east, to the summits of the Rocky Mountains on the west. Over that territory, larger than the empire of Napoleon, when, at the head of the grand army, he gazed upon that 'ocean of flame' that wrapped the minarets, turrets, and towers of the ancient capital of the czars, the republic, on the 6th of March, 1820, engraved in letters of living light the sacred words, 'Slavery shall be and is forever prohibited.' Slavery, with hungry gaze, glared upon the forest and prairie, hill and mountain, lake and river, of that magnificent region it was forever forbidden to enter. Fixing its glittering eye upon that paradise, consecrated by the nation to freedom and free institutions for all, hallowed forever to free men and free labor, the slave-power, in the person of the late president of the Senate, the soul of these border aggressions, demanded that this heritage of free labor should be opened to the withering footsteps of the bondman. Sir, with hot haste you grasped this domain of freedom, and flung it to the slave propaganda. Your administration, in answer to the stern protest of the free laboring-men of the country, whose heritage it was, mocked them with the delusive promise that the actual settlers were to shape, mould, and fashion the institutions of Kansas and Nebraska. Two years have passed, and your 'squatter sovereignty' is proved a delusion and a cheat. Laws more inhuman than the code of Draco, forced upon the actual settlers of Kansas by armed invading hosts from Missouri, are now to be enforced by United-States dragoons. The Constitution, framed by a convention of the people, is spurned from the halls of Congress ; the convention that formed it is pronounced ' spurious ' by the senator from Connecticut ; and the people who ratified it are branded as traitors by the administration and its subalterns.

" By the theory of the Kansas-Nebraska Act, Mr. President, the actual settlers were to decide the transcendent question, whether freedom should bless, or slavery curse, the virgin soil of those vast Territories lying in the central regions of the continent. The sons of the free States, of Puritan New England, of the great central States, and of the North-west, — men who call no man master, and who wish to make no man a slave, — were invited to plant upon the soil of Kansas those institutions that have blessed, beautified, and adorned the homes of their childhood. The sons of the South — from regions once teeming with the rich fruits of fields now blasted, blighted, and withered by the sweat of untutored and unrewarded toil — were invited to plant, if they could, the institutions that had dishonored labor in their own native States upon the unbroken soil of Kansas. Sir, the people of the North and the people of the South had a legal and moral right to go there when they pleased, how they pleased, and with whom they pleased ; in companies, or in single families ; under their own direction, or under the auspices of emigrant-aid societies in the North or the South.

"Sir, the honorable senator from Missouri (Mr. Geyer), in his remarks the other day upon the resolution of inquiry submitted by me, made the extraordinary declaration, that the ' disorders ' which he admits have existed on the borders ' are to be attributed to an extraordinary organization, called an ' Emigrant-aid Society,' — the first attempt in the history of this country to take possession of an organized Territory, and exclude from it the inhabitants of other portions of the Union.' I am amazed that the senator from Missouri should make such a declaration on the floor of the Senate. When and how did the Emigrant-aid Society ' attempt to take possession of an organized Territory, and to exclude from it the inhabitants of other portions of the Union ' ? Will the senator tell us when that ' attempt ' was made ? Will he tell us where it was made ? Will he tell us how it was made ? I challenge the senator to give us one single fact to sustain the declaration he has so unjustly made against men of stainless purity. The senator avows that men from his State ' have passed over the borders ; ' but they have done so, he tells us, ' to protect the ballot-box from the attempt of armed colonists to control the elections there.' When and how were the ballot-boxes assailed by ' armed colonists ' from the North ? I call upon the senator from Missouri, I challenge any senator, to furnish one fact, one single authenticated fact, to sustain this assumption.

"Sir, the Emigrant-aid Society of New England has violated no law, human or divine. Standing here before the Senate and the country, I challenge the senator from Missouri, or any other senator, to furnish to the Senate one fact, one authenticated fact, to show that the Emigrant-aid Society has performed any illegal act, any act inconsistent with the obligations of patriotism, morality, or religion. The President of the United States has arraigned before the country these emigrant-aid societies; the organs of the administration have assailed them; and now the senator from Missouri here, on the floor of the Senate, renews the assault. Sir, I defy any supporter of the administration, any apologist of Atchison, Stringfellow, and their followers, to give us one act of the directors of the New-England Emigrant-aid Society hostile to law, order, and peace. I know most of these gentlemen thus wantonly assailed; and I know them to be law-abiding, order-loving, conservative men. I defy the senator from Missouri, the senator from Connecticut, or the chief magistrate at the other end of the avenue, to show, here or elsewhere, that the Emigrant-aid Society ever violated a law of this country, or performed an act which could not receive the sanction of the laws of God and man. They have sent no paupers or criminals to Kansas: they have simply organized a system by which persons wishing to go to Kansas may go in small companies; and by going together, and starting at a particular time and place, may have the cost of their fare reduced about thirty-three per cent. This company has built a hotel in Kansas; has sent some saw-mills there; has aided in establishing schools and churches. That is the extent of offence, — no more, no less.

"Mr. President, on the 29th of July, 1854, within sixty days after the passage of the Kansas-Nebraska Act, a meeting was called at Weston, Mo., by the 'Platte-county Self-defensive Association.' Resolutions were adopted, declaring that the association, whenever called upon by any of the citizens of Kansas Territory, will hold itself in readiness to assist in removing any and all emigrants who go there under the auspices of the Northern emigration-aid societies.

" Before the feet of the first emigrants who went there under the auspices of the Emigrant-aid Society pressed the soil of Kansas, this ' Platte-county Self-defensive Association,' under the guidance of B. F. Stringfellow, proclaimed to the world its readiness to cross into Kansas and remove actual settlers from their new homes. Under the lead of this lawless association other meetings were held in Western Missouri, and resolutions adopted in favor of carrying slavery into Kansas, and in denunciation of emigrants from the free States who should go there under the auspices of the emigrant-aid societies.

" On the 9th of August, more than two months after the Kansas-Nebraska Act was passed, a few persons went into that Territory from the East. They went there under the auspices of that society referred to the other day so unjustly by the senator from Missouri. Early in the autumn of 1854 the Missouri guardians of Kansas crossed over into the Territory, and, by force of arms, endeavored to drive from their homes the few persons who had begun the little settlement at Lawrence. But these Platte-county-Association heroes found a little band of about thirty New-England men, under the lead of Charles Robinson, — the Miles Standish of Kansas, — ready to meet the issue with powder and ball; and they retreated to their homes, preferring to live to fight another day.

" The senator from Connecticut referred with an air of triumph to the election which took place on the twenty-ninth day of November, 1854. On that day Mr. Whitfield was

elected — and triumphantly elected — a delegate from that
Territory. No one ever questioned the fact that he had
a majority of the legal voters of the Territory on that day;
but, in addition to that fact, men familiar with the Terri
tory declare that he received the votes of more than a
thousand inhabitants of Missouri who crossed the line and
voted on that occasion.

"I hold in my hand, sir, a paper drawn up and signed by
Gen. Pomeroy, — a gentleman of intelligence, of personal
honor, whose veracity no man who knows him can ever
question. From this memorial, addressed to Congress, I
quote the following words concerning the election of the
29th of November, 1854: —

"'The first ballot-box that was opened upon our virgin
soil was closed to us by overpowering numbers and impending force. So bold and reckless were our invaders, that they
cared not to conceal their attack. They came upon us,
not in the guise of voters to steal away our franchise, but
boldly and openly, to snatch it with a strong hand. They
came directly from their own homes, and in compact and
organized bands, with arms in hand, and provisions for the
expedition, marched to our polls; and, when their work was
done, returned whence they came. It is unnecessary to
enter into the details: it is enough to say, that in three
districts, in which by the most irrefragable evidence there
were not a hundred and fifty voters, — most of whom
refused to participate in the mockery of the elective
franchise, — these invaders polled over a thousand votes.'

"An examination of details will reveal the extent of this
fraud. In the seventh election district of Kansas, six
hundred and four votes were cast on the 29th of November, 1854: of these Whitfield received five hundred and
ninety-seven, — all but seven. Three months afterwards

14

the census was taken, and there were only fifty-three
voters in the seventh district.   Who went there to vote ?
Organized, armed, disciplined men from the State of
Missouri ; and all the votes but seven in that district
were given for Mr. Whitfield.   Does the senator from
Missouri call that 'protecting the ballot-box against
armed colonists' ?   In the eleventh district, on the same
day, two hundred and thirty-seven votes were given.   In
February following, when the census was taken, there
were but twenty-four voters in that district, which, three
months before, had given Whitfield two hundred and
thirty-seven votes, — all but three of the whole number
cast; and, within thirty days after the census was taken,
three hundred and twenty-eight votes were given in this
district having only twenty-four voters.   Yet the senator
from Missouri gravely informs the Senate that Missourians only crossed over the borders ' to protect the ballot-
boxes against armed colonists' sent there under the
auspices of emigrant-aid societies.   That these Missourians crossed the line and voted on that day for Whitfield,
no one doubted ; but he had a majority of the voters of
the Territory, and *for that reason his election was not
contested*.   That is the answer to the senator from Connecticut, who has built his argument on that fact.

"The character of this invasion will appear in an extract from a speech made by one of these modern heroes
(Gen. Stringfellow), who, according to the senator
from Missouri, crosses over into Kansas ' to protect the
ballot-boxes from the armed colonists' from the free
States.   This speech was made just before the elec
tion of Nov. 29, 1854, to which the senator from
Connecticut has referred with so much confidence, at St.
Joseph, Mo.   In that speech, Gen. Stringfellow said, —

" ' I tell you to mark every scoundrel among you that is the least tainted with free-soilism or abolitionism, and *extermino'e* him. Neither give nor take quarter from the damned rascal. I propose to mark them in this house, and on the present occasion, so that you may *crush them out.*'

" ' Crush them out' is the language. You will remember, sir, that the Attorney-General of the United States — a man who spent the dew of his youth and the vigor of his early manhood in assailing democratic statesmen, and who is now giving the mature years of his life to undermining and perverting democratic principles — sent an edict to Massachusetts, pending the election in 1853, that the president ' was up to the occasion,' and intended ' to crush out the element of abolitionism.' Gen. Stringfellow, like the president, is ' up to the occasion.' He has caught up the word of the attorney-general. He is going to mark the free-soilers, he says, that you may ' crush them out.' I think his success, sir, will be about equal to the success which followed the efforts of the president and Gen. Cushing in ' crushing out the element of abolitionism.' The elections of the last two years have shown who is the crusher and who is the crushed. Gen. Stringfellow continues : —

" ' To those who have qualms of conscience as to violating laws, state or national, the time has come when such impositions must be disregarded, as your rights and property are in danger ; *and I advise you, one and all, to enter every election district in Kansas, in defiance of Reeder and his vile myrmidons, and vote at the point of the bowie-knife and revolver.* Neither give nor take quarter, as our cause demands it. It is enough that the slaveholding interest wills it, from which there is no appeal. What right has Gov. Reeder to rule Missourians in Kansas? His proclamation and prescribed oath must be repudiated. It is your interest to do so. Mind that slavery is established where it is not prohibited.'

"'Qualms of conscience as to violating laws, state or national.' No, sir, that will never do! 'Such impositions must be disregarded.' 'Every election district in Kansas must be entered by one and all,' and they must 'vote at the point of the bowie-knife and revolver.' Is that the way these border gentlemen pass over the line, according to the senator from Missouri, 'to protect the ballot-boxes against the armed colonists'?

"'Qualms of conscience about violating laws, state or national,' were given up; and they 'entered into every election district in Kansas, in spite of the proclamation of Reeder,' and made the election of Whitfield doubly sure. The Senate will remember that the senator from Missouri assures us that Missourians only crossed the borders to 'protect the ballot-boxes against the armed colonists' from the East. Sir, I commend to the especial consideration of the senator from Missouri the advice of Gen. Stringfellow, to give up all 'qualms of conscience as to violating laws, state or national,' and to 'enter every election district in Kansas.' Is that the way Missourians 'protect the ballot-boxes over the borders'?

"I proceed now with the facts. The census of Kansas was taken, by the direction of Gov. Reeder, in February, 1855; and then there were eight thousand five hundred inhabitants, and two thousand eight hundred and seventy-seven legal voters, in the Territory. At the ensuing election, — on the 30th of March, 1855, — four thousand voters from the State of Missouri passed into that Territory and gave their votes. Lawrence, according to the census, was entitled to less than five hundred votes. But, sir, nine hundred and fifty were cast; although nearly one-half the legal voters of Lawrence, if we are to believe the testimony of some of their most respectable citizens, refused to vote on that day. More than eight hundred Missourians, armed to the teeth, led by Col. Young, a lawyer of Western Missouri, went to Lawrence, the home of the New-England men so often assailed and so much misrepresented in the documents before us. Col. Young made a speech declaring that he would vote, or would shed his blood. He took the precaution, however, to swear in his vote. He had more regard for his life than he had for his conscience.

"'In the Lawrence district, speeches were made to them by leading residents of Missouri, in which it was said that they would carry their purpose, if need be, at the point of the bayonet and bowie-knife; and one voter was fired at as he was driven from the election-ground. Finding they had a greater force than was necessary for that poll, some two hundred men were drafted from the number, and sent off, under their proper officers, to another district; after which they still polled from this camp over seven hundred votes.'

"Gen. Pomeroy says that in the fourth and seventh districts, along the Sante Fé road, —

"'The invaders came together in one armed and organized body, with trains of fifty wagons, besides horsemen, and, the night before election, pitched their camp in the vicinity of the polls; and having appointed their own judges in place of those who, from intimidation or otherwise, failed to attend, they voted without any proof of residence. In these two election-districts, where the census shows one

14*

hundred voters, there were polled three hundred and fourteen votes.'

" In the Leavenworth district, hundreds of men breakfasted in Missouri, voted in Kansas, and returned on the same day to Missouri. While the voting was going on, one of their leaders made a speech, in which he told the Platte-county boys that they must stand aside, and let the Clay-county boys vote first, because they had the farthest to go in returning to their homes ; and the Platte-county boys of Missouri stood aside, and allowed the Clay-county boys of Missouri to vote first and go home.

" This memorial declares that

" ' Hundreds of men came together in the sixteenth district, crossing the river from Missouri the day before election, and encamping together, armed and provisioned, made the fiercest threats against the lives of the judges, and during the night called several times at the house of one of them for the purpose of intimidating him, declaring in the presence of his wife that a rope had been prepared to hang him : and although we are not prepared to say that these threats would have been carried out, yet they served to produce his resignation, and give these invaders, in the substitution, control of the polls ; and, on the morning of the election, a steamboat brought from the town of Weston, Mo., to Leavenworth, an accession to their number of several hundred more, who returned in the same boat after depositing their votes. There were over nine hundred and fifty votes polled, besides from a hundred to a hundred and fifty actual residents who were deterred or discouraged from voting ; while the census returns show but three hundred and eighty-five votes in the district a month before. Not less than six hundred votes were here given by these non-residents of the Territory, who voted without being sworn as to their qualifications, and, immediately after the election, returned to Missouri ; some of them being the incumbents of important public offices there.'

" I will now, sir, quote what Gen. Pomeroy says of the election in the eighteenth district ; and I ask the attention of the senator from Missouri to this statement : —

" ' In the eighteenth election district, where the population was sparse, and no great amount of foreign votes was needed to overpower it, a detachment from Missouri, from sixty to a hundred, passed in with a train of wagons, arms, and ammunition, making their camp the night before the election near Moorestown, the place of the polls, without even a pretext of residence, and returning immediately to Missouri after their work was done ; their leader and captain being a distinguished citizen of Missouri, but late the presiding-officer of the Senate of the United States, and who had bowie-knife and revolver belted around him, apparently ready to shed the blood of any man who refused to be enslaved. All these facts we are prepared to establish, if necessary, by proof that would be considered competent in a court of justice.'

" Gen. Pomeroy expresses the opinion

" ' That not less than three thousand votes were given by these armed invaders, who came organized in bands, with officers and arms, and tents and provisions, and munitions of war, as though they were marching upon a foreign foe instead of their own unoffending fellow-citizens. Upon the principal road leading into our Territory, and passing several important polls, they numbered not less than twelve hundred men ; and one camp alone contained not less than six hundred. They arrived at their several destinations the night before the election, and having pitched their camps, and placed their sentries, waited for the coming day. Baggage-wagons were there, with arms and ammunition enough for a protracted fight, and among them two brass field-pieces ready charged.   They came with drums beating, and flags flying; and their leaders were of the most prominent and conspicuous men of their State.'

"How very considerate it was, Mr. President, in these 'prominent and conspicuous men,' with their baggage-wagons and cannons and rifles and drums and flying flags, to lead the men of Western Missouri over into the forests and prairies of Kansas to protect the ballot-boxes from those dangerous men, the armed colonists of New England!

"Sir, the gentleman from Connecticut wishes to know why the seats of the legislators elected by the Missourians were not contested.   I will tell him.   Mr. Phillips, a young lawyer of Leavenworth, not himself a candidate, took measures to have the seat of the member from the sixteenth district contested; and what was the result?   He was taken over into Missouri and lynched, because he dared, simply on patriotic grounds, to dispute the right of the member to his seat, into which he had been voted by these armed men from Missouri.

"Sir, the whole power and patronage of this government, from the time when the Kansas and Nebraska Act went into operation to this hour, has been given to crush out the freemen of Kansas, and to plant the institution of slavery upon that virgin soil.

"The officers of the United States in the Territory of Kansas — the judges, the district-attorney, the secretary, and the marshal — are all slave-State men; and their influence has been given in favor of making Kansas a slave State.   Gov. Reeder, who undertook to protect the people in their legal rights, was stricken down under the pretence that he had been speculating in the public lands.   Of twenty-one officers of the Federal Government in the Territory, nineteen are slave-State men, and one is a free-State man ; but already he is marked by Atchison, and another designated for his place. Within the last ten days, men from Kansas have called upon the executive to remonstrate against this striking-down of a public officer simply for the crime of being in favor of free institutions.

" When I yielded the floor yesterday for an adjournment, I was speaking of the election of the 30th of March, 1855. The result of that election was, that the nineteen districts in Kansas were carried by the proslavery party, and that more than six thousand votes were given in that Territory, where, thirty days before, there were less than three thousand voters.

" The question was put yesterday by the honorable senator from Connecticut, why the governor gave certificates of election on that occasion. I will simply say, that Gov. Reeder, in the cases brought before him, did refuse to deliver the certificates ; that he made the refusal in the presence of the men who claimed them with bowie-knives and revolvers in their belts, and amidst threats of his life ; and, while he read the statement, he held a cocked revolver in his hand for necessary self-defence. There were a few devoted friends around him, expecting to see him murdered on that occasion. In the cases not at the time contested in the cases where at the time no one dared to raise a question, in the cases where at the time a contest was neglected, the certificates were given. A new election was ordered in those cases where the certificates were set aside ; and, in pursuance thereof, the people elected representatives and councillors, and commissions were issued to them. They met on the second day of July at Pawnee ; and both branches of the legislature, without examining the facts, and positively refusing to do so, voted out the men chosen by the people of Kansas, and voted in the men originally chosen by the Missouri invaders. This legislature thus chosen moved the place of meeting from Pawnee to Shawnee Mission against the consent of the governor, who refused afterwards to recognize it as a legislature. They went on, and passed the laws which are now brought he e. Some of those laws are as inhuman as any code ever presented for the government of a conquered people.

" When the legislature assembled, when it turned out the men who had been legally chosen, when it brought in the men imposed on the Territory by armed invaders from a neighboring State, when it removed to the Shawnee Mission, when it was repudiated by your governor sent there by this administration, then it was that the freemen of Kansas assembled in their primary meetings, and declared against the legality of this legislature and its acts. A convention of the people was called. That convention assembled, and framed a constitution; the people ratified it; and that constitution is now submitted for the action of the Congress of the United States. The senator from Connecticut denounces it as a ' spurious convention.' Sir, this convention was the act of the people of Kansas in their sovereign primary capacity. They accepted the doctrine of squatter sovereignty. They accepted the doctrines laid down by Madison, by Marshall, by Story, by Judge Wilson, by Buchanan and Wright, and the chiefs of the Democratic party, in the days when the Democratic party paid some little regard to the principles of popular government.

" Sir, the senator from Connecticut denounced this act of the people as a ' spurious convention.' In 1836, the freemen of Michigan, disregarding the action of their legislature, came together in their primary capacity, framed a constitution, sent that constitution to Congress, and that constitution was carried through the Senate by the votes of Benton, Buchanan, Wright, and the chiefs of the Democratic party; but that was in the days of Andrew Jackson, when it was supposed the people of this country had retained the rights guaranteed to them by the fundamental laws of the country. Sir, Andrew Jackson did not denounce the movement as an insurrectionary one, although they refused to receive the officer whom he sent to them. The Congress of that day did not denounce those men as traitors to the country, as the men of Kansas are denounced in the documents before us, ten thousand extra copies of which we are asked to publish. No, sir; no! This is the first time in the history of this country when the people have assembled in their primary capacity, and exercised their right — their inborn, natural right — to change their government at their pleasure, and have, for such an act, been held up as traitors by the government of the country.

" Sir, the Democracy in both branches of Congress sustained the doctrines maintained by the suffrage party in Rhode Island; and it so happens, that, when Gov. Dorr took refuge in the old Granite State, among the first who recognized the doctrines which he maintained was the man who is chief magistrate of the United States, and who now denounces the freemen of Kansas, and holds up to the country, as violators of the law, men who are, on the 4th of March next, to be arrested if they dare assemble in their legislative capacity and choose two United-States senators to come and implore us to receive Kansas into this sisterhood of States, and thus save this fair Territory from bloodshed and ruin. Yes, sir, this man, who now characterizes as ' revolutionary ' what has already been done by the people of Kansas, and warns them that further action ' will become treasonable insurrection,' welcomed Gov. Dorr to the capital of New Hampshire on the 14th of December, 1842, in a series of resolutions, declaring, that, ' when the people act in their original sovereign capacity, they are not bound to conform to forms not instituted by themselves;' that ' the day of free government would never dawn upon the eyes of oppressed millions if the friends of liberty should wait for leave from tyrants to abolish tyranny.'

"Sir, in pursuing this history, I have followed the order of time; and I am now brought to speak of another invasion from Missouri, — an invasion which took place on the 1st of October last, when Gen. Whitfield was elected. I state here — on the authority of gentlemen, some half-dozen of whom are within the sound of my voice, and who will prove it under oath before your committee if you will permit them to do so — that hundreds of men went over from Missouri, and voted in that election.

"The invasion — the fourth invasion, of which we have heard so much in these papers from the executive department — grew out of the cold-blooded murder of a man by the name of Dow, at Hickory Point, by one Coleman. Mr. Branson and his neighbors took the mortal remains of the murdered Dow from the highway, where he had lain for hours, and consigned them to his last resting-place. The murderer has never been tried nor arrested. Branson, with whom Dow had lived, was arrested on a peace-warrant by Sheriff Jones, and rescued by some fifteen of his neighbors and friends. Then it was that the stories were manufactured, that a thousand men were organized at Lawrence, armed with

Sharpe's rifles and cannon, ready to resist the authorities. There were not then more than three hundred Sharpe's rifles in Lawrence, and not one cannon. There was no armed soldiery in Lawrence when these charges were made: there were armed men there; but they were not embodied. Of the men who aided in the rescue of Branson, — an act which might take place in any State, at any time, without any governor thinking of calling out the armed militia, much less the forces of the United States, — only two ever lived in Lawrence; and they were not in Lawrence at that time. The reports mentioned in these despatches about burning buildings have turned out to be exaggerated and misrepresented.

"On the strength of these reports, however, Gov. Shannon sent his letter of the 28th of November to the president; and on the next day he issued that fatal proclamation, which fomented, at the time, the invasion from Missouri; and this was followed by his telegraphic despatch of the 1st of December. Here let me say, that in this letter, proclamation, and despatch, Gov. Shannon shows that he is not a man who comprehends his position or his duties. He was excited and frightened by the reports and rumors he relied upon. During this period, when he ordered out the militia and telegraphed the president, despatches, founded on rumors, were sent into Missouri: and the result was, that from one thousand to two thousand armed men came from Missouri into Kansas; and they were incorporated into that 'little force of less than four hundred men,' spoken of in these despatches from Kansas, which rallied to the call of the officers of the militia. Sir, if the people of Kansas had been with the governor, if they had sympathized with him in his ill-starred movements, if they had believed

15

that law and order were in danger, would they not have rallied to his support? On that occasion, the arsenal of the United States in Western Missouri was broken open; arms were stolen, and carried into Kansas. Nothing is said about this robbery in these reports. Missourians broke open this arsenal, and stole cannon, ammunition, and muskets, for the purpose of going on a .marauding invasion; and the late president of the Senate was compelled — so great was the danger — to hasten after them to keep them from hurting somebody! Yet not a word is said about it in these despatches. Sir, if the freemen of Kansas had broken open that arsenal, and had stolen even a gun-flint, you would have had a proclamation from your governor and your president, and the army of the United States would have been called out to put them down. But it was the organized men of the blue lodges in Western Missouri who did it. They have been, and now are, permitted to violate all law with impunity. Woodson, the secretary of Kansas, urged on these lawless men from Missouri by assuring them that 'there is no doubt in regard to having a fight; and, if we are defeated this time, the Territory is lost to the South.'

"The invading hosts from Missouri encamped on the Wakarusa, within about six miles of beleaguered Lawrence. In marked contrast to the inconsiderate folly of Shannon was the prudent, firm, and heroic bearing of Gen. Robinson. Throughout the whole contest his prudence was signally manifested; and, in the opinion of many, the country was saved from bloodshed and civil war by his action. On the 7th of December your governor tells you he went to Lawrence; but he does not tell you the whole story. He did go to Law-

rence, and he met the Lawrence men, and the Lawrence
women too ; and he saw the inflexible determination of
the one, and the calm devotion of the other. He told
gentlemen who directed the affairs of Lawrence, that
they had been misrepresented ; that they misunderstood
each other ; and then, after two days of conference and
negotiation, he made a treaty. The first sentence of the
treaty acknowledges that the governor and the people of
Lawrence had not understood each other. Here is a
man who asked the president for the army of the United
States ; who ordered out the militia, and incorporates
into the militia of Kansas, by the showing of these papers,
from a thousand to fifteen hundred Missourians ; and
then, after doing this, he went to Lawrence. And what
did he find ? People who flew to arms simply to protect
their homes and their firesides against an armed invasion
of two thousand men who were threatening with oaths
to burn their city and to blot them out from existence.
I say, Gov. Shannon made a treaty with Gen. Lane
(known to some senators here) and with Gen. Robinson
(a man who, I hope, is hereafter to be known to senators) : and this treaty closes with the agreement, on the
part of Gov. Shannon, that he ' will use his influence to
secure to the citizens of Kansas remuneration for any
damages sustained by the sheriff's posse in Douglas
County ; that he has not called upon persons residents of
any other States to aid in the execution of the laws ;
and that he has not any authority or legal power to do
so, nor will he exercise any such power ; and that he
will not call on any citizen of another State who may be
here.' In these negotiations he agreed to waive the
question of the validity of the laws of the Territorial legislature. Then he issued an order to Lane and Robinson

to incorporate into the service of Kansas the militia of
Lawrence, and directed them ' to use the enrolled force
for the preservation of the peace, and the protection of
Lawrence and vicinity' against the armed men on the
banks of the Wakarusa.

" Mr. President, this treaty, which Shannon signed
with Lane and Robinson on Sunday, the 9th of December, 1855, will stand a perpetual confession of his incapacity and folly; this order, giving Lane and Robinson
authority ' to use the enrolled force ' — with those famed
Sharpe's rifles — ' for the preservation of peace, and the
protection of Lawrence and vicinity' against the armed
bands his fatal proclamation had summoned, will stand a
living testimony that the men of Lawrence were the
guardians of law. Yes, sir, that treaty and that order
will stand, an eternal expression at once of error and
repentance.

" After signing these evidences of his own humiliation,
he returned to the camp on the Wakarusa, and then,
to the leaders of the crew he had drawn together, proclaimed his truce with the men of Lawrence. Back to
their homes in Missouri sauntered these baffled bands of
lawless desperadoes, cold, sullen, dispirited. They came
to the banks of the Wakarusa big with threats of vengeance upon the free-State men of Lawrence: they
returned with bitter curses upon the imbecile governor
whose proclamation had drawn them from their homes.
Gen. Stringfellow, whose pure taste the senator from
South Carolina can vouch for, denounced the treachery
of Shannon. Capt. Leonard, the leader of one of these
gangs of border banditti, through the columns of ' The
St. Joseph Gazette ' declares that your governor ' raises
a storm; and then, to quell it, Judas-like professes his

special friendship, first for one party, and then, I conjecture, for the other. But, however this may be, he descends to the despicable position of a common liar both to the one party and the other.'

"You may search the records of the country from the settlement at Jamestown to this day, and you can find no instance of such incapacity, folly, and superadded criminality, as Wilson Shannon displayed on that occasion, or such an utter disregard of the rights of the people as was manifested by the border settlers of Missouri.

"This administration has now clothed Wilson Shannon — whose incompetency has been made manifest to the world — with the civil and military authority, and with all the power of the government to execute the laws and to maintain order in the Territory. The duties assigned this officer in the present critical condition of affairs on your frontiers are of the gravest and most weighty character. Sir, your administration — by the wanton repeal of the Missouri prohibition, by the failure to protect the actual residents of Kansas in their rights, and by the blundering acts and criminal remissness of the official authorities — has brought the nation to the perilous edge of civil strife. Sir, this administration owes it to the country, whose peace is in danger this day, to intrust the responsible and delicate duties of governor of Kansas to a prudent, judicious, sagacious statesman, — a man of individual honor and personal character, in whom the people can place the fullest confidence. Wilson Shannon is not that man. The man who could descend to degrading companionship around the gaming-tables of those saloons. of San Francisco (described by that experienced traveller, Madame Ida Pfeiffer, as the most dissolute she had ever seen in her tour

15*

of the globe) with Mexican greasers, the escaped convicts of the British penal colonies, and the desperadoes of the Old World and the New; the man who could — while Kansas was overrun by armed bands summoned around Lawrence by his own reckless letters, despatches, and proclamations; while civil war lowered over the people intrusted to his care; while an honored citizen, stricken down by the assassin, lay cold in death, and a devoted wife was weeping over his mortal remains — make himself the humiliating object of the derision of his enemies, and of the pity of his friends, by an exhibition of gross intoxication, — is not the man to whom the American people would intrust the affairs of Kansas.

"I call the attention of the Senate, Mr. President, to another forray over the borders, — to the fifth Missouri invasion: I mean the irruption into Kansas on the 15th of December, when the people were called upon to vote upon the constitution framed by that convention the senator from Connecticut is pleased to pronounce 'spurious.' Along the Missouri border the people in several of the voting precincts were overawed by threats of impending violence, and meetings were not holden. At Leavenworth the election was broken up by the lawless brutality of men, many of whom had been ordered to Leavenworth on that day to be formally discharged from service in the Kansas militia, into which they had been incorporated. At the dinner-hour, while most of the people were absent from the polls, these 'border ruffians' rushed upon the officers, broke up the meeting, beat to the earth Witherell the clerk, whose life was saved by the heroic daring of Brown, since foully murdered, who rushed to his rescue at a moment when the uplifted axe of the assassin was about to descend upon his prostrate form.

"On the 22d of December another forray was made upon freedom at Leavenworth; and the press of Mr. Delahay, which barely escaped on the 15th, was destroyed. Mr. Delahay is a native of Maryland, and has been a slaveholder in his native State, in Alabama, and in Missouri,—a man who has little sympathy with antislavery men. He is simply one of those moderate, conservative men who believe that 'free labor is honorable, and slave labor is dishonorable,' and that the permanent interests of Kansas would be promoted by making it a free commonwealth.

"On the 15th of January the people of Kansas were called upon to elect officers under the constitution adopted on the 15th of December. Another assault upon the freedom of the ballot-box was made at Easton by armed men. The people attempted to resist the destruction of the ballot-boxes by these marauding squads that were prowling over the country, insulting the people, and robbing them of their means of defence. Peaceable, law-abiding citizens were hunted down, fired upon, and their lives put in imminent peril. Some of them had to flee to Lawrence, as to a city of refuge, to save themselves from the vengeance of the prowling assassins. A party of these lawless desperadoes captured Mr. Brown — who so bravely rescued Witherell at Leavenworth — and several others; robbed them of their arms; and then, with hatchets and knives, they fiendishly hacked and cut Brown to pieces, flung him in a dying condition into a carriage, and bore him to his home to breathe out his life in the arms of his distracted wife, another sacrifice to the dark spirit of slave propagandism.

"To-day, sir, unless they are on their march, there are arming and organizing in Western Missouri, in the blue

lodges, in the secret camps, hosts of men for another
invasion. Sleepless eyes are upon these movements
organized by Atchison and his subalterns. Gen. Lane
and Gen. Robinson sent to the president, on the 21st of
January, a telegraphic despatch. Gen. Lane — a man
who trod the battle-field of Buena Vista; a man who
knows something of what war is; who knows something
of the threats that have been made, and the preparations
that are now making, on the borders of Western Missouri, for another lawless invasion of Kansas — has appealed to the president for protection. He is no fanatic.
Sir, you cannot call him an abolitionist; at least, not
yet.

"The senator from New Hampshire (Mr. Hale) says
he will be one soon. The scenes through which he is
passing are calculated to abolitionize men made of the
hardest natures. John Quincy Adams once said that a
man ' has the right to be an abolitionist; and, being an
abolitionist, he violates no law, human or divine.' Gen.
Lane may be an abolitionist; but, sir, he is not one now.
On the 21st of January he asked the president to send
the military force stationed at Fort Leavenworth to protect the people of Kansas against an invasion which is
' organizing on our border, amply supplied with artillery,
for the avowed purpose of invading our Territory, de-
molishing our towns, and butchering our unoffending
free-State citizens.'

"Two days after, — on Jan. 23, — Gen. Lane and
Gen. Robinson asked the president to issue his proclamation forbidding this lawless invasion of their Territory.
The senator from Connecticut flatters himself that those
of us who do not approve the course of the administration will be greatly disappointed to find that the lead-

ers of the free-State movement in Kansas have implored the executive to issue his proclamation. Let not the senator from Connecticut lay the flattering unction to his soul that we are chagrined by the disclosure of this correspondence. Robinson and Lane, in behalf of the imperilled people of Kansas, asked the president to issue ' his proclamation immediately, forbidding the invasion, which, if carried out as planned, will stand forth without a parallel in the world's history.' They did not ask the president for his proclamation against the wronged and oppressed people of Kansas. They asked for bread; the president gave them a stone : they asked for a fish ; the president gave them a serpent.

"The president, sir, has issued his proclamation ; but that proclamation is chiefly and mainly directed against Lane and Robinson, and the liberty-loving, law-abiding free-State men of Kansas. Like his annual message, in which he softly spoke of the long series of outrages you will scarcely find paralleled in the history of Christian States as ' irregularities;' like that special message, in which the aggressive acts of the Missouri invaders were covered over with mild and honeyed phrases, and the defensive measures of the actual settlers treated as insurrectionary acts, demanding executive censure, — this proclamation will be received on the Western borders, by the men who by their votes and by their resolves have dictated law to Kansas, with shouts of approval. Sir, this proclamation will carry no terror into the blue lodges and secret clubs of Western Missouri.

" But, sir, we were congratulated yesterday by the senator from Connecticut that the laws were to be executed, and order preserved. I call the attention of the Senate and of the country to the order of the secretary of war. What does this order say to Col. Sumner? Does it clearly and expressly command him to arrest, at all hazards, any aggressive movement upon Kansas from Missouri? The secretary of war informs Col. Sumner that

" ' The president has, by proclamation, warned all persons combined for *insurrection, or invasive aggression,* against the organized government of the Territory of Kansas, or associated to resist the due execution of the laws therein, to abstain from such revolutionary and lawless proceedings.'

" Does the secretary, then, direct Col. Sumner to defend Kansas against ' invasive aggression ' ? No, sir; no! The secretary then issues the orders of the government to Col. Sumner in these terms : —

" ' If, therefore, the governor of the Territory, finding the ordinary course of judicial proceeding and the powers vested in the United-States marshals inadequate for the suppression of *insurrectionary combinations,* or *armed resistance to the execution of the law,* should make requisition upon you to furnish a military force to aid him in the performance of that official duty, you are hereby directed to employ for that purpose the forces under your command.'

" Sir, this is not a direction to Col. Sumner to use his forces against the armed Missouri invaders. The secretary tells the colonel that the president has sent out his proclamation against those movements ; but, when he comes to direct the commander of the force of the United States what to do, he does not order him to use that force if there shall be an invasion from the State of Missouri. The secretary shrinks from putting himself against the lawless men who represent a power in this country that sustains them in their aggressive acts. Sir, the secretary bends to that power; he bows to these men, who have no 'qualms of conscience as to violating laws, state or national;' and we have had nothing but bows to these men for the last eighteen months from the other end of the avenue.

"The reason why the government has not used its proper legitimate influences in Kansas for peace, for order, and for liberty, is the same reason which originally snatched that four hundred and fifty thousand square miles of free soil, — consecrated forever to the laboring millions of this country, — and flung it open to the slave-extending interests.

"Sir, I know that men in the confidence of the administration have expressed the idea that the administration intends, if the people's legislature meets on the 4th of March, to arrest the members the moment they take the oath of office. It is a well-known fact, sir, — known by those who know any thing about affairs in Kansas, — that they do not intend to pass laws, or interfere in any way with the legislation of the country; that they intend merely to assemble, state their grievances to the country, and choose senators to come here to implore us in God's name to carry out the wishes of the people, and allow Kansas to take her place in this Union of free commonwealths. I understand these to be the intentions of the tried and trusted leaders of the free-State men in Kansas. You may arrest Gov. Robinson and the leaders of the free-State party; you may imprison them if you will; you may shed the blood of the actual settlers of Kansas: but you cannot break their spirits, or crush out their hopes. The people of Kansas are for a free State; and, if it is made a slave State, it

will be by the criminal remissness or direct interposition
of this administration.   Leave the people of Kansas free,
uninfluenced by your slave-State officials you have thrust
upon them, uninfluenced by foreign interposition, and
they will bring her here clothed in the white robes of
Freedom.

" The senator from Missouri said to us the other day
that the colonists from the East wished to keep others
out; that they wished to get possession of the Territory.
Armed men, he said, had crossed from Missouri to protect
the ballot-boxes against the armed colonists sent there by
the Emigrant-aid Society.   Did they protect the ballot-
boxes on the 29th of November, 1854, when they went over
and gave fifteen hundred votes?   Did they protect the
ballot-boxes when they marched into Kansas on the 30th
of March, with cannon, with revolver, and with rifle, dis-
placed the election of officers, and delivered their hundreds
of votes, and, in a place where there were but fifty-three
voters, cast over six hundred?   Did they protect the
ballot-boxes when they went there on the 15th of December, and broke up the meeting at Leavenworth?   Did
they protect the ballot-boxes on the 15th of January,
when Brown was murdered in revenge for standing by
the ballot-boxes and protecting them against them?

" Sir, men aided to go there by the Emigrant-aid Society have never — no, sir, never — at any time, or on
any occasion, interfered with the freedom of voting.

> ' Whatever record leaps to light,
>   They never can be shamed.'

" Sir, I see that in the South there are movements from
all quarters to get up emigrant-aid societies.   The senator from Mississippi (Mr. Brown), always frank and manly

on these questions, proposes that Mississippi shall send three hundred of her young men and three hundred of her bondmen into that Territory to plan and shape its future. I say to the honorable senator from Mississippi, Send your Mississippi young men and your Mississippi bondmen: you will never find, on the part of the men who went there from the North under the auspices of emigrant-aid societies, one single unlawful act to keep you out or rob you of one of your lawful rights. The men who charge the emigrants from the North with aggressions upon the men of other sections of the country utter that which has not the shadow of an element of truth in it; and they know it, or they are grossly ignorant of Kansas affairs. This proposition of the senator from Mississippi was followed by a letter from a representative from South Carolina (Mr. Brooks), offering to give a hundred dollars, — one dollar for every man they will send from his section. I say to the senators from South Carolina, that if the offer of their colleague in the other House is accepted, and if the hundred men go from South Carolina to Kansas, they will never be interfered with in the exercise of their legal rights by the men who have gone there from New England or from the North.

"Atchison, the organizer and chief of those border movements, thus appeals to the citizens of Georgia to come to the rescue; for 'KANSAS MUST HAVE SLAVE INSTITUTIONS, OR MISSOURI MUST HAVE FREE INSTITUTIONS.'

"Sir, to appease the unhallowed desires of the slave propaganda, you complied with Atchison's demands, and repealed the Missouri prohibition. You then told the laboring-men of the republic, whose heritage you thus put in peril, that they could shape, mould, and fashion the institutions of those future commonwealths. Animated

16

by motives as pure and aims as lofty as ever actuated the founders of any portion of the globe, the sons of the North wended their way to this region beyond the Mississippi. These emigrants did not all go there under the auspices of emigrant-aid societies: for it is estimated that not more than one-fourth of the settlers of Kansas are from New England and New York; that nearly one-half of the dwellers in that Territory are from Pennsylvania and the North-west.

"Only about one-fourth of the actual residents of Kansas are from the slaveholding States; and many of these settlers from the South, perhaps a majority of them, are in favor of making Kansas a free State. That many of these emigrants from the South are in favor of rearing free institutions will surprise no one who understands their condition. Most of these emigrants are poor men, and have felt in their native homes the malign influences which bear with oppressive force upon free labor. Thirty-five per cent of the emigration of the slave States has sought homes in the free States; while less than ten per cent of the emigration from the free States and from the Old World find homes in the slave States, although those States embrace the largest as well as the fairest regions of the country east of the Rocky Mountains.

"Coming from fields blasted by the sweat of artless, untutored, unpaid labor; from regions once teeming with the products of a prolific soil, now 'exhibiting,' to quote the language applied 'with sorrow' to his native country by the senator from Alabama (Mr. Clay), 'the painful signs of senility and decay apparent in Virginia and the Carolinas;' witnessing the prosperity of free, educated labor, — many of these sons of the South meet the men of the North, and stand with them, shoulder to shoulder, in upholding the institutions of freedom.

" Within the Territory, the men of the North and the men of the South meet together in council. Northern and Southern men stood side by side in those assemblages of the people that put the brand of condemnation upon the acts of the legislature imposed upon them ; Northern and Southern men sat in council in that Constitutional Convention the senator from Connecticut now pronounces ' spurious ;' and Northern and Southern men stood side by side in the trenches of beleaguered Lawrence.

" Leave these men now in Kansas free from Missouri forrays and administration corruption, and, in spite of the inhuman, unchristian, and devilish acts to be found in the past legislation of the Territory, they will bring Kansas here, as they have done already, robed in the garments of Freedom. Men of the South ; you who would blast the virgin soil of Kansas with the blighting, withering, consuming curse of slavery ; you who would banish the educated, self-dependent, free laboring-men of the North, to make room for the untutored, thriftless, dependent bondmen of the South, — vote down the free-State men of Kansas, if ·you can ; but do not send ' border ruffians' to rob or burn their humble dwellings, and murder brave men, for the crime of fidelity to their cherished convictions."

Replying, April 14, to Mr. Douglas, who had stigmatized Mr. Wilson and his party as " black Republicans," he uses these heroic, telling words : —

" The senator from Illinois may denounce us as black Republicans, as abolition agitators, if he thinks such language worthy of the Senate or of himself; but the issue is being made up in the country between the people and the slave propaganda. He told us the other day that he intended to subdue us. I say to that senator, We accept your issue. Nominate some one of your scarred veterans; some one who is committed, fully committed, to your policy. You want a candidate that is scarred with your battles. Well, sir, if he goes into the battle of 1856, he will not come out of it without scars. You have made the issue: put your chieftains at the head. No man fitter to lead than the honorable senator himself in this contest; for his position has the merit at least of being bold; and I like a bold, brave man who stands by his declarations. Now, I say to senators on the other side of the chamber, We will accept your issues. You may sneer at us as abolition agitators. That may have some little effect in some sections of the North, but very little indeed. We have passed beyond that. The people of this country are being educated up to a standard above all these little sneering phrases. We will accept your issue; but you will not, can not, subdue us. I tell the honorable senator he may vote us down, but subdue us never. We belong to a race of men that never were subdued; and, if anybody undertakes that work, he will find he has taken a rather costly contract. Subdue us! subdue us! Sir, you may vote us down; but we stand with the fathers. Our cause is the cause of human nature. The star of duty shines upon our pathway; and we will pursue that pathway, looking back for instructions to the great men who founded the institutions of the republic, looking up to Him whose ' hand moves the stars and heaves the pulses of the deep.' I tell the senator that this talk about subduing us and conquering us will not do. Gentlemen, you cannot do it. You may vote us down; but we shall live to fight another day. (Laughter.)

Mr. DOUGLAS. —

> " He who fights and runs away
> May live to fight another day."

Mr. WILSON. — " We shall not run away to live : we shall live to run. (Laughter.) We shall go into the conflict in the coming contest like the Zouaves at Inkermann, ' with the light of battle on our faces.' If we fall, we shall fall to rise again ; for the arm of God is beneath us, and the current of advancing civilization is bearing us onward to assured triumph.

" Now, I will tell you what we intend to do. We shall stand here and vote to defeat the bill reported by the senator from Illinois, because we believe, by the provisions of that bill, Kansas can be and will be invaded and conquered. We shall vote for the admission of this petition, for the admission of all petitions, from the people of Kansas ; we shall vote for the admission of Kansas into this Union as a free State. If we fail, if you vote us down, we shall go to the country with that issue. We shall appeal to the people, to the toiling millions whose heritage is in peril, to come to the rescue of the people of Kansas, struggling to preserve their sacred rights. Madness may rule the hour; the black power, now enthroned in the National Government, may prolong for another Olympiad its waning influence : but we shall ultimately rescue the republic from the unnatural rule of a slaveholding aristocracy. Before the rising spirit of liberty this domination will go down.

" A quarter of a century ago the conquest and subjugation of the republic was complete. Institutions of learning, benevolence, and religion, political organizations, and public men, ay, and the people themselves,

16*

all bowed in unresisting submission to the iron dominion of the slave-power. Murmurs of discontent sometimes broke upon the ear of the country : here and there a solitary voice uttered its feeble protest against the domination of a power which had inthralled the heart, conscience, and intellect of the conquered North ; but the overshadowing despotism of that power was complete. Twenty-five years have not yet closed since a few heroic men raised the banner of impartial liberty. Then we had not a single member of the Senate or House of Representatives. Not a single State legislature was with us. The political press of the country covered the humble movement with ridicule and contempt ; always excepting 'The New-York Evening Post,' then conducted by that inflexible Democrat, William Leggett, who went to a premature grave cheered by the assurance that he ' had written his name in ineffaceable letters on the abolition record.'

"Twenty years ago the public sneered at and defied the few proscribed and hunted followers who rallied around the humble leaders that inaugurated the movement, which, within two years, has secured a popular majority in the free States of more than three hundred thousand. We have an overwhelming majority there to-day against your policy ; and, if that majority is united, we can control the policy of the country. We shall triumph ; we shall enlarge this side of the chamber ; we shall thin out the other. (Laughter.) We have done some of that work recently in New England. We shall have a majority in this chamber yet ; we shall have a majority in the other House ; and we shall have a man at the other end of the avenue. We shall take the government of this country, and we shall govern the country as the true Democratic party.

"Now, sir, I have told the senator from Illinois what we intend to do; and we have no doubt of doing it. If the honorable senator wishes, through the coming weeks of this debate, to throw on this side of the chamber the taunting epithets of ' black Republicans ' and ' abolition agitators,' he may find that it is a game that two can play at. I think he and I and others had better discuss these grave questions without the application of taunts and epithets."

On the twenty-second day of May, 1856, Preston S. Brooks, member of the House from South Carolina, came into the Senate-chamber and made a dastardly assault on Mr. Sumner, who fell prostrate, under the repeated blows, upon the floor. This act of violence was occasioned by the senator's able speech, entitled "The Crime against Kansas," on Mr. Seward's bill for the admission of the State of Kansas into the Union. Mr. Wilson, at that moment in the room of Mr. Banks, immediately came into the Senate-chamber, where he found his colleague stricken down, and weltering unconscious in his blood. He aided in carrying him to his chamber, placing him upon his couch, and alleviating his pain. The next day he appropriately called the attention of the Senate to the assault upon his colleague.

On motion of Mr. Seward, a committee was appointed: and on the morning of the 27th instant, the floor and galleries being filled with anxious listeners, Mr. Wilson rose, and in a few fearless words characterized the assault upon his colleague as " brutal, murderous, and cowardly; " when

Mr. Butler of South Carolina, with whose family Brooks the assailant was connected, rudely interrupted him; and cries of " Order, order! " rang through the

tumultuous assembly. Threats of personal violence arose
in the confusion; but they had no terror for him who
knew no fear. In the evening he went to Trenton to
speak before the State Convention; and on the morning
of the 29th inst. he received, by the hand of Gen.
Joseph Lane of Oregon, a challenge from Mr. Brooks.
Taking up his pen, he at once replied in words which
are memorable as embodying the views of Northern men
upon duelling.

WASHINGTON, May 29, half-past ten o'clock.
Hon. P. S. BROOKS.

Sir,—Your note of the 27th inst. was placed in my
hands by your friend Gen. Lane at twenty minutes past
ten o'clock to-day.

I characterized on the floor of the Senate the assault
upon my colleague as brutal, murderous, and cowardly.
I thought so then : I think so now. I have no qualifications whatever to make in regard to those words.

I have never entertained or expressed, in the Senate
or elsewhere, the idea of personal responsibility in the
sense of the duellist.

I have always regarded duelling as the lingering relic
of a barbarous civilization, which the law of the country
has branded as a crime. While, therefore, I religiously
believe in the right of self-defence in its broadest sense,
the law of my country and the mature civilization of my
whole life alike forbid me to meet you for the purpose
indicated in your letter.

Your obedient servant,

HENRY WILSON.

This reply to Brooks, so firmly, so tersely, and so
serenely expressed, touched the very key-note of public

sentiment, and was most enthusiastically received through the whole Northern country. While the right of self-defence was not yielded, the unlawful practice of duelling was condemned as the remains of barbarism, and the three strong, pointed words of rebuke, " brutal, murderous, and cowardly," sent back fearlessly to the challenger. The press, the pulpit, and men of every political complexion, at the North, indorsed the action ; and those few words, written in a moment from the impulse of an honest heart, have done something to drive the idea of duelling from the mind of the nation.

The " cowardly conclave " still beset the steps of Mr. Wilson, as the following letter indicates; but they had not the courage to strike : —

Hon. H. WILSON. WASHINGTON, June 2, 1856.

Sir, — A gentleman in constant association with the South-Carolina members sent to my house last night to inform me that it was intended to attack you this morning.

Brooks did not leave town on Friday evening, but was parading among the groups at the president's house on Saturday afternoon. He probably does not intend to leave until after the action of the House upon the outrage. I mention these facts for your information, and to say that you had better be on your guard.

Very truly, E. HARTE.

On the 13th of June Mr. Wilson made a brave and manly reply to Mr. Butler's speech of the two preceding days assailing Mr. Sumner and the State of Massachusetts. The passages we present will show its spirit and its forensic power : —

" Mr. PRESIDENT, — I feel constrained by a sense of duty to my State, by personal relations to my colleague and friend, to trespass for a few moments upon the time and attention of the Senate.

" You have listened, Mr. President, the Senate has listened, these thronged seats and these crowded galleries have listened, to the extraordinary speech of the honorable senator from South Carolina, which has now run through two days. I must say, sir, that I have listened to that speech with painful and sad emotions. A senator of a sovereign State, more than twenty days ago, was stricken senseless to the floor for words spoken in debate. For more than three weeks he has been confined to his room upon a bed of weakness and of pain. The moral sentiment of the country has been outraged, grossly outraged, by this wanton assault, in the person of a senator, on the freedom of debate. The intelligence of this transaction has flown over the land, and is now flying abroad over the civilized world ; and wherever Christianity has a foothold, or civilization a resting-place, that act will meet the stern condemnation of mankind.

" Intelligence comes to us, Mr. President, that a civil war is raging beyond the Mississippi ; intelligence also comes to us, that, upon the shores of the Pacific, lynch law is again organized ; and the telegraph brings us news of assaults and murders around the ballot-boxes of New Orleans, growing out of differences of opinion and of interests. Can we be surprised, sir, that these scenes, which are disgracing the character of our country and our age, are rife, when a venerable senator — one of the oldest members of the Senate, and chairman of its Judiciary Committee — occupies four hours of the important time of the Senate in vindication of and apology for an assault unparalleled in the history of the country ? If lawless violence here in this chamber, upon the person of a senator, can find vindication, if this outrage upon the freedom of debate finds apology, from a veteran senator, why may not violent counsels elsewhere go unrebuked ?

"The senator from South Carolina, through this debate, has taken occasion to apply to Mr. Sumner, to his speech, to all that concerns him, all the epithets " —

Mr. BUTLER. — "I used criticism, but not epithets."

Mr. WILSON. — "Well, sir, I accept the senator's word, and I say ' criticism.' But, I say, in his criticism he used every word that I can conceive a fertile imagination could invent, or a malignant passion suggest. He has taken his full revenge here on the floor of the Senate — here in debate — for the remarks made by my colleague. I do not take any exception to this mode. This is the way in which the speech of my colleague should have been met, — not by blows, not by an assault.

"The senator tells us that this is not, in his opinion, an assault upon the constitutional rights of a member of the Senate. He tells us that a member cannot be permitted to print, and send abroad over the world, with impunity, his opinions ; but that he is liable to have them questioned in a judicial tribunal. Well, sir, if this be so, — he is a lawyer ; I am not, — I accept his view ; and I ask, Why not have tested Mr. Sumner's speech in a judicial tribunal, and let that tribunal have settled the question whether Mr. Sumner uttered a libel or not ? Why was it necessary, why did the ' chivalry ' of South Carolina require, that for words uttered on this floor, under the solemn guaranties of constitutional law, a senator should be met here by

violence ?   Why appeal from the floor of the Senate, from
a judicial tribunal, to the bludgeon ?   I put the question
to the senator, to the ‘ chivalry ’ of South Carolina, ay, to
‘ the gallant set,’ to use the senator’s own words, of ‘ Ninety-
six,’ why was it necessary to substitute the bludgeon for the
judicial tribunal ?

“ The senator complained of Mr. Sumner for quoting
the Constitution of South Carolina ; and he asserted over
and over again, and he winds up his speech by the declaration, that the quotation made is not in the Constitution.
After making that declaration, he read the Constitution,
and read the identical quotation.   Mr. Sumner asserted
what is in the Constitution ; but there is an addition to it
which he did not quote.   The senator might have complained because he did not quote it ; but the portion not
quoted carries out only the letter and the spirit of the portion quoted.   To be a member of the House of Representatives of South Carolina, it is necessary to own a certain
number of acres of land and ten slaves, or seven hundred
and fifty dollars of real estate free of debt.   The senator
declared with great emphasis — and I saw nods, Democratic nods, all around the Senate — that ‘ a man who was
not worth that amount of money was not fit to be a representative.’   That may be good Democratic doctrine, — it
comes from a Democratic senator of the Democratic State
of South Carolina, and received Democratic nods and
Democratic smiles, — but it is not in harmony with the
democratic ideas of the American people.

“ The charge made by Mr. Sumner was, that South
Carolina was nominally republican, but in reality had
aristocratic features in her constitution.   Well, sir, is not
this charge true ?   To be a member of the House of
Representatives of South Carolina, the candidate must

own ten men, — yes, sir, ten men, — five hundred acres of land, or have seven hundred and fifty dollars of real estate free of debt; and, to be a member of the Senate, double is required. This legislature, having these personal qualifications, placing them in the rank of a privileged few, is elected upon a representative basis as unequal as the rotten-borough system of England in its most rotten days. That is not all. This legislature elects the governor of South Carolina and the presidential electors. The people have the privilege of voting for men with these qualifications upon this basis; and they select their governor for them, and choose the presidential electors for them. The privileged few govern: the many have the privilege of being governed by them.

"Sir, I have no disposition to assail South Carolina. God knows that I would peril my life in defence of any State of this Union if assailed by a foreign foe. I have voted, and I will continue to vote while I have a seat on this floor, as cheerfully for appropriations, or for any thing that can benefit South Carolina or any other State of this Union, as for my own Commonwealth of Massachusetts. South Carolina is a part of my country. Slaveholders are not the tenth part of her population: there is somebody else there besides slaveholders. I am opposed to its system of slavery, to its aristocratic inequalities, and I shall continue to be opposed to them; but it is a sovereign State of this Union, — a part of my country, — and I have no disposition to do injustice to it.

"Sir, the senator from South Carolina has undertaken to assure the Senate and the country to-day that he is not the aggressor. I tell him that Mr. Sumner was not the aggressor; that the senator from South Carolina was the aggressor. I will prove this declara-

17

tion to be true beyond all question. Mr. Sumner is not a man who desires to be aggressive towards any one. He came into the Senate 'a representative man.' His opinions were known to the country. He came here knowing that there were but few in this body who could sympathize with him. He was reserved and cautious. For eight months here he made no speeches upon any question that could excite the animadversion even of the sensitive senator from South Carolina. He made a brief speech in favor of the system of granting lands for constructing railways in the new States, which the people of those States justly applauded; and I will undertake to say that he stated the whole question briefly, fully, and powerfully. He also made a brief speech welcoming Kossuth to the United States. But, beyond the presentation of a petition, he took no steps to press his earnest convictions upon the Senate; nor did he say any thing which could by possibility disturb the most excitable senator.

"On the twenty-eighth day of July, 1852, after being in this body eight months, Mr. Sumner introduced a proposition to repeal the Fugitive-slave Act. Mr. Sumner and his constituents believed that act to be not only a violation of the Constitution of the United States and a violation of all the safeguards of the common law which have been garnered up for centuries to protect the rights of the people, but at war with Christianity, humanity, and human nature, — an enactment that is bringing upon this republic the indignant scorn of the Christian and civilized world. With these convictions he proposed to repeal that act, as he had a right to propose. He had made no speech. He rose and asked the Senate to give him the privilege of making a speech. 'Strike, but

hear,' said he, using a quotation. I do not know that
he gave the authority for it. Perhaps the senator from
South Carolina will criticise it as a plagiarism, as he
has criticised another application of a classical passage.
Mr. Sumner asked the privilege of addressing the Senate.
The senator from South Carolina, who now tells us that
he had been his friend, an old and veteran senator here,
instead of feeling that Mr. Sumner was a member standing almost alone, with only the senator from New York
(Mr. Seward), the senator from New Hampshire (Mr.
Hale), and Gov. Chase of Ohio, in sympathy with him,
objected to his being heard. He asked Mr. Sumner
tauntingly if he wished to make an ' oratorical display,'
and talked about ' playing the orator ' and ' the part
of a parliamentary rhetorician.' These words, in their
scope and in their character, were calculated to wound
the sensibilities of a new member, and perhaps bring
upon him what is often brought on a member who maintains here the great doctrines of Liberty and Christianity,
— the sneer and the laugh under which men sometimes
shrink.

"Thus was Mr. Summer, *before he had ever uttered a
word on the subject of slavery here,* arraigned by the
senator from South Carolina, not for what he ever had
said, but for what he intended to say; and the senator
announced that he must oppose his speaking, because he
would attack South Carolina. Mr. Sumner quietly said
that he had no such purpose; but the senator did not
wish to allow him to ' make the Senate the vehicle of
communication for his speech throughout the United
States to wash deeper and deeper the channel through
which flow the angry waters of agitation.'

"Now, I charge here on the floor of the Senate, and

before the country, that the senator from South Carolina was the aggressor ; that he arraigned, in language which no man can defend, my colleague before he ever uttered a word on this subject on the floor of the Senate, and in the face of his express disclaimer that he had no purpose of alluding to South Carolina. This was the beginning."

After citing other instances of personal insult and abuse with which Mr. Butler sought to blacken Mr. Sumner, Mr. Wilson says, —

"He again talks about ' sickly sentimentality ; ' and he charges that this ' sickly sentimentality now governs the councils of the Commonwealth of Massachusetts.' Yes, sir, the senator from South Carolina makes five distinct assaults upon Massachusetts. Massachusetts councils governed by sickly sentimentality ! Sir, Massachusetts stands to-day where she stood when the little squad assembled on the 19th of April, 1775, to fire the first gun of the Revolution. The sentiments that brought those humble men to the little green at Lexington, and to the bridge at Concord ; which carried them up the slope of Bunker Hill ; and which drove forth the British troops from Boston, never again to press the soil of Massachusetts, — that sentiment still governs the councils of Massachusetts, and rules in the hearts of her people. The feeling which governed the men of that glorious epoch of our history is the feeling of the men of Massachusetts of to-day.

"Those sentiments of liberty and patriotism have penetrated the hearts of the whole population of that Commonwealth. Sir, in that State, every man, no matter what blood runs in his veins, or what may be the color of his skin, stands up before the law the peer of the proudest that treads her soil. This is the sentiment of the people of Massachusetts. In equality before the law they find their strength. They know this to be right if Christianity is true, and they will maintain it in the future as they have in the past; and the civilized world, the coming generations, those who are hereafter to give law to the universe, will pronounce that in this contest Massachusetts is right, inflexibly right, and South Carolina and the senator from South Carolina wrong. The latter are maintaining the odious relics of a barbarous age and civilization, — not the civilization of the New Testament, not the civilization that is now blessing and adorning the best portions of the world.

"'We cannot be hurt by attempted assassination!' exclaims the senator from South Carolina.

"Attempted assassination?

"It ill becomes the senator from South Carolina to use these words in connection with Massachusetts or the North. The arms of Massachusetts are Freedom, Justice, Truth. Strong in these, she is not driven to the necessity of resorting to 'attempted assassination' either in or out of the Senate.

"But the whole story is not yet told. I wish to refer to another assault made by the senator, which I witnessed myself a few days after I took a seat in this body. On the 23d of February, 1855, on one of the last days of the last session, to the bill introduced by the senator from Connecticut (Mr. Toucey) Mr. Sumner moved an amendment providing for the repeal of the Fugitive-slave Act. He made some remarks in support of that proposition. The senator from South Carolina rose and interrupted him, saying, 'I would ask him one question, which he perhaps will not answer *honestly*.' Mr. Sumner said, 'I will answer any question.' The senator went

17*

on to ask questions, and received his answers; and then he said, speaking of Mr. Sumner, 'I know he is not a tactician, and I shall not take advantage of the infirmity of a man who does not know half his time exactly what he is about.' This is indeed extraordinary language for the senator from South Carolina to apply to the senator from Massachusetts. I witnessed that scene. I then deemed the language insulting: the manner was more so. I hold in my hands the remarks of 'The Louisville Journal,' a Southern press, upon this scene. I shall not read them to the Senate; for I do not wish to present any thing which the senator may even deem offensive. I will say, however, that his language and his deportment to my colleague on that occasion were aggressive and overbearing in the extreme. And this is the senator who never makes assaults! But, not content with assaulting Mr. Sumner, he winds up his speech by a taunt at 'Boston philanthropy.' Surely no person ever scattered assault more freely.

"Thus has Mr. Sumner been, by the senator from South Carolina, systematically assailed in this body from the 28th of July, 1852, up to the present time, — a period of nearly four years. He has applied to my colleague every expression calculated to wound the sensibilities of an honorable man, and to draw down upon him sneers, obloquy, and hatred, in and out of the Senate. In my place here, I now pronounce these continued assaults upon my colleague unparalleled in the history of the Senate.

"I come now to speak for one moment of the late speech of my colleague, which is the alleged cause of the recent assault upon him, and which the senator from South Carolina has condemned so abundantly. That speech, — a thorough and fearless exposition of what Mr. Sumner entitled the 'Crime against Kansas,' — from beginning to end, is marked by entire plainness. Things are called by their right names. The usurpation in Kansas is exposed, and also the apologies for it, successively. No words were spared which seemed necessary to the exhibition. In arraigning the *crime*, it was natural to speak of those who sustained it. Accordingly, the administration is constantly held up to condemnation. Various senators who have vindicated this crime are at once answered and condemned. Among these are the senator from South Carolina, the senator from Illinois (Mr. Douglas), the senator from Virginia (Mr. Mason), and the senator from Missouri (Mr. Geyer). The senator from South Carolina now complains of Mr. Sumner's speech. Surely it is difficult to see on what ground that senator can make any such complaint. The speech was indeed severe, — severe as truth, — but in all respects parliamentary. It is true that it handles the senator from South Carolina freely; but that senator had spoken repeatedly in the course of the Kansas debate, once at length and elaborately, and at other times more briefly, foisting himself into the speeches of other senators, and identifying himself completely with the *crime* which my colleague felt it his duty to arraign. It was natural, therefore, that his course in the debate, and his position, should be particularly considered. And in this work Mr. Sumner had no reason to hold back, when he thought of the constant and systematic and ruthless attacks, which, utterly without cause, he had received from that senator. The only objection which the senator from South Carolina can reasonably make to Mr. Sumner is that he struck a strong blow.

"The senator complains that the speech was printed before it was delivered. Here, again, is his accustomed inaccuracy. It is true that it was in the printers' hands, and was mainly in type; but it received additions and revisions after its delivery, and was not put to press till then. Away with this petty objection! The senator says that twenty thousand copies have gone to England. Here, again, is his accustomed inaccuracy. If they have gone, it is without Mr. Sumner's agency. But the senator foresees the truth. Sir, that speech will go to England; it will go to the continent of Europe; it has gone over the country, and has been read by the American people as no speech ever delivered in this body was read before. That speech will go down to coming ages. Whatever men may say of its sentiments, — and coming ages will indorse them, — it will be placed among the ablest parliamentary efforts of our own age, or of any age.

"The senator from South Carolina tells us that the speech is to be condemned; and he quotes the venerable and distinguished senator from Michigan (Mr. Cass). I do not know what Mr. Sumner could stand. The senator says he could not stand the censure of the senator from Michigan. *I could;* and I believe there are a great many in this country whose powers of endurance are as great as my own. I have great respect for that venerable senator; but the opinions of no senator here are potential in the country. This is a Senate of equals. The judgment of the country is to be made up on the records formed here. The opinions of the senator from Michigan, and of other senators here, are to go into the record, and will receive the verdict of the people. By that I am willing to stand.

"The senator from South Carolina tells us that the speech is to be condemned. It has gone out to the country. It has been printed by the million. It has been scattered broadcast amongst seventeen millions of Northern freemen who can read and write. The senator condemns it; South Carolina condemns it. But South Carolina is only a part of this Confederacy, and but a part of the Christian and civilized world. South Carolina makes rice and cotton; but South Carolina contributes little to make up the judgment of the Christian and civilized world. I value her rice and cotton more than I do her opinions on questions of scholarship and eloquence, of patriotism or of liberty.

"Mr. President, I have no desire to assail the senator from South Carolina, or any other senator in this body; but I wish to say now, that we have had quite enough of this asserted superiority, social and political. We were told some time ago by the senator from Alabama (Mr. Clay), that those of us who entertained certain sentiments fawned upon him and other Southern men if they permitted us to associate with them. This is strange language to be used in this body. I never fawned upon that senator. I never sought his acquaintance; and I do not know that I should feel myself honored if I had it. I treat him as an equal here; I wish always to treat him respectfully: but, when he tells me or my friends that we fawn upon him or his associates, I say to him that I have never sought, and never shall seek, any other acquaintance than what official intercourse requires with a man who declared on the floor of the Senate that he would do what Henry Clay once said 'no gentleman would do,' — hunt a fugitive slave.

"The senator from Virginia, not now in his seat (Mr.

Mason), when Mr. Sumner closed his speech, saw fit to tell the Senate that his hands would be soiled by contact with ours. The senator is not here: I wish he were. I have simply to say that I know nothing in that senator, moral, intellectual, or physical, which entitles him to use such language towards members of the Senate, or any portion of God's creation. I know nothing in the State from which he comes, rich as it is in the history of the past, that entitles him to speak in such a manner. I am not here to assail Virginia: God knows I have not a feeling in my heart against her or against her public men. But I do say, it is time that these arrogant assumptions ceased here. This is no place for assumed social superiority, as though certain senators held the keys of cultivated and refined society. Sir, they do not hold the keys, and they shall not hold over me the plantation-whip.

" I wish always to speak kindly towards every man in this body. Since I came here, I have never asked an introduction to a Southern member of the Senate; not because I have any feelings against them (for God knows I have not); but I knew that they believed I held opinions hostile to their interests, and I supposed they would not desire my society. I have never wished to obtrude myself on their society, so that certain senators could do with me as they have boasted they did with others, — refuse to receive their advances, or refuse to recognize them on the floor of the Senate. Sir, there is not a cooly in the guano islands of Peru who does not think the Celestial Empire the whole universe. There are a great many men, who have swung the whip over the plantation, who think they not only rule the plantation, but make up the judgment of the world, and hold the keys not only to political power, as they have done in this country, but to social life.

"The senator from South Carolina assails the resolutions of my State with his accustomed looseness, as springing from ignorance, passion, prejudice, excitement. Sir, the testimony before the House committee sustains all that is contained in those resolutions. I know Massachusetts; and I can tell him, that, of the twelve hundred thousand people of Massachusetts, you cannot find in the State one thousand, administration office-holders included, who do not look with loathing and execration upon the outrage on the person of their senator and the honor of their State. The sentiment of Massachusetts, of New England, of the North, approaches unanimity. Massachusetts has spoken her opinions. The senator is welcome to assail them, if he chooses; but they are on the record. They are made up by the verdict of her people; and they understand the question; and from their verdict there is no appeal."

After this speech of Mr. Wilson, Mr. Butler indulged in some discursive remarks, and ended by saying, —

"As I suppose the senator (Mr. Wilson) is to be considered, in some sense, the historian of his State, I desire to ask him how many battles were fought in Massachusetts during the Revolutionary war."

Mr. WILSON. — "I will answer the senator. The battles fought in Massachusetts during the Revolution were few, because they were not necessary. Our Massachusetts men met the enemy at Lexington, at Concord Bridge, at Bunker Hill, and on the heights of Dorchester. They would have met them on every spot in Massachusetts; but the enemy took good care right early to get and keep out of that State.

"The senator said yesterday, as I understood him, that 'South Carolina had shed hogsheads of blood where Massachusetts had shed gallons' during the Revolution."

Mr. BUTLER. — "On the battle-fields of the two States."

Mr. WILSON. — "I heard no such limitation. I understood the senator to mean that South Carolina had contributed hogsheads of the blood of her sons, where Massachusetts had only contributed gallons, to the Revolution. Sir, South Carolina furnished five thousand five hundred soldiers; Massachusetts, sixty-nine thousand; and they drove the enemy, and followed the enemy, and met the enemy on the battle-fields of the Revolution, from the northern to the southern boundaries of the republic, from the St. Lawrence to the St. Mary's. There were but few battles fought on the soil of Massachusetts, for the reason that the enemy thought it was safer to leave Massachusetts, and go to South Carolina. The British army thought it was not safe to be very near the battle-fields of Concord, of Lexington, and of Bunker Hill; and it left Massachusetts, and took good care to keep out of a Commonwealth where friends always find a welcome, and foes are apt to find a grave.

"During the Revolution, a portion of the people of South Carolina — the Gadsdens, the Rutledges, the Laurenses, the Sumters, the Marions — made as great sacrifices for the cause of independence as any patriots in any portion of the land; but the fact cannot be denied, — and all these patriots, including even Marion, convict South Carolina of the fact, — that she had a large lot of Tories. There was a civil war in that State; and, more than that, thousands and tens of thousands of her sons sought protection under the British flag. When the army of Greene was starving, the British army in Charleston was receiving

all that the fertile valleys of South Carolina could produce, carry into Charleston, and exchange for British
gold. When Greene and his patriot army wanted oxen
and horses to carry supplies, they were hustled off into
the forest by people who had, to quote the words of
Gen. Greene to Gen. Barnwell, 'far greater attachment to
their interests than zeal for the service of their country.'"

Mr. BUTLER. — "Let me ask the gentleman who fed
Greene's army at that time."

Mr. WILSON. — "'Who fed Greene's army?' That
army was hardly fed at all: at any rate, it was but poorly
fed, and scantily clothed. I apprehend, sir, that Greene's
army — like the schoolboy's whistle, that whistled itself —
fed itself.

"I have no disposition to assail the senator's State. I
should blush if I could say aught against the patriots of
South Carolina, or even cease to feel gratitude for their
efforts, their prompt response to the patriots of my own
State, in the early days of the Revolution. But, sir, Gads-
den, Burke, Marion, Ramsay, Barnwell, and the patriots
of that period, have borne this evidence, — that South Carolina was weakened in that contest by the existence of
slavery. That was what Mr. Sumner charged, and, on a
former occasion, demonstrated; and that, I take it, no
man here or elsewhere can deny.

"The senator tells us that he has complimented the
battle-fields of Massachusetts, — the fields of Lexington,
Concord, and Bunker Hill. That senator, and the constituents of that senator, can stand upon those sacred
spots, and breathe something of the spirit of liberty that
makes them immortal; he can utter his sentiments, —
sentiments so little in harmony with the gallant dead
that sleep beneath those hallowed sods, or the living who

18

now guard them under the protection of law and a public sentiment nurtured and sustained by free speech. I should be proud to tread the battle-fields of South Carolina, hallowed by patriot blood. Yes, sir, it would afford me intense gratification to stand upon those stricken fields, so dear to every true American heart; but I do not know that I could do so without suppressing those cherished sentiments of liberty, for the vindication of which patriot blood was poured out at Camden, Guilford, Eutaw, and Hobkirk Hill.

"But all these allusions and reflections upon the history of the past afford me no gratification. I say to the senator from South Carolina, that he and I and all of us had far better turn from the past, cease to reflect upon the services of our States in the Revolutionary era, and deal with the living questions which we must meet in this age, — questions that have great issues, involving the interests of our common country and the rights of human nature. He and I and all of us here ought to strive to settle these great issues for the good of our common country, and the whole people of the country, bond and free."

Many letters of congratulation were received after the delivery of this speech, and among them one from the patriotic poet J. G. Whittier, in which he says, —

"Thy reply to Butler after the outrage upon our noble friend Sumner was eminently 'the right word in the right place.'"

The departure of Mr. Sumner from the Senate (from which he was absent several years) left a heavier burden upon Mr. Wilson; yet with dauntless vigor he pressed on, meeting the Southern members with a clear head and lion heart on the great questions then at issue, and repelling by unanswerable arguments the assaults upon the North.

He would not interfere with slavery in the Southern States; but with invincible determination he stood opposed to its extension over the Territories of the West, and to the doctrine of the "squatter sovereignty" advanced by Mr. Douglas, and maintained by the pro-slavery propagandists.

In a noble speech, July 9, on a report for printing twenty thousand extra copies of the bill to enable Kansas to form a constitution, he said, —

" Sir, for framing this constitution, this free constitution, for organizing under it a State government, and choosing senators to urge its adoption here, the people of Kansas have been denounced as ' traitors' by the senator from Illinois and those who follow his lead in and out of the Senate. This chamber has rung with your words of rebuke, denunciation, and reproof of the people of Kansas, whose only crime is devotion to freedom, resistance to the monstrous tyranny of usurped power. I charge upon the administration the crime of abandoning the people of Kansas to the merciless rule of their conquerors. Ay, sir, I go farther, and I charge upon the administration and upon its supporters here the crime of aiding and abetting their conquerors in their unhallowed deeds.

" Mr. President, the administration and its supporters — the senators from Illinois, Pennsylvania, and Georgia — snatched Kansas from the exclusive possession of the free laboring-men of the republic, North and South, and flung it open to the footprints of the slave and his master. You deluded the people with the idea of popular sovereignty: you have seen that sovereignty cloven down by invading hordes of armed men ; you have seen the people robbed of their rights, and oppressed; you have seen them struggle to recover their lost rights; and in all their wrongs and struggles you have basely abandoned them; ay, you have joined their oppressors, and aided them in the enforcement of their usurped powers and unhallowed decrees. Sir, I hold the administration, I hold the majority here, I hold the Democratic party, up to the stern verdict of the civilized world for this abandonment of the people of Kansas, this collusion with their oppressors.

"The people of Kansas, Mr. President, have not only been defrauded of their legal and political rights, oppressed by laws imposed upon them by foreign force, and denied all redress, but they have been invaded, hunted down, by armed bands of thieving marauders, their dwellings burned, their property stolen, and many of their number treated with personal violence, and some of them brutally murdered. Dwellings have been battered with cannon, houses have been fired, presses destroyed, oxen, horses, and other property, stolen, and men foully murdered; and the administration and its officials in the Territory have no time to spare from the infamous work of subduing the friends of free Kansas for the arrest and punishment of the men who have illumined the midnight skies with the lurid light of sacked and burning dwellings of the people, — men who have inaugurated the era of robbery, violence, and murder."

In enumerating the outrages committed upon the peaceable citizens of Kansas, he held up a musket-ball to the Senate, and touchingly said, —

"The ball I hold in my hand was shot through a boy eighteen years old, the son of a widow. On his way home from Westport, Mo., he was stopped by these gentry who keep guard over the passes' into the Territory, and

required to give up what he had.   He gave up his arms.
They then required him to give up his horse; but he told
them he would not do it.   For that he was shot down;
and this ball was taken out of his lifeless body by a friend
of mine."

In an effective speech in the Senate, Aug. 27, against
sending military supplies to subjugate freemen in Kansas,
he said, —

" Let the army be disbanded forever rather than enforce
those infamous enactments or uphold the usurpation in
Kansas. Almost every township of the North has furnished
actual settlers to Kansas.   Are senators on the other side
infatuated enough to believe that the people will sustain
them in their career of madness in forcing down the
throats of their kindred and friends, with the sabre and
bayonet, these enactments?   When the brutal boast of
the British officer, that he would cram the stamps down
the throats of our fathers with the hilt of his sword, is
applauded by their descendants, then, and not till then,
will the people of the free States applaud your efforts to
cram these unchristian, inhuman, and fiendish laws down
the throats of their brethren in distant Kansas with the
sabre of the dragoon, — enactments which the senator
from Delaware (Mr. Clayton) declares would send even
John C. Calhoun to the penitentiary."

18*

CHAPTER XI.

JOHN C. FRÉMONT was nominated as the Republican candidate for president in the convention held at Philadelphia, June 17, 1856, on a platform opposing the repeal of the Missouri Compromise, the extension of slavery into the free Territories, the policy of the pro-slavery administration of Mr. Pierce, and in favor of a railroad to the Pacific, and the admission of Kansas as a free State into the Union. Mr. Wilson, though not a delegate, was present at the convention, where he was most cordially received, and where he brought forward Mr. Dayton for vice-president. On his return from Congress, he went into the presidential contest with his usual ardor, delivering powerful speeches before immense audiences, in which he rebuked the aggressive spirit of the South and the pusillanimity of the administra-

210

tion, and developed the principles of the Republican party.

In a festival of the Sons of New Hampshire, held at Natick Aug. 18, he was greeted with tremendous applause, and his senatorial course commended. The indignity cast on Massachusetts by the dastardly assault on Mr. Sumner, and the arrogance of the border ruffians, were converting rapidly her conservatives to Republicanism; and great enthusiasm for the liberal candidates was manifested, especially by the working-people.

It was generally admitted that Mr. Frémont would be elected; and mutterings were heard, that, in such event, the South would dissolve the Union. Senator Butler said, "If he should be chosen, I shall advise my legislature to go at the tap of the drum;" and Mr. Toombs of Georgia, that "the Union would be dissolved, and ought to be dissolved."

But the action of the third party in the nomination of Mr. Fillmore brought James Buchanan into the executive chair. The large vote cast, however, for the Republican candidate, revealed the strength of the party, the sentiment of the North, and abundantly repaid the exertion which the contest cost.

On entering Congress in December, Mr. Wilson introduced a bill to organize the Territory of Kansas and Nebraska on the 16th inst.; and on the 19th made a speech of masterly ability in defence of the acts and principles of his organization, which had an immense circulation through the country, and fully sustained his reputation as an orator, a statistician, and a statesman. In it he said, —

"On the 4th of November last, more than thirteen hundred thousand men, intelligent, patriotic, liberty-loving, law-abiding citizens of New England, the great Central States, and of the North-west, holding with our republican fathers that all men are created equal, and have an inalienable right to liberty ; that the Constitution of the United States was ordained and established to secure that inalienable right everywhere under its exclusive authority; denying ' the authority of Congress, of a Territorial legislature, of any individual, or association of individuals, to give legal existence to slavery in any Territory of the United States while the present Constitution shall be maintained,'— pronounced through the ballot-box that ' the Constitution confers upon Congress sovereign power over the Territories of the United States ; and that, in the exercise of this power, it is both the right and the duty of Congress to prohibit in the Territories those twin relics of barbarism, polygamy and slavery.' Believing with Franklin, that ' slavery is an atrocious debasement of human nature ;' with Adams, that ' consenting to slavery is a sacrilegious breach of trust ;' with Jefferson, that ' one hour of American slavery is fraught with more misery than ages of that which we rose in rebellion to oppose ;' with Madison, that ' slavery is a dreadful calamity,' — that ' imbecility is ever attendant upon a country filled with slaves ;' with Monroe, that ' slavery has preyed on the vitals of the community in all the States where it has existed ;' with Montesquieu, 'that even the very earth, which teems with profusion under the cultivating hand of the free-born laborer, shrinks into barrenness from the contaminating sweat of a slave,' — they pronounced their purpose to be to save Kansas, now in peril, and all the Territories of the republic, for the free laboring-men of the North and the South, their children, and their children's children, forever.

" Accepting the Declaration of Independence and the Constitution of the United States as their political charts ; avowing their purposes to be to maintain the Constitution, the Federal Union, and the rights of the States ; proclaiming everywhere their purpose not to make war upon the South, not to interfere with the legal and constitutional rights of the people of any of the States, — they gave their votes with the profoundest conviction that they were discharging the duties sanctioned by humanity, patriotism, and religion."

He thus denied the charges of the president : —

" Assuming, Mr. President, that his policy has been sanctioned by the election, the president proceeds to accuse more than thirteen hundred thousand American citizens of an attempt to organize a sectional party, and usurp the government of the country. He proceeds to arraign more than thirteen hundred thousand citizens of the free North, and to charge them with forming associations of individuals, 'who, pretending to seek only to prevent the spread of slavery into the present or future inchoate States, are really inflamed with a desire to change the domestic institutions of existing States;' with seeking 'an object which they well know to be a revolutionary one ;' with entering 'a path which leads nowhere, unless it be to civil war and disunion ;' with being 'perfectly aware that the only path to the accomplishment' of the change they seek 'is through burning cities and ravaged fields and slaughtered populations;' with endeavoring 'to prepare the people of the United States for civil war, by doing every thing in their power to deprive the Constitution and the laws of moral authority, and to undermine the fabric of the Union by appeals to passion and sectional prejudice, by indoctrinating its peo-

ple with reciprocal hatred, and by educating them to stand
face to face as enemies.'

"Sir, I deny each, every one, ay, all, of these charges.
There is not the semblance of truth in them. If the
serpent that stole into Eden, that beguiled our first mother,
which the angels

'Found
Squat like a toad at the ear of Eve,'

had glided into the executive mansion, that serpent could
not have hissed into the president's ear words more skil-
fully adapted to express the precise and exact opposite of
truth. Sir, these accusations against as intelligent and
patriotic men as ever rallied around the standard of Freedom are untruthful and malignant, showing that the
shafts hurled in the conflict through which we have just
passed rankle in his bosom."

Of the issues and the real agitator he said, —

"Surely senators cannot be surprised at the discussion
of questions so vast as those which grow out of the slavery
of nearly four millions of men in America. American
slavery, our connections with it, and our relations to it,
and the obligations these connections and relations impose
upon us as men, as citizens of the States and the United
States, make up the overshadowing issues of the age in
which we live. Philanthropists, who have sounded the
depths and shoals of humanity; scholars, who have laid
under contribution the domain of matter and of mind,
of philosophic inquiry and historical research; statesmen,
who are impressing their genius upon the institutions
of their country and their age, — all are now illustrating, by their genius, learning, and eloquence, the vast
and complicated issues involved in the great problems we
of this age, in America, are working out. The transcend-

ent magnitude of the interests involved in the existence and expansion of the system of human bondage in America is arresting the attention of the people, and stirring the country to its profoundest depths.

"The senator from Tennessee (Mr. Jones) quoted a remark of mine, to the effect that this agitation of the slavery question would never cease while the soil of the republic should be trod by the foot of a slave. That sentiment I repeat here to-day. I believe it. GOD is the great agitator. While his throne stands, agitation will go on until the foot of a slave shall not press the soil of the Eastern or Western continent."

Of the Union sentiment of his party he remarked, —

"Then we are charged in the message with having entered upon a path which has no possible outlet but disunion. When the Republican party was organized, the avowal was made that the Union must be maintained. The declaration of Mr. Webster, 'Liberty and Union, now and forever, one and inseparable;' the declaration of Andrew Jackson, 'The Union must be preserved,' — were borne throughout the canvass on all our banners. In the public press, and before the people everywhere, the doctrine was maintained that we were for the Union; and if any men, North or South, laid their hands upon it, they should die, if we had the power, traitor deaths, and leave traitor names in the history of the republic."

He thus rebuked the sneer of "bleeding Kansas:"—

"Sir, the senator from Texas spoke sneeringly of 'bleeding Kansas.' Throughout the canvass, our efforts in favor of making Kansas a free State, and protecting the legal rights of the people, were sneered at as 'shrieks for Freedom' and for 'bleeding Kansas.' I remember that on the evening when the news came to New York that

Pennsylvania was carried, in October, the Empire Club came out with cannon, banners, and transparencies. The Five Points, where the waves of abolition fanaticism have never reached, — the inhabitants of that locality, like the people of the Lower Egypt of the West, stood fifty to one by the Democracy; the Five Points and the Sixth Ward were out; and upon a transparency, borne through the streets of the great commercial capital of the Western world, was the picture of three scourged black men; and on that transparency were the words, 'Bleeding Kansas.' I thought then that it was a degradation which had reached the profoundest depths of humiliation; but even that degradation has been surpassed here in the national capital. In that procession which passed along these avenues but a few evenings before we came here — a procession formed under the immediate eyes of the chiefs of the executive departments of the government, and filled with their retainers, led by government officials — was borne upon a transparency the words, 'Sumner and Kansas, — let them bleed!'

"The senator from Texas may sneer, and others may sneer, at 'bleeding Kansas;' but I tell him one thing, — that the next day at ten o'clock, after the presidential election, there was an assemblage of men, continuing through two days, in the city of Boston, from several States, and from 'bleeding Kansas,' — men, some of whom you guarded through the summer months for treason, — assembled together to take measures to save Kansas; and I assure that senator, and others who may think this struggle for Kansas is ended with the election, that more money has been contributed since that election than during any three months of the whole controversy. Thousands of garments have been sent to clothe that suffering people. We have resolved, — and we mean to keep that resolution, — that if by any lawful effort, any personal sacrifice, Kansas can be saved to Freedom, it shall be saved in spite of your present administration, or any thing that your incoming administration can do."

Respecting freedom of speech, he spoke as follows: —

"But we are charged by the president with inculcating a spirit which would lead the people of the North and South to stand face to face as enemies. Sir, I repel that charge as utterly and wholly false. There is no such feeling in the Northern States towards the people of the South. But a few months ago, the senator from Georgia (Mr. Toombs), whose views upon this question of slavery are known to be extremely ultra, went to the city of Boston, and lectured before one of the most intelligent audiences that ever assembled in that section of our country. He was received by all with that courtesy and that kindness of feeling which every Southern man who visits that section receives, and to which they bear testimony. Mr. Benton is in the North now, lecturing in favor of the Union, — 'carrying coals to Newcastle.' He is everywhere sought after, everywhere listened to, everywhere treated kindly, although he holds views in regard to slavery that not one man in ten thousand in that section approves.

"Can we utter in the South the words which the fathers of the South taught us? Could the senator from New York (Mr. Fish), whose father fought at Yorktown, go to that field, and utter the sentiments which were upon the lips of all the great men of Virginia when Cornwallis surrendered? Could the senators from New Hampshire stand on that spot once baptized by the blood of Alexander Scammell, and there utter the sentiments of Henry,

or of Jefferson, or of Mason?   Could one of us go down
to Mount Vernon, which slavery has converted into a sort
of jungle, and there repeat the words of Washington, —
'No man desires more earnestly than I do to see slavery
abolished : there is only one proper way to do it, and
that is by legislative action; and for that my vote shall
never be wanting'?   Could we go to Monticello, could
we stand by the graves of Jefferson, of Madison, of Henry,
of the great men of Virginia, and utter the sublime
thoughts which they uttered for the liberty of the bondmen?   Could we stand by the grave of Henry Clay, and
declare, as he declared, slavery to be ' a curse,' ' a wrong,'
a ' grievous wrong to the slave, that no contingency could
make right'?

" In the slaveholding States, free speech and a free press
are known only in theory.   A slaveholding, slavery-ex-
tending Democracy has established a relentless despotism.
We invited you of the South to meet us in national convention to restore the government to the policy of the
fathers.   Mr. Underwood of Virginia did go to Philadelphia.   He united with us in our declaration of principles ;
he united with us in the nomination of John C. Frémont:
and for this offence he was banished from Virginia.   He
returned a few days since, and was notified, that, if he
remained, he must run the risk of being dealt with by an
indignant community.   He has left there, and I believe is
now here in the city of Washington.   When the Frémont
flag was raised in Norfolk, the civil authorities took it
down.   Mr. Stannard, a merchant of Norfolk, a native of
Connecticut, went up to the ballot-box, and quietly handed
in his vote for Frémont.   It was handed back to him.
They would not receive it.   He was driven from the polls,
and compelled to hide himself for days, until he could find

an opportunity to escape from the State to preserve his life."

Of the despotism of slavery he said, —

" Sir, I have said that you have no freedom of speech at the South. Senators have denounced us as sectional because we have no votes in the South. That reminds me of the Dutch judge in old democratic Berks, who kicked the defendant out of doors, locked the door, and then entered a judgment for default. (Laughter.) Your native sons stand on electoral tickets, or vote our principles, at the peril of life. Then, when you are able with your iron despotism to crush out all there who would go with us, you turn round and tell us we are getting up a sectional party. I assure you, there are tens of thousands of men in the South whose sympathies are with us ; but they have no opportunity so to vote. In the city of St. Louis, nearly three thousand Germans, to show their devotion to liberty, went to the ballot-boxes, when they could get up no State ticket for Frémont, and voted for Millard Fillmore, the Know-Nothing candidate, with the word ' Protest ' printed on their ballots, — an act which illustrates your despotism, and shows that these men, who were true to liberty in the Old World, will not be false to their cherished convictions in the New.

" Even here in the national capitol, that vacant seat (pointing to Mr. Sumner's chair) is an evidence that freedom of speech is not always tolerated, — not always safe."

To the charge of fanaticism he replied, —

" If you believe that the people are fanatics, or that their leaders deceive them, remember one thing, — that, in 1850, there were in the United States nearly eight hundred thousand free persons above twenty years of age who could not read or write. Only ninety-four thousand out of this eight hundred thousand happen to live in the States which Frémont has carried. Remember another thing, — that the State of Massachusetts, which you consider so ultra, — a people so easily deluded, — prints within a few thousand, and circulates, more newspapers within the State than all the fifteen Southern States of the Union. Remember, they have more volumes in their public libraries than all the slave States. Remember, they give away more money to the Bible and Missionary and other benevolent societies, every year, than the entire slaveholding States ; and they have done so during the last quarter of a century.

"I tell you, sir, that the people are ahead of us; and that is what you fear. You say that they are deceived by us; and then you turn round and declare that you cannot rely on our disclaimers, because the people will pass beyond the direction and control of political leaders. The people understand this question, sir : they know their responsibilities, their powers, and their duties."

He closed by these brave words : —

"I give you notice to-day, gentlemen, what we intend to do. If the incoming administration sends into this body the nomination of a single man who ever threatened the dissolution of the Union, we intend to camp on this floor, and to resist his confirmation to the bitter end. I give you notice now, that we shall resist the coming into power of all that class of men, as enemies of the Constitution and the Union.

" We go farther. We mean to hold the incoming administration responsible if it gives confidence or patronage to your 'Richmond Enquirers' and 'Examiners,' your 'Charleston Mercuries' and 'Standards,' your 'New-

Orleans Deltas ' and your ' South-side Democrats,' or any Democratic journal in the United States which threatened the dissolution of the Union in the event of our success. We intend here in our places to defend that Union which makes us one people against the men of your party who have threatened to subvert and destroy it. We intend to go a little farther. Your slave propagandist journals have denounced the independent laboring-men of the North as ' greasy mechanics,' ' filthy operatives,' ' small-fisted farmers,' ' moon-struck theorists.' We mean to hold you responsible if you bestow your confidence and patronage upon journals which maintain that ' the principle of slavery is itself right, and does not depend on difference of complexion.'

"Senators have told us they want peace; they want repose. Well, sir, I want peace; I want repose.. The State I represent wants peace; wants repose. Tens of millions of our property are scattered broadcast over the Southern States. The business-men, the merchants, the manufacturers, of my State want peace as much as you can want it. You can have it. But you cannot have it if you want to extend slavery over the free Territories. You cannot have it if you continue your efforts to bring Kansas here a slave State. If you want peace, abandon your policy of slavery extension. Cease all efforts to control the political destinies of the country through the expansion of slavery as an element of political power. Plant yourselves upon your reserved constitutional rights, and we will aid you in the vindication of those rights. Turn your attention from the forbidden fruits of Cuban, Central-American, or Mexican acquisitions, to your own dilapidated fields, where the revegetating forests are springing up, and where, in the language of Gov. Wise,

19*

'you have the owners skinning the negroes, the negroes skinning the land, until all grow poor together.' Erase from your statute-books those cruel laws which shock the sensibilities of mankind. Place there humane and beneficent legislation, which shall protect the relations of husband and wife, parent and child; which shall open darkened minds to the elevating influence of Christian culture. You will then have the generous sympathies, the sincere prayers, of men who reverently look to Him whose hand guides the destinies of the world. You will have the best wishes of the friends of liberty all over the globe. Humanity and Christianity will sanction and bless your efforts to hasten on that day, though it may be distant, when freedom shall be the inalienable birthright of every man who treads the soil of the North-American continent."

Mr. Wilson visited Canada for the first time in the autumn, and was present at the banquet in Montreal at the opening of the Grand-Trunk Railroad, where to the third toast, which was to the chief magistrate of the United States, he made this admirable response: —

"MR. MAYOR AND FELLOW-CITIZENS, — I thank you, in behalf of the citizens of the United States who have come to join you on this great festival, for the sentiment you have given for the chief magistrate of the United States. (Cheers.) I am sure, sir, that I speak the sentiments of every American here to-day, when I say that we not only thank you for proposing a sentiment to the chief magistrate of our country, but I thank you for saying that you trust that the people of the United States and the people of British America will always meet as friends. (Cheers.) Difficulties have arisen, have frequently arisen, between Great Britain and the United

States. These difficulties, sir, between our governments, we all trust, are in process of settlement, so that peace, perpetual peace, may be preserved between Great Britain and America. (Great applause.) Let me say here to-day,—what I know every son of New England, New York, and, in an especial manner, the sons of the mighty West, will sustain me in saying,—that we witness the development and the prosperity of the British Colonies in North America (cheers) not only without jealousy, but we witness them with pride and admiration. (Cheers.) Go on, brethren; improve and develop all the mighty resources of British America. Your prosperity is our prosperity. (Applause.) We are bound together by a thousand associations of blood and of kindred. We are connected together by those mighty improvements which we are met here to-day to commemorate. We are bound together by a treaty of reciprocity, mutually beneficial to you and to us. We are beginning to understand each other, to value each other, to be proud of each other's prosperity and success; and may God grant that the sons of British America and the sons of the North-American republic may never meet again on the banks of the St. Lawrence, on river, on lake, on land, in any other way than that in which we are all met to-day,—to grasp each other's hands in friendship, and to aid, to encourage each other in the development of the resources of the North-American continent! (Great applause.) Sir, the governor-general has alluded to Lord Durham,—a statesman in whose premature grave were buried many of the high hopes of the reformers of England. He uttered a sentiment that every statesman, whether in the service of England or America, should respond to; and that was this,—'that he never saw an hour pass over recognized and unreformed abuses without profound regret.' (Cheers.) Gentlemen, I give you in conclusion this sentiment: 'Prosperity to the people of the Canadas, and success to their government.'" (Great applause.)

Mr. Wilson's Congressional career in 1857, though characterized by no striking effort in debate, was nevertheless marked by incessant and effective labor. We find him, in addition to his arduous duties in the Military Committee, always abreast of the questions of the times, and vigorously advocating liberal and progressive measures. This may be seen from a brief record of his doings in the Senate for the month of February, here presented: On the 4th inst. he spoke in favor of disposing of the alternate sections of land along the railroads aided by the government, not to speculators, but to actual settlers on the lines. Twenty-one millions of acres had been granted to the States for railroad-purposes: by selling to the cultivators of the soil, a population would arise to support the roads, and make them really serviceable to the country. On the 10th he presented a resolution against the repeal of the fishing bounty; on the 12th, a resolution to inquire into the cause of the failure of the mails at Washington, this having occurred thirty-eight times within seventy-two days; on the 17th inst. he spoke in favor of increasing the pay of officers of a rank lower than lieutenant-colonels in the army; on the 18th he advocated the introduction of a bust of Chief Justice William Cushing, as an offset to that of Mr. Rutledge; on the 21st he made an argument in favor of admitting Minnesota, "clothed," as he said, "in the white robes of Freedom," into the Union; on the 26th he declared himself in favor of a sub-marine telegraph; on the 27th he spoke in favor of a telegraphic line between the Atlantic and Pacific States; and on the 28th he introduced a bill for the erection of a court-house in the city of Boston. Such were some of his labors for the month; and, by a reference to "The Congressional Globe," it will be seen that the interests of the Commonwealth he represented did not suffer in his hands.

On the Lecompton Constitution, and the admission of Kansas into the Union under it, Mr. Wilson declared his sentiments in forcible language on the 3d and 4th of February, 1858. Replying to Mr. Brown, he asks, —

" Why is this act to be consummated, when we know, that, on the 4th of January, twelve thousand men of that Territory voted against this constitution ; and that there were only six thousand votes cast for it on the 21st of December, of which three or four thousand were unquestionably fraudulent?

" There is only one power on this continent which could thus control, direct, and guide men: and that is that gigantic slave power which holds this administration in the hollow of its hand ; which guides and directs the Democratic party ; and which has only to stamp its foot, and the men who wield the government of this country tremble, submit, and bow to its will. Senators talk about the dangers of the country. Great God ! what are our dangers ? The danger is that there is such a power — a local, sectional power — that can control this government, can ride over justice, ride over a wronged people, consummate glaring and outrageous frauds, and trample down the will of a brave and free people. That is the danger. The time has come when the freemen of this country, looking to liberty, to popular rights, to justice to all sections of the country, should overthrow this power, and trample it under their feet forever. The time has come when the people should rise in the majesty of conscious power, and hurl from office and from places of influence the men who thus bow to this tyranny.

" Senators are anxious about the Union. The senator from Delaware (Mr. Bayard) to-day thought it was in peril. Well, sir, I am not alarmed about it. I am in the Union; my State is in the Union: we intend to stay in it. If anybody wants to go out, Mexico and Central America, and the valley of the Amazon, are all open to emigration: let them start. I shall not hold them back, nor mourn over their departure. But all this continent now in the Union is American soil, and a part of my country; and my vote and my influence, now and hereafter, will be given to keep it a part of my country."

The following letter from the late Hon. George T. Bigelow indicates the spirit with which liberty-loving men responded to the sentiments which the Massachusetts senator expressed : —

BOSTON, Feb. 22, 1858.

DEAR SIR, — I had read a report of your remarks in the Senate in reply to Messrs. Brown and Green before I received your pamphlet edition of them. I trust that you will not think it intrusive in me to say that I was highly gratified by the matter, as well as by the tone and temper which pervade them. They are manly and dignified; sufficiently bold and resolute, without being vituperative or personal; maintaining the truth fearlessly, and resisting the disposition of the Southern men to overawe and browbeat in the right spirit. The South will soon learn that their bastard chivalry is worth but little when opposed to such courageous assaults.

I suppose that there is but little, if any, hope of successfully resisting the admission of Kansas under the Lecompton Constitution. There is no scheme of fraud and violence which the South will not adopt to secure their ends, and which the Northern Democracy will not subserviently support. I cannot doubt, however, that the flagrant wrong and injustice of the whole proceeding will arouse the spirit of the North and North-west to a united effort against the slavery propagandism of the party in power. The great danger is that the enthusiasm of the people of the free States will expend itself in electing a Republican majority in the next Congress, and will then die away, so that we shall lose the presidential election of 1860. However this may be, the only way is to fight on in the confident hope that the day of triumph will surely come.

I am, with great respect,
Your friend and servant,
G. T. BIGELOW.

Another letter, dated Feb. 22, says in relation to this speech, —

"It adds to your laurels; and I congratulate you on your successful encounter with our enemies in the Senate. Your whole course since you have been a member of the Senate has been highly honorable to you, and gratifying to the great body of your constituents. You have manifested not only the most distinguished ability, but a fearlessness that has raised you amazingly in the good opinion of Northern men. I hear but one sentiment expressed in regard to you; and that is friendly and respectful. You never held so elevated a position as you do at the present time. We all feel proud that we have at least one representative who is both able and willing to take a defiant stand against the tyranny which is making our country worthless to us and a mockery to the world.

   " Yours very truly,

       " G. R. RUSSELL."

CHAPTER XII.

Character of his Reply to Mr. Hammond. — " Cotton is King." — Southern
Institutions. — A Contrast. — Social Condition of the North and South. —
Mud-sills. — Free Labor of the North. — Conclusion of his Argument. —
Reply to Mr. Gwin's Challenge. — The Affair amicably adjusted.

ON the 20th of March (1858) following, Mr. Wilson made a most eloquent speech in reply to Mr. Hammond of South Carolina, who had proclaimed that " Cotton was king," and most insolently characterized the Northern working-men as " mud-sills " and " essentially slaves." In Mr. Wilson's array of facts, his cogent arguments, his bold invective, he confounds this chivalric defender of the servile institution, and presents the noblest plea for the Northern laborer ever uttered in the halls of Congress. By all his sympathies, by the whole training of his life, he was prepared for the contest. In some respects this speech is a model of invective eloquence, and has endeared its author to the hearts of millions of the working - people. We regret that but a few extracts can be given here.

To his vaunting assertion that " Cotton was king," he says, " The senator, filled with magnificent visions of Southern power, crowns Cotton ' king ; ' and tells us, that, if they should stop supplying cotton for three years, 'England would topple headlong, and carry the whole civilized world with her, save the South'! What presumption! The South, — which owns lands and slaves, the price fluctuating with the production, use, and price of cotton, — having no other resource or means of support, would go harmless; while the great commercial centres of the world, with the vast accumulations of capital, the products of ages of accumulation, with varied pursuits and skilled industry, would 'topple' to their fall. Sir, I suppose the coffee-planters of Brazil, the tea-growers of the Celestial Empire, and the wheat-growers on the shores of the Black Sea and on the banks of the Don and the Volga, indulge in the same magnificent illusions. I would remind the senator that the commercial world is not governed by the cotton-planters of the South, the coffee-planters of Brazil, the tea-growers of China, nor the wheat-producers of Eastern Europe. I tell the senator that England, France, Germany, Western Europe, and the Northern States of the Union, are the commercial, manufacturing, business, and monetary centres of the world; that their merchants, manufacturers, and capitalists grasp the globe; that cotton and sugar and tea and coffee and wheat, and the spices of the isles of the Oriental seas, are grown for them. Sir, the cotton-planters of the South are their agents. I would remind the senator that the free States in 1850 produced eight hundred and fifty million dollars of manufactures, and that only fifty-two million dollars of that vast production — about one-seventeenth part of it — was made up of cotton. Our manufactures and mechanic arts now must exceed twelve hundred million dollars; and cotton does not make up more than seventy million dollars. Does the senator think the free States would 'topple' down if they should lose one-seventeenth part of their productive industry?

"The productive industry of Massachusetts, a State that manufactures more than one-third of all the cotton manufactured in the country, was, in 1855, three hundred and fifty million dollars: only twenty-six million dollars, one-thirteenth part of it, was cotton. Does the senator believe that a State which has a productive industry of three hundred and fifty million dollars — about two hundred and eighty dollars per head for each person — would perish if she should lose twenty-six million dollars of that vast production?

"It is no matter of surprise that gentlemen who live away off on cross-roads, where the cotton blooms, should come to believe that cotton rules the world; but a few months' association with the great world would cure that delusion. 'You are our factors,' exclaims the senator; 'you bring and carry for us. Suppose we were to discharge you; suppose we were to take our business out of your hands: we should consign you to anarchy and poverty.' Sir, suppose, when the senator returns from this chamber to his cotton-fields, his slaves should in their simplicity say to him, 'Massa, you only sells de cotton: we plants; we hoes; we picks de cotton. 'Spose we discharge you, massa!' The unsophisticated 'mud-sills' would be quite as reasonable as the senator. The senator seems to think that the cotton-planters hold us in the hollow of their hands: if they shake them, we tremble; if they close them, we perish."

To his boasting of the excellence of Southern social and political institutions Senator Wilson replies, —

"The senator from South Carolina, after crowning Cotton as king, with power to bring England and all the civilized world 'toppling' down into the yawning gulfs of bankruptcy and ruin, complacently tells the Senate and the trembling subjects of his cotton-king that 'the greatest strength of the South arises from the harmony of her political and social institutions;' that 'her forms of society are the best in the world;' that 'she has an extent of political freedom, combined with entire security, seen nowhere on earth.' The South, he tells us, 'is satisfied, harmonious, and prosperous:' and he asks us if we 'have heard that the ghosts of Mendoza and Torquemada are stalking in the streets of our great cities; that the Inquisition is at hand; and that there are fearful rumors of consultations for vigilance committees.' Sir, this self-complacency is sublime. No son of the Celestial Empire can approach the senator in self-complacency. That 'society the best in the world' where more than three millions of beings created in the image of God are held as chattels, — sunk from the lofty level of humanity to the abject condition of unreasoning beasts of burden! That 'society the best in the world' where are manacles, chains, and whips, auction-blocks, prisons, bloodhounds, scourgings, lynchings, and burnings; laws to torture the body, shrivel the mind, and debase the soul; where labor is dishonored, and laborers despised! 'Political freedom' in a land where woman is imprisoned for teaching little children to read God's holy Word; where professors are deposed and banished for opposing the extension of slavery; where public men are exiled for quoting in a national convention the words of Jefferson; where voters are mobbed for appearing to vote for free territory; and where booksellers are driven from the country for selling that masterly work of genius, 'Uncle Tom's Cabin'! A land of 'certain security,' where patrols, costing, as in

Old Virginia, more than is expended to educate her poor children, stalk the country to catch the faintest murmur of discontent; where the bay of the bloodhound never ceases; where, but little more than a year ago, rose the startling cry of insurrection; and where men, some of them owned by a member of this body, were scourged and murdered for suspected insurrection! 'Political freedom' and 'certain security' in a land which demands that seventeen millions of freemen shall stand guard to seize and carry back fleeing bondmen!"

Contrasting the desolation of the South with the prosperity of the North, he says, —

"De Bow's 'Resources of the South,' from Fenno's 'Southern Medical Reports,' speaks of 'decaying old tenements' in Georgia; 'red old hills, stripped of their native growth and virgin soil and washed into deep gullies, with here and there patches of Bermuda grass and stunted pine-shrubs struggling for subsistence on what was once the richest soil of America.' Millions of acres of the richest soil of the Western world have been converted into barrenness and desolation by the untutored, unpaid, and thriftless labor of slaves. This exhaustion of Southern soil tilled by bondmen; this deterioration, decay, and desolation, now visible in what was once the fairest portion of the continent, — stands confessed by the most eminent writers of the South. These descriptions of the decay and desolation of some of the fairest portions of the sunny South remind us of the desolating effects of slavery upon the rich fields of classic Italy in the days of Tiberius Gracchus, as described by the brilliant and philosophic pen of Bancroft in his masterly article on Roman slavery.

20*

"Turning, Mr. President, from this contemplation of the desolations of slavery to the rugged soil and still more rugged clime of the free North, we shall see that the farms tilled by free, educated men are annually blooming with a fresher and richer verdure ; that they annually wave with larger harvests of the varied products which find markets in the cities and villages which commerce, manufactures, and the mechanic arts, create, beautify, and adorn.   While the plantations of the South echo the sound of the lash by which unpaid toil is driven on in the blighting process of exhausting the richest soils, the farms of the free States are increasing in value, fertility, and beauty : they are nursing a race of noble and independent men, where

> 'The lowliest farm-house hearth is graced
>   With manly hearts, in piety sincere ;
> Faithful in love, in honor stern and chaste,
> In friendship warm and true, in danger brave ;
> Beloved in life, and sainted in the grave.' "

In respect to the comparative educational and literary and scientific condition of the two sections of the Union, he remarks, —

"In the slave States, laws forbid the education of nearly four millions of her people : in the free States, laws encourage the education of the people, and public opinion upholds and enforces those laws.   In 1850 there were sixty-two thousand schools, seventy-two thousand teachers, two million eight hundred thousand scholars, in the public schools of the free States : in the slave States there were eighteen thousand schools, nineteen thousand teachers, and five hundred and eighty thousand scholars.   Massachusetts has nearly two hundred thousand scholars in her public schools, at a cost of a million three hundred thousand dollars. South Carolina has seventeen thousand scholars in her public schools: seventy-five thousand dollars is paid by the State; and the governor in 1853 said, that, 'under the present mode of applying it, it was the profusion of the prodigal rather than the judicious generosity which confers real benefits.' New York has more scholars in her public schools than all the slave States together. Ohio has five hundred and two thousand scholars in her public schools, supported at an expense of two million two hundred and fifty thousand dollars. Kentucky has seventy-six thousand scholars, supported at an expense of a hundred and forty-six thousand dollars.

" The free States had, in 1850, more than fifteen thousand libraries, containing four million volumes: the slave States had seven hundred libraries, containing six hundred and fifty thousand volumes. Massachusetts, the land of 'hireling operatives,' has eighteen hundred libraries, which contain not less than seven hundred and fifty thousand volumes, — more libraries and volumes than all the slave States combined. The little State of Rhode Island, a mere patch of thirteen hundred square miles on the surface of New England, has more volumes in her libraries than have the five great States of Georgia, Florida, Alabama, Mississippi, and Louisiana. De Bow — good Southern authority — says, that, in every country, the press must be regarded as a great educational agency. The free States had, in 1850, eighteen hundred newspapers, with a circulation of three hundred and thirty-five million: the slave States had, at that time, seven hundred newspapers, with a circulation of eighty-one million. The free States have seven times as many religious papers, and twelve times as many scientific papers, as the South. Mas-

sachusetts has more religious papers than all the slaveholding States of the Union. She has a circulation of
two million for her scientific papers: the South has but
three hundred and seventy-two thousand. The 'hireling
operatives, mechanics, and laborers,' the very 'mud-sills'
of society, read five times as many copies of scientific
papers as the entire South, including that class which,
the senator tells us, leads 'progress, civilization, and
refinement.' Nine-tenths of the book-publishers of the
United States are in the free States. 'The Charleston
Standard'—good authority with the senator—tells us 'that
their pictures are painted at the North, their books published at the North, their periodicals printed at the North;
that should a man rise with the genius of Shakspeare or
Dickens or Fielding, or all three combined, and speak
from the South, he would not receive enough to pay
the cost of publication.' That class, that favored class,
which leads, as the senator tells us, 'progress, civilization, and refinement,' forces the literary talent to the
North, the home of hireling operatives, to find not only
publishers, but readers also.

"Of the authors mentioned in Duyckinck's 'Cyclopæ-
dia of American Literature,' eighty-seven were natives of
slave States, and four hundred and three were natives
of the free North,—the land of the 'hireling laborers.'
Of the poets mentioned in Griswold's 'Poets and Poetry
of America,' seventeen were natives of the land where
they have that other class, which leads 'progress, civilization, and refinement,' and a hundred and twenty-three
were natives of the land of 'hireling operatives,'—the
'mud-sills' of society. Of the poets whose nativity is
given by Mr. Reed in his 'Female Poets of America,'
eleven are from the South, seventy-three from the North.

Nine-tenths of all the books written in America fit to be read, nine-tenths of all the books published in America fit to be published, are written and published, not in the land of that privileged class of which the senator boasts, but in the free States, unblessed by that privileged class. Nearly all the authors whose names grace and adorn the rising literature of America, whose names are known in the literary and scientific world, find their homes in the free States of the North. Irving, Ticknor, Sparks, Bancroft, Prescott, Hildreth, and Motley, whose contributions to the historical literature of America are recognized by the literary world; Dana, Bryant, Halleck, Longfellow, Sprague, Whittier, Lowell, and Willis, the recognized poets of our country; Hawthorne, Emerson, Curtis, Melville, and Mitchell, whose names grace the light literature of our times; and Silliman, Agassiz, and Peirce, names associated with American science, — find their homes, not in the land of the privileged class that the senator from South Carolina tells us leads 'progress, civilization, and refinement;' but they dwell in the land of 'small-fisted farmers, greasy mechanics, and filthy operatives,' — the 'mud-sills' of society. The sculptors and the painters and the artists — they, too, find their homes, not in the sunny South, but in the free land of the North. In literature, in science, in the arts, the superiority of the North is beyond all question. Men who have been, or who now are, 'hireling laborers,' in some forms, in the North, have contributed more to the arts, the science, the literature of America than the whole class of slaveholders now living in the South.

"I would not, Mr. President, underrate the influence of the slave States in the councils of the republic. Bound together by the cohesive attraction of a vast interest, from which the civilization of the age averts its face, the privileged class have won the control and direct the policy of the government. In the council and in the field, the representatives of this privileged class have assumed to direct and to guide; but in accumulating capital, in commerce, in manufactures, in the mechanic arts, in educational institutions, in literature, in science, in the arts, in the charities of religion and humanity, in all the means by which the nation is known among men, the free States maintain a position of unquestioned pre-eminence. In all these the South is a mere dependency of the North. India and Australia are not more the dependencies of England than are the slaveholding States the dependencies of the free States. Sir, your fifteen slave States are but fifteen suburban wards of our great commercial city of New York. Beyond the political field this dependency is everywhere visible, even to the most blind devotees of 'King Cotton.' Mr. Perry, in an address before the South-Carolina Institute in 1856, says of the State represented by the senator, 'The dependence of South Carolina upon the Northern States for all the necessaries, comforts, and luxuries which the mechanic arts afford, has drained her of her wealth, and made her positively poor.' "

Mr. Wilson thus nobly speaks of the condition of free labor at the North: —

"Mr. President, the senator from South Carolina tells us that 'all the powers of the world cannot abolish the thing' he calls slavery: 'God alone can do it when he repeals the fiat, "The poor ye have always with you." For the man who lives by daily labor, and your whole class of hireling manual laborers and operatives, are essentially slaves. Our slaves are black, happy, content, unaspiring: yours are white; and they feel galled by their degradation. Our slaves do not vote : yours do vote ; and, being the majority, they are the depositaries of all your political power ; and if they knew the tremendous secret, that the ballot-box is stronger than " an army with banners," and could combine, your society would be reconstructed, your government overthrown, and your property divided.'

" ' The poor ye have always with you.' This fiat of Almighty God, which Christian men of all ages and lands have accepted as the imperative injunction of the common Father of all to care for the children of misfortune and sorrow, the senator from South Carolina accepts as the foundation-stone, the eternal law, of slavery, which ' all the powers of the earth cannot abolish.' These precious words of our heavenly Father, ' The poor ye have always with you,' are perpetually sounding in the ears of mankind, ever reminding them of their dependence and their duties. These words appeal alike to the conscience and the heart of mankind. To men blessed in their basket and their store they say, · Property has its duties as well as its rights.' To men clothed with authority to shape the policy or to administer the laws of the State they say, ' Lighten, by wise, humane, and equal laws, the burdens of the toiling and dependent children of men.' To men of every age and every clime they appeal by the divine promise, that ' he that giveth to the poor lendeth to the Lord.' Sir, I thank God that I live in a Commonwealth which sees no warrant in these words of inspiration to oppress the sons and daughters of toil and poverty. Over the poor and lowly she casts the broad shield of equal, just, and humane legislation. The poorest man that treads her soil, no matter what blood may run in his veins, is protected in his rights, and incited to labor by no other force than the assurance that the fruits of his toil belong to himself, to the wife of his bosom, and the children of his love.

"The senator from South Carolina exclaims, 'The man who lives by daily labor, your whole class of manual laborers, are essentially slaves: they feel galled by their degradation.' What a sentiment is this to hear uttered in the councils of this democratic republic! The senator's political associates, who listen to these words which brand hundreds of thousands of the men they represent in the free States and hundreds of their neighbors and personal friends as 'slaves,' have found no words to repel or rebuke this language. This language of scorn and contempt is addressed to senators who were not nursed by a slave ; whose lot it was to toil with their own hands ; to eat bread earned, not by the sweat of another's brow, but by their own. Sir, I am the son of a 'hireling manual laborer,' who, with the frosts of seventy winters on his brow, 'lives by daily labor.' I, too, have lived by daily labor ; I, too, have been a 'hireling manual laborer.' Poverty cast its dark and chilling shadow over the home of my childhood ; and Want was there sometimes, an unbidden guest. At the age of ten years, to aid him who gave me being in keeping the gaunt spectre from the hearth of the mother who bore me, I left the home of my boyhood, and went to earn my bread by 'daily labor.' Many a weary mile have I travelled

'To beg a brother of the earth
To give me leave to toil.'

"Sir, I have toiled as a 'hireling manual laborer' in the field and in the workshop ; and I tell the senator from South Carolina that I never 'felt galled by my degradation.' No, sir; never! Perhaps the senator who represents that 'other class, which leads progress, civilization, and refinement,' will ascribe this to obtuseness of intellect and blunted sensibilities of the heart. Sir, I was conscious of my manhood: I was the peer of my employer. I knew that the laws and institutions of my native and adopted States threw over him and me alike the panoply of equality: I knew, too, that the world was before me; that its wealth, its garnered treasures of knowledge, its honors, the coveted prizes of life, were within the grasp of a brave heart and a tireless hand; and I accepted the responsibilities of my position, all unconscious that I was a 'slave.' I have employed others, — hundreds of 'hireling manual laborers.' Some of them then possessed, and now possess, more property than I ever owned; some of them were better educated than myself, — yes, sir, better educated, and better read too, than some senators on this floor; and many of them, in moral excellence and purity of character, I could not but feel, were my superiors.

"I have occupied, Mr. President, for more than thirty years, the relation of employer or employed; and, while I never felt 'galled by my degradation' in the one case, in the other I was never conscious that my 'hireling laborers' were my inferiors. That man is a 'snob' who boasts of being a 'hireling laborer,' or who is ashamed of being a 'hireling laborer;' that man is a 'snob' who feels any inferiority to any man because he is a 'hireling laborer,' or who assumes any superiority over others because he is an employer. Honest labor is honorable; and the man who is ashamed that he is or was a 'hireling laborer' has not manhood enough to 'feel galled by his degradation.'

"Having occupied, Mr. President, the relation of either

21

employed or employer for the third of a century; having lived in a Commonwealth where the 'hireling class of manual laborers' are 'the depositaries of political power;' having associated with this class in all the relations of life, —I tell the senator from South Carolina, and the class he represents, that he libels, grossly libels them, when he declares that they are 'essentially slaves.' There can be found nowhere in America a class of men more proudly conscious or tenacious of their rights. Friends and foes have ever found them

'A stubborn race, fearing and flattering none.'

"But the senator from South Carolina tells us, that, if the hireling laborers knew the 'tremendous secret' of the ballot-box, our 'society would be reconstructed, our government overthrown, and our property divided.' Does not the senator know that an immense majority of the 'hireling class of manual laborers' of New England possess property? Does he not know that the man who has accumulated a few hundred dollars by his own toil, by the savings of years, who has a family growing up around him upon which his hopes are centred, is a conservative? Does not the senator know that he watches the appropriation-bills in the meetings of those little democracies, the towns, as narrowly as the representative from Tennessee in the other House (George W. Jones) watches the money-bills on the private calendar? I live, Mr. President, in a small town of five thousand inhabitants. Nearly half of the population are employed as operatives and mechanics for the manufacture of shoes for the Western and Southern markets. In 1840 we had thirteen hundred inhabitants, and the property valuation was about three hundred thousand dollars. Last May we had fourteen hundred names on our poll-list, two-thirds of them 'hireling mechanics,' and a property valuation of over two millions of dollars. Those 'hireling laborers,' on town-meeting days, make the appropriations for schools, for roads, and for all other purposes. Do they not know 'the tremendous secret of the ballot-box'? Have they proposed to divide the property they themselves created? No, sir; no! But I will tell the senator what they have done. Since 1850 they have built seven new schoolhouses, with all the modern improvements, at an expense of about forty thousand dollars; one house costing more than fourteen thousand. They have established a high school, where the most advanced scholars of the common schools are fitted for admission to the colleges, or for the professions, the business, and the duties of life. They have established a town-library, freely accessible to all the inhabitants, containing the choicest works of authors of the Old World and the New, of ancient and modern times. The poorest 'hireling manual laborer,' without cost, can take from that library to his home the works of the master-minds, and hold communion with

'The dead but sceptred sovereigns, who rule
Our spirits from their urns.'

"The senator tells us, Mr. President, that their slaves are 'well compensated.' South Carolina slaves 'well compensated'! Why, sir, the senator himself, in a speech made at home for home consumption, entered into an estimate to show that a field-hand could be supported for from 'eighteen to nineteen dollars per annum' on the rice and cotton plantations. He states the quantity of corn and bacon and salt necessary to support the 'well-compensated' slave. And this man, supported by eighteen dollars per annum, with the privilege of being flogged at discretion, and having his wife or children sold from him at the necessity or will of his master, the senator from South Carolina informs the Senate of the United States, is 'well compensated'! Sir, there is not a poor-house in the free States where there would not be a rebellion in three days if the inmates were compelled to subsist on the quantity and quality of food the senator estimates as ample 'compensation' for the labor of a slave in South Carolina.

"Turning from his 'well-compensated' slaves, the senator tells us that our 'hireling laborers,' our 'mud-sills,' are scantily 'compensated.' Mr. Clingman of North Carolina, in urging the establishment of cotton manufactories in the South, says the wages of labor at the North are one hundred per cent higher than wages in the same pursuits in the South. The wages of labor in iron mills in South Carolina were thirteen dollars per month in 1850; in Massachusetts they were thirty. Sir, these hands of mine have earned, month after month, two dollars per day in manual labor; and I have paid that sum to 'hireling manual laborers' month after month, and year after year. Financial and commercial revulsions sometimes come upon us, and press heavily upon all branches of the mechanic arts and manufactures; but labor is generally well employed and well paid. At any rate, the laboring-men of the free States have open to their industry all the avenues of agriculture, commerce, manufactures, and the multifarious mechanic arts, where skilled labor is demanded, and where they do not have to maintain, as the senator in his address before the institute of his own State tells us the white men of South Carolina have to maintain, 'a feeble and ruinous competition with the labor of slaves.'

" Borrowing, Mr. President, an idea found in a speech

made in the other House by Mr. Pickens of his own State more than twenty years ago, in which he threatened to preach insurrection to Northern laborers, the senator asks 'how we would like for them to send lecturers and agitators to teach our hireling laborers' the 'tremendous secret of the power of the ballot-box,' and 'to aid in combining them and to lead them.' Sir, I tell the senator we would welcome him, his lecturers and agitators; we would bid them welcome to our hearth-stones and our altars. Ours are the institutions of freedom; and they flourish best in the storms and agitations of inquiry and free discussion. We are conscious that our social and political institutions have not attained perfection; and we invoke the examination and the criticism of the genius and learning of all Christendom. Should the senator and his agitators and lecturers come to Massachusetts on a mission to teach our 'hireling class of manual laborers,' our 'mud-sills,' our 'slaves,' the 'tremendous secret of the ballot-box,' and to help 'combine and lead them,' these stigmatized 'hirelings' would reply to the senator and his associates, 'We are freemen; we are the peers of the gifted and the wealthy; we know the "tremendous secret of the ballot-box;"' and we mould and fashion these institutions that bless and adorn our proud and free Commonwealth. These public schools are ours, for the education of our children; these libraries, with their accumulated treasures, are ours; these multitudinous and varied pursuits of life, where intelligence and skill find their reward, are ours. Labor is here honored and respected, and great examples incite us to action. All around us, — in the professions; in the marts of commerce; on the exchange, where merchant-princes and capitalists do congregate; in these manufactories and workshops, where the products of every clime are fashioned into a thousand

21*

forms of utility and beauty; on these smiling farms, fertilized by the sweat of free labor; in every position of private and of public life, — are our associates, who were but yesterday "hireling laborers," "mud-sills," "slaves." In every department of human effort are noble men, who sprang from our ranks, — men whose good deeds will be felt, and will live in the grateful memories of men, when the stones reared by the hands of affection to their honored names shall crumble into dust. Our eyes glisten and our hearts throb over the bright, glowing, and radiant pages of our history, that record the deeds of patriotism of the sons of New England, who sprang from our ranks, and wore the badges of toil. While the names of Benjamin Franklin, Roger Sherman, Nathanael Greene, and Paul Revere, live on the brightest pages of our history, the mechanics of Massachusetts and New England will never want illustrious examples to incite us to noble aspirations and noble deeds. Go home: say to your privileged class, which, you vauntingly say, "leads progress, civilization, and refinement," that it is the opinion of the "hireling laborers" of Massachusetts, if you have no sympathy for your African bondmen, in whose veins flows so much of your own blood, you should at least sympathize with the millions of your own race, whose labor you have dishonored and degraded by slavery. You should teach your millions of poor and ignorant white men, so long oppressed by your policy, the "tremendous secret, that the ballot-box is stronger than 'an army with banners.'" You should combine, and lead them to the adoption of a policy which shall secure their own emancipation from a degrading thraldom.'"

He concludes his argument with these strong and earnest words of counsel: —

"Duty to the government now prostituted and polluted,

to the country now dishonored in the face of the civilized world, summons the liberty-loving and patriotic men of the republic, of every name and creed, to 'forget, forgive, and unite,' and rally to the overthrow of this venal, cringing, and inglorious administration, and to the utter annihilation of the oligarchic Democracy. To the men of the North, ay, and the men of the South, who loathe fraud, paltry trickery, venality, and servility, who believe that 'righteousness exalteth a nation,' this summons alike appeals. But to no men does this summons appeal with such irresistible and imperative force as to the 'whole hireling class of manual laborers and operatives,' now disdainfully stigmatized as the 'slaves,' the 'very mud-sills,' of that society upon which that privileged class assumes to rest which now claims to control this government, and 'to lead progress, civilization, and refinement' in America. It appeals to them to repel the libellous aspersions cast upon the toiling millions of America, by taking, through the ballot-box, the reins of power from the grasp of the slaveholding aristocracy of the South and their servile allies of the North; rebuking the arrogance of the one by banishment from usurped power, and the servility of the other by putting upon their breasts the 'Scarlet Letter' of dishonor. It appeals to them to place in every department of the Federal Government statesmen who cherish a profound reverence and an inextinguishable love for humanity; who are animated by lofty motives, aims, and purposes; guided by wise, comprehensive, and patriotic counsels; and who will put the republic in harmony with the sacred and inalienable rights of mankind."

During this session Mr. Wilson received a challenge from Mr. Gwin of California for some words spoken hastily in debate. He replied to it, as he had done to that of Mr. Brooks, by saying, that, while he held to the right of self-defence, he did not, as was well known, accept the code of the duellist. He was willing to refer the difference between Mr. Gwin and himself to any three members of the Senate, and abide by their decision. Messrs. Seward, Crittenden, and Davis were selected, who on the 12th of June drew up the following agreement: —

WASHINGTON, June 12, 1858.

GENTLEMEN, — We have made ourselves acquainted with the circumstances and facts involved in the case submitted to us.

The remarks of Mr. Gwin, imputing unworthy motives — namely, those of demagogism — to Mr. Wilson, although general, certainly were objectionable and unparliamentary; and yet they by no means justified or warranted Mr. Wilson in using the very opprobrious epithet with which he retaliated. Mr. Gwin's rejoinder in contumelious terms is to be regarded as a passionate expression, naturally provoked by the offensive language of Mr. Wilson. We think, therefore, that Mr. Wilson ought to regard himself in fact as having committed the first real personal offence; and therefore he should make such reparation as is now in his power. We are possessed of the fact, — which, indeed, is apparent on the face of the reported debate, — that Mr. Wilson, in using the epithet employed, did not impute any want of personal integrity or honor to Mr. Gwin, but merely reflected upon his course in legislation in regard to California, which Mr. Wilson deemed extravagant and wasteful; although the expression is obviously liable to an offensive and dishonoring construction. With this disclaimer adopted by Mr. Wilson, we hold that Mr. Gwin is bound to withdraw the reproachful language in which he replied to Mr. Wilson. The disavowal required of Mr. Wilson, and the withdrawal demanded from Mr. Gwin, shall be deemed to have been made by them, respectively, when they shall have expressed in writing their assent to this report.

J. J. CRITTENDEN.
WM. H. SEWARD.
JEFFN. DAVIS.

To Messrs. WILSON and GWIN.

I assent to the above.
HENRY WILSON.

I assent to the above.
WM. M. GWIN.

The parties were satisfied with the mutual explanation and concession; and thus the matter ended. Duelling belongs to the mediæval ages; and so this Northern senator again decided.

CHAPTER XIII.

RE-ELECTION TO THE UNITED-STATES SENATE. — PACIFIC
RAILROAD. — ORATION AT LAWRENCE. — THE JOHN
BROWN RAID. — THE SLAVE-TRADE.

Re-elected by a Large Majority. — Reasons for it. — His Industry. — Patronage. — Advocates Central Route for the Pacific Railroad. — Extract from
his Speech. — A Radical Southern Party. — A Personal Interview. — His
Course. — Temperance Meeting. — Printers' Banquet. — Paul Morphy. —
Fourth of July at Lawrence. — His Address. — His Course in respect to the
Raid of John Brown. — Meeting at Natick. — Reply to Mr. Iverson. — Vote
of Thanks by the General Court. — Speech on the Slave-Trade.

IN January, 1859, the General Court re-elected Mr.
Wilson to the United-States Senate for six years
from the 3d of March in that year; the higher branch
giving him thirty-five out of forty votes, and the lower
a hundred and ninety-nine out of two hundred and
thirty-five votes. His record had been clear, his labors
arduous; his legislative experience now was large; his
courage had been tested. The times demanded men of
steady nerve; and hence this strong majority was given
to him. The expectation was not disappointed; for he is
one of the very few whom life at Washington does not
corrupt.

In looking over the files of " The Congressional Globe,"
we find him with tireless industry taking part in the dis-

cussions on the questions of the day, advocating retrench-
ment in postal, naval, and every other department of
the government.

In respect to patronage he truly said, "I think it should
be the interest of all parties to get clear of patronage; for
patronage is only weakness, if you have any principles to
carry."

Of the projects for internal improvement at that time
before Congress, one of the most important was the construction of a railroad across the continent. Mr. Davis had
caused extensive explorations to be made, and three routes
for the road were indicated. The Southerners advocated
the line through Arizona, called the "Disunion route,"
because some senators had avowed that they should own
it on the dissolution of the Union. The administration
favored them; but, on the eleventh day of January, Mr.
Wilson, in a speech displaying vast research and great ability, clearly pointed out the impracticability of that line, and
advocated the adoption of the central route, which was
finally agreed upon, through Nebraska and Nevada. Economy, freedom, and the business of the country, alike demanded that the road should run in this direction; and
the gigantic scheme could not be carried into effect, he
said, without the liberal aid of government. From the
array of facts which he presented, one might have thought
that "railroading" had been the principal study of his life,
and travelling in the "Far West" his diversion. This
speech turned the attention of the public more directly to
the central line, and greatly encouraged the friends of progress in the East to enter upon the construction of the
road. The Hon. A. A. Sargent of California, who, like
Mr. Wilson, is a self-made, practical man, subsequently
pressed with the same energy the construction of the Cen-

tral Pacific road ; and, after years of persevering effort, the driving of the golden spike connecting the Union Pacific with that road gave these two gentlemen inexpressible delight. We regret that we can give but a single extract from Mr. Wilson's admirable speech : —

"I think," said he, "the course I have proposed is that suggested by sound policy ; and I should like to recommit this bill, or in some way put it in such a shape, that we shall, as a government, undertake the construction of a railroad starting between the mouths of the Big Sioux and Kansas Rivers, crossing the continent to San Francisco on a line north of the thirty-fifth or thirty-sixth parallel, and south of the forty-third parallel. Let that be a great national work : for the idea of the country is to go to San Francisco, where there is population ; not to Puget Sound, where there is none ; and not to San Diego, where there never can be any. Then let us give our Southern friends, those gentlemen who want a road on which they can go to the Pacific Ocean when they dissolve the Union, all the lands they want south of the thirty-fourth parallel, and let them make the most of them. I hope they may make a hundred million dollars out of them ; for I should rejoice in their prosperity. Then let us give lands on the northern line, and carry out the ideas suggested by the senator from Minnesota and the senator from Wisconsin. What they want in that vast northern region is a people. They want settlers : and a policy of this kind will carry settlers from Lake Superior a thousand miles to the Rocky Mountains ; and, if the engineers who went over this route are to be believed, even in the Rocky Mountains is to be found good land. Beyond the Rocky Mountains, to Puget Sound, there will be found not only a great country, but across that line, in time, I do not doubt we are to have a great commercial route connecting the northern lakes with Puget Sound.

"These are my views. I am for a Pacific railroad; but I do not believe in the idea of attempting to construct a road to the Pacific Ocean merely by grants of land within any reasonable period. If we make a grant to the northern line, I do not expect a road to be built there for some time. I do not even expect it to be commenced at once. I know it cannot be done in earnest in the present financial condition of the world. Neither do I expect any such thing over the southern line. But we want a central road; we want it begun now; we want it completed as speedily as possible; and, to do that, let us take the money of the government, and build it as cheaply as cash can build it, and keep the lands, reserving their proceeds as a sinking fund to meet the bonds, which may be made due thirty or forty years hence. We shall then have seventy or eighty million people; and their redemption will be but a light tax on such a nation. During that period, in my judgment, it will have added hundreds of millions to the wealth of the country; and the addition it will make to the power and strength of the Union is beyond the calculation of the human intellect."

On the 18th of February he thus referred to the existence of a party, little thought of at the time, which was ready to dissolve the Union : —

"I am glad to hear the declarations made by the senator from South Carolina; and I have no doubt they are substantially correct. No doubt, a large portion of the people of the Southern States are opposed to the African slave-trade : but that there is a party, young, vigorous, and active, that wishes to open the slave-trade; a party that wishes to extend the country into the tropics; a

22

party that believes not only in compulsory labor in the tropics, but everywhere else ; a party that wishes to govern this country under that policy, and, failing to do that, to establish a Southern confederacy, and dissolve this Union, — there is evidence. There is such a party. Now, I want the Senate, I want Congress, to sustain the contract made by the president : and let it be understood in the North and in the South, by all parties, that this country has branded the slave-trade ; that it can never be opened ; that the power and influence of this nation shall be used to put it down ; and that we will go to the full extent, not only of the letter of the law, but the spirit of the law, to sustain this policy."

In a personal interview with one of his friends, April 25, 1859, Mr. Wilson, speaking of the members of the Senate, said, "Mr. Collamer of Vermont knows the most of politics, but has no oratory ; Fessenden of Maine is the best debater, but has no facts ; Seward is very able, and may run for president ; Toombs is indomitable ; Davis is high-spirited ; Yulee and Gwin are mercenary ; and John P. Hale is wide-awake, but not sufficiently industrious. The Senate of to-day is abler than the Senate of twenty years ago : few then entered into debate ; but all at present take a part, and evince ability. My own course for the last sixteen years has been one and straight : my constant aim has been to do the very best thing I could against slavery. In every party I have used my influence for this purpose. I aim to move straight forward in the Senate ; and my highest ambition is to have it said, when my career is over, ' He acted for the good of humanity and the rights of man.' I am no orator ; but my memory is retentive, and facts and principles I try to state with accuracy and clearness." He was then in the best of health and spirits, and preparing speeches — one on Cuba, another on the District of Columbia — for the coming session.

Although Mr. Wilson was so profoundly occupied in national affairs, he still took time to attend the gatherings and to mingle in the innocent diversions of the people. Of ceaseless activity, he seemed sometimes almost ubiquitous. Now we find him addressing the people at a picnic, now present at the examination of a school, and now telling stories at a temperance festival; never seeking pleasure, but imparting it to multitudes of his fellow-men as he went along.

We meet him in May at a temperance festival at the Adams House, where to this sentiment, "Our country, — with wisdom in her councils, and temperance among her people, she shall command the respect and admiration of the world," — he is thus reported to have responded : —

"The hand of intemperance had, from his childhood, been laid upon him, and very early in life he had resolved to be temperate himself at all times. Twenty-seven years ago he signed the pledge, which he had ever since kept. He alluded to the intemperance which prevailed among the statesmen of the country, and said many of those men were sinking under the baleful and withering curse. He wished that the words of the sentiment to which he had been called upon to respond had been reversed, and that it had read, 'wisdom among her people, and temperance in her councils.' He spoke in the highest terms of the Sons of Temperance in general, and the Crystal-fount Division in particular."

Now we see him in the same month at the printers' banquet held at the Revere House, where to the sentiment, "The National Legislature, — the right arm of

the American people," — he made this appropriate re
sponse : —

" The National Legislature deserved all that was said of
it in that sentiment. If there was a class of men who
voted long speeches a bore, it was printers. He would,
therefore, be short. He spoke of his knowledge of printers
as gathered from his connection with a newspaper nine or
ten years ago. There was no class of men that toiled with
more fidelity, or should receive more support from every
citizen. He saw here men from all parts of the country,
and especially the men from other States who often set up
very unpleasant allusions to him (laughter) : he welcomed
them warmly, one and all, and closed with, —

" The National Printers' Union, — May its laudable
efforts to promote the interests, elevate the position, and
improve the characters, of the printers of the United States,
be crowned with abundant success ! "

A few days afterwards (June 1) he was present at a
meeting in honor of Mr. Paul Morphy, the American
chess-player, at the same hotel, where, on the announcement of the tenth regular toast, " Our national representatives, — their position gives them a special interest in
national success," — he most fittingly replied, " I suppose we
all feel proud of the achievements of our American representatives in the Old World. We all unite to do honor
to him who has achieved honor for the American nation
abroad. As we have read of his brilliant achievements
with pride and admiration, we have loved him because he
has been throughout a modest and quiet American gentleman. Surrounded as Mr. Morphy has been by royalty,
learning, and genius, in all his splendid triumphs he has
borne himself with modesty, and he ought to be welcomed
by every American. We have witnessed here to-night

his modest demeanor and noble carriage with pleasure. In conclusion, he gave this sentiment: "The modest bearing of your guest, — worthy the imitation of American scholars, artists, jurists, and statesmen, who uphold the intellectual character of America among the nations."

Among other labors in the summer of this year, Mr. Wilson delivered an eloquent oration on the celebration of the 4th of July by the civil authorities and people of the city of Lawrence, Mass. The preparations for the occasion were extensive, the expectations of the vast throng of people high; but they were more than realized in the patriotic fervor and the manly eloquence of the speaker. His introduction breathes the very spirit of the founders of our civil liberty. In it he says, —

"To-day, fellow-citizens, the golden light of the eighty-third anniversary of 'the day of deliverance' is above and around us; to-day 'the rays of ravishing light and glory,' which gladdened the soul of the impassioned 'Colossus of independence' amidst the storm and blood of civil war, flash upon the glowing faces of twenty-five millions of American freemen, whose hearts swell with patriotic pride on the return of this anniversary of the birthday of the republic. Over this broad land, from the shores which first welcomed the weary feet of the Pilgrims to the golden sands which have lured their descendants to the distant shores of the Pacific, throughout the vast breadth of our ever-expanding republic, age with its ripe and rich experiences, manhood in the maturity and vigor of its powers, and youth with its fresh hopes and glowing aspirations, are joyfully mingling in the scenes, associations, and memories of this 'anniversary festival' of the 'most memorable epoch in the history of America.' To-day the teeming millions of America, in her cities, vil-

22*

lages, and hamlets, on her broad prairies, rich valleys, and laughing hillsides, and by her mountains, lakes, and rivers, welcome with exultant hearts this day, on which we give a truce to the strifes of sentiment and opinion, passion and interest, and remember only that we are all Americans, the citizens of the foremost republic of the world."

Having described the spirit which prompted the Declaration of Independence, he proceeds : —

"These sublime ideas of the Declaration of Independence express the whole creed of the equality of humanity, the basis of government, and the rights of the people. They speak to the universal heart of mankind. They declare to kings and princes, and nobles and statesmen, ' Governments are instituted among men, deriving their just powers from the consent of the governed, to secure the inalienable rights of men to liberty ; ' they proclaim to toiling millions, ' Whenever any form of government becomes destructive of these ends, it is the right of the people to alter or abolish it ; ' they utter in the hungry ears of lowly bondmen, ' All men are created equal,' and ' endowed with the inalienable rights of liberty and the pursuit of happiness.' These ' self-evident truths ' may be hated and spurned by the monarch, in the arrogance of unrestricted power ; they may be scoffed at and jeered at by the noble, hedged about with ancient privileges ; they may be limited, qualified, or denied, by the ignoble politician, whose apostasy is revealed and rebuked by the brilliancy of their steady light ; they may be sneered at as ' glittering generalities ' by the nerveless conservative, who ' has ever opposed every useful reform, and wailed over every rotten institution as it fell : ' but they live in the throbbing hearts of the toiling millions, and they nurse the wavering hopes of hapless bondmen amidst the thick gloom of rayless oppression. When the Christian shall erase from the book of life the precious words, ' Do unto others as ye would that others should do unto you,' ' Love thy neighbor as thyself,' then may the sincere lover of human freedom blur, blot, and erase from the language of humanity these immortal words embodied by our fathers in the Declaration of the 4th of July, 1776. These words, these ideas, which underlie the institutions of the republic, associate the name of America with the cause of universal freedom and progress all over the globe. We may be recreant to these ideas ; we may ignobly fail: but the incorporation of these sacred ideas with the charter of national independence will bear the name of the North-American republic down to coming ages, and win for it the grateful homage and lasting remembrance of mankind."

Announcing his theme as " Our country at that period and our country of to-day," he said, —

" How wonderful the contrast ! The thirteen colonies of that day have expanded into thirty-three sovereign commonwealths, — glittering constellations that revolve in their orbits round the great central sun of the North-American Union. The two and a half millions of British colonists that timidly clung to the shores of the seas have multiplied into twenty-five millions of freemen, who have crossed the ridges of the Alleghanies, spread over the broad basin of the Great Lakes, the Mississippi, and the Missouri, and passed through the defiles of the Rocky Mountains to the golden shores of the Pacific. The weak confederacy of dependent colonies has developed into a central Union, — a National Government, — whose name is known to the nations, and whose power is acknowledged by all mankind. Upon the soil where stood two and a half millions of colonists to meet the shock of battle in defence of perilled lib-

erty stand two and a half millions of enrolled men, ready to
leap at the summons of patriotism, to hurl into the seas any
force that shall press the soil of the republic with hostile
feet.

" The territory embraced in the thirteen colonies on the
Atlantic slope of the Alleghanies on the 4th of July, 1776,
contained less than three hundred thousand square miles :
to-day the territory embraced within the boundaries of the
Union exceeds three millions of square miles.   The boundaries of the republic are to be still farther extended.
Unroll the map of North America, trace out upon that
map the boundaries of other powers, study their position,
and comprehend their condition and character, and the
conviction will flash upon the mind that expansion is the
destiny of the United States.   God grant that this inevi-
table expansion may be in harmony with justice, with a
scrupulous regard for the rights of other nations and races,
and with the equal rights of mankind !

" Great as has been the extension of the limits of the
country, population has kept abreast of that extension.
The sun of the 4th of July, 1776, went down on less
than two and a half millions of freemen : to-day the sun
casts his beams on twenty-five millions of freemen in
America.   The accumulation of wealth has more than
kept pace with the extension of territory and the increase
of population.   The wealth of the thirteen colonies in 1776
did not exceed the wealth of the young Commonwealth of
Ohio in 1859 : the value of the real and personal property
in the United States is now estimated at eleven thousand
millions of dollars.   Under the restrictive and repressive
colonial policy of England, the annual productive industry
of the colonies was small indeed : now it is estimated at
three thousand millions of dollars, five hundred millions

of which are exchanged between the States, and three hun. dred millions exported to foreign lands. This extension of territory, this increase of population, this accumulation of wealth, far transcends all the most comprehensive minds ever conceived, and baffles even the predictions of enthusiasts.

" At the dawn of the Revolution, agriculture was the chief occupation of the people ; but the condition of the colonies limited the quality and value of production : now more than three hundred millions of acres are devoted to agriculture; these farms and plantations are valued at four thousand millions, tilled by four millions of men, and produce nearly eighteen hundred millions of products.

" The narrow colonial and commercial policy of England limited the variety, checked the production, and depressed the value, of manufactures and the mechanic arts in America. British manufacturers demanded the monopoly of the colonial markets ; British navigation demanded the monopoly of the carrying-trade of the colonies. Manufactures and mechanic arts, commerce and navigation, languished under the depressing effects of British legislation. The ships the mechanics of New England and New York launched upon the deep were not permitted to carry to their markets the rice, indigo, and tobacco of the South ; and these ships were forced to seek the products of Continental Europe, of Asia, and the Orient, in the storehouses of England.

" In 1850 the capital invested in more than a hundred thousand establishments was five hundred and thirty millions, the number of persons employed more than a million, and the value of the production more than a thousand millions. In 1776 the cotton-plant bloomed ungathered, and its manufacture was hardly known : now more than seven hundred thousand acres, tilled by nearly nine hundred thousand persons, are devoted to its culture; and the capital invested in its manufacture is more than eighty millions, the number of persons engaged in its manufacture a hundred thousand, and the value of the production seventy millions. At the opening of the war of independence, the imports and exports, burdened by the repressive commercial policy of England, did not exceed the trade with the British Provinces on the north at this time; and these imports and exports were chiefly monopolized by British navigation: now our imports and exports amount annually to six hundred millions of dollars; and the annual arrivals and clearances are forty thousand, with an inward and outward tonnage of eleven millions of tons. The tonnage of the United States is more than five millions of tons, — equal to the tonnage of the Britsh empire.

"When the Declaration was sent abroad over the land, the means of transportation, communication, and travel, were of the most limited description. Beyond the shores of the seas and the banks of the streams, mere bridle-paths, often following the trails of the sons of the forest, were the avenues of travel. Now the avenues of transportation have multiplied almost beyond comprehension. Five thousand miles of canals, thirty thousand miles of railway, forty-five thousand miles of telegraph, five million tons of shipping, fifteen hundred steamers, which annually transport forty millions of passengers, afford the amplest facilities for rapid communication. . . .

"Then religious strifes, growing out of the conflicting claims of rival sects for supremacy in some of the colonies, and the poverty and scattered condition of the people in others, limited the means of moral instruction: now religion is wholly divorced from the corruptions of power; all forms of faith are protected by equal laws; and forty thousand churches — costing nearly a hundred millions of dollars, in which fifteen millions of people may be seated, and in which more than thirty thousand clergymen instruct the people in the duties of life — point their spires toward the skies. Religious and philanthropic associations annually scatter among the people millions of publications for the moral culture of the people. Humane institutions, almost unknown when the nation commenced its independent existence, have been founded, where the children of misfortune, the blind, the deaf, the dumb, the insane, and the sons and daughters of toil, find shelter from the storms of life. . . .

" When independence was proclaimed, less than forty newspapers spread the immortal words among the people; and these journals were small in size, and of limited circulation: on this eighty-third anniversary, nearly three thousand newspapers are printed in America, having a circulation of six millions, and annually scattering broadcast nearly six hundred millions of copies, — more copies than are printed by the two most powerful nations of the globe, France and England. At the dawn of the Revolution, periodical literature was hardly known: now two hundred periodicals, devoted to literature, science, and art, to religion, law, politics, manufactures, commerce, agriculture, mechanics, and the moral, intellectual, and material interests of society, are published; and the circulation of these periodicals is immense, amounting to many millions annually. These three thousand periodicals and journals, which the prolific press of America scatters among the people, give to them the ideas, inventions, discoveries, arts, facts, and events, at rates so low as to bring them within the reach of the toiling masses.

"At the opening of the Revolutionary contest, books were rare and dear, — beyond the reach of the masses of the people; only a few small libraries had been created: now the public libraries, exclusive of those of schools and institutions of learning, contain more than six millions of volumes. The rarest and choicest works find a place in the private libraries which the increasing wealth, taste, and refinement of the people are creating. The American press, hardly a power at the opening of the contest for national existence, now annually publishes more than a thousand new works, and more than nine millions of volumes. The works of the profoundest and the ripest intellects in the Old World and the New, in ancient and modern times, are now, by the ceaseless activity of the American press, placed before the people at prices so low, that all can hold communion with the mighty minds of the living and with the dead. The great living authors of England and of France are read hardly less in America than in their native lands. Before the Revolution, there were a few scholars of research and learning, of genius and taste; but they had contributed little to literature, science, or art. America has achieved a position in the republic of letters which gives assurance of a brilliant future; and she has given to the world some of the noblest names that grace the literature, science, and art of the age.

. "These statistics of wealth, of production, of material advancement, of churches, schools, libraries, and journals, give us some idea of the vast resources and abounding means now possessed by the people of America for moral and intellectual culture and physical well-being.

"This rapid advancement of the republic in all the elements of power, this lofty position achieved within the brief space of one human life, this consummated result,

which places America among the foremost powers of the
globe, make the hearts of our countrymen, wherever they
may be, on the ocean or on the land, throb with patriotic
joy and pride ; and they give this day to memory, exultation, and hope."

Referring to the subject ever uppermost in his mind, he
said, —

" But to the thoughtful patriot who loves his country,
who would make that country an example to the nations ;
to the lover of human freedom, who would extend its sway
over the globe ; to the Christian philanthropist, whose
heart ever throbs for the welfare of the children of men, —
this hallowed anniversary, so glorious in its memories of
the past, its realities of the present, and its hopes of the
future, is not one of unmingled joy.   Within the limits of
the republic, four millions of mankind are bending to-day
beneath the nameless woes of perpetual servitude ; and,
while the self-evident truths of the great charter of rights
are upon our lips, the humiliating consciousness flashes
upon our souls, that fleeing bondmen are shrinking away
in the glens and forests from the echoes of the glad voices
of general rejoicing, watching for the going-down of the
sun, so that their weary eyes may gaze upon the north
star, whose steady light they anxiously hope will guide
their aching feet to that land beyond the Great Lakes and
the St. Lawrence, where the shackle falls and the voice
of the master is not heard.

" This ' odious and abominable trade,' this ' inhuman
and accursed traffic,' which Daniel Webster summoned the
country to ' put beyond the circle of human sympathies
and human regards,' now flourishes in defiant mockery of
the laws of the country and the public opinion of the
Christian and civilized world."

23

He closed his eloquent address with these hopeful words : —

" Though deeds of injustice, inhumanity, lawlessness, and oppression, darken our horizon, casting their saddening influences over the festivities of this anniversary, the lesson of this day is the lesson of hope, not of despair.   Upon America, our country, and, with all her faults, the land of our affections and pride, are centred the best hopes of mankind.   To what portion of the globe, to what land under the whole heavens, can the friend of human progress, of equal and universal liberty, this day turn with more of hope and confidence than to this magnificent continental empire, this broad land of wondrous fertility, where Providence has garnered illimitable resources to be developed for human prosperity, power, and happiness ; this democratic republic, with achieved free institutions based upon the rights of human nature, with millions of people trained in self-government, and in full possession of the citadel of consummated power, — the ballot-box ; where the loving heart, the enlightened conscience, the unclouded reason, of man, can utter their voices for humane and equal laws, and for their wise and impartial administration ?   ' Our country,' said that illustrious supporter of the rights of mankind, John Quincy Adams, ' began her existence by the proclamation of the universal emancipation of man from the thraldom of man.'   In support of that glorious proclamation, our fathers were summoned to walk the path of duty ; and they obeyed the call, though it was swept by British cannon, darkened by the storm of battle, and sprinkled with the blood of falling comrades. We honor their sublime devotion ; we applaud their heroic deeds.   Their bright example of devotion to principle, and fidelity to duty, should incite us of this age in America to accept joyfully and bravely the responsibilities of our position, and, like them, be ever ready

> ' To take
> Occasion by the hand, and make
> The bounds of freedom wider yet.' "

To the raid of John Brown into Virginia in October (1859), causing wild excitement through the South, and terminating in the death of the invader, Mr. Wilson was from principle opposed. He had often made the declaration, that even Congress had no right to interfere with slavery in the slave States; and in this position he firmly stood. An attempt was made in the Senate, Dec. 6, to prove that he was in sympathy with those who would resort to force for the liberation of the slave, by showing that he was present at a meeting of the citizens of Natick on the 29th of November, in which was passed, without opposition on his part, the resolution, " That it is the right and duty of the slaves to resist their masters." To this imputation he replied : —

" During the canvass in New York, I spent two weeks there, and addressed tens of thousands of people; and my speeches were reported in full two or three times. In those speeches I expressed my views in regard to this raid of John Brown at Harper's Ferry fully and explicitly. I returned to my home on the day preceding the election in my State; and I addressed a very large meeting of the citizens of my town for two hours on general political topics, and fully on this matter in regard to the Harper's-Ferry affair. . . . In the town where I live we have more than a thousand voters. We have some ten or twenty men who are radical abolitionists. Some of them were present. They did not interrupt me nor the meeting.

When the meeting had ended, they said to their neighbors and friends, and some of them came to me and said, that they disagreed with me entirely, and would have somebody there to put the other side of the question. A short time afterwards, Mr. Henry C. Wright, a Garrison abolitionist, who is a professed disunionist, a no-government man, a non-resistant, came to speak in my town. The population of the place went to hear him, and crowded the hall. Most of the active Democrats in the town were present. The postmaster was present, and sat close by me. The resolutions were offered by Mr. Wright; and he made a non-resistant speech in favor of resistance. (Laughter.) He went on to explain how the thing could be done. He said he would not shed a drop of human blood to free every slave in the country.

"After he closed his speech, the question was put, and perhaps fifteen or twenty persons in that meeting of seven or eight hundred voted for the resolution. All the rest, feeling that Mr. Wright's friends had paid for the hall, and got up the meeting for him and for themselves, took no part for or against him. They did not interrupt the meeting; believing as they did, and as we do in our part of the country, in the absolute right of free discussion of all questions. When the meeting adjourned, the general expression was that the resolution was a very foolish one, and for which Mr. Wright and his friends were alone responsible. Nine-tenths of that meeting took no part in it. They did not wish to interrupt the meeting, or interfere with it in any way whatever, or be responsible for it. There were present gentlemen as sound on the slavery question as the senator from Mississippi could desire. The postmaster of that town is as sound on the slavery question as the senator from Mississippi, and often manifests his zeal in defence of the policy of the slave power; but he did not say a word, nor did those who act with him, because nobody wished to interfere with those who had invited the speaker there, and who agreed with him in his general opinions. Senators should remember that the right to hold meetings, and to utter opinions upon all matters of public concern, is an acknowledged right in my section of the country. They should remember, also, that the people in that section often attend meetings where subjects are discussed in a way they do not sanction; but they do not think it becomes gentlemen to interrupt such meetings, or interfere with those who differ from them. Often do I attend such meetings, and listen to what is said, without feeling myself in any way responsible for what is said or done: so do the people of my State. I wish the people of other sections of the country would thus cherish the sacred right of free discussion."

So, in reply to the remarks of Mr. Iverson, he said in the Senate, Dec. 8, —

"The sentiment in my State approaches unanimity in condemnation of the raid of John Brown. If there be any man in Massachusetts, especially any Republican in Massachusetts, who upholds or justifies that act, he has my unqualified opposition and condemnation. But, sir, I wish to deal frankly with senators on the other side, and to say that the sentiment of my State approaches unanimity in sympathy for the fate of the leader of that invasion. It springs mainly and chiefly from what happened after that event, during his imprisonment, his trial, and his execution. His words, his letters, his bearing, every thing about him, extorted admiration from friends and foes."

Such had been Senator Wilson's steady, able, and consistent defence of the rights of the Northern people and of

23*

those in bondage, that on the twelfth day of June, 1860, both branches of the General Court of Massachusetts passed a resolution honorable alike to the sentiment of the representatives of the people and to him : —

" *Resolved*, That the thanks of this legislature, acting as the agents of the people, be and are hereby tendered to the Hon. HENRY WILSON for his able, fearless, and always prompt defence of the great principles of human freedom while acting as a senator and a citizen of the Old Bay State."

" Approved June 16, 1860 :

"NATHANIEL P. BANKS."

On his amendment to the Naval Appropriation Bill for the purchase of three steam-vessels for the suppression of the African slave-trade, Mr. Wilson, true to his noble record, made on the 18th of June, 1860, a strong speech, in which he presents a mass of startling facts in respect to the re-opening of this iniquitous business. " The senator from Virginia (Mr. Mason) asks how it is," says he, " that the slave-trade has been revived in the cities of the North. He does not understand why this traffic in men should be re-renewed at this time by persons residing in this country. I think, sir, it is all very plain. We have had in this country during the past six years an immense pressure for the extension of slavery into the Territories, and for the supremacy of slavery in the councils of the government. To extend slavery, to secure its controlling influence over the government, ancient restrictions have been abrogated, and lawless violence and frauds have been resorted to by unscrupulous men ready to sacrifice every right that stood in the way of their schemes of expansion and dominion.

The senator from Virginia himself proclaimed on this floor that the slaveholding States had the right to the natural expansion of slavery on this continent as an element of political power. Does the senator suppose that these efforts to expand human slavery over this continent for the avowed purpose of strengthening the power of slave-masters over the National Government have no influence over men ever ready to do any work of inhumanity or crime to fill their coffers with gold?

"Sir, these efforts to extend human slavery in America, these attempts to increase the power of slavery in the councils of the nation, these discussion sin these halls and in the public journals, these deeds of fraud and violence, have had their demoralizing effects upon the country. When the senator from Virginia finds that men engaged in this inhuman traffic cannot be convicted, that juries fail, that judges pervert the laws, that public journals and public men demand the abrogation of treaty stipulations and the modification or repeal of all laws branding the slave-trade as piracy, why should he be surprised that in Northern commercial cities, in the great city of New York, there should be found men to invest capital to fit out ships, to send vessels to the coast of Africa, to engage in a traffic, which, if successful, fills their purses with coveted gold? Why should not men be found in that great commercial city as ready to violate law, the rights of human nature, and feelings of humanity, to win gold, as to aid in the work of slavery expansion and dominion in America for the poor boon of official patronage? Surely the experienced senator from Virginia cannot be surprised at the readiness of men to do mean and wicked deeds for slavery. The senator has often seen how ready men are, even in these chambers, to do whatever slavery requires of them.

The senator, the other day, reported in favor of returning to my colleague a petition presented by him of colored citizens of Massachusetts. In this the senator had the ready support of the senator from Indiana (Mr. Fitch). When the honorable senator from Virginia finds the senator from Indiana not only ready to engage in an act like that, — an act which violates the constitutional rights of men and the rights of a senator of a sovereign State, — but willing to make an insulting motion, accompanied by impertinent remarks toward the senator who, in the discharge of public duty, presented the petition, why should he not suppose that other men can be found willing to do any work in the interests of slavery? When the senator from Virginia sees the pliancy and alacrity of the senator from Indiana in this work of suppressing the petitions of the colored citizens of a sovereign Commonwealth, why should he not suppose that men may be found in other Northern States ready to engage in the slave-trade?

"It cannot be matter of surprise to senators that men in our great commercial cities, especially New York, should engage with renewed zeal in the slave-trade. Men ever ready to clutch at every opportunity to fill their purses with gold, no matter how it is to be won, could not fail to be influenced to embark in the unlawful and inhuman slave-trade by the change which has been going on in the public mind in regard to this traffic in men. We cannot disguise the fact, that a great change of sentiment has been going on in this country with regard to the slave-trade."

CHAPTER XIV.

THE NOMINATION OF MR. LINCOLN. — THE PARAMOUNT
QUESTION BETWEEN THE PARTIES. — HOW SHOULD
WORKING-MEN VOTE ? — HIS COURSE IN THE EVENT
OF DISUNION. — HIS RELATIONS TO MR. DAVIS. —
THE CRITTENDEN COMPROMISE. — LETTERS.

ABRAHAM LINCOLN was nominated for the presidency by the Republicans in convention at Chicago in the month of May, 1860 ; and John C. Breckinridge in April following, at Charleston, S.C., by the proslavery Democrats. The other candidates were John Bell and Stephen A. Douglas. The main question between the two leading parties was freedom, or slavery, in the immense Territories of the Union ; or, in other words, shall free, or servile, labor have the ascendency in this country ? Long and carefully, both in and out of Congress, had Mr. Wilson studied this question under every form and bearing ; long had he contemplated the tremendous interests involved in the issue of the question ; and he therefore threw himself into the contest with unfaltering energy, addressing vast and enthusiastic audiences in many States with eloquent and effective words of warning, counsel, and encouragement. In an address at Myrick's Junction, Mass., on the 18th of September, in reference to the paramount question of the parties, he said, —

"Issues growing out of the existence of human slavery in America are now the paramount issues before the nation. Shall slavery continue to expand? shall it continue to guide the counsels of the republic? or shall its expansion be arrested, its power broken, and it forced to retire under the cover of the local laws under which it exists? These issues loom up before the nation, dwarfing all other issues, and subordinating all other questions. Public men and political organizations are forced to accept the transcendent issues growing out of the existence of slavery in America.

"The American Democracy, which for twenty-five years has borne the banners of slavery, won its victories, and shared in its crimes against humanity, though broken into fragments, struggles on, faithful still to the interests of slavery. Breckinridge and Lane accept the creed of slavery expansion, slavery protection, and slavery domination; Douglas 'don't care whether slavery is voted up or voted down;' and Johnson, commended by the Massachusetts Democracy at Springfield for his 'honest and fearless promulgation of Democratic truth,' proclaims that it 'is best that capital should own labor.' The American Democracy, demoralized by slavery, has ceased to speak of the rights of man: it now speaks only of the rights of property in man. The Republican party, brought into existence by the aggressions of slavery upon freedom, cherishing the faith of the founders of the republic, and believing with their chosen leader, Abraham Lincoln, that '*he* who would be no slave must consent to *have* no slave,' pledges itself, all it is, all it hopes to be, to arrest the extension of slavery, banish it from the Territories, dethrone its power in the National Government, and force it back under the cover of State sovereignty."

After giving the proslavery record of Mr. Bell, he closed by these strong words : —

" Men of old Puritan and Revolutionary Massachusetts, upon whose pathway the star of duty casts its radiant and steady light, — you who believe with Benjamin Franklin, that ' slavery is an atrocious debasement of human nature ;' with John Adams, that ' consenting to slavery is a sacrilegious breach of trust ; ' with John Quincy Adams, that ' slavery taints the very sources of moral principle ; ' with Daniel Webster, that ' slavery is a continual and permanent violation of human rights,' ' opposed to the whole spirit of the gospel and to the teachings of Jesus Christ,' — reject, I pray you, reject with loathing, the false and guilty doctrine, that, in this crisis of the republic, ' it is the part of patriotism and duty to recognize no political principle ; ' turn from a candidate whose record is blurred, blotted, and stained with words and deeds for human slavery ; spurn with scorn all affiliation with men who in the South are vying with the slave-code Democracy in fealty to the slave propagandists, — who in the North are scoffing and jeering at the sacred cause of liberty, organizing Democratic-aid societies, peddling and dickering with Democratic factions, to defeat men whose only offence is their unswerving fidelity to the cause of human nature now in peril in America, and ' consecrating,' in the words of Whittier,

> ' their baseness to the cause
> Of Constitution, Union, and the Laws.'

" Rally, men of Massachusetts, to the standard of a party that proclaims its principles and its policy, — a party that would engrave in letters of living light upon the arches of the skies, so that the nations might read it, its undying hostility to the domination and extension of slavery in America. Rally to the support of a candidate for the chief magistracy of the republic who penned these noble words : ' This is a world of compensations; and he who would *be* no slave must consent to *have* no slave. Those who deny freedom to others deserve it not for themselves ; and, under a just God, cannot long retain it.' "

On the question, " How ought working-men to vote ? " Mr. Wilson said, contrasting free with servile labor, in a speech of signal force delivered at East Boston on the 24th of October, —

" Self-interest, self-respect, the love he bears his wife, and the hopes centred in those who inherit his blood and bear his name, all urge, press, command, the poor man, the mechanic, the laboring-man, to rush to the ballot-box on the 6th of November, and vote to take the government of his country from the unhallowed grasp of men, who, by word and deed, have proved themselves the mortal enemies of free labor and free-laboring men, and to place that government in the hands of statesmen who will maintain the rights, interests, and dignity of free labor.

" Glancing over this assemblage of the freemen of East Boston, I see before me the manly forms of toiling men, who, through weary days and sleepless nights of personal toil, have won for themselves positions of independence, or who now, by the scanty wages of manual labor, support themselves and the dear and loved ones of their household. And I say to you, men of Massachusetts, slavery is the unappeasable enemy of the free laboring-men of America,

of the North and of the South. Ay, I repeat, slavery is the unappeasable enemy of the free laboring-men
of America, of the North and of the South. The party
that upholds slavery in America, that would extend its
boundaries, increase its influence and its power, is the mortal enemy of the free white laboring-men of the United
States. I declare to you, men of Massachusetts, and, if I
could be heard, I would proclaim it in the ear of every
laboring-man in America, the slavery of the black man
has degraded labor and the white laboring-man of the
South, and dishonored the white laboring - man of the
North. Some writer (I think it was Carlyle) has said that
the Indian away on the shores of Lake Winnipeg cannot
strike his dusky mate but the world feels the blow. Put
the brand of degradation upon the brow of one working-
man, and the toiling millions of the globe share in that
degradation. Slavery makes labor dishonorable, puts the
brand of degradation upon the brow of manual labor, free
as well as slave, blights the homes of the free laboring
white men of the South, and casts its baleful shadows over
the homes, the fields, and the workshops of the laboring-
men of the North.

"In 1620 — two hundred and forty years ago — freedom
and slavery came to the shores of America. Freedom
took the rugged soil and still more rugged clime of the
North : slavery took the genial clime and sunny lands of
the South. Freedom, starting from Plymouth, has advanced with steady step westward, crossed the Rocky
Mountains to the shores of the Pacific seas, founding commonwealths which 'recognize the eternal laws of man's
being : slavery, starting from Jamestown, has advanced
westward and southward into the depths of the continent,

24

founding States of privilege and caste. The results of these two antagonistic systems are plain to the comprehension of all men.

" Here, in these free commonwealths, are twenty millions of freemen, with free speech, free press, free schools, free churches, and free institutions. Here all questions that concern humanity are examined and discussed by the unfettered press and the free thoughts and words of men. Here ' labor,' in the words of Daniel Webster, ' looks up and is proud in the midst of its toil.' Here the laboring-man, who daily goes forth with a brave heart to toil for his loved ones, wins not only bread by the sweat of his face, but the applauding voice of men who honor labor, who believe the laborer is worthy of his hire. Here the toil of the working-man is lightened by ennobling motives, by aspirations which expand the mind and elevate the soul. The toil which wearies his arm is to make glad the home of wife and children; to smooth adown the declivity of life the steps of parents to whom he owes his being; to lift the burdens of life from brother, sister, or friend ; or to win for him competence, independence, positions of power, the lofty and glittering prizes of ambition. Here the laboring-men in all the fields of manly toil are working out a con-dition of society for the toiling masses more elevated than can be found in any other portion of the globe. Here agriculture, commerce, manufactures, the mechanic arts, churches, schools, libraries, the institutions of a refining civilization, flourish in vigor and strength. Such are the magnificent results of freedom in the North.

" The results of slavery in the South glare upon us from every rood of the land stained by its existence. The fruits of slavery are bitter to the taste, and sickening to the soul of man. There are auction-blocks, where man made in the image of God is sold like the beasts that perish; there are chains and fetters for human limbs, whips to scourge and torture the body, and laws to debase and brutalize the mind and soul of man. There labor is dishonored, laborers degraded, despised. 'To work,' said William Ellery Channing, 'in sight of the whip, under menace of blows, is to be exposed to perpetual insult and degrading influences. Every motion of the limbs which such a menace urges is a wound to the soul.' To work beside the bondmen urged on to toil by the menace of blows degrades the poor white laborer to the abject condition of the slave. To continually eat the bread of enforced and unrequited toil, to look upon labor extorted by the menace of the lash, upon the laborer thus degraded, excites in the bosom of the slave-master that scorn for manual labor, and that contempt for laboring-men, now so manifest in the slave States of republican America.

The deterioration, exhaustion, and desolation of the soil of the South, under the culture of unskilled, untutored, unrewarded slave-labor, stands confessed by even the champions of that cleaving curse. Thousands of square miles, millions of acres of the best soil of the Western world, have been blighted, blasted, desolated, by the polluting footsteps of the bondman. The champions of slavery, men who would eternize it, extend its boundaries and its dominion over the National Government, have borne testimony to the desolating effects of the Southern system of agriculture, which means the Southern slave-labor system, upon the most prolific soil of the continent. . . .

" Breckinridge," he said, " bears aloft the banner of slavery expansion, slavery protection, and slavery domination; and around that black flag rallies the Democratic masses of the South, and the men of the North who believe with Mr. Buchanan that 'the master has the right to take his slaves into the Territories as property, and have it protected there under the Federal Constitution;' that 'neither Congress nor the Territorial legislature, nor any human power, has any authority to annul or impair that vested right.' Benjamin F. Hallett tells the assembled Breckinridge Democracy of Massachusetts that there can never be a successful Democratic party in the free States: so he goes with the slave-code Democracy of the South. There can never be a successful Democratic party in the North! What an admission is this! There can never be a successful Democratic party in the land of free speech, free press, free schools, free labor, and free educated working-men trained in self-government! Successful Democracy buds and blooms only in the land of bondage, where the right to think, to discuss, to act, is not recognized; where labor is dishonored, and laboring-men despised! Surely the working-men of the North can not, will not, sustain by their suffrages that false, foul, profane Democracy which draws its life, its soul, from slavery.

"Douglas 'don't care whether slavery is voted down or voted up.' To him it is a matter of supreme indifference whether a million and a half of the square miles of America shall be gladdened by the footsteps and beautified by the hands of freemen, who acknowledge no man master; or whether they shall be seared, blasted, desolated, by

> The old and chartered lie,
> The feudal curse, whose whips and yokes.
> Insult humanity.'

"The laboring-men of the North, ay, and of the South too, should never forget nor forgive that heartless decla-

ration.   The peerless Washington cared whether slavery
was voted down or voted up in the Territories ; for he
' trusted we should have a confederacy of free States,' and
he deemed the ordinance of 1787 ' a wise measure.'   The
working-man who votes the Douglas and Johnson ticket
votes for a president who ' don't care whether slavery is
voted down or voted up,' and for a vice-president who
' believes capital should own labor.'   Can a working-man,
who eats his bread in the sweat of his face, give such a
vote ?   Such a vote would be a betrayal of the cause of
the toiling masses of America, an act of self-humiliation
which should bring the blush of conscious shame to the
cheek.

   " The Republican party, brought into being by the neces-
sities of the country and the needs of the age, rejects the
wicked dogma, that slaves, the creatures of local law, are
recognized by the Constitution as property, that the Constitution of republican America carries slavery wherever
it goes, and that the national flag protects slavery wherever
it waves.   The Republican party ' cares whether slavery
is voted down or voted up ' in the Territories, rejects with
horror the idea that ' capital should own labor,' disowns the
craven declaration that ' it is the part of patriotism and of
duty to recognize no principle,' and bravely and hopefully
accepts the duties now imposed upon the people of the
United States by the providence of Almighty God.   The
Republican party proclaims its living faith in the self-evident truths of the Declaration of Independence, now scoffed
at and jeered at by the leaders of the slave Democracy as
' rhetorical flourishes,' ' glittering generalities,' ' self-evident
lies,' ' farragoes of nonsense,' pronounced by Breckinridge
' abstractions,' which, if carried into practice, would ' lead
our country rapidly to destruction,' and declared by Doug-

24*

las to mean only that ' British subjects on this continent were equal to British subjects born and residing in Great Britain.'

" The Republican party believes with its chosen leader, Abraham Lincoln, that ' these expressions ' of apostate Democratic politicians, ' differing in form, are identical in object and effect, — the supplanting of the principles of free government, and restoring those of classification, caste, and legitimacy ; ' that ' they would delight a convocation of crowned heads plotting against the people ; ' that ' they are the vanguard, the sappers and miners, of returning despotism.' The Republican party believes too, with its noble candidate, that the ' abstract truth ' of the Declaration is ' applicable to all men and all times ; ' that ' to-day, and in all coming days, it shall be a rebuke and a stumbling-block to the harbingers of re-appearing tyranny and oppression.' Accepting as its living faith the creed of the equality of mankind, the Republican party recognizes the poor, the humble, the sons of toil, whose hands are hardened by honest labor, whose limbs are chilled by the blasts of winter, whose cheeks are scorched by the suns of summer, as the equals, before the law, of the most favored of the sons of men.

" Believing with the republican fathers of the North and of the South, with Washington and Franklin, Adams and Jefferson, Henry and Jay, Morris and Mason, Madison and Hamilton, King and Munroe, Pinckney and Martin, and their illustrious associates, that slavery is ' a sin of crimson dye,' ' an atrocious debasement of human nature,' ' a dreadful calamity,' which ' lessens the sense of the equal rights of mankind, and habituates us to tyranny and oppression ; ' believing with Henry Clay, that ' slavery is a wrong, a grievous wrong no contingency can make right,'

— the Republican party is opposed to slavery everywhere. Recognizing the rights of the States, it does not claim power to abolish slavery in the States by Congressional legislation : but it claims the power to exclude slavery from the Territories ; and, by the blessing of God, it will use every legal power and make every honorable effort to expel slavery from every rood of the territory of the republic.

" Working-men of Massachusetts, you who eat your bread in the sweat of the face, would you make the self-evident truths of the charter of independence again the active faith of America ; would you weaken the influences of slavery and the power of the slave-masters over the National Government ; would you expel slavery and its degrading influences from the Territories ; would you bring Kansas as a free commonwealth into the Union ; would you suppress the reviving African slave-trade, now dishonoring the nation ; would you erase from the statutes of New Mexico the inhuman slave-code, and the more infamous code authorizing employers to degrade white laboring-men with blows, while it denies all means of protection by closing the courts against their appeals for redress ; would you set apart the public domain for homesteads for the landless ; would you construct a railroad across the central regions of the continent to the Pacific ; would you adjust the revenue-laws so as to incidentally favor American labor ; would you win back our lost influence with the nations south of us on this continent, and thus increase and develop our manufacturing and commercial interests ; would you reform existing abuses, strengthen the ties of interest and affection which bind these sister States together, and put the republic in the van of advancing nations, — then commit, fully and unreservedly commit, yourselves to the cause of republicanism, to the support of the Republican party and its tried and trusted candidates. Born in the ranks of the toiling masses, reared in the bosom of the people, trained in the hard school of manual labor, Abraham Lincoln and Hannibal Hamlin are true to the rights, the interests, and the dignity of the working-men of the republic; worthy to lead their advancing hosts to victory for the vindication of rights as old as creation, and as wide as humanity."

Mr. Schuyler Colfax and many others wrote to the author, thanking him for this speech; and the general tenor of the letters may be seen from this: —

BIDDEFORD, ME., Nov. 19, 1860.

DEAR SIR, — You have made but very few political speeches during your life that I have not read. No one appreciates more than I do the herculean labors that you and your noble colleague and associates have made in enlightening the national mind and heart upon the aggressions of the slave-power. What a glorious triumph you have achieved! What a revolution has been effected, and how peacefully! I have many times expressed to my family and friends the thought so eloquently enforced by our mutual friend, Henry Ward Beecher, in his recent sermon on the times (which I think is the greatest speech he has ever made), — that hereafter the 6th of November, 1860, will be ranked by the historian as an era of equal importance with the 22d of December, 1620, and the 4th of July, 1776.

I subscribe myself, with high respect and regard,

Your obedient servant,

CHARLES PACKARD.

On the triumph of the Republicans in Mr. Lincoln's election in November, the South, led on by Messrs. Mason, Hammond, Davis, Floyd, and other kindred spirits, who foresaw that freedom, so persistently resisted, was now coming into the ascendant, inconsiderately passed, State after State, the ordinance of secession, and gradually withdrew its representatives from Congress.

Mr. Wilson clearly saw the magnitude of the proceeding and the tremendous stake at issue : he knew the strength of the North in numbers, wealth, and principle ; he knew the weakness of the South ; and hence he had no fear for the ultimate result : but from the unity of sentiment, from the *animus* of the South, he openly avowed to his associates that the struggle would be desperate and terrible.

With calm and manly earnestness he performed his senatorial duties, ever protesting that his party had no design to interfere at all with the domestic institutions of the States, and that, if they fell, it would be in consequence of their impetuous action, and upon their own responsibility.

He had already fearlessly expressed his mind in a speech in the Senate on the 25th of January preceding, in which he refers to the following remark of Mr. Clingman of North Carolina : " As from this Capitol so much has gone forth to inflame the public mind, if our countrymen are to be involved in a bloody struggle, I trust in God that the first-fruits of the collision may be reaped here." He said, —

" This language, Mr. President, admits of but one interpretation.   Gentlemen from the South who are in favor of a dissolution of the Union do not intend, in so doing, to secede from this Capitol, nor surrender it to those who

may remain within the Union. Having declared, that, if
lives are to be sacrificed, it will be poetically just that they
should be sacrificed here on this floor; and that, as so
much has gone forth from this Capitol to inflame the public
mind, it is but proper that the first-fruits of the struggle
should be reaped here, the senator gives us, therefore,
distinctly to understand that there may be a physical
collision, 'a bloody struggle;' that the scene of this conflict is to be the legislative halls of this Capitol. To
simply say, in reply to this threat, that Northern senators
cannot thus be intimidated, is too tame and commonplace
to meet the exigency. Therefore I take it upon myself
to inform the senator from North Carolina that the people
of the free States have sent their representatives here, not
to fight, but to legislate; not to mingle in personal combats,
but to deliberate for the good of the whole country; not
to shed the blood of their fellow-members, but to maintain
the supremacy of the Constitution, and uphold the Union:
and this they will endeavor to do here, in the legislative
halls of the Capitol, at all events and at every hazard. In
the performance of their duties they will not invade the
rights of others, nor permit any infringement of their own.
They will invite no collision; they will commence no
attack: but they will discharge all their obligations to their
constituents, and maintain the government and institutions
of their country in the face of all conceivable consequences.
Whoever thinks otherwise has not studied either the
history of the people of the free States, or the character of
the men dwelling in that section of the Union, or the philosophy of the exigency which the senator from North
Carolina seems to invoke. The freemen of the North have
not been accustomed to vaunt their courage in words: they
have preferred to illustrate it by deeds. They are not

fighting-men by profession, nor accustomed to street broils, nor contests on the 'field of honor' falsely so called, nor are they habitual wearers of deadly weapons. Therefore it is, that when driven into bloody collisions, and especially on sudden emergencies, it is as true in fact as it is sound in philosophy, that they are more desperate and determined, and more reckless of consequences to themselves and to their antagonists, than are those who are more accustomed to contemplate such collisions. The tightest band, when once broken, recoils with the wildest power. So much for the people of the free States. As to their representatives in this Capitol, I will say, that if, while in the discharge of their duties here, they are assaulted with deadly intent, I give the senator from North Carolina due notice here to-day, that those assaults will be repelled and retaliated by sons who will not dishonor fathers that fought at Bunker Hill and conquered at Saratoga, that trampled the soil of Chippewa and Lundy's Lane to a bloody mire, and vindicated sailors' rights and national honor on the high seas in the second war of independence. Reluctant to enter into such a contest, yet, once in, they will be quite as reluctant to leave it. Though they may not be the first to go into the struggle, they will be the last to abandon it in dishonor. Though they will not provoke nor commence the conflict, they will do their best to conquer when the strife begins. So much their constituents will demand of them when the 'bloody struggle' the senator contemplates is forced upon them; and they will not be disappointed when the exigency comes. I say no more: I wait the issue, and bide my time."

Mr. Wilson for a long period had been serving on the Military Committee of the Senate, of which Mr. Jefferson Davis was chairman; and had thus become familiar with his schemes for strengthening the military condition of the South : he had not, however, anticipated that secession from the Union was so close at hand. Though opposed to each other in principle, the personal relations between himself and Mr. Davis were at that time pleasant; and once at least, when Mr. Wilson closed a strong speech in the Senate, the Mississippi senator came across the floor, and thanked him cordially for the manly expression of his views. It was while on the Military Committee that Mr. Wilson, in opposition to the chairman, carried the "Signal-service Bill" through Congress, and thus conferred a lasting benefit upon the country. It is not probable that Mr. Davis himself, until the election in November, imagined the secession of the slave States very near. South Carolina had always led the van in opposition to the North ; and now, in the culmination of the long argument, it was for her to cast the fatal die. Mr. Wilson, with his Northern friends, deplored her folly ; but he foresaw that her first shot would break the chain of the slave, and that, in spite of the tongues of soothsayers, the Union and the Constitution still would stand.

He knew, perhaps as well as any man, the comparative strength of the contending parties. He saw in Mr. Lincoln's overwhelming vote in the electoral college the sentiment of the nation. He well understood that the struggle was, and had been, whether free, or servile, labor should rule the country ; and that his party, which had arisen from a small band branded by the name of Abolitionists in 1840 to place by such a vast majority a president in the chair in 1860, had grown too slowly, fought too steadily on the line of sacred principle, to be intimidated by an ordinance, or even by the cannon of seceders from the Union. He pointed out the impending danger, yet hoped,

that, by the policy of the incoming president, some reconciliation might be made without recourse to arms.

But the vantage-ground now reached must be maintained. An indignant people had at the polls declared that
slavery must not be extended. By that declaration he
must stand. He would not interfere with the "peculiar
institution" in the States; he would exhibit courtesy, for-
bearance, and fraternity to the South: but the vast Territories of the Union must not be surrendered to the
domination of the slaveholding power. In this position,
he, with his associates, stood intrenched: so that when
Mr. Crittenden's compromise, which made concessions to
the South, came up in the Senate, he opposed it in a
manly speech delivered on the 21st of February, 1861.
With the clearest apprehension of the situation, with the
history of the whole struggle fresh in memory, with the
ominous prospect of disunion rising up before him, and with
a spirit fired by the love of human freedom, he meets the
question in a strain of fervid eloquence, vindicates the
friends of liberty, and unfolds the iniquity of the offered
compromise.

After an eloquent introduction, he thus describes the
distracted state of the nation : —

"One year ago these chambers rang with passionate and
vehement menaces of disunion. Statesmen to whom were
committed the destinies of United America, with the oath
of fidelity to the Constitution fresh upon their lips, insolently, scornfully, defiantly threatened to shiver the noblest edifice, the fairest fabric, of free government ever
erected by the toil or blessed by the hopes and prayers
of humanity, if the people, the people of the free North,
dared through the ballot-box assume the control of the
affairs of the republic. These disloyal avowals were

25

flashed over the wires, scattered broadcast over the land. Timid conservatives shrank appalled before these angry mutterings of meditated treason, and, with 'bated breath and whispering humbleness,' counselled submission. But these treasonable menaces unnerved not the souls of the ever loyal freemen of the North: they fired the hearts and rekindled the patriotism of the unselfish masses, — of the farmers who till their own fee-simple acres, unpolluted by the foot of the bondman; of the mechanics whose hands are skilled by art; of the laborers who recognize no master but Almighty God. Impelled by the fervid and unextinguishable impulse of freedom, by the purest and most unselfish patriotism, the unseduced, unpurchased, unawed freemen of the North calmly thronged to the ballot-box, and struck from faithless, corrupt, and disloyal hands the reins of power.

" The treasonable words of last year have now hardened into deeds. Madness and folly rule the hour. Treason holds it carnival here in the national Capitol. . Men high in the national councils plot conspiracies against the government they are sworn to defend, and clasp the hands of the assassins of the Union. Men to whom have been intrusted official duties and responsibilities talk of the dismemberment of the republic, not in the sad accents of patriotism, but with the gleeful chuckle of an irrepressible joy. States vauntingly proclaim their withdrawal from the Union made by the fathers, recall their representatives in these chambers, capture the fortresses of the nation, insult, dishonor, and fire upon the flag of the republic, seize the public property, and even erase from their festive days the hallowed anniversary of national independence, with all its glorious associations and thrilling memories. Never, no, never, since the morn of creation, has the historic pen recorded a conspiracy against the rights of man and democratic institutions so utterly causeless, so wicked in its purpose, so regardless of the judgment of the civilized world and the approval of Almighty God."

He makes this reference to Mr. Benton's views: —

" But, sir, this wicked plot for the dismemberment of the Confederacy, which has now assumed such fearful proportions, was known to some of our elder statesmen. Thomas H. Benton ever raised his warning voice against the conspirators. I can never forget the terrible energy of his denunciations of the policy and acts of the nullifiers and secessionists. During the great Lecompton struggle in the winter of 1858, his house was the place of resort of several members of Congress, who sought his counsels, and delighted to listen to his opinions. In the last conversation I had with him, but a few days before he was prostrated by mortal disease, he declared that ' the disunionists had prostituted the Democratic party;' that ' they had complete control of the administration ; ' that ' these conspirators would have broken up the Union if Col. Frémont had been elected ;' that ' the reason he opposed Frémont's election was that he knew these men intended to destroy the government, and he did not wish it to go to pieces in the hands of a member of his family.' "

Repelling the reiterated charge that " Massachusetts hates the South," he said, —

" In the halls of Congress, in the public journals, before the people, everywhere, the Christian people of the North are accused of hatred towards their countrymen of the South ; and these oft-repeated accusations have penetrated the ears and fired the hearts of the men of the South to madness. The people of Massachusetts, of New England,

of the North, hate not their countrymen of the South.   I
know Massachusetts; I know something of the sentiments
and feelings of her people.   During the past fifteen years
I have traversed every portion of the State, from the sands
of the capes to the hills of Berkshire; spoken in nearly
every town; sat at the tables and slept beneath the roofs
of her people.   Around those tables and beneath those
roofs I have heard prayers to Almighty God for blessings
on slave and on master.   From thousands of Christian
homes in Massachusetts, New England, the North, tens
of thousands of men and women daily implore God's blessing upon the whole country, — upon the poor slave and
his proud master.   Around the firesides of the liberty-
loving, God-fearing families of Massachusetts, I have often
heard the men, stigmatized as 'malignant, unrelenting
enemies of the people of the South,' on their bended knees,
with open Bible, implore the protection and blessing of
Almighty God upon both master and slave, upon the people of the whole country.   Gentlemen of the South visiting Massachusetts on pleasure or business are ever treated
by all her people with considerate kindness and fraternal
regard.   The public men of the South are ever welcomed
to Massachusetts, treated with courtesy by all, and sometimes with 'complimentary flunkeyism' by the few.   I
assert positively, without hesitation or qualification, that
the people of Massachusetts, ay, of New England, manifest
more kindness and courtesy towards their fellow-countrymen of the South sojourning among them than they do
towards their fellow-countrymen of the central States and
of the West.   Yancey, Henry, Hilliard, and other distinguished sons of the South, were, during the late canvass,
listened to in New England with attention and the utmost
courtesy; and that, too, when quiet citizens of Massachu-

setts were, in portions of the South, subjected to the greatest indignities. . . .

"Not one, no, not one, in a thousand of the men who voted for Abraham Lincoln, cherishes in his heart a feeling of hatred towards the South, or the wish to put the brand of inequality or degradation upon the brow of his countrymen of that section of the Union. They would as generously contribute of their treasure, they would as freely pour out their blood, for the defence of the South, as they would for the protection of their own Northern homes. Believers in that Christianity which unites all men as brethren, which makes man unutterably dear to his fellowman, which impels its disciples to raise the fallen, and to labor for the elevation of the poor and the lowly of the children of men, oppose the wrong, yet hate not the wrongdoer."

He thus defends his constituents from the imputation of fanaticism : —

"The distinguishing opinion of Massachusetts concerning slavery in America is often flippantly branded in these halls as wild, passionate, unreasoning fanaticism. Senators of the South, tell me, I pray you tell me, if it be fanaticism for Massachusetts to see in this age what your peerless Washington saw in his age, — 'the direful effects of slavery.' Is it fanaticism for Massachusetts to believe as your Henry believed, that 'slavery is as repugnant to humanity as it is inconsistent with the Bible and destructive to liberty'? Is it fanaticism for her to believe as your Madison believed, that 'slavery is a dreadful calamity'? Is it fanaticism for her to believe with your Monroe, that 'slavery has preyed upon the vitals of the Union, and has been prejudicial to all the States in which it has existed'? Is it fanaticism for her to believe with your

25*

Martin, that 'slavery lessens the sense of the equal rights of mankind, and habituates us to tyranny and oppression'? Is it fanaticism for her to believe with your Pinckney, that 'it will one day destroy the reverence for liberty which is the vital principle of a republic'? Is it fanaticism for her to believe with your Henry Clay, that 'slavery is a wrong, a grievous wrong; no contingency can make it right'? Surely senators who are wont to accuse Massachusetts of being drunk with fanaticism should not forget that the noblest men the South has given to the service of the republic in peace and in war were her teachers.

"Massachusetts in her heart of hearts loves liberty, loathes slavery. I glory in her sentiments; for the heart of our common humanity is throbbing in sympathy with her opinions. But she is not unmindful of her constitutional duties, to her obligations to the Union, and to her sister States. Up to the verge of constitutional power she will go in maintenance of her cherished convictions; but she has not shrunk, and she does not mean to shrink, from the performance of her obligations as a member of this confederation of constellated States. She has never sought, she does not seek, to encroach by her own acts, or by the action of the Federal Government, upon the constitutional rights of her sister States. Jealous of her own rights, she will respect the rights of others. Claiming the power to control her own domestic policy, she freely accords that power to her sister States. Conceding the rights of others, she demands her own. Loyal to the Union, she demands loyalty in others. Here and now, I demand of her accusers that they file their bill of specifications, and produce the proofs of their allegations, or forever hold their peace."

Thus grandly he speaks of the spirit of the State he represents : —

"In other days, when Adams, Webster, Davis, Everett, Cushing, Choate, Winthrop, Mann, Rantoul, and their associates, graced these chambers, Massachusetts was then, as she is now, the object of animadversion and assault. I have sometimes thought, Mr. President, that these continual assaults upon the Commonwealth of Massachusetts were prompted, not by her faults, but by her virtues rather; not by the sense of justice, but by the spirit of envy and jealousy and uncharitableness. Unawed, however, by censure or menace, she continues to move right on, upward and onward, to the accomplishment of her high destinies. She is but a speck, a mere patch, on the surface of America, hardly more than one four-hundredth part of the territory of the republic, with a rugged soil, and still more rugged clime. But on that little spot of the globe is a Commonwealth where common consent is recognized as the only just basis of fundamental law, and personal freedom is secured in its completest individuality. In that Commonwealth are a million and a quarter of freemen, with skilled hand and cultivated brain ; with nine hundred millions of taxable wealth, and an annual productive industry of three hundred and fifty millions ; with mechanic arts and manufactures on every streamlet, and commerce on the waves of all the seas ; with institutions of moral and mental culture open to all, and art, science, and literature illustrated by glorious names ; with benevolent institutions for the sons and daughters of misfortune and poverty, and charities for humanity the wide world over. The heart, the soul, the reason of Massachusetts send up perpetual aspirations for the unity, indivisibility, and eternity of the North-American republic : but if it shall be rent, torn, dissevered, she will not lose her faith in God and humanity; she will not 'go down with the falling fortunes of her country without making a struggle to preserve and perpetuate free institutions. So long as the ocean shall roll at her feet, so long as God shall send her health-giving breezes and sunshine and rain, she will endeavor to illustrate, in the future as in the past, the daily beauty of freedom secured and protected by law."

On the money question he truly says, —

"But the senator from Texas tells us that money is the sinew of war; that we of the North have no money; that they gather gold in hundreds of millions from the stalk of the cotton-plant. They send the negro, he says, to the field: he gathers cotton from the stalk, brings it to the gin-house, puts it through the necessary process, and rolls out a bale of five ten-dollar gold-pieces. But the senator did not tell us that it might have cost six ten-dollar gold-pieces to get this bale of five ten-dollar gold-pieces. The senator seems to belong to that class of political economists that never count the cost of maintaining 'King Cotton.' I would remind the senator that we of the North take this bale of cotton the negro picks, pay the five ten-dollar gold-pieces, stamp upon it our skill, art, civilization, send it back, and they of the South promise to give five bales of the next crop for it; but I regret to say, sir, we are often forced to take fewer than are promised. I would remind the boastful senator that the people of the cotton confederacy are in debt to the amount of millions; that they are not paying fifty cents on the dollar of their indebtedness; that the proceeds of the last cotton-crop will not extinguish that indebtedness. I would remind the senator, who tells us we of the North have no money, that they pick it by millions from the stalk of the cotton-plant, that the working-men of Massachusetts, whom gentlemen of the South predicted would be in a state of starvation and insurrection ere this, have on deposit, in the savings-banks alone, forty-five millions of dollars, — millions more than are deposited in all the banks of the seven seceding States by merchants, bankers, planters, and all classes of their people."

Of the compromise he remarks, —

"The senator proposes to amend the Constitution so as to provide that 'in all the territory now held or hereafter acquired, situate north of latitude thirty-six degrees and thirty minutes, slavery or involuntary servitude is prohibited; and, in all territory now held or hereafter acquired south of that line of latitude, slavery shall be recognized as existing, and shall be protected by the territorial legislature during its territorial existence.' This, sir, is called a compromise of the slavery question in the Territories of the United States. A compromise! — a compromise of the slavery question in the Territories! It is, sir, a cheat, a delusion, a snare. It is an unqualified concession, a complete surrender of all practical issues concerning slavery in the Territories, to the demands of slave propagandism."

He closes this masterly effort in these comprehensive words: —

"But the senator from Kentucky asks us of the North, by irrepealable constitutional amendments, to recognize and protect slavery in the Territories now existing or hereafter acquired south of thirty-six degrees thirty minutes; to deny power to the Federal Government to abolish slavery in the District of Columbia, in the forts, arsenals, navy-yards, and places under the exclusive jurisdiction of Congress; to deny to the National Government all power to hinder the transit of slaves through one State to another; to take from persons of the African race the elective franchise; and to purchase territory in South America or Africa, and to send them, at the expense of the treasury of the United States, such free negroes as the States may desire removed from their limits. And what does the senator propose to concede to us of the North? The prohibition of slavery in Territories north of thirty-six degrees thirty minutes, where no one asks for its inhibition; where it has been made impossible by the victory of freedom in Kansas and the equalization of the fees of the slave commissioners. And this — this plan of concession — is called a compromise, — the Crittenden Compromise, — to be supported by the representatives of millions of Northern freemen, on pain of having their fidelity to the Union questioned by the senator from Illinois, and his confederates in and out of this chamber.

"Such, Mr. President, are the propositions of the senator from Kentucky, which we of the North are asked to put into the Constitution of the United States beyond the power of the American people ever to change or repeal. The unclouded reason, the enlightened conscience, the love of country and of our race, — all, all, forbid that Northern freemen should commit these crimes against mankind, our country, and the cause of popular freedom and republican institutions. We can not, no, sir, we dare not, do so. We fear — should we consummate these wrongs to our country, to our race — the perpetual reproaches of insulted reason and violated conscience, the irreversible judgment of earth and of heaven. We fear that our names will be enrolled, not with the benefactors of mankind, but with those who have betrayed the cause of the people. We fear — should we assent to this eter-

nization of slavery in the Constitution our fathers framed
to secure the blessings of liberty — that we shall sink, 'after
life's fitful fever,' into dishonored graves, amid the curses
of a betrayed people ; and that our names will be consigned
to what Grattan, the great Irish orator, called 'oppression's
natural scourge, — the moral indignation of history.'"

This speech drew forth expressions of admiration from
all sections of the country, which appeared in the public
journals, or in resolutions, or in private letters. Mr. Whittier the poet wrote as follows : —

AMESBURY, 23d 2d mo., 1861.

MY DEAR WILSON, — I have this moment finished
reading thy admirable and timely speech. It is as I wished
it, — manly, frank, and dignified. Especially I was gratified
by the portion of it directed to Crittenden's plan. The
tribute to the colored citizens is a very noble and eloquent
one, and ought to shame every Massachusetts man whose
name is on the Crittenden petitions.

Very truly thy friend,
JOHN G. WHITTIER.

The gifted Mrs. L. M. Child wrote thus : —

MEDFORD, March 10, 1861.

DEAR AND HONORED REPRESENTATIVE OF THE FREE
OLD COMMONWEALTH, — I have just finished reading
aloud to my husband your speech on Mr. Crittenden's
proposed amendment to the Constitution ; and I cannot
refrain from writing to thank you for it with my whole
heart. Eloquent, able, true, brave words, such as the
times need. I had seen extracts from your speech which
made my heart throb with a generous joy. I was *almost*
afraid to read the entire speech, lest some word, *meant* for

conciliation, but which *would* be compromise, should abate somewhat my exultation in the honest and true expression of Massachusetts feeling ; but, as I proceeded, the reading was only interrupted by exclamations of " Well done, Wilson ! " " That *is* manly ! " " *That's* a good hit ! " &c. You have made many able speeches ; and I have often felt grateful to you for true, manly utterance. In your speech, " Are working-men slaves ? " I greatly admired the dignified frankness with which you announced *yourself* a working-man ; for no feeling in my soul is stronger than respect for labor. The physical courage and moral bravery you manifested on the subject of duelling commanded my unqualified respect. You stood firmly in your position, took back no word you had uttered, but simply said, " Duelling is a *barbarism;* my conscience and reason are opposed to it ; the conscience and reason of my constituents are opposed to it ; and no force of example shall degrade me to its level." That is what I have always *wanted* Northerners to say. If all Northern men would manifest the same moral courage, slaveholders would be compelled to respect freedom of speech, or resort to assassination. They could no longer murder their opponents, or threaten it, under the painted mask of " laws of honor."

But, much as I have admired several of your former speeches, you have never so completely gained my heart as in this last one. I have so often closed the reading of Republican speeches with the remark, " Ah ! they think only of the interests of *white* men : they ignore the monstrous and perpetual wrongs that we are *helping* the South to inflict upon the *colored* race."

Yours with great respect and gratitude,

L. Maria Child.

Hon. H. Wilson, U. S. Senator.

From Gerrit Smith the following letter was received: —

Hon. HENRY WILSON.   PRINCETON, Feb. 26, 1861.

My dear Sir, — I have just finished reading your manly, bold, strong, and eloquent speech of the 21st instant. Heaven bless you for it! Let there be no compromise with men whilst they are in the attitude of rebels. When they shall have returned to their allegiance, then deal with them not only justly, but generously. If *the people* of the slave States — not merely *the politicians* — shall tell us that they wish to leave us, then let them go, if they will go peaceably and decently. But we can never consent to their going in a way that will disgrace us, demoralize and destroy our government. Nor can we consent to a small secession on any terms. We cannot let the Gulf States go unless most of the other slave States go with them. We cannot consent, for the gratification of a few States, to lose the mouth of the Mississippi, and to leave ourselves comparatively defenceless on the south.

Give my love to dear Sumner, and tell him that I hope to read a grand speech from him before the session closes.

With great regard, your friend,

GERRIT SMITH.

Mr. Amasa Walker wrote as follows: —

NORTH BROOKFIELD, March 11, 1861.

DEAR SIR, — I have received your speech on the Crittenden Compromise, and read it with great satisfaction.

You have met the true issue fully and ably, and will receive the approbation of all your constituents, and, I doubt not, of the Republican party generally.

Your friend and servant,

AMASA WALKER.

Hon. HENRY WILSON, U. S. Senator, Washington, D.C.

26

But perhaps, of all the testimonials of gratitude which the senator received for his great speech, none was more acceptable than the following from an association of that race whose wrongs he had been so long struggling to remove : —

At a regular meeting of the Union Progressive Association, — a literary society composed of young colored men, — held at their rooms Feb. 27, the following vote of thanks was unanimously adopted : —

Whereas, The adoption by Congress of that monstrous proposition known as the Crittenden Compromise would extend, perpetuate, and give the sanction of law to that infernal system which keeps four millions of our brethren in bondage, and would deprive us young colored men of Massachusetts of prospective rights, the enjoyment of which we have looked forward to with the most ardent anticipations ; and

Whereas, In this hour of our peril, when there are so few men occupying places of trust who have the moral courage to plead our cause and defend our rights when they are assailed, we should be recreants to our race and to ourselves did we not recognize the value and importance of words spoken in our behalf by our friends at this time : therefore

Resolved, That the grateful thanks of this association are tendered to the honorable senator from Massachusetts, Henry Wilson, for his able analysis and lucid exposition of the enormities of the " Crittenden Surrender," and also for his manly recognition and eloquent enumeration of the services of our patriot fathers in the war for American independence. We shall ever hold his name in grateful remembrance for the noble and generous words uttered on that occasion, worthy as they are of a son of old Massachusetts.

WILLIAM C. NELL, *President.*

R. Z. GREENER, *Secretary.*

To the Honorable Senator from Massachusetts, HENRY WILSON.

BOSTON, Feb. 27, 1861.

CHAPTER XV.

THE inaugural of Mr. Lincoln was conciliatory, but
decided. It echoed the sentiment of the Republican
party, declaring that the Constitution should be faithfully
regarded, and the rights of Southern men respected. It
served, however, but to inflame the animosity of the secessionists; and, on the afternoon of April 12, the fearful
drama opened by the cannonade upon Fort Sumter.
" Those guns proclaim the doom of slavery," said Mr.

Wilson; "but a tremendous conflict is before us." He and Mr. Walbridge of New York advised the president (May 1) to call for three hundred thousand instead of seventy-five thousand men; and, persuading the secretary of war to double the number of men apportioned to the State he represented, he telegraphed immediately to Gov. Andrew, requesting that one brigade be sent at once to Washington. Returning home, he received intelligence that the Sixth Massachusetts Regiment, under Col. Edward F. Jones, had been fired upon while passing through the streets of Baltimore. Spending a sleepless night, he started on the following day for Washington. Learning that communication with that city had been closed, he left New York on April 21, and went by water with the troops to Annapolis. On finding Gen. Butler here in want of cannon to defend the place, he returned immediately to New York, obtained some heavy pieces of artillery, and then, as soon as possible, went to Washington, where he continued laboring day and night in making preparations for the coming conflict. In the hospital, the camp, the cabinet, his cheerful voice was heard encouraging and counselling; and, by his earnest exhortations, many persons in those dark days of doubt and indecision were induced to ignore minor differences, and to stand fast by the Union. As the rebellion strengthened, Mr. Lincoln saw that more efficient measures must be taken to subdue it; and he therefore called an extra session of Congress, which assembled on the fourth day of July, and at once proceeded to important business.

As chairman of the Military Committee of the Senate, Mr. Wilson entered on a course of ceaseless toil and vigilance. It was a post of vast responsibility, demanding clear conception, solid judgment, great executive ability, and a practical knowledge of military affairs. An army was to be raised, equipped, and officered; supplies and hospitals were to be provided, and funds for carrying on the war obtained. It was fortunate that the government found in Mr. Wilson one who, by long experience in legislative and military life, by comprehensive views, by good sound common sense, and by celerity of execution, was qualified to meet the occasion.

With an energy unparalleled in the annals of legislation, he engaged in making preparations for the coming conflict.

On the 6th of July he introduced into the Senate the important bill authorizing the president to call for five hundred thousand volunteers, which on the 21st of that month became a law; also the bill to "increase the military establishment of the United States," which was approved by the president on the 29th of July; and the bill providing for the "better organization of the military establishment." It contained twenty-five sections, and received the signature of the president on the third day of August. .

Of the last bill Mr. Wilson said, "I have labored night and day for many days and nights to fit and prepare this bill to meet the actual wants of the country; and, in doing so, I confess that in every step of it I have had to meet the interests, the jealousies, or the prejudices of men connected with the army of the United States: but, in framing it, I have endeavored to be governed wholly by the public interest."

On the 22d of July he introduced the bill authorizing the president "to accept of the services of volunteers, either as cavalry, infantry, or artillery, in such numbers as the exigencies of the public service might in his opinion demand." This bill became a law on the 26th of the same month. On the 29th be brought forward a bill to provide for the purchase of arms, ordnance, and ordnance-stores, which was approved by the president on the third day of August; and on the last day of July he presented the bill for the appointment of additional aides-de-camp, which was enacted on the 5th of August. By a provision of this act, the barbarous custom of flogging was abolished in the army. On the first day of August he introduced the bill for making an appropriation of a hundred thousand dollars for contingencies for fortifications, and on the next day the "bill to authorize an increase in the corps of engineers and topographical engineers."

On the 5th of the same month he introduced an important bill to increase the pay of privates in the army from eleven to thirteen dollars per month; also to extend the provisions of the act "for the relief of the Ohio volunteers and other volunteers" to all volunteers, no matter for what term of service they might have been accepted. He also added an amendment to the bill, that all the acts, proclamations, and orders of the president after the 4th of March, 1861, respecting the army and navy, be legalized and made valid. This received the approval of Mr. Lincoln on the 6th of August.

To frame, explain, and defend these various bills, which called into being, organized, and provisioned a vast army, demanded an extent of information, a constructive ability, and a rapidity of execution, such as but few law-makers possess. In view of these herculean labors, Gen. Scott remarked that "Senator Wilson had done more work in that short session than all the chairmen of the military committees had done for the last twenty years." He afterwards addressed to him the following note of thanks:—

WASHINGTON, Aug. 10, 1861.

DEAR SIR, — In taking leave of you some days ago, I fear that I did not so emphatically express my thanks to you, as our late chairman of the Senate Committee, as my feelings and those of my brother-officers of the army (with whom I have conversed) warranted, for your able and zealous efforts to give to the service the fullest war development and efficiency. It is pleasing to remember the pains you took to obtain accurate information, wherever it could be found, as a basis for wise legislation; and we hope it may be long before the army loses your valuable services in the same capacity.

With great esteem,

Yours very truly,

WINFIELD SCOTT.

Hon. H. WILSON, Chairman Senate Military Committee.

Such strenuous action for the soldier in the Senate-chamber, camp, and hospital, such cordial sympathy with him in his toils and sufferings, gained for Mr. Wilson the enviable name of "THE SOLDIER'S FRIEND."

Mr. Wilson was personally present at the disastrous battle of Bull Run, July 21, aiding and encouraging officers and privates as he had opportunity. Attempts were made by the confederates to secure his person; but he returned to Washington in safety. Undismayed by the repulse, he said to one of his friends on Monday following, "This is our chastisement for fighting on the sabbath. But we are right in principle: God is on the side of right; and we shall win if we obey him. We want more men; we must go to work for them; and, just as soon as possible, I intend to raise a regiment in Massachusetts."

On the adjournment of Congress, the president was desirous that Mr. Wilson should be appointed brigadier-general of volunteers; but, as this would compel the resignation of his seat as senator, he preferred to carry out his original design of raising a regiment of men at home. Obtaining authority for this, he returned to Massachusetts, issued an address, held an enthusiastic meeting in Faneuil Hall, and commenced recruiting. Such was his popularity, that, in the space of forty days, he raised nearly two thousand three hundred men. They were strong, intelligent farmers, mechanics, and tradesmen, from the good families of the Commonwealth. Out of them were formed the Twenty-second Regiment, a part of the Twenty-third Regiment, one company of sharpshooters, and two batteries of artillery. The first company went into camp at Lynnfield on the second day of September; and on that day Mr. Wilson received his commission from the governor as colonel, with the distinct understanding, however, that his senatorial duties would permit him to remain with the regiment only for a brief period; and that he would, on leaving it, endeavor to find some able commander to assume his place. On the eighth day of October, the regiment, with full ranks, and armed with Enfield rifles, together with the company of sharpshooters and the third battery of light artillery, left for Washington. Previous to his departure, Mr. Wilson received as a present from some friends a fine Morgan horse, with saddle and housings, as a testimonial of their confidence and regard; and a splendid flag was presented by Robert C. Winthrop to the regiment on Boston Common. On their way to Washington, these troops were most enthusiastically greeted by the people. In New York a banquet was prepared for them, attended by eminent men of every party. A beautiful flag was presented to the regiment by the late distinguished lawyer, James T. Brady. They arrived at Washington on the eleventh day of October; and two days later, crossing the Potomac, went into camp with Gen. Martindale's brigade in Fitz-John Porter's division at Hall's Hill in Virginia. His duties in connection with the Senate rendered it necessary for Mr. Wilson to leave his fine regiment: and he therefore gave up his commission on the 28th of October; and the accomplished Jesse D. Gove (killed June 27, 1862, at Gaines's Mills, Va.) was appointed to fill the vacancy.

When the regiment, after the unfortunate battle of Ball's Bluff, Oct. 29, was expected to advance to an engagement with the enemy, Mr. Wilson offered to share the danger; but, as circumstances changed, his personal presence was not demanded.

This regiment, and especially the third battery under the command of the able and heroic Augustus P. Martin, performed effective service in many warm engagements during the Rebellion. "The valuable and efficient service you have rendered your country," said Gen. Charles Griffin in a letter to the commander of the regiment at the expiration of its term of service in October, 1864, "during the past three years of its eventful history, is deserving of its gratitude and praise."

Mr. Wilson always took the liveliest interest in this regiment, and provided for the intellectual and moral advancement, as well as for the personal comforts, of the men; for he believed that "bayonets which think fight best." The manner in which its officers and men regarded him may be seen from the following letter, dated —

HALL'S HILL, VA., Oct. 21, 1861.

MY DEAR SIR, — I know not what I am going to write : but I know what is in my heart; and that is, a deep respect and affection for yourself.

My father died more than four years since ; and I have not met, until I knew you, one whom I could look up to with that mingled respect and affection which is due to a father. You have chidden only when it was for our good, and have exhibited a kindness and benevolence of heart which no man shall ever dare to deny to you before me.

Be assured, sir, that I fully appreciate your acts of kindness to me; and they have been many, — so many, indeed, that I have come slowly to the conclusion that a man may, even in these days, occupy a high position without abandoning his good qualities. May God prosper you in your labors for our beloved country ! I tremble when I think what power is in your hands to do our country good or evil, and only pray that you may never be swerved from that bright pathway along which you are now journeying. WM. S. TILTON.

On resigning his position as colonel of the Twenty-second Regiment, Mr. Wilson, by the pressing invitation of the secretary of war, took position for a brief period as an aide-de-camp on Gen. McClellan's staff, in order that he might, by practical observation of the condition of the army, increase its power and efficiency by his labors in the legislative hall. The organization of fresh forces on so vast a scale demanded practical knowledge of the art of war ; and the best place to obtain it was at head-quarters on the field. But senatorial duties soon compelled him to return to Washington ; and, in the letter accepting his resignation as an aide-de-camp, Gen. Williams said, " The reasons assigned in your letter (Jan. 9) are such, that the general is not permitted any other course than that of directing the acceptance of your resignation. He wishes me to add that it is with regret that he sees the termination of the pleasant official relations which have existed between you and himself, and that he yields with reluctance to the necessity created by the pressure upon you of other and more important public duties."

He cheerfully bore his own expenses while raising his regiment, and received no pay whatever for his services as colonel or as Gen. McClellan's aide-de-camp.

To the infamous charge of W. H. Russell of " The London Times," that Senator Wilson was interested in large shoe contracts, and had taken better care of himself and his fortunes than of a suffering nation, he made the following distinct and unequivocal reply : —

"NATICK, Nov. 9, 1861.

" To the Editor of ' THE BOSTON JOURNAL:'—

" I ask you, and other conductors of public journals in Massachusetts willing to do me a personal favor, to publish this explicit denial of the truthfulness of the story some person or persons have invented and put in circulation, that I have a government contract for a million pairs of shoes, by which I am to realize the sum of a quarter of a million of dollars. This story, in all its parts and in every form, is utterly false ; and the person or persons originating it knew it to be a false and wicked slander. I have no contract, I have had no contract, with the government, either directly or indirectly, for shoes, or for any thing else ; nor have I now, nor have I had, any interest in any contract of any person whatever with the government. I not only .have no contract with the government, nor interest in the contracts of others, but no man now has, nor has had, any contract with the government through any agency or influence of mine. The government, since the 4th of March, has made no contract with any man, for any purpose whatever, through any agency or influence of mine; and it never will make contracts through any agency or influence of mine. As a senator of Massachusetts, mindful of her interests, I have sometimes reminded the department of the manufacturing and mechanical skill of her people; of their losses by this wicked Rebellion; of their readiness to furnish men and money to sustain the national cause; of their capacity to furnish the army, at the lowest rates, needed articles: and I have expressed the hope that the agents of the government, in their purchases, would not forget the people of my State. This much I have said; this much I felt I had a right to say; and this much I felt it my duty to say. But to all men, who have asked me by word or letter to aid them in obtaining contracts of the government, I have said that my sense of propriety would not permit me to have any thing to do with contracts; that I could not, in any way, aid in procuring contracts; that no man ever had, or ever would have, contracts through my agency or influence. This has been, now is, and will ever be, my position."

While many men in power most shamefully enriched themselves and families by "the spoils of war," the record of Henry Wilson is absolutely clean and clear. "I am not worth enough," said he in one of his addresses, "to buy a pine coffin for my burial." Immaculate as an old Roman patriot, he stands unscathed by any charge of bribery, venality, or corruption.

Eleven States were now in open rebellion against the government. A Southern confederacy had been formed, with Jefferson Davis at the head; many forts and arsenals had been seized, and a vast confederate army was in the field. Old landmarks had been broken down, and a new order of things had begun. Four million slaves were panting to be free. The capital of the nation had become a camping-ground, and open war was the order of the day.

It was forced upon the government: the South must take the consequences. The president had, on the sixteenth day of August, declared a state of insurrection; and the leading questions were, " How shall the Union be preserved? " " How increase and officer, and impart efficiency to, the army? " " What shall be done with slaves and rebel property? " " How, at the least expense of blood, crush the Rebellion? "

Rapid, efficient, and decisive legislation was demanded for the exigency; and it was fortunate for the country that strong men were in the halls of Congress. For the most part they were true reformers, educated in the school of freedom, and prepared for the tremendous issue. Among them Henry Wilson stood prominent. He had studied America, her spirit and her institutions; he saw distinctly where the merit of the question lay; and, though he shuddered at the sacrifice, he felt certain of the ultimate result.

Entering with indomitable industry upon business at the second session of the Thirty-seventh Congress, he introduced, and carried to enactment, many bills and resolutions which had an immediate bearing on the efficiency of the army and the government. Among the more important measures was a bill providing for the appointment of persons to procure from volunteers their respective allotments of pay for their families, which was enacted Dec. 24, 1861; a bill regulating courts-martial in the army; "a bill to provide for the better organization of the signal department of the army," approved on the twenty-second day of February, 1862.; a bill for the "appointment of sutlers in the volunteer service;" a bill "to increase the efficiency of the medical department of the army;" a bill to facilitate the discharge of enlisted men for physical disability; a joint resolution providing for "the presentation of medals of honor to the enlisted men of the army and volunteer forces who may distinguish themselves in battle;" a bill, introduced on the eighth day of July, "to amend the act calling forth the militia to execute the laws, suppress insurrections, and repel invasions," which became a law on the 17th of July, 1862.

By this important act the president is authorized to receive persons of African descent for any military service for which they are competent; and all Africans rendering such service shall be free. This act authorized, for the first time, the drafting of negroes, and their regular introduction as soldiers into the service of the United States.

Mr. Wilson also, on the 23d of December, introduced the bill into the Senate, dismissing from the service officers guilty of surrendering fugitive slaves to their masters. After much discussion, it became a law March 13, 1862.

It was framed to protect those slaves, who, as our armies advanced into the rebel States, fled to them for refuge, and who offered, in the words of Mr. Wilson, "to work and fight for the flag whose stars for the first time gleamed upon their vision with the radiance of liberty."

On resigning his office as secretary of war during this session, Mr. Cameron addressed to him the following letter : —

WASHINGTON, Jan. 27, 1862.

MY DEAR SIR, — No man, in my opinion, in the whole country, has done more to aid the war department is preparing the mighty army now under arms than yourself; and, before leaving this city, I think it my duty to offer to you my sincere thanks as its late head.

As chairman of the Military Committee of the Senate, your services were invaluable. *At the first call for troops, you came here; and up to the meeting of Congress, a period of more than six months, your labors were incessant. Sometimes in encouraging the administration by assurances of support from Congress, by encouraging volunteering in your own State, by raising a regiment yourself when other men began to fear that compulsory drafts might be necessary, and in the Senate by preparing the bills, and assisting to get the necessary appropriations, for organizing, clothing, arming, and supplying the army, you have been constantly and profitably employed in the great cause of putting down the unnatural Rebellion.

For the many personal favors you have done me since the beginning of this struggle I shall ever be grateful.

Your friend truly,

SIMON CAMERON.

Hon. HENRY WILSON.

On the 16th of December, 1861, he introduced a bill "for the release of certain persons held to service or labor [that is, for the abolition of slavery] in the District of Columbia." "If it shall become a law of the land," said Mr. Wilson, "it will blot out slavery forever from the national capital, transform three thousand personal chattels into freemen, obliterate oppressive, odious, and hateful laws and ordinances which press with merciless force upon persons, bond or free, of African descent, and relieve the nation from the responsibilities now pressing upon it. An act of beneficence like this will be hailed and applauded by the nations, sanctified by justice, humanity, and religion, by the approving voice of conscience, and by the blessing of Him who bids us "break every yoke, undo the heavy burden, and let the oppressed go free."

This bill met with bitter opposition from the secession element in Congress, but was finally passed; and the president gave it his approval on the sixteenth day of April, 1862. The freedmen then assembled in their churches, and offered thanks to God for their deliverance.

In the enactment of this law Mr. Wilson saw the realization of those hopes which he had expressed in his first public speech, made a full quarter of a century before, in Strafford (N. H.) Academy. He surely had been led in a way he knew not to the accomplishment of a part in rending the chain of the bondman, for which his name will ever be held by the friends of freedom in grateful remembrance.

The following letters from two eminent philanthropists express the general sentiment of the North in respect to Mr. Wilson's course: —

NEW YORK, April 28, 1862.

Hon. HENRY WILSON, Senator in Congress from Massachusetts.

My dear Sir, — I have to day read your speech of March 27, "On the Bill to abolish Slavery in the District of Columbia," for the second time, and must drop you a line to say that it deserves to be written in letters of gold, and be put into the hands of every citizen of the United States. To you, especially, is the country indebted for the passage of this bill. May the country ever be grateful! and may the blessing of the God of the oppressed rest upon you! As a native of Massachusetts, and the son of a Massachusetts mechanic, I feel thankful that one of her senators has, under the divine blessing, accomplished such a humane deed.

Although it will at all times give me pleasure to hear from you, I do not expect, that, amidst your arduous labors, you can acknowledge the receipt of the many letters addressed to you. My object is not now, more than heretofore, to draw from you a response, but to assure you of the very grateful sense I have of your successful services in the case to which I have alluded, and of the eminent services rendered to your country throughout your whole senatorial career.

Respectfully and truly yours,
LEWIS TAPPAN.

THE JAY HOMESTEAD, KATOUCH,
N.Y., April 17, 1862.

MY DEAR GEN. WILSON, — I must thank you, and congratulate you that our National Government sits, at last, in a free capital. Your part in the accomplishment of this great triumph of national justice and national dignity will be long remembered by a grateful people ; and, if you had not done so much else for the country, you might safely rest your historic fame on that single act and your sturdy efforts to crown it with success.

For myself, I can hardly recall without emotion my boyish efforts to arouse attention to the atrocity of slavery in Washington, commenced nearly thirty years ago, and those of my father, which I find, from one of his petitions, commenced in 1826, as I read the record of the vote in the House, and the president's message, and thank God that the work of abolition has begun, and the first great step boldly taken towards the position of a free republic.

I trust the good work will be pushed speedily.   Slavery is doomed ; and it is worse than useless to prolong the agony of dissolution.

Always faithfully yours,

JOHN JAY.

CHAPTER XVI.

THE REBELLION. — SENATORIAL LABORS. — SPEECH IN
PHILADELPHIA, 1863. — DEATH OF SLAVERY THE
LIFE OF THE NATION. — HIS PERSISTENT
EFFORTS TO CARRY ON THE WAR.

The Conflicting Powers. — The Army and Congress. — Position of Mr. Wilson.
— Bill for Sutlers. — Signal Service. — Pay to Officers. — Medical Department. — Volunteers. — Seniority of Commanders. — Storekeepers. — District
of Columbia. — Medals. — Pay in Advance. — Abolition in District of Co-
lumbia. — The Confederates. — Militia Bill. — President's Proclamation. —
Rosecrans. — Bureau of Emancipation. — Enrolment Bill. — Remarks. —
Colored Youth. — Wounded Soldiers. — Corps of Engineers. — Letter of Dr.
Silas Reed. — Fall of Vicksburg. — Conference with the Cabinet. — Battle
of Gettysburg. — Gen. Grant. — Address before the Antislavery Society. —
Thanks to the Army. — Bounties. — Ambulances. — Colored Soldiers Free.
— Thirteenth Amendment. — Speech. — Appropriation Bill. — Wives and
Children of Colored Soldiers Free. — Fourth of July at Washington. — Gen.
Grant. — "New-Bedford Mercury." — A Letter.

AT the commencement of the year 1862 the Union
was coming slowly and steadily up to bear the tremendous strain of the Rebellion; and the moral grandeur
of the scene has never been surpassed in any crisis of a
distracted nation. On the one hand were dissolution and
anarchy; on the other hand, the Constitution and the liberation of the slave. The destinies of unborn millions
were in the conflict. Will the government meet the exigency? Yes; for, while our loyal soldiers were bravely

320

gathering to roll back the tide of war upon the field, our loyal Congress-men were as bravely toiling to sustain them, and to break the chains of servitude in the halls of legislation. Here, indeed, the battles are really fought. The army is but an exponent of power: the power itself is in the principles that move the army; and these are settled by the action of the people's representatives. As one of those noble men whose doings will render the Thirty-seventh and Thirty-eighth Congresses ever memorable, Mr. Wilson exhibited clear-sightedness which no intricacies could baffle, hope which no disasters could repress, courage which no danger could appall, and patriotism which no bribe could bend.

In the full confidence of the government, he gave his whole energies of heart and hand to its support, and still brought forward measure after measure for the prosecution of the war, and for the overthrow of a system, which, recognizing the right of property in man, had caused the war. But little more than a bare enumeration of the measures which he introduced can here be given.

On the 2d of January, 1862, he presented the bill appointing sutlers and defining their duties in the volunteer service; which, after several amendments, became a law on the 19th of the following March. On the 9th of January he introduced a bill for the better organization of the signal department of the army, which was approved on the 22d day of February; and on the 28th of January a bill to define the pay and emoluments of certain officers of the army, and for other purposes, which, after a long discussion, became a law on the 17th of July, 1862. On the 7th of February he brought forward a bill to increase the efficiency of the medical department of the army, which, after several amendments, became a law on the sixteenth day of April, 1862. A joint resolution for the payment of the moneys of any State to its volunteers was introduced by him on the 11th of March, and became a law on the nineteenth day of April following ; and also another, on the 14th of March, assigning command in the same field or department to officers of the same grade without regard to seniority, which was enacted on the 4th of April, 1862. On the 7th of May his bill for the appointment of medical storekeepers was brought forward, and approved by the president on the 20th of the same month. Ever anxious for the improvement of the colored people in the District of Columbia, Mr. Wilson, on the 8th of May, moved, as an amendment to Mr. Grimes's educational bill, that all persons of color in that District shall be amenable to the same laws, and tried in the same manner, as the free white people, which received the approval of the president on the eleventh day of July, 1862 ; and thus the "black code" was abolished forever in the national capital. Ever mindful of the services of the soldier, he reported, on the thirteenth day of May, a joint resolution for the preparation of two thousand medals of honor, "with suitable devices, to be presented to such non-commissioned officers and privates as should distinguish themselves by gallantry in action and other soldier-like qualities ;" and this became a law on the twelfth day of July, 1862. For the further encouragement of enlistments, he introduced a joint resolution on the 4th of June (enacted on the 21st of the same month), that the soldier who enlisted might receive one month's wages in advance ; and on the 12th of June he brought forward an additional bill for the abolition of slavery in the District of Columbia, which, after being amended, received the signature of Mr. Lincoln on the twelfth day of July, 1862.

The activity of the rebels in Tennessee, the retreat of

Gen. Banks upon the Potomac, and the indecisive battles of Gen. McClellan in front of Richmond, all conspired to dishearten loyal men, and to fill the government with gloomy apprehensions. Mr. Wilson urged upon the Senate prompt and decided action. Of the confederates he said, " They have appealed to their people, — to their passions, to their prejudices, to their hate; they have organized their people; they have issued their conscriptions, using every man who could do any thing, — no matter how halt or maimed he might be, if he could strike a blow; they have carried on their military operations with great administration and military ability. We are in one of the darkest periods of the contest; and we had better look our position in the face, meet the responsibilities of the hour, rise to the demands of the occasion, pour out our money, summon our men to the field, go ourselves if we can do any good, and overthrow this confederate power, that feels to-day, over the recent magnificent triumphs, that it has already achieved its independence. Bold and decisive action alone in the cabinet and in the field can retrieve our adverse fortunes, and carry our country triumphantly through the perils that threaten to dismember the republic."

Actuated by such sentiments, he introduced on the twelfth day of July his effective bill into the Senate, authorizing the president to call forth the militia of the country; enrolling all able-bodied men between the ages of eighteen and forty-five years; to accept a hundred thousand volunteers as infantry for nine months, and volunteers for twelve months, with fifty dollars bounty; to fill up the old regiments: also to establish army corps, and to receive into the army persons of African descent to perform any service for which they may be competent; and providing that persons performing such service shall be forever free, and also the mothers, wives, and children of such persons as may be owing service to any men engaged in the Rebellion. This important measure, after strenuous opposition by Messrs. Davis of Kentucky, Saulsbury, Powell, and others, was enacted July 17, 1862, and was another heavy blow to that institution which had brought the country into such a bloody contest.

But why stop with the emancipation of the colored soldiers in the army? Are not three millions longing to be free? Will not the strength of the confederates be lessened by their manumission? Will not such an act serve to harmonize the feelings of the North? Has not the South, by its revolt, invited it? The president saw the situation, and the readiness of Congress and the army to sustain him, and on the first day of January, 1863, sent forth his glorious proclamation, which declared " forever free " the slaves in the Confederate States. Of the representatives at Washington, none hailed that grand announcement with more joy than Henry Wilson: none had labored for it more persistently; none saw with clearer vision the encouraging effect it would produce upon the spirit of the people, and the aid which it would render in the prosecution of the war.

At the commencement of the year (1863) the hopes of the Union men were brightened by the victory of Gen. Rosecrans over the rebel forces under Gen. Bragg at Murfreesborough, Tenn.; and on the 8th of January Mr. Wilson introduced a resolution tendering thanks to the general and his army for their distinguished gallantry in that action, and it received the signature of the president on the third day of the following March. On the twelfth day of January he presented in the Senate a memorial of the Emancipation League of his State for a bureau of emancipation, and entered into the discussions upon this philanthropic measure, which was to aid, protect, and elevate " the children of the government."

To bring up the power of the republic to meet the exigencies of the war, Mr. Wilson, on the ninth day of February, introduced his great bill for enrolling and calling out the national forces, and for other purposes. It consisted of thirty-six sections, the first of which declared that " all able-bodied male citizens in the United States (with certain exceptions) between the ages of eighteen and forty-five shall constitute the national forces, and be liable to military duty at the call of the president." By the eighteenth section, a bounty of fifty dollars was given to present volunteers who re-enlist for one year. This important measure was framed with great administrative ability; and, in defence of it, Mr. Wilson said, " I am confident the enactment of this bill, embodying so many provisions required by the exigencies of the public service, will weapon the hands of the nation, fire the drooping hearts of the people, thrill the wasting ranks of our legions in the field, carry dismay into the councils of treason, and give assurance to the nations that the American people have the sublime virtue of heroic constancy and endurance that will assure the unity and indivisibility of the republic of the United States. We have endeavored to frame this bill so as to bear as lightly as possible upon the toiling masses, and to put the burdens, so far as we could do so, equally upon the more favored sons of men."

On a motion of Mr. Cowan of Pennsylvania to exempt members of Congress from the law, he said, " Its adoption would weaken the moral force of the law. He wanted every one to feel that this measure was a necessity forced upon us by the needs of the country; that to be drafted to carry this country through the impending struggle was the most honorable thing that can fall upon an American citizen : " and the motion was not carried. After several amendments, this great measure was approved by the president on the third day of March; and the army was thus brought into order for the reception of the confederate forces on the field of Gettysburg in July following.

On the 17th of February he brought forward the bill to incorporate " the institution for the education of the colored youth " in the District of Columbia, which was approved by the president on the 3d of March; and on the 10th of February a bill to increase the number of major and brigadier generals in the army, which became a law on the second day of March. His resolution " to facilitate the payment of sick and wounded soldiers," and also his bill to promote the efficiency of the corps of engineers and of the ordnance department, and for other purposes, were approved by the president on the third day of March, 1863.

At this period, Mr. Wilson, following up the proclamation of the president, entered warmly into the senatorial debates on the question of rendering aid to Missouri and other semi-loyal States for the liberation of their slaves. In response to Mr. Henderson of Missouri, he said, " Let us stamp upon her now war-desolated fields the words, ' Immediate emancipation;' and these blighted fields will bloom again, and law and order and peace again will bless the dwellings of her people."

The following letter from a prominent citizen of that State will indicate how his services were there regarded: —

UNITED-STATES GENERAL HOSPITAL,
JEFFERSON BARRACKS, Mo., Feb. 24, 1863.

Hon. H. WILSON, U. S. Senate.

Sir, — Excuse the liberty I take in expressing my gratification at the manner in which you treat the *traitors* in the Senate.

I have also to thank you from the bottom of my heart for the interest and zeal you have manifested in securing compensated emancipation for Missouri.

With this measure successful, this State, in a year or two, might almost thank the rebels for their efforts to ruin us ; but without it we must sink almost as low as Virginia in financial woe and general desolation.

All good men in Missouri pray daily that Congress may see the wisdom of perfecting this aid to loyal slave-owners of the State. It is not material, perhaps, what sum Congress appropriates, if the maximum be three hundred dollars for the best slaves, and graduated in proportion for females, children, and aged persons.

I feel the utmost confidence that it will not take ten million dollars to pay all *loyal* owners, if three hundred dollars is the highest price to be paid, and a proportionate price for the young, aged, and all other classes. I know of no slave in Missouri now that would command at private sale three hundred dollars, unless the purchaser were misled by an impression that he might obtain more by virtue of the proposed act of Congress.

Emancipation in Missouri would soon make it one of the greatest States in the Union, and the disinthralment of her antislavery population would enable us to show the traitors in the old free States whether New England is ever to be severed from the States of the West. Congress is on the right war-path this winter ; and *God be praised* for the bright prospect of soon crushing out the life of the Rebellion.

I am, dear sir, very truly,

Your obedient servant,

SILAS REED, M.D.

During the recess of Congress, Mr. Wilson labored with ceaseless activity to sustain the administration in the prosecution of the war. Moving from point to point, he was now assisting the Sanitary Commission, now writing letters to the soldiers, now examining the claims of rival officers to promotion, now suggesting more vigorous measures to the cabinet, now urging moneyed men to aid the government, and now addressing vast audiences in support of the Union cause. In the great rejoicings at Washington, July 7, on the surrender of Vicksburg, he participated, and addressed a vast multitude in front of the presidential mansion. On the same day, with Senators Fessenden and Morrill, he had a conference with the cabinet, which resulted in the ordering of five vessels to protect the seaboard from Nantucket to the British Provinces.

Mr. Wilson also shared with the administration in the profound anxiety for the issue of the bloody conflict at Gettysburg (July 1, 2, and 3), and put forth his best efforts to assuage the sufferings of wounded soldiers.

The delay of Gen. Meade in following up his victory led the government soon to turn attention to the victorious GRANT as the man to lead the army on to Richmond; and Mr. Wilson urged his nomination as commander.

On his way to resume his seat in Congress in December, on the 9th of July, he took part in the celebration of the thirtieth anniversary of the American Antislavery Society.

and made an address remarkable for its earnestness and vigor. Contrasting the antislavery cause at the institution of the society with what it was in the closing month of 1863, he eloquently said, —

"Then a few unknown and nameless men were its apostles : now the most accomplished intellects in America are its champions. Then a few proscribed and hunted followers rallied around its banners : now it has laid its grasp upon the conscience of the nation, and millions rally around the folds of its flag. Then not a statesman in America accepted its doctrines, or advocated its measures : now it controls more than twenty States, has a majority in both Houses of Congress, and the chief magistrate of the republic decrees the emancipation of three millions of men. (Applause.) Then every free State was against it : now West Virginia, Delaware, Maryland, and Missouri pronounce for the emancipation of their bondmen. Then the public press covered it with ridicule and contempt : now the most powerful journals in America are its organs, scattering its truths broadcast over all the land. Then the religious, benevolent, and literary institutions of the land rebuked its doctrines, and proscribed its advocates : now it shapes, moulds, and fashions them at its pleasure. Then political organizations trampled disdainfully upon it : now it looks down in the pride of conscious power upon the wrecked political fragments that float at its feet. Then it was impotent and powerless : now it holds public men and political organizations in the hollow of its hand. (Applause.) Then the public voice sneered at and defied it : now it is master of America, and has only to be true to itself to bury slavery so deep that the hand of no returning despotism can reach it. (Great applause.)

"The way to triumph," he continued, "is to assume

that the proclamation of Abraham Lincoln, emancipating three million three hundred thousand slaves in the ten rebel States, is the irrepealable law of this land; that this Christian nation is pledged to every slave, to the country, to the world, and to Almighty God, to see that every one of these bondmen is free forever and forevermore. (Great applause.) Let the loyal men of America assume, as the eternal law of the land, that slavery does not now exist in the disloyal States; that every black man there is free; that the President of the United States has pledged the physical power of all America to enforce the proclamation of freedom; that seven hundred thousand loyal bayonets bear that proclamation upon their glittering points." (Applause.)

He thus referred to Gen. Grant: —

"Sir, I saw the other day a letter from Gen. Grant, who has fought so many battles for the republic, and won them all (enthusiastic applause), — the hero who hurled his legions up the mountains before Chattanooga, and fought a battle for the Union above the clouds. (Applause.) The hero of Vicksburg says, 'I have never been an anti-slavery man; but I try to judge justly of what I see. I made up my mind when this war commenced that the North and South could only live together in peace as one nation, and they could only be one nation by being a free nation. (Applause.) Slavery, the corner-stone of the so-called confederacy, is knocked out; and it will take more men to keep black men slaves than to put down the Rebellion. Much as I desire peace, I am opposed to any peace until this question of slavery is forever settled.' That is the position of the leading general of our armies. . . .

"The crimes of two centuries have brought this terrible

war upon us; but if this generation, upon whom God has laid his chastisements, will yet be true to liberty and humanity, peace will return again to bless this land now rent and torn by civil strife. Then we shall heal the wounds of war, enlighten the dark intellect of the emancipated bondman, and make our country the model republic, to which the Christian world shall turn with respect and admiration."

"The speaker retired," says "The Chronicle," "amid the deafening plaudits of the audience."

In the Senate, on the 14th of December, Mr. Wilson introduced resolutions expressing the thanks of Congress to Gens. Hooker, Meade, Howard, and Banks, their officers and men, for gallantry at Gettysburg and Port Hudson; which received the signature of the president. He also introduced at the same time a bill " to increase the bounty to volunteers, and the pay of the army; " and also, on the 23d of the same month, the bill "to establish a uniform system of ambulances in the United States," which was indorsed by eminent generals, commanders in the army, and became a law on the 11th of March, 1864.

Among the numerous measures introduced by Mr. Wilson into Congress in 1864, we may cite as of great importance an amendment in the bill enacted on the 24th of February, declaring that every colored soldier, on being mustered into the service, should, not by the act of his master, but by the authority of government, be made forever free. By this provision, more than twenty thousand slaves in Kentucky alone received their freedom.

In the exciting debates on the Thirteenth Amendment of the Constitution, the first article of which is, " Neither slavery nor involuntary servitude, except as a punishment for crime whereof the party shall have been duly con-

victed, shall exist within the United States, or any place
subject to their jurisdiction," Mr. Wilson most earnestly
engaged. His speech in the Senate on the 28th of March
has in it the ring of a clarion. In some respects, it is a
master-piece of eloquence. Intensely earnest, fervid, fearless, it grasps the question with Websterian vigor, and
strikes the fated institution with gigantic blows. The
speech, as circulated, has for its significant title, " THE
DEATH OF SLAVERY IS THE LIFE OF THE NATION ; " and
this the nation now believes. It closes with these grandly-
impressive words : —

" But, sir, the crowning act in this series of acts for the
restriction and extinction of slavery in America is this
proposed amendment to the Constitution, prohibiting the
existence of slavery forevermore in the republic of the
United States. If this amendment shall be incorporated
by the will of the nation into the Constitution of the
United States, it will obliterate the last lingering vestiges
of the slave system — its chattelizing, degrading, and
bloody codes ; its dark, malignant, barbarizing spirit ; all
it was and is ; every thing connected with it or pertaining
to it — from the face of the nation it has scarred with moral
desolation, from the bosom of the country it has reddened
with the blood and strewn with the graves of patriotism.
The incorporation of this amendment into the organic law
of the nation will make impossible forevermore the re-
appearing of the discarded slave system, and the returning
of the despotism of the slave-masters' domination.

" Then, sir, when this amendment to the Constitution
shall be consummated, the shackle will fall from the limbs
of the harmless bondmen, and the lash drop from the
weary hand of the taskmaster. Then the sharp cry of
the agonizing hearts of severed families will cease to vex

the weary ear of the nation, and to pierce the ear of Him whose judgments are now avenging the wrongs of centuries. Then the slave-mart, pen, and auction-block, with their clanking fetters for human limbs, will disappear from the land they have brutalized, and the schoolhouse will raise to enlighten the darkened intellect of a race imbruted by long years of enforced ignorance. Then the sacred rights of human nature, the hallowed family relations of husband and wife, parent and child, will be protected by the guardian spirit of that law which makes sacred alike the proud homes and lowly cabins of freedom. Then the scarred earth, blighted by the sweat and tears of bondage, will bloom again under the quickening culture of rewarded toil. Then the wronged victim of the slave system, the poor white man, the sand-hiller, the clay-eater, of the wasted fields of Carolina, impoverished, debased, dishonored by the system that makes toil a badge of disgrace, and the instruction of the brain and soul of man a crime, will lift his abashed forehead to the skies, and begin to run the race of improvement, progress, and elevation. Then the nation, 'regenerated and disinthralled by the genius of universal emancipation,' will run the career of development, power, and glory, quickened, animated, and guided by the spirit of the Christian democracy that ' pulls not the highest down, but lifts the lowest up.'

" Our country is now floating on the stormy waves of civil war. Darkness lowers, and tempests threaten. The waves are rising and foaming and breaking around us and over us with ingulfing fury; but, amid the thick gloom, the star of duty casts its clear radiance over the dark and troubled waters, making luminous our pathway. Our duty is as plain to the clear vision of intelligent patriotism as though it were written in letters of light on the bending arches of the skies. That duty is, with every conception of the brain, every throb of the heart, every aspiration of the soul, by thought, by word, and by deed, to feel, to think, to speak, to act, so as to obliterate the last vestiges of slavery in America, subjugate rebel slave-masters to the authority of the nation, hold up the weary arm of our struggling government, crowd with heroic manhood the ranks of our armies that are bearing the destinies of the country on the points of their glittering bayonets, and thus forever blast the last hope of the rebel chiefs. Then the waning star of the Rebellion will go down in eternal night, and the star of peace ascend the heavens, casting its mild radiance over fields now darkened by the storms of this fratricidal war. Then, when 'the war-drums throb no longer, and the battle-flags are furled,' our absent sons, with the laurels of victory on their brows, will come back to gladden our households and fill the vacant chairs around our hearthstones. Then the stars of united America, now obscured, will re-appear, radiant with splendor, on the forehead of the skies, to illume the pathway and gladden the heart of struggling humanity."

Ever intent on justice, and earnest for equal rights, Mr. Wilson succeeded in introducing into the appropriation bill enacted on the fifteenth day of June, 1864, a provision to the effect that "all persons of color who had been or might be mustered into the military service should receive the same uniform, clothing, rations, medical and hospital attendance, and pay," as other soldiers, from the beginning of 1864. He fought persistently to obtain justice for the colored troops of Massachusetts; and finally succeeded, in face of stanch opposition, in carry-

ing through Congress his important and humane measure, making the wives and children of those whose husbands and fathers were fighting for the Union forever
free.

In support of this resolution he said, "It is estimated
that from seventy-five to a hundred thousand wives and
children of these soldiers are now held in slavery. It is a
burning shame to this country. . . . Wasting diseases,
weary marches, and bloody battles, are now decimating our
armies. The country needs soldiers, must have soldiers.
Let the Senate, then, act now. Let us hasten the enactment of this beneficent measure, inspired by patriotism and
hallowed by justice and humanity, so that, ere merry
Christmas shall come, the intelligence shall be flashed over
the land to cheer the hearts of the nation's defenders and
arouse the manhood of the bondman, that, on the forehead
of the soldier's wife and the soldier's child, no man can
write 'Slave.'"   This measure became a law on the third
day of March, 1865; and, six months afterwards, Gen.
Palmer estimated that by its operation nearly seventy-five
thousand women and children had, in Kentucky alone,
been made free.

At the celebration of the 4th of July by the freedmen
in the District of Columbia this year, he was present,
and made an encouraging address. "I predict," said he
to them, "that, before five years have rolled around, you
will be allowed to vote, and right here in Washington
too." Scarcely half that time passed before his hopeful
words were realized.

Mr. Wilson's policy, from the beginning of the war, was
to crush the Rebellion just as quick as possible. He dep-
recated the delay of the generals in command, and ever

urged a forward movement. He voted for the confirmation of Gen. Grant, March 2, in the Senate, because he felt assured that he would allow the enemy no time to rally from his repulses; and yet his motives were continually misinterpreted. To a statement in "The New-York Herald," that he had been to Washington to urge an armistice, he made this distinct reply in a letter dated Natick, Aug. 20, 1864 : —

"There is not the slightest foundation for the report, as I never entertained for a moment any other thought than that of conquering a peace by the defeat of the rebel armies."

At this time "The New-Bedford Mercury" said of him, "Henry Wilson has, from the day he entered the Senate to the present moment, in our judgment, and we believe in the judgment of the great body of the people of the State, been an able public servant. No man has been more laborious in the committee-room, more ready in the Senate-chamber, and we believe more single-hearted and unselfish in purpose to sustain the government in its trial-hours, than Henry Wilson."

The following, among hundreds of letters received from all parts of the country, will also indicate how the soldiers and the people viewed his senatorial course : —

"I cannot close this letter, my dear sir, without thanking you for the upright and manly course you have pursued all through this terrible war; for your grand, good words, and the strong blows you have given to the cause of all our woe, — slavery. At last your efforts and those of your noble colleagues are telling, and the government seems about to act justly towards our colored soldiers.

God grant this tardy justice may help to prevent more massacres!

"I am, sir, with profound respect, very truly yours."

His friends urged Mr. Wilson to accept the nomination for vice-president this year; but he declined to be a candidate.

29

CHAPTER XVII.

RE-ELECTION TO UNITED-STATES SENATE. — HIS VIEW OF
ABRAHAM LINCOLN. — ADDRESS AT WASHINGTON. —
SILVER WEDDING. — ANTISLAVERY MEASURES IN
CONGRESS.

IN February, 1865, Mr. Wilson was re-elected United-
States senator for the term of six years. There was some
delay in the election on the part of the conservative branch
of the General Court, instigated, said " The Journal," " by
a few eminently respectable parties who cannot forget that
Mr. Wilson was once a shoemaker. We should like to see
them," it continued, " go before the people on that issue.
They would hear such a response as would convince them

that Massachusetts esteems the sterling qualities of a self-made man, an astute statesman, and an active patriot, over the finest strain of blood or the most eminent respectability."

In March of this year, Mr. Wilson, from the Committee of Conference, reported a new bill for the establishment of a freedman's bureau, whose object was the supervision and relief of the freedmen and refugees. This important bill was carried through both Houses against strenuous opposition, and received, immediately on its passage, the president's approval.

As, by the Constitution, the appointment of officers by the president must receive the confirmation of the Senate, it was called to act upon ten thousand eight hundred and ninety-one military nominations, ranging from second lieutenants up to Lieut.-Gen. Grant, during the four years of the Rebellion; and this vast amount of labor fell upon that small Military Committee of which Mr. Wilson was and still is chairman.

In the crowning of the Union arms with success by the surrender of Gen. Lee in April, Mr. Wilson saw with inexpressible gratitude the realization of his hopes and labors carried on twenty years for the overthrow of the gigantic slave power in America; and he left Washington to be present at the raising of the Union flag once more to float above Fort Sumter. While on board the boat off Hilton Head, he heard the startling news that the president of the nation, Abraham Lincoln, had been stricken down by the ruthless hand of J. Wilkes Booth; and he immediately hastened back to Washington to assist in the emergency, and to share in the sorrows of the afflicted people. With Mr. Lincoln his relations had been intimate, and for his honesty and ability he entertained profound respect. In an address (May 3) before the New-England Historic-Genealogical Society, of which he became a member in 1859, he said of Mr. Lincoln, that "he would pass into history as the foremost man of his age. He was a genuine product of our democratic institutions, and had a living faith in their permanency. His sympathy for the poor and the oppressed was hearty and genuine. Of his mind, one characteristic was the power of stating an argument clearly, and of quickly detecting a fallacy. He had also a felicity of expression. There were many phrases of power and beauty in his letters." The speech at Gettysburg was instanced as containing some of the noblest utterances of any age.

He also said of him in his address in Chicago, September, 1866, "Abraham Lincoln was always patriotic, always true to liberty, justice, humanity, and Christian civilization. He was true to his friends, and always considerate. If he moved slowly, he always moved. His face was always in the right direction."

Mr. Wilson attended the colored people's celebration in the presidential grounds at Washington, July 4, 1865, and said in his address to them, —

"I am not here to find fault with the government, however; though I fear that the golden moment to secure justice, and base our peace on the eternal principle of right, was not taken. I have faith in the motives and purposes of the administration, and shall keep my faith, unless it shall be broken by future deeds. I have faith in the motives and purposes of Pres. Johnson, who told the colored men in the capital of his own Tennessee that he would be their Moses. Andrew Johnson will, I am sure, be to you what Abraham Lincoln would have been had he been spared to complete the great work of emancipation and enfranchisement.

" Pardoned rebels, and rebels yet unpardoned, flippantly tell us that they hold in their hands, yet red with loyal blood, the rights of loyal colored men, of the heroes scarred and maimed beneath the dear old flag. I tell these repentant and unrepentant but conquered and subdued rebels, that, while they hold the suffrage of the loyal black men in their hands, we, the loyal men of America, hold in our hands their lost privilege to hold office in the civil service, army, or navy. The Congress of the United States has placed upon the statute-book a law forever prohibiting any one who has borne arms against the country, or given aid, comfort, and countenance to the Rebellion, from holding any office of honor, profit, or emolument, in the civil, military, or naval service of the United States. . . .

" You, sir, invited Mayor Wallach to be here to-day; but I don't see him. I have a sort of dim idea, that, if you held the right of suffrage, Mayor Wallach, and perhaps the whole city government, would be here. (Cheers.) To insure the attendance of the Mayor of Washington next year, I would suggest that you early send your petitions to Congress asking for the ballot. (' We will.') I am a Yankee, and have the right to guess; and I guess you will get it." (Great applause.)

But from the appointments of the president for the South, from his sympathy for the men so recently engaged in the Rebellion, and from his treasonable declarations, the senator saw that the question of slavery was by no means settled, and that the great impediment in the way of settlement was in the executive chair.

His fears were openly expressed in an eloquent speech at the Academy of Music, Brooklyn, N.Y., Oct. 25, wherein he describes the recent rapid growth of insurrectionary

29*

sentiment in the Confederate States under the fostering patronage of the president.

"Let the late slave-masters, from the Potomac to the Mexican line, fully understand that you are amenable to the same laws as themselves; that you are to be tried for their violation in the same manner, and punished in the same degree. (Cheers.) Let them know that henceforth you will utter your own thoughts, make your own bargains, enjoy the fruits of your own labor, go where you please throughout the bounds of the republic, and none have the right to molest or make you afraid. (Applause.) If my voice to-day could penetrate the ear of the colored men of my country, I would say to them, that the intelligence, character, and wealth of the nation imperatively demand their freedom, protection, and the recognition of their rights. I would say to them, 'Prove yourselves, by patience, endurance, industry, conduct, and character, worthy of all that the millions of Christian men and women have done and are doing to make for you — that Declaration of Independence, read here to-day — the living faith of United America.'" (Loud and prolonged cheering.)

On the twenty-fifth anniversary of their marriage, Oct. 27, 1865, the friends and neighbors of Mr. and Mrs. Wilson assembled at their house in Natick for the celebration of their "silver wedding." Although the night was stormy, a large number of ladies and gentlemen from their own and from the neighboring towns were present; and with mutual congratulations, speeches, poetical recitations, instrumental music, and the singing of songs, a bountiful collation, and the outflow of good will, the festival was full of life and pleasure. Among those present were Messrs. Hannibal Hamlin, Charles Sumner, Anson Burlingame, Oakes Ames, William Claflin, Ginery Twitchell, Charles

W. Slack, and Mrs. Julia Ward Howe. Mrs. Wilson received her guests with her usual unaffected grace and courtesy, and received a purse of four thousand dollars, presented by the hand of William Claflin. An address was made by the Rev. C. M. Tyler, Mr. Wilson's pastor at that time; and a poem by Mrs. Julia Ward Howe was sung, from which we cite the following stanza:—

> "But Wilson from the lowlier base,
>   The silver vantage gaining,
> Climbs ever towards the golden grace,
>   With labor uncomplaining."

Another poet, referring to Mrs. Wilson, wrote:—

> "Thus every wish his heart could frame
>   In her reality became:
> Affection, undiminished still
> By clouded brow or wayward will;
> And that still lovelier, holier grace
> That beams upon a mother's face,—
> These round his path have shed a light
> Mild as the moon of summer's night."

Many elegant articles of silver were presented to Mr. and Mrs. Wilson, among which was a very beautiful silver tea-service from the citizens of Natick. On subscribing for this, one of them characteristically said, "That is for the MAN, not for his principles." As a man, Mr. Wilson's townsmen, even those bitterly opposing his political opinions, have always held him high in their regard and honor. His son, Lieut.-Col. Henry Hamilton Wilson, was at this time in command of the Hundred-and-fourth Regiment of United-States colored troops at Beaufort. S.C. One of his friends on the occasion truly said or sung,—

' A silver wedding claims a silvery verse;
And WILSON well deserves a poet's lay:
But I in humbler measure must rehearse
How fairly earned the honors of this day.
For friendship here puts on more public guise:
The man we love has been the people's friend:
Not wedded faith more sacred in his eyes
Than Truth to champion, and the poor defend."

Mr. Wilson gave the world this year a work of great and permanent value, bearing the title of " History of the Anti-slavery Measures of the Thirty-seventh and Thirty-eighth United-States Congresses, 1861–65. By Henry Wilson." It contains four hundred and twenty-four pages octavo, and most lucidly exhibits the course of national legislation on the slave question, from the opening of the Rebellion until the overthrow of the system by the adoption of the anti-slavery amendment to the Constitution of the United States. The work is written with great candor by one who, as we have seen, took part in the legislation, framing several of the most important measures, and carrying them, against persistent opposition, through Congress. The style is dignified and manly ; the speakers present their views in their own language ; and the grounds on which the bills are framed are very ably and distinctly stated. The abstract of the work accomplished by the fearless advocates of freedom in the closing pages gives with clearness the results accomplished, and a just idea of the burden taken by this legislation from the bondman and the Union.

"This volume," says "The Atlantic Monthly," " is a labor-saving machine of great power to all who desire or need a clear view of the course of Congressional legislation on measures of emancipation ;" and Mrs. Stowe characterizes it as "exhibiting the magnificent morality, the dauntless courage, the unwearied faith, hope, and charity, that are the crown jewels of the republic."

The closing summary of the achievements of the friends of freedom given in this work is so well made, and is such a valuable historical record, that we think it worthy of transcription.

" The annals of the nation," says the author, " bear the amplest evidence that the patriots and statesmen who carried the country through the Revolution from colonial dependence to national independence, framed the Constitution, and inaugurated the Federal Government, hoped and believed that slavery would pass away at no distant period under the influences of the institutions they had founded. But those illustrious men tasted death without witnessing the realization of their hopes and anticipations. The rapid development of the resources of the country under the protection of a stable government, the opening-up of new and rich lands, the expansion of territory, and perhaps, more than all, the wonderful growth and importance of the cotton culture, enhanced the value of labor, and increased many-fold the price of slaves. Under the stimulating influences of an ever-increasing pecuniary interest, a political power was speedily developed, which early manifested itself in the National Government. For nearly two generations, the slaveholding class, into whose power the government early passed, dictated the policy of the nation. But the presidential election of 1860 resulted in the defeat of the slaveholding class, and in the success of men who religiously believe slavery to be a grievous wrong to the slave, a blight upon the prosperity, and a stain upon the name, of the country. Defeated in its aims, broken in its power, humiliated in its pride, the slave-holding class raised at once the banners of treason. Retiring from the chambers of Congress, abandoning the seats of power to men who had persistently opposed their aggressive policy, they brought to an abrupt close the record of half a century of SLAVERY MEASURES IN CONGRESS. Then, when slavery legislation ended, antislavery legislation began. . . .

" When the Rebellion culminated in active hostilities, it was seen that thousands of slaves were used for military purposes by the rebel forces. To weaken the forces of the Rebellion, the Thirty-seventh. Congress decreed that such slaves should be forever free.

" As the Union armies advanced into the rebel States, slaves, inspired by the hope of personal freedom, flocked to their encampments, claiming protection against rebel masters, and offering to work and fight for the flag whose stars for the first time gleamed upon their vision with the radiance of liberty. Rebel masters and rebel-sympathizing masters sought the encampments of the loyal forces, demanding the surrender of the escaped fugitives; and they were often delivered up by officers of the armies. To weaken the power of the insurgents, to strengthen the loyal forces, and assert the claims of humanity, the Thirty-seventh Congress enacted an article of war, dismissing from the service officers guilty of surrendering these fugitives.

" Three thousand persons were held as slaves in the District of Columbia, over which the nation exercised exclusive jurisdiction: the Thirty-seventh Congress made these three thousand bondmen freemen, and made slave-holding in the capital of the nation forevermore impossible.

" Laws and ordinances existed in the national capital that pressed with merciless rigor upon the colored people:

the Thirty-seventh Congress enacted that colored persons should be tried for the same offences in the same manner, and be subject to the same punishments, as white persons ; thus abrogating the ' black code.'

" Colored persons in the capital of this Christian nation were denied the right to testify in the judicial tribunals; thus placing their property, their liberties, and their lives, in the power of unjust and wicked men : the Thirty-seventh Congress enacted that persons should not be excluded as witnesses in the courts of the District on account of color.

" In the capital of the nation, colored persons were taxed to support schools from which their own children were excluded ; and no public schools were provided for the instruction of more than four thousand youth : the Thirty-eighth Congress provided by law that public schools should be established for colored children, and that the same rate of appropriations for colored schools should be made as are made for schools for the education of white children.

" The railways chartered by Congress excluded from their cars colored persons, without the authority of law : Congress enacted that there should be no exclusion from any car on account of color.

" Into the Territories of the United States — one-third of the surface of the country — the slaveholding class claimed the right to take and hold their slaves under the protection of law : the Thirty-seventh Congress prohibited slavery forever in all the existing territory, and in all territory which may hereafter be acquired ; thus stamping freedom for all, forever, upon the public domain.

" As the war progressed, it became more clearly apparent that the rebels hoped to win the border slave States ; that rebel sympathizers in those States hoped to join the rebel States; and that emancipation in loyal States would bring repose to them, and weaken the power of the Rebellion: the Thirty-seventh Congress, on the recommendation of the president, by the passage of a joint resolution, pledged the faith of the nation to aid loyal States to emancipate the slaves therein.

"The hoe and spade of the rebel slave were hardly less potent for the Rebellion than the rifle and bayonet of the rebel soldier. Slaves sowed and reaped for the rebels, enabling the rebel leaders to fill the wasting ranks of their armies, and feed them. To weaken the military forces and the power of the Rebellion, the Thirty-seventh Congress decreed that all slaves of persons giving aid and comfort to the Rebellion, escaping from such persons, and taking refuge within the lines of the army; all slaves captured from such persons, or deserted by them; all slaves of such persons, being within any place occupied by rebel forces, and afterwards occupied by the forces of the United States, — shall be captives of war, and shall be forever free of their servitude, and not again held as slaves.

"The provisions of the Fugitive-slave Act permitted. disloyal masters to claim, and they did claim, the return of their fugitive bondmen: the Thirty-seventh Congress enacted that no fugitive should be surrendered until the claimant made oath that he had not given aid and comfort to the Rebellion.

"The progress of the Rebellion demonstrated its power, and the needs of the imperilled nation. To strengthen the physical forces of the United States, the Thirty-seventh Congress authorized the president to receive into the military service persons of African descent; and every such person mustered into the service, his mother, his wife and children, owing service or labor to any person who should give aid and comfort to the Rebellion, was made forever free.

"The African slave-trade had been carried on by slave pirates under the protection of the flag of the United States. To extirpate from the seas that inhuman traffic, and to vindicate the sullied honor of the nation, the administration early entered into treaty stipulations with the British Government for the mutual right of search within certain limits; and the Thirty-seventh Congress hastened to enact the appropriate legislation to carry the treaty into effect.

"The slaveholding class, in the pride of power, persistently refused to recognize the independence of Hayti and Liberia; thus dealing unjustly towards those nations, to the detriment of the commercial interests of the country: the Thirty-seventh Congress recognized the independence of those republics by authorizing the president to establish diplomatic relations with them.

"By the provisions of law, white male citizens alone were enrolled in the militia. In the amendment to the acts for calling out the militia, the Thirty-seventh Congress provided for the enrolment and drafting of citizens, without regard to color; and, by the Enrolment Act, colored persons, free or slave, are enrolled and drafted the same as white men: the Thirty-eighth Congress enacted that colored soldiers shall have the same pay, clothing, and rations, and be placed in all respects upon the same footing, as white soldiers. To encourage enlistments, and to aid emancipation, the Thirty-eighth Congress decreed that every slave mustered into the military service shall be free forever; thus enabling every slave fit for military service to secure personal freedom.

"By the provisions of the fugitive-slave acts, slave-masters could hunt their absconding bondmen, require the people to aid in their recapture, and have them returned at the expense of the nation : the Thirty-eighth Congress erased all fugitive-slave acts from the statutes of the republic.

" The law of 1807 legalized the coastwise slave-trade : the Thirty-eighth Congress repealed that act, and made the trade illegal.

" The courts of the United States receive such testimony as is permitted in the States where the courts are holden ; several of the States exclude the testimony of colored persons : the Thirty-eighth Congress made it legal for colored persons to testify in all the courts of the United States.

" Different views are entertained by public men relative to the reconstruction of the governments of the seceded States and the validity of the president's proclamation of emancipation : the Thirty-eighth Congress passed a bill providing for the reconstruction of the governments of the rebel States, and for the emancipation of the slaves in those States ; but it did not receive the approval of the president.

" Colored persons were not permitted to carry the United-States mails : the Thirty-eighth Congress repealed the prohibitory legislation, and made it lawful for persons of color to carry the mails.

" Wives and children of colored persons in the military and naval service of the United States were often held as slaves ; and, while husbands and fathers were absent fighting the battles of the country, these wives and children were sometimes removed and sold, and often treated with cruelty : the Thirty-eighth Congress made free the wives and children of all persons engaged in the military or naval service of the country.

" The disorganization of the slave system, and the exigencies of civil war, have thrown thousands of freedmen upon the charity of the nation: to relieve their immediate needs, and to aid them through the transition period, the Thirty-eighth Congress established a bureau of freedmen.

" The prohibition of slavery in the Territories, its abolition in the District of Columbia, the freedom of colored soldiers and their wives and children, emancipation in Maryland, West Virginia, and Missouri, and, by the reorganized State authorities, of Virginia, Tennessee, and Louisiana, and the president's Emancipation Proclamation, disorganized the slave system, and practically left few persons in bondage; but slavery still continued in Delaware and Kentucky, and the slave codes remained unrepealed in the rebel States. To annihilate the slave system, its codes and usages; to make slavery impossible, and freedom universal, — the Thirty-eighth Congress submitted to the people an antislavery amendment to the Constitution of the United States. The adoption of that crowning measure assures freedom to all.

" Such are the 'ANTISLAVERY MEASURES' of the Thirty-seventh and Thirty-eighth Congresses during the past four crowded years. Seldom in the history of nations is it given to any body of legislators or lawgivers to enact or institute a series of measures so vast in their scope, so comprehensive in their character, so patriotic, just, and humane.

" But, while the Thirty-seventh and Thirty-eighth Congresses were enacting this antislavery legislation, other agencies were working to the consummation of the same end, — the complete and final abolition of slavery. The president proclaims three and a half millions of bondmen in the rebel States henceforward and forever free. Mary-

land, Virginia, and Missouri adopt immediate and uncon-
ditional emancipation.   The partially re-organized rebel
States of Virginia and Tennessee, Arkansas and Louisiana, accept and adopt the unrestricted abolition of slavery.
Illinois and other States hasten to blot from their statute-
books their dishonoring ' black codes.'   The attorney-
general officially pronounces the negro a citizen of the
United States.   The negro, who had no status in the Supreme Court, is admitted by the chief justice to practise
as an attorney before that august tribunal.   Christian men
and women follow the loyal armies with the agencies of
mental and moral instruction to fit and prepare the enfranchised freedmen for the duties of the higher condition
of life now opening before them."

In these labors Mr. Wilson bore a prominent and honorable part; and to no man living are the colored people of
this country under higher obligation for their liberty.

CHAPTER XVIII.

CONTEST BETWEEN THE PRESIDENT AND CONGRESS. — MR. WILSON'S VIEWS OF RECONSTRUCTION. — REPLY TO MR. COWAN. — SPEECH ON MR. STEVENS'S RESOLUTION, ETC. — RELIGIOUS VIEWS. — MILITARY MEASURES IN CONGRESS.

Course of the President. — Reconstruction Difficult. — Mr. Wilson's View. — No Desire to degrade the South. — Bill to maintain the Rights of the Freedmen. — Supports Mr. Trumbull's Bill to enlarge the Freedmen's Bureau. — What he means by Equality. — Honorable Sentiments. — Joint Resolution for disbanding Military Organizations. — Speech on the Resolution of Mr. Stevens against the Admission of Southern Representation. — The Nature of the Struggle. — Condition of Freedmen. — Mistake of the President. — Gen. Grant. — Legislative Labors. — Speech in Boston. — Natick. — Defection of the President. — Massachusetts. — Congress a Co-ordinate Branch of the Government. — Tour through the West. — Speech at Chicago. — Elective Franchise in the District of Columbia. — Corporal Punishment. — Buying and selling Votes. — Address on Religion. — Testimony of Statesmen to Christianity. — An Admonition. — Death of his Son. — Monument. — Address at Quincy. — Good Advice. — His Work on Military Legislation in Congress. — Its Character.

WHEN, by the death of Mr. Lincoln, Andrew Johnson came into the executive chair, the senators of our State had strong hopes that he would carry out the policy of their party, and maintain the vantage-ground so nobly won by the untiring valor of the national army. The States lately in rebellion were now prostrate, their governments dissolved, and their military organizations demoralized and

disbanded. The Union flag was floating over them ; and
the leaders were ready to accept such terms of reconstruction and restoration as the president and Congress might
deem advisable.   It was a golden opportunity for the
friends of freedom.   The power of re-organization was in
their hands : but the work to be accomplished was of no
small magnitude ; and from the peculiar relations between
the loyalists, the freedmen, and the confederates, it was as
delicate as it was difficult and great.

Forgetting that his province was to execute, not frame,
the laws, and assuming that the power of reconstruction
was in his hands alone, the president began the work
by what he termed an " experiment ; " which, during the
recess in Congress, became a settled governmental policy.
By his unwarrantable course, he so revived the hopes of
the disloyal States, that on the opening of the Thirty-ninth
Congress in December, 1865, a demand was made for
the immediate admission of senators and representatives
holding rebel sentiments from the disaffected States.   This
demand, encouraged by Mr. Johnson, the Republicans persistently resisted ; and the struggle between the legislative
and the executive branches of the government thence became intensely earnest, and so continued till the term of
the experimenting president expired.

In the reconstruction of the States, Mr. Wilson's counsel
was for a generous yet decisive course of action.   Let
loyal men alone assume control ; let freedmen be protected ; let the governments be constructed on the basis of
equal rights for every citizen, and loyalty to the Union.
He desired not to crush, but to elevate and improve, the
Southern people ; asking only security for the future of
the nation.   Congress alone has the power to reconstruct
the States ; and, when so reconstructed, they may have,

and not till then, a representation in this body. In support of his bill to maintain the freedom of the inhabitants of the States lately in rebellion, he said in the Senate on the 13th of December, 1865, " I have never entertained a feeling of bitterness or of unkindness to the Southern people. Notwithstanding all that has taken place, I have always regarded those persons as my countrymen; nor do I wish to impose upon the many things that would be degrading or unmanly : but I wish to protect all the people there, of every race, the poorest and the humblest; and, while I would not degrade any of them, neither would I allow them to degrade others. . . . To turn these freedmen over to the tender mercies of men who hate them for their fidelity to the country is a crime that will bring the judgment of Heaven upon us."

Two days after the announcement that the States had ratified the constitutional amendment abolishing slavery, Mr. Wilson introduced, Dec. 21, 1865, another bill, — " to maintain and enforce the freedom of the inhabitants of the United States;" which was nearly the same in substance as Mr. Trumbull's Civil-rights Bill, enacted over the veto of the president on the 9th of April, 1866.

On the 22d of January, 1866, he made an effective speech in support of Mr. Trumbull's bill for the enlargement of the Freedmen's Bureau, which was also vetoed by the president. Replying to Mr. Cowan, — a Republican in name, but Democrat in action, who had insolently demanded what the honorable senator from Massachusetts meant in saying that " all men in this country must be equal," — he said, " Does he " (the senator from Pennsylvania) " not know that we mean that the poorest man, be he black or white, that treads the soil of this continent, is as much entitled to the protection of the law as the richest and the proudest man in the land? Does he not know that we mean that the poor man, whose wife may be dressed in cheap calico, is as much entitled to have her protected by equal law as is the rich man to have his jewelled bride protected by the laws of the land? Does he not know that the poor man's cabin, though it may be the cabin of a poor freedman in the depths of the Carolinas, is entitled to the protection of the same law that protects the palace of a Stewart or an Astor? He knows that we have advocated the rights of the black man, because the black man was the most oppressed type of the toiling men of this country. The man who is the enemy of the black laboring-man is the enemy of the white laboring-man the world over. The same influences that go to crush down and keep down the rights of the poor black man bear down and oppress the poor white laboring-man. . . . , I tell the senator from Pennsylvania that I know we shall carry these measures. God is not dead, and we live; and standing upon the eternal principles of his justice, with a Christian nation behind us, with God's commands ever ringing in our ears, we shall in the future, as we have in the twenty-five years of the past, march straight forward to battle and to victory over all opposition."

Such sentiments the State which Mr. Wilson represents indorses. They accord with Solon's high conception of true liberty, — " A commonwealth where an injury to the meanest member is an injury to the whole."

As some new military organizations in the insurrectionary States were commanded by veterans in the Rebellion, and refused to carry the Union flag, Mr. Wilson, on the 19th of February, 1866, introduced a joint resolution providing that they should be forthwith disbanded, and such organizations prohibited in the future. This became a law, preventing that exhibition of disloyal purpose, and protecting peaceable citizens from abuse.

On the resolution of Mr. Stevens against the admission of senators and representatives from any rebel State until Congress shall have declared such State entitled to such representation, he made, March 2, an eloquent speech, in which his views on many points of reconstruction are presented. On the nature of the struggle he asserted that

" A loyal people instinctively see, amid the turmoil and excitement of the present, that this is not a struggle for the re-admission of the rebel States into the Union, but a struggle for the admission of rebels into the legislative branches of the government; not a struggle to put rebels under the laws of the country, but a struggle to enable rebels to frame the laws of the country. A loyal people see that the Confederate States, reconstructed since the surrender of the rebel armies, are as completely in the hands of rebels now as on the day Jeff. Davis was incarcerated at Fortress Monroe."

Of the condition of the freedmen under the new order of things he remarked, —

" The poor freedmen, who a few months ago were leaping and laughing with the joy of new-found liberty, invoking the blessings of Heaven upon the government that had stricken the galling manacles from their limbs, are now trembling with apprehension, everywhere subject to indignity, insult, outrage, and murder. During the past four months, in Alabama alone, fourteen hundred cases of assault upon freedmen have been brought before the Freedmen's Bureau. Thousands and tens of thousands of harmless black men, from the Potomac to the Rio Grande, have been wronged and outraged by violence, and hundreds upon hundreds have been murdered. The

offices and the agencies of the Freedmen's Bureau, of the
officers of our armies, and the office of Judge-Advocate
Gen. Holt, are filled with the records of outrage and
murder.   The local authorities screen the murderers; the
people protest against the punishment of white men for
the murder of black men; and the murderers go unpun-
ished."

Of the great mistake of the president he said, —

"Thoughtful men, anxious to heal the wounds of civil
war, and bury in forgetfulness the memories of old contests, were speaking for universal amnesty and universal
suffrage, for forgiving and restoring all.   The nobler sentiments of the liberty-loving men of the country at that
time are caught and expressed in the verse of Whittier: —

> 'From you alone the guaranty
>   Of union, freedom, peace, we claim:
>   We urge no conquerer's terms of shame.
>
> Alas! no victor's pride is ours,
>   Who bend above our triumphs won
>   Like David o'er his rebel son.
>
> Be men, not beggars; cancel all
>   By one brave, generous action; trust
>   Your better instincts, and be just.
>
> Make all men peers before the law;
>   Take hands from off the negro's throat;
>   Give black and white an equal vote.
>
> Keep all your forfeit lives and lands,
>   But give the common law's redress
>   To labor's utter nakedness.'

"If the President of the United States had seized that
golden moment, — that grand opportunity then vouchsafed
by Providence to weapon the hand of the new-made free-

man with the ballot, — these sectional controversies would
have perished forever ; the representatives of the rebellious
States would, ere this, have filled these vacant chairs ; and
the heavens would be raining their choicest blessings upon
the nation for a deed so wise and so just.   But the president, though frankly avowing himself in favor of qualified
suffrage, declined to asssume the responsibility which the
condition of the country imposed upon him ; and the great
opportunity God gave the nation to destroy caste, to clothe
the emancipated race with power to guard their own liberties, rights, and interests without a struggle, passed by,
perhaps forever. . . .

"The loyal people of the United States, who have
poured out so much blood and given so much treasure for
its preservation, are in favor of fully protecting the people
of the rebellious States, white and black, loyal and disloyal ; but they have the right to demand, and they
should demand, before intrusting the legislation of the
country to the framers and administrators of confederate
governments, and to the soldiers who have met their
sons on bloody battle-fields, ample security for the rights
of loyal men of every race, and for the money loaned
the country in its hour of need to arm, clothe, feed, equip,
and pay the defenders of the republic."

In the closing paragraph of this spirited speech he thus
prophetically pointed to Gen. Grant as the next president.
He said, —

" Two years ago, in a trying hour of the country, we
placed a great soldier at the head of all our armies ; and
he led those armies to victory, and the country to peace.
Perhaps a patriotic and liberty-loving people, if disappointed in their aspirations and their hopes, may again
turn to that great captain, and summon him to marshal
them to victory."

In addition to various resolutions, reports, and private bills which he brought forward during the Thirty-ninth Congress, Mr. Wilson spoke on the bills for the admission of Nebraska and Colorado, for which he voted; also in advocacy of the protection of the national cemeteries, of the establishment of a department of education, of the incorporation of the orphans' home, of appropriations for soldiers' bounties, and for other important measures. He was never idle; yet he often said, as in the war, that he was not accomplishing what he would or could.

Such is a brief outline of some of the legislative labors which Mr. Wilson performed in that series of Congressional measures which culminated in the suppression of the Rebellion and the liberation of the slave; and which, for wisdom, efficiency, and humanity, will ever command the admiration of the world. Since that period Mr. Wilson has been steadily at his post in Congress, battling for the rights of the freedmen and for restoration of tranquillity to the Union on the basis of the Declaration of Independence and the Constitution. The pages of "The Congressional Globe" bear ample witness to his unremitting industry, as well as to the practical views he entertained and the manly sentiments he expressed upon the various questions which arose in Congress.

His views of the policy of the president Mr. Wilson expressed in a large meeting in Tremont Temple, Boston, on the 6th of August.

After alluding to what had been accomplished the last six years, he said we had yet work to do. Of the honorable men who, in November, 1864, re-elected Abraham Lincoln president, and Andrew Johnson vice-president, ninety-nine out of a hundred were to-day bowing their heads in disappointment and sorrow. This was because the vice-president, who became president by an act that needed not naming, has disappointed our expectations, turned his back upon the men who elected him, upon the principles he then professed, and is to-day the inspiration of wrong and outrage upon loyal white men and upon loyal black men South.

In the same month, by an invitation signed by a hundred and fourteen of the citizens of Natick, he addressed the people of that town, who always throng the hall to hear him, upon the variance between the president and Congress; and urged his hearers in words of glowing eloquence to vote for the amendment to the Constitution, as essential to the liberties of the people and the rights of the unprotected freedmen.

" After the surrender of Lee," he said, " the rebels were absolutely under the control of the military authorities of the government. They were then ready to accept any terms the nation chose to give. But to-day the rebels have possession of Virginia, of its government, of North Carolina, South Carolina, Georgia, Florida, Alabama, Mississippi, Louisiana; and on Thursday next they will take possession of the government of Texas in the person of their rebel governor, Gen. Throckmorton. How came this so? Andrew Johnson, elected by the votes of loyal men who carried the country through the fire and blood of four years of war, has put these States in the hands of rebels.

" And what have the legislatures elected under his policy done? That of Virginia inaugurated no State officers unless they were well-known rebels. North Carolina has elected a delegation to Congress, that, with one exception, are rebels. South Carolina has elected a rebel delegation, and has a rebel governor, — one of the leading men in establishing the confederacy. Georgia has elected Alexan-

der II. Stephens to the Senate of the United States, and
an unbroken rebel delegation to the House. Florida has
a rebel governor, one rebel and one loyal senator, whose
term will expire on the 4th of next March; and there is
no prospect of his being re-elected. Mississippi and Alabama have sent to Congress men who cannot take the
oath. . . .

"These States want admission into Congress; and for
what purpose? To take part in the government of the
United States; and not only to govern these States, but
to direct and control the policy of the nation. And they
present themselves with the declaration, that they acquiesce
in their defeat because they cannot help it. They are not
sorry for their revolt against the country, and that they
murdered more than three hundred thousand men fighting
to uphold the old flag. We should never consent to surrender into rebel hands the government for which these
loyal soldiers died."

He closed by paying an eloquent tribute to the patriotism of Massachusetts.

"He had no doubt that Massachusetts would be all right:
she had always been. Among the first and foremost has
she been for the rights of man, and in the bloody Rebellion
through which we have just passed. The bones of her
sons lie upon many a battle-field; her maimed heroes are
here among us; her brave men who have come from
battle-fields forever made immortal are here. I believe
they will vote in the future as they have fought in the past.
I believe that the loyal men who carried the country
through the war will stand by this constitutional amendment, — stand by the action of Congress now, and elect
one that will be true to them and that in 1868. The unity
of the country will be assured, and the liberties of all races
and conditions of men forever established in America."

Senator Wilson spoke an hour and a half, and was frequently applauded.

Addressing a vast assembly at Philadelphia, Sept. 4, — for we find him ever moving, ever speaking, in defence of human rights, — he said he "could tell the president and his cabinet that Congress was not a subordinate, but a co-ordinate branch of the government (cheers); that backed up by the country, as it had been, now was, and would be, it would speak for itself, and fix the time and conditions in which it would admit the representatives of rebel constituencies to the Senate and House of Representatives. (Cheers.) It wanted the rebel States represented at the earliest possible moment, not by such men as had met here a few weeks ago, but by such men as were in the city to-day (cheers), and who were true to the country and to liberty."

Referring to the assertion that the president was pursuing the policy of Mr. Lincoln, which Mr. Wilson pronounced as black a falsehood as ever fell from human lips, he said, "Abraham Lincoln sought to put the rebel States into the hands of loyal men; but Andrew Johnson put them back into the hands of rebels; and loyal men were under the hoof of those rebels as much now as when Jefferson Davis was President of the Southern Confederacy."

In the autumn of this year Mr. Wilson made a tour through the West, where he met with most cordial receptions, and addressed many large and enthusiastic audiences in six Western cities on the questions then at issue. In this journey he travelled over three thousand miles, and in one instance spoke to a throng of about thirty thousand people. In his speech at Chicago on the twenty-eighth day of September, he said, —

"You will remember that army after army surrendered,

and those composing each one hastened to their homes; that the rebels were humiliated, subjugated, conquered, and powerless at our feet, ready to accept any policy the government chose to impose upon them. We all know that these conquered rebels in every portion of the country were ready and willing to accept at the hands of this government just such a policy as the government believed the good of the country required. `

"You will remember how kind, humane, and generous our people were. We did not wish their lands, money, or blood; but we desired security for the future. We wanted that the fruits of the war should be gathered: that was all. Our capitalists were ready to send their money there. Our young men were ready to go there and develop that portion of the country. Our noble women, who rushed to the hospitals and bound up the wounds of our soldiers, were ready to go there and instruct the darkened intellects of an emancipated race. All over the loyal States there was a desire, not to punish, to crush out, or to crush down, this people, but a desire to lift up and improve that section of the country, and to demand only security for the future of the nation.

"Now, this was the feeling in the spring of 1865; but what is the condition of that portion of the country now? These men, then humble and penitent, and making excuses for their actions, are now boasting of their deeds against the country, and are scornfully defiant. Why? Who is responsible? I say that Andrew Johnson alone is responsible for this change in the condition of affairs. Our brave soldiers struck the weapons from the rebel hands, and Andrew Johnson has restored them to them. Every one of the States which he has reconstructed has passed into the hands of unrepentant rebels. The other day, after he had put the government of Texas into the hands of a rebel general, he issued a proclamation declaring that peace had come. Order reigned in Warsaw then. Peace come, when the last great rebel State was put back again into the hands of the rebels! And these States are in rebel hands to-day.

"The president demands the admission of their representatives into Congress. Now, only five of the men elected in those ten rebel States can take the oath of office. Five only! The others are unrepentant traitors, though some of them are pardoned ones. Now, it is demanded that they shall be admitted into the Congress of the United States. They went out when it pleased them to go out: they shall come back when we please to let them back. They went out against our pleadings. We almost went upon our knees and implored them to remain with us, to follow the old flag, and stand by the common country; but they turned their backs upon us, and went out undertaking to establish a government. They said they would go out, and we said they should not. They fought to go out, and we fought to keep them in; and, thanks be to God, they are to-night part and parcel of our common country, within the Union, and under the authority of the laws. The old flag is there waving over them. The boys in blue are there to maintain the authority of the government. They have to pay their taxes and obey the laws. They are subject to the authority of the nation. All there is about it is this: their senators and representatives are not yet permitted to go into Congress and legislate for the country; and we mean, when we have taken ample security for the future, to let them in, and not until we have taken it.

"This body of men, 'calling itself a Congress,' that

31*

Andrew Johnson says ' is hanging on the verge of the government,' — this body of men has framed a constitutional amendment. We have submitted it to the people: and I tell you that this nation has resolved it; it has proclaimed it; it is recorded that that amendment shall be incorporated into the Constitution of the country, and the representatives of these traitors shall sit no more in the Congress of the United States. If they want to be represented, let them adopt that constitutional amendment; let them choose men who believe in it, who are for it, and who will guard it; let them choose men who will in the future be with their country and for their country, — men who give all they have, and all they hope to be, to the cause of unity and a free country, — a country that recognizes the equality of all men, and the equal privileges of all men; and then the seats are ready for them in the Senate and House of Representatives, and not until that day.

"You have recently had a visit from the chief magistrate of the country. Let me say that I think that chief magistrate has gone back to Washington a sadder, if not a wiser man. He believed that he could do what he started to do in May, 1865; ay, before Abraham Lincoln had been laid in his grave at Springfield: and that was, to build up a great personal party; that he should be the founder of a great political party, as were Jefferson and Jackson. He has labored from May, 1865, until the present time, to create, build up, organize, and develop such a party in America; and what is the result? He has the whole power and patronage of this government brought to bear. He has shaken in the face of the loyal people of the land the vast patronage of the government. I told them in the Senate last winter, that a nation that had buried three hundred thousand of its children to save the country was in no temper to be bought off by patronage."

The bill for extending the elective franchise to the freedmen of the District of Columbia received Mr. Wilson's cordial support during its tardy progress through the Senate. Speaking on one of the amendments to the bill, he thus declared (Dec. 13, 1866) his views on the right of suffrage : " Sir, I believe in the right of suffrage for my country. I believe in it far more for the poor, ignorant man. I believe that he is more of a man when he has it, and that he will use it in the future as he has in the past, — generally for the elevation and the protection of the poor and lowly and dependent. No loyal man who has the right of suffrage shall ever have it taken away or abridged by me, unless for crime. No poor laboring-man shall ever accuse me before the bar of man or of God of voting against giving him the same right that I possess to go to the ballot-box."

Ever espousing the cause of the oppressed, Mr. Wilson, in the Senate, on the 20th of December, 1866, introduced a joint resolution authorizing the president to prevent the infliction of corporal punishment in the States lately in rebellion. Its object was, especially, to defend the freedmen in their helplessness from a mode of punishment which he considered barbarous in its infliction, and degrading in its tendencies.

Surely such sentiments — and they are the rule of the heart and the life — entitle the senator to his honored name of " the poor man's friend."

An amendment by Mr. Wilson, making it unlawful to buy or sell votes, was incorporated in the bill, which, over the veto of the president, became a law on the eighth day

of January, 1867; and was the first of these great measures giving the elective franchise to the entire nation.

Although upright and honorable in his dealings with his
fellow-men, consistent in his walk and conversation, a
regular attendant on the services of the sanctuary, and a
supporter of the institutions of religion, Mr. Wilson did
not, until the autumn of 1866, avow himself a follower of
the Saviour. But, in a large assembly held in the Congregational church in Natick on the 28th of October, he declared in a very touching address, that, within a few past
weeks, he had come to a knowledge of his own personal
salvation through the merits of the Redeemer. All who
knew him felt that he would stand firmly to the position
he had taken ; and many prayers ascended to the seat of
mercy that the richest blessings of our heavenly Father
might attend the future course of the beloved senator.

On his return from Washington, he addressed, Dec. 23,
the Young Men's Christian Association of Natick on " The
Testimonies of American Statesmen and Jurists to the
Truths of Christianity," which was afterwards published in
a tract for general circulation. He said, —

" God has given us existence in this Christian republic,
founded by men who proclaim as their living faith, amid
persecution and exile, ' We give ourselves to the Lord
Jesus Christ, and the word of his grace, for the teaching,
ruling, and sanctifying of us in matters of worship and
conversation.' · Privileged to live in this age, when the
selectest influences of the religion of our fathers seem to
be visibly descending upon our land, we too often hear the
providence of God, the religion of our Lord and Saviour
Jesus Christ, the inspiration of Holy Writ, doubted, questioned, denied. With an air of gracious condescension we
are sometimes reminded that this religion of the crucified

Redeemer may do for women, for children, for weak-minded men, but not for men of experience, observation, reflection. Men who see not God in our own history have surely lost sight of the fact, that, from the landing of ' The Mayflower ' to this hour, the great men whose names are indissolubly associated with the colonization, rise, and progress of the republic, have borne testimonies to the vital truths of Christianity.

" These utterances, not of the great teachers of Christianity, but of men of varied and large experience, accustomed to the classification and comparison of facts, the sifting and weighing of evidences, cannot pass unheeded by the young men of the land who cherish their names and revere their memories."

After citing the testimonies of the distinguished states-men of America to the truth and value of the Scriptures, he closed his beautiful address by these admonitory words : —

" Young men of this Christian association, remember, ever and always, that your country was founded, not by ' the most superficial, the lightest, the most unreflective of all the European races,' but by the stern old Puritans, who made the deck of ' The Mayflower ' an altar of the living God, and whose first act, on touching the soil of the New World, was to offer on bended knees thanksgiving and prayer to Almighty God. Remember, too, that the great men of your country — Washington, Franklin, Jefferson, the Adamses, Hamilton, Jay, Marshall, Kent, Webster, and their illustrious compeers — possessed the intellectual ' force and severity necessary to carry far and long the greatest conception of the human understanding, the idea of God.' Never forgetting the religious character of our national origin, and the humble and pious recognition of the hand of God in our affairs by the immortal statesmen and jurists who moulded and fashioned the institutions of our country, we will continue to indulge the hope that it shall never be said of any considerable portion of our countrymen, by poet, philosopher, or statesman, of our country, that their minds are too superficial, too light, too unreflective, to conceive 'the profoundest and weightiest idea of which the human intelligence is capable.' "

A few days afterwards, the sad intelligence of the death of his only son, Lieut.-Col. Henry Hamilton Wilson, which occurred in Austin, Tex., on Dec. 24, came to fill his home with sorrow, which nothing but an abiding trust in Him "who doeth all things well" was able to assuage. The remains of this brave young soldier were brought home, and with many tears consigned to their final resting-place in Dell-park Cemetery, where a marble monument has been raised over them, bearing this inscription. On the front, —

"LIEUT.-COL. HENRY HAMILTON WILSON.

Born in Natick, Nov. 11, 1846; died at Austin, Tex., Dec. 24, 1866.

Army of the Potomac."

On the reverse, —

"He the young and strong, who cherished
Noble longings for the strife,
By the roadside fell and perished,
Weary with the march of life.

Department of the South.
Department of the Gulf."

Addressing a Christian convention at Quincy soon after his bereavement, he gave some account of the Congressional prayer-meeting, and then said, "In military life it is the duty of the soldier to be on the alert at all times, and always to be present at the roll-call : so should Christians always be present at prayer-meetings. It is said that prayer-meetings are sometimes dull ; but, if all Christians attend who can, they never will be dull. With the room well filled, and all engaged in one cause, there will be no lack of interest.

" Christians should act from principle and deep conviction. They should forsake all that tempts others away from duty, should abandon all that will leads others astray. If a glass of wine leads the young to stumble, Christians should throw it away. If going to theatres leads others to wrong, Christians should keep away from theatres. If a Christian feels that his staying away from prayer-meeting causes others to stay away, then he should go, even if he only expected to meet his God there. Nothing but sickness should keep a man from the sabbath-meeting ; and all should go to the prayer-meeting who could.

" Christians should not neglect their duty because they are depressed in spirit: they should always be up and doing. They should always act from principle, and always do right. He said he looked to the young men as the hope of the country ; and they should catch the spirit of the age, and carry it forward. They should act now as they did in the war. The gigantic evil which had overspread the South had been overcome ; and now that region is a missionary field for Christian young men. The next thirty years has a mortgage on the efforts of every Christian young man and woman. ·

" Although that gigantic evil had been overcome, here in Massachusetts there was a greater evil than slavery had ever been : that was intemperance.

" The church wants the same earnestness that the country carried into the war; wants men and money to enroll in the ranks, and be ever ready to respond to the call, morning, noon, or night." Alluding to the death of his son, an only child, who had been brought home a corpse from Texas, he said, with much feeling, that he would give his life to-day if he had been able to say to his dear boy what he was now able to say to young men; and he begged of them, as they loved their parents, as they loved their country, to love their Saviour also. They knew not when they might be brought back to their friends as his son had been. In conclusion, he urged, that no matter what base motives might be charged, no matter what might be said, all should do their duty, and serve their Master, and in life and death have the proud consciousness of having done right.

In 1866 Mr. Wilson found time to enrich the legislative history of his country by the publication of a very valuable work, under the title of "Military Measures of the United-States Congress, 1861–1865. By Henry Wilson, Chairman of the Committee on Military Affairs." It is printed in double columns royal octavo, contains eighty-eight pages, and forms a part of Frank Moore's "Rebellion Record." It presents a clear and connected view of the course and character of Congressional legislation in respect to the calling-forth and organization of the grand army of the republic. It is a record of what our patriotic Congressmen accomplished, in a military point of view, for the salvation of the State, when imperilled by the most tremendous conflict ever known. The heart of the nation was on fire; the actors were in earnest; most momentous interests were at stake; vast plans and movements were inaugurated; gigantic blows were struck, and hundreds of thousands bravely fell. The organizing and constructing power was

Congress : hence the history of its herculean labors through that memorable period will ever command the attention of the world ; and it is fortunate that one who shared those labors, and who knew their magnitude, was led to make of them such an impartial, vivid, and distinct record. The work is worthy of the subject and the man.

32

CHAPTER XIX.

REPLY TO MR. NYE. — CONGRESSIONAL TEMPERANCE
SOCIETY. — WELCOME TO BOSTON. —SOUTHERN TOUR.
— CONVENTION AT · WORCESTER. — SPEECH AT
MARLBOROUGH. — BANGOR. — FANEUIL
HALL. — WORKING-MEN. — HISTORY OF
THE RECONSTRUCTION. MEASURES
IN CONGRESS.

Peonage. — Whipping. — Colored Persons in the Militia. — Bill to facilitate Resto-
ration. — Speech thereon. — Feelings toward the Rebels. — Temperance in
Congress. — Hon. Richard Yates. — Reception at Tremont Temple. — Re-
marks of W. B. Spooner. — Mr. Wilson's Address. — Mr. Yates's. — Liquors
banished from the Capitol. — Enforcement of the Law. — Visit to the South.
— At Richmond, Va. — Petersburg. — Animosity of Goldsborough, N.C. —
Reception at Wilmington. — Mr. Robinson. — At Charleston, May 2. — New
Orleans. — Gen. Longstreet's Opinion. — Declines going to Europe. — Bill
vacating Offices. — Appointing Civilians incorporated in Mr. Trumbull's
Bill. — Remarks on its Passage. — President of Convention at Worcester. —
Speech. — Gen. Sheridan. — Hopeful View of the Republic. — Speech at
Marlborough. — Effects of Intemperance. — Who are Weak? — Strong
Appeal. — Speech at Bangor. — Gen. Grant. — Speech in Faneuil Hall. —
Friend of Working-Men. — Reconstruction Measures. — Style and Subject
Matter. — A Wedding.

THE system of peonage, or servitude, for debt, was
in force in the Territory of New Mexico, and
about two thousand persons were held in thraldom. Mr.
Wilson saw that it was inconsistent with the spirit of our
liberal institutions, and therefore introduced a bill on the

twenty-sixth day of January, 1867, for its abolition, which, on the 2d of the following March, became a law; and thus was the last vestige of human servitude in this land obliterated.

On the twelfth day of February, 1867, he reported two bills in the Senate, — one of which, in its eleventh section, prohibited whipping in the reconstructed States; and the other, that the word "white" should be stricken from the militia-laws, so that colored persons might become a part of the militia of the United States.

In order to carry into effect the measures of reconstruction already passed, Mr. Wilson, on the 7th of March, 1867, introduced an important bill supplementary to the act providing for "the more efficient government of the rebel States, and to facilitate restoration;" which, after long discussion in both Houses, became a law over the veto of the president on the twenty-third day of the same month. In a sharp encounter during the progress of this bill with Mr. Nye of Nevada, who was very severe in denouncing the rebels, and thought Mr. Wilson was extending his Christian charity too far towards them, he thus, in the spirit of wise and liberal statesmanship, replied: —

"I remind that senator in the outset that this nation has been engaged in a mighty contest of ideas, a bloody struggle, in which all the passions of this people, South and North, have been aroused. That bloody struggle is ended; that contest of ideas is closed. Patriotism, humanity, and Christianity bid us of the North and of the South subdue, hush, and calm the passions engendered by the terrific conflicts through which we have passed, and to call the dews of blessing, not the bolts of cursing, down upon each other. We should remember the words of one of our own poets of freedom and humanity: —

'Always he who most forgiveth
In his brother is most just.'

"Whatever the champions of the lost cause in the South
may do, we of the North, whose cause is triumphant in the
fields of war and of peace, should appeal, not to the passions
and prejudices and hatreds of the people, but to the heart
and conscience and reason. Unreasoning passion may
applaud violent appeals to-day; but unclouded reason will
utter its voice of condemnation to-morrow.

"The honorable senator from Nevada is pleased to tell
me that I am anxious to welcome rebels here. I do not
propose to welcome rebels here; but I do desire to welcome tried and true men of the South, the representatives
of the seven hundred thousand enfranchised black men,
the ever-loyal white men of the South, and the men compromised by the Rebellion, whose affections are again given
to their native land, and who would now peril their lives
for the unity of the republic and the triumph of the old
flag. I believe that the enfranchised black men of the
rebel States, the men who have ever been loyal, and the
men reluctantly compromised by the Rebellion, who are for
their country, and many fiery, generous, deluded young
men of the South, who have seen their political illusions
vanish in the smoke of lost battle-fields, can immediately
take the direction and control of these rebel States. I believe these States must pass into the hands of patriotic men,
who comprehend in their affections the whole country; of
liberty-loving men, who believe in the sublime creed of
human equality. I believe these States will soon pass into
the hands of radical and progressive men who are true to
country, true to the equal rights of man, true to the laws
of human development and progress. I would facilitate
that great work; I would welcome these men into these

chambers with heart and hand. Does the senator from Nevada wish to keep such men out of these chambers ? . . . The honorable senator from Nevada, and those who agree with him, fear our enemies, and distrust our friends. I do not fear our enemies, and I have confidence in our friends. This is the difference between the honorable senator from Nevada and myself.

" The honorable senator from Nevada deems it matter of reproach, now the bloody contest is over, the rebels beaten, and their cause lost forever, that I should not entertain and express toward my defeated and fallen countrymen of the South the same stern condemnation, the same sentiments of censure and reproach. They are not alien enemies ; they are not of another lineage and language : they are our countrymen. These States must continue for ages to come to be a part of our common country ; and these people, their children, and their children's children, must continue to be our countrymen. I do not consider it either generous, manly, or Christian, to nourish or cherish or express feelings of wrath or hatred toward them. At this time, when these misguided and mistaken countrymen of ours have been conquered, when we have absolutely established our ideas, which must pervade and be incorporated into their system of public policy, it seems to me to be a duty sanctioned by humanity and religion to heal the wounds of war. Sir, I have fought the battle for the country, I have fought this battle for the equal rights of man, not to pull down anybody, nor to be the personal enemy of anybody on earth. That is my position now, and it will be my position hereafter. Our words should not rekindle the prejudices, passions, and hatreds engendered by the bloody struggles of civil war ; but our words should be fitted

32*

to the changed condition of affairs and the needs of our country."

Anxious to save some of his associates at Washington from the baleful influence of strong drink, Mr. Wilson, early this year (1867), instituted the Congressional Temperance Society, of which he was chosen president. At the first meeting the hall of the House of Representatives was densely crowded, many standing in the aisles and at the doors. On taking the chair, Mr. Wilson said, —

" Several senators and representatives, mindful of the numerous evils and sorrows of intemperance, had formed a society, in which they had pledged each to the other, and all to the country, to put away from them forever the intoxicating cup, and to commit themselves and all they have to the holy cause of temperance. They humbly trusted in the providence of Almighty God that they might contribute to arrest the evils of intemperance which were sweeping over our land."

Among those who spoke was Senator Yates of Illinois, who had been, like many others, reclaimed by the kind efforts and example of the president of the society. His remarks were very touching, and were listened to with sincere delight. A noble man had come to his right mind. He ascribed his taking the pledge to Mr. Wilson, who came to him " in the kindness and goodness of his big heart," and said to him, " Governor, I want you to sign a call for a temperance meeting." He replied, " With all my heart," but did not wait for the meeting before he signed the pledge. He had now " promised the State, and all who loved him, Katy, and the children, that he would never more touch, taste, or handle, the unclean thing."

For his eloquent words and earnest efforts on behalf of temperance at Washington the citizens of Boston tendered

Mr. Wilson a public reception, on the fifteenth day of April, at the Tremont Temple. The building was crowded, and the utmost enthusiasm prevailed. On taking the chair, the president (William B. Spooner), said, —

" You have been invited to come here this evening to give a cordial welcome to Mr. Wilson, and to receive words of encouragement and wisdom from one who has always been true to this subject, to this cause, as he has always been true to the cause of the weak, suffering, and down-trodden, on all occasions. (Applause.)

" He has never forborne to speak his mind on this sub-ject, whenever occasion called ; he has never failed, in low places or in high places, wherever he has been, to give his example in favor of temperance. I have known him thirty years. When quite a young man, I used then to be with him in the temperance movement. He was always ready, and did not stop to ask whether the cause were popular. He asked whether it were right (applause). He asked, ' Can I do any good ? Can my example, my word, in favor of the cause, benefit my fellow-man ? ' That it has done good is manifest. His example is one which in this State, if a man wishes for promotion, he had better follow ; that is, do whatever is right under all circumstances. (Applause.) He asked only the questions, ' Is it right ? Can I do any good ? ' His recent efforts at the capital of the country in forming a total-abstinence society among the members of Congress and the other officers of the government have turned the attention of his state and of the country anew to him as an advocate of temperance." Mr. Wilson was introduced amid the most enthusiastic applause, and then made an address of remarkable force and fervor. In the course of his speech, he said, —

" You have made mention to-night, sir, of the organiza-

tion of the Congressional Temperance Society.   Sir, I
claim no honor for that.   At the last session of Congress
we organized a Congressional Temperance Society, composed of some of our ablest, truest, and best men; and I
thank God to-night that it lives in the strength of its purpose and its power.   (Applause.)   Judging from the
words that come to us from all parts of the country, it has
contributed something to advance the holy cause of temperance throughout the land.   I say to you to-night, what I
believe to be true, that there is no city of the Union where
there are, in proportion to the numbers, more true, earnest,
and devoted temperance men than in the city of Washington.   (Applause.)   There are more than six thousand
members of temperance organizations in that city (applause); and such men as Gen. Howard (applause), one
of our noblest, bravest, and best, are giving their influence
to advance the cause.   More than seven hundred liquor-
shops have been closed in that city, not by law, but starved
out by the people; and there are hundreds of other shops
that are eking out a precarious existence. . . .

   " The prairies of Illinois are all aflame in favor of the
cause, following in the grand movement their loved and
honored senator, Richard Yates.   (Applause.)   He has
been one of the victims of the curse of intemperance.
Every man and woman and child in his State knew it.
Last winter he came to me, or rather I went to him,
and asked him if he would sign a call for a temperance
meeting to organize a Congressional society; and he said
he would do it with all his heart.   Before I could get up
the meeting, he became earnest in the matter, and committed himself to the cause; and, by the blessing of
Almighty God, I believe he will stand to it.   He goes
home in a few days, and will be welcomed at Chicago as

you welcome me here to-night. (Applause.) His influence will tell with powerful effect in that State, where he is honored and loved for his devotion to his country, to freedom, and for his generous personal qualities.

"Two years ago, after the humiliating scene of the inauguration, I secured the passage of a resolution in the Senate, forbidding the sale of intoxicating liquors in the Capitol. In spite of that resolution, liquors were brought into the committee-rooms and into other places. Again I introduced the subject of banishing liquors from the Capitol; and Congress adopted a joint rule forbidding the sale, and empowering the sergeants-at-arms of the two Houses to keep all kinds of liquors out of the Capitol of the nation. (Applause.) No more can intoxicating liquors be brought into, sold, or given away in, that magnificent edifice. This banishment of liquors has been followed by the adoption of a rule requiring the members of the Capitol-police to sign the total-abstinence pledge; and they all have done it (applause), and more than four-fifths of the Senate employés have signed the pledge." (Applause.)

He closed his grand address by saying, —

"I thank you, ladies and gentlemen, for this generous welcome and these applauding voices; I thank you, Mr. Chairman, for your words of kindness and approval: and I close with the expression of the hope that the hallowed cause of temperance will be advanced in the state and nation. In this hour of trial let us invoke upon it the blessing of Almighty God, and the prayers of all whose hearts throb in sympathy with tempted and struggling humanity." (Prolonged applause.)

In order to examine the condition of the South, encourage the colored people, and defend the policy of his party,

Mr. Wilson made, in the spring of 1867, a tour through the Southern States. At Richmond, Va., he addressed some six thousand people from the steps of the Capitol. He was introduced to them by Gov. Pierpont, and assured his hearers that the Reconstruction Bill had in view the highest good of the whole country, and advised all classes to unite on the basis of the Republican party. "The Richmond Times" announced him as "a Puritan radical under the shadow of the monument of the great Virginia rebel."

At Petersburg, April 4, he spoke as openly as he would have done on Bunker Hill. The mayor presided at the meeting, which numbered several thousands. In respect to the war, he said, —

"It had to come; it was unavoidable. It came, and we fought it out; and, when the last gun was fired, I was in favor of forgetting all the bitterness engendered by the contest, and of marching with you shoulder to shoulder in favor of a united country. . . . There was only one cause of the war, — human slavery in America." To the colored people he said, "Go for the schoolhouse and the church. Get homes and lands, however humble they may be. Touch not the bowl whose contents degrade humanity."

At Goldsborough, N.C., the white people manifested signs of animosity; and one rebel declared that he should like to put a bullet through his head. He spoke, however, with fearlessness, and no violence was attempted.

At Wilmington, N.C., which he reached on the first day of May, he met with an enthusiastic reception. The public buildings were decorated with the national flag, streamers, &c.; and mottoes were suspended across the streets in many places. A procession of the colored men was formed with music, and marched to Dudley's Grove, a short distance from the city, where a public meeting was held. Among the mottoes noticed upon the banners borne in the procession was the following: "Equal rights before the law: we will ask no more; we will take no less."

Gen. Estes was president of the meeting. Resolutions were adopted, thanking Congress for passing the Military Reconstruction Bill; promising to reconstruct North Carolina with loyal men; to give colored men the right to sit on juries; and to secure rights and privileges for the poor white men by establishing a Republican party in the State.

Mr. Wilson spoke about two hours. He declared that the Republican party was not responsible for one life lost in the war; but, before God and history, the supporters of slavery were responsible for every life sacrificed and every dollar spent in it. He invited the colored people to vote with the Republican party, declaring it vitally important that there should be no black party or white party formed.

In reply to Mr. Robinson, editor of "The Despatch," who endeavored to throw the responsibility of the war upon antislavery agitators, Mr. Wilson declared that the abolition of slavery by the General Government was the result of the Rebellion. He congratulated Mr. Robinson upon the change already effected in his views by his willingness to have the colored people educated; and thought, that, in a few months more, Mr. Robinson would be fully affiliated with the Republican party.

As to colored men not holding commissions in the colored army, he declared that his own son, who died recently, served as a lieutenant, captain, and lieutenant-colonel in a regiment whose major was as black as any man in the audience.

He arrived at Charleston, S.C., on the second day of May, where he was cordially received by many distinguished citizens. He addressed a vast audience on Citadel Green, and was serenaded in the evening. He visited and addressed the citizens of Savannah and Augusta, Ga., Montgomery, Ala. (May 11), and New Orleans; and, although he was sharply questioned by the disloyal men, he was, in general, heard with attention, and treated with courtesy and respect. In a letter dated New Orleans, June 3, 1867, Gen. James Longstreet said of him, " I was much pleased to have the opportunity to hear Senator Wilson, and was agreeably surprised to meet such fairness and frankness in a politician whom I have been taught to believe uncompromisingly opposed to the white people of the South."

Mr. Wilson's impressions of the South were favorable; and, on arriving home, he spoke hopefully of the future prospects of the Southern people.

His friend Mr. Pierce had invited him to embark for Europe on the nineteenth day of June; but the continued illness of Mrs. Wilson led him to postpone his foreign tour.

Still distrusting the policy of the president, Congress, after taking a recess, assembled on the third day of July, 1867; when Mr. Wilson introduced a bill vacating the offices held under the pretended State governments, and for other purposes, which was not carried. His amendment authorizing district commanders to appoint civilians to perform the duties of persons removed from office was, however, incorporated in Mr. Trumbull's bill, which became a law over the veto of Mr. Johnson on the

19th of July, 1867. " The passage of the bill," said
Mr. Wilson, " would complete the work of restoration.
I rise now," continued he, " to express the hope, that,
throughout that part of our country, men of all parties
and of all sentiments and feelings will clearly understand, that, if they comply with the terms and conditions
of these three reconstruction laws honestly and faithfully, all obstacles will be removed, and they will be
admitted into these chambers."

On the 11th of September Mr. Wilson was chosen
president of the Republican Convention at Worcester,
and, on taking the chair, presented his views of the condition of the country in an earnest and felicitous speech,
during which he paid the following compliment to the
gallant Gen. Sheridan : —

" Not appeased by striking down the great war
secretary, Andrew Johnson has laid his hand of violence
on that brilliant, honored, and loved soldier, Philip H.
Sheridan, whose record in the field glitters with glorious
achievements, whose record in the fifth military district
is instinct with patriotism and justice. This brilliant
hero of the Valley of the Shenandoah, and of battle-
fields made immortal by his genius and valor, is sent
from his department, hurried away to the distant plains,
to the gorges of the Rocky Mountains, to chase the wild
Indian, with an admonition that his energies will there
find a fitting field for action. Time, it is said, brings
about its revenges. Perhaps it may so happen that an
outraged nation, that is master of presidents, congresses,
and generals, may bid this man — drunk at least with
unreasoning passion — descend from that lofty position
from which he smites down her honored statesman and
her brilliant general, and go back to that famous Ten-

nessee village, where his abilities will find an appropriate sphere of action in filling once again the office of village alderman. It is not given to men of the capacity or character of Andrew Johnson, however lifted up to exalted positions, to belittle Edwin M. Stanton or Philip H. Sheridan. The illustrious commander of our army, who is now enduring the burden imposed by patriotism, as did his predecessor through weary months, uttered the voice of loyal America when he expressed his appreciation of the 'zeal, patriotism, firmness, and ability' with which Edwin M. Stanton had discharged the duties of secretary of war. I remember, too, — for I could not forget it, — the generous tribute the same great commander paid a few weeks ago to the genius of Sheridan. 'The people,' he said, 'do not fully appreciate Sheridan. I think him the greatest soldier the war developed. Were we to have a great war, and to call out a million of men, I think Sheridan the best fitted to command them. Some persons say I have done a great deal for him; but I never did any thing for him: he has done much for me.' Such is the statesman and such is the general Andrew Johnson has thrust from posts of duty, and striven to disgrace."

He closed by this hopeful view of the republic: —

"If the Republicans of Massachusetts and of other States subordinate minor issues, personal ambitions and interests, and rise to the full comprehension of the high duties now imposed upon them, the complete unity of the country, and the perfect equality of the rights of the people, will speedily come. Then the republic, redeemed and purified, the people free to run the race and win the glittering prizes of life, will daily illustrate the power and beauty of free institutions. Then the people of the

North and the people of the South will vie with each other in fidelity to the country, and devotion to liberty. Then the bitter memories of the stern conflicts of civil war will fade away in the prosperity and renown of the great republic. Then the sons of patriots and the sons of rebels, whose fathers fought and fell on bloody fields, will glory in the name and fame of their common country, and cherish, honor, and love their countrymen. Inspired by these lofty purposes, animated by these exalted hopes, we, the Republicans of old Massachusetts, here and now call the battle-roll anew, and move forward to the conflicts of the future with the light of victory on our faces."

Though detained at home considerably this season to watch at the bedside of his sick wife, Mr. Wilson made many public speeches on behalf of temperance in various towns and cities of this State. In a grand address at Marlborough in November, he said, —

" I was born in a section of the country where New-England rum was used at births and at funerals; used to keep out the heat of summer and the cold of winter ; sold openly at the cross-road groceries, where too many of the companions of my boyhood were wont to assemble, instead of going to lyceums and associations for mental and moral improvement, and spend their evenings in drinking poor rum. I have seen the effects of the use of intoxicating liquors on the farm, in the workshop, and in the halls of legislation. I have found that in the field in the heats of summer, in the forests in winter, in the mechanic's shop, in our own State legislature, in the Congress of the United States, everywhere, the men who use intoxicating drinks are the first to fail in the performance of duty. During fourteen sessions in the Senate of the United States I have witnessed many severe contests, lasting through the hours of the night until daylight streamed into the windows; and I have always found that the men who resorted to intoxicating liquids for strength found weakness, — were always the first to retire to their rooms or their homes."

During the summer and autumn of 1868, Mr. Wilson heartily advocated the election of Gen. Grant and the course of the Republican party. On the 27th of August he spoke to a vast throng in Bangor, Me., on what the Republican and Democratic parties have done, and what they propose to do. Referring to what the former organization had accomplished, he said, —

"It was said of Wilberforce that he went to God with the shackles of eight hundred thousand West-India slaves in his hands. The Republican party enters the forum of the nations with four million and a half of riven fetters in one hand, and four million and a half of title-deeds of American citizenship in the other. These broken fetters, these title-deeds, it holds up to the gaze of the living present and the advancing future. In the progress of the ages, it has been given to few generations, in any form or by any modes, to achieve a work so vast, so grand, so sure to be recorded by the historic pen, or flung upon the canvas in enduring colors. Defeat and disaster may come upon the Republican party; it may perish utterly from the land it saved and made free: but its name will be forever associated with the emancipation of millions of a poor, friendless, and hated race, their elevation to the heights of citizenship, their exaltation to equality of civil rights and privileges, and, crowning act of all, the prerogative ' to vote and to be voted for.' These beneficent deeds will live in the hearts of coming generations, and 'brighter glow and gleam immortal, unconsumed by moth or rust.'"

Speaking of the coming contest, he said, — and his prediction time and events have verified, —

"In November there is to be another struggle between these two parties for the control of the national administration. The Republican party met at Chicago, re-affirmed its policy of reconstruction, pronounced against all forms of repudiation, for the reduction and equalization of taxation, for the equal protection of American citizens, for the recognized obligations to our soldiers and to the widows and orphans of the gallant dead, and for the removal of restrictions imposed upon rebels as rapidly as the safety of the loyal people will admit. The convention than presented the name of Gen. Grant, the great captain who has so often marshalled our armies to victory; and Schuyler Colfax, a statesman of pure life, stainless honor, and commanding influence. If success crowns its efforts, if the administration shall be intrusted to Gen. Grant, with a House of Representation to sustain that administration, the policy of reconstruction will be perfected, the States will all be speedily restored to their practical relations to the General Government, equal rights will be assured and disabilities removed, the nation's faith will be untarnished, its currency and credit improved, and 'Peace,' in the language of Mr. Lincoln, ' will come to stay.' Then the blood poured out like autumnal rains will not have been shed in vain; for then united and free America, with liberty for all and justice to all, will enter upon a career of development, culture, and progress, that shall insure a ' future grand and great.'"

His speech in Faneuil Hall on the 14th of October most

33*

clearly exhibits him as an earnest, strong, and sensible defender of the interests of the working-people. He stands upon the side, as he has ever done, of those who bear the heat and burden of the day. He said, —

"To provide for the expenses of that Democratic rebellion, the Republican party were compelled to take the responsibility of arranging a system of taxation; and they so adjusted that taxation as to make the burden bear as lightly as possible on the productive interests of the country and upon the working-men of the country. More than one-half of the duties levied on imports are assessed on wines, brandies, silks, velvets, laces, and other articles of luxury, chiefly consumed by the more wealthy portion of our countrymen. The duties imposed on the necessaries of life — upon tea, coffee, sugar, and other articles entering into the consumption of the masses of the people — are made as low as possible; and discrimination is made in favor of our mechanical and manufacturing industry.

"The Republican party spurns this Democratic doctrine of taxing every species of property according to its value. It believes in discriminating in favor of poor, toiling men, and of putting the burden of taxation on accumulated capital and large incomes. In time of war, when the nation needed money so much, the Republicans exempted nineteen out of every twenty dollars of the incomes of the people. This was done to relieve the working-men, whose small incomes were required for the support of their families and the education of their children. We exempted all incomes under six hundred dollars; and this exemption included the incomes of nearly all the laboring-men, mechanics, and small farmers, of the country. We taxed all incomes from six hundred to five thousand dollars five per cent, and all incomes over five thousand dollars ten per cent. That was not *equal* taxation : but it was *just* taxation ; for it was based on the sound policy of putting the burden upon capital, and taking the burden from labor. Now we have taken the tax from all incomes less than a thousand dollars, and we tax all incomes above a thousand dollars five per cent, thus relieving the working-men and nearly all the mechanics and farmers from taxation on incomes. We Republicans intend to stand or fall by this policy, which discriminates in favor of the poor, the mechanics, the small farmers, and the working-men, of the country. We serve notice on the Democratic party, on all the supporters of this anti-democratic doctrine of the equal taxation of every species of property according to its value, that we Republicans will never agree to the taxation of the little earnings of working-men at the same rate we tax the incomes of the Stewarts and the Astors, the great corporations and capitalists, of the country. We give the Democracy notice that we will never tax sugar, coffee, and tea at the same rates we tax silks and wines and brandies ; that we will never tax a gallon of milk as high as we tax a gallon of whiskey. We give the Democracy notice that we will not tax the tools of the mechanic, the horse of the drayman, the little homes and farms of the poor, and the incomes of working-men needed for the support of themselves and the support of their households. We Republicans will never consent to the putting of the burdens of the government equally on the small accumulations of the poor and the great capitals and large interests of the country. That is the position of the Republican party ; and it is a position in favor of the productive interests of the nation and the interests of the working-men : and we

Republicans mean to stand by it, or fall by it ; live by it, or die by it. Every laboring-man in America, every mechanic, every farmer, and every business-man, who desires to develop the mighty resources of this country, and carry it upward and onward in a career of power and prosperity, should trample upon this democratic doctrine of equal taxation, which is against labor, and in favor of capital ; against the loyal, and in favor of the disloyal, portions of the land."

Inured to steady and persistent intellectual labor, Mr. Wilson finds in it his chief delight. To him idleness is misery. He is a working-man, who believes in actual work : and his system being, by his temperate habits, always in good working-order, he turns off work with astonishing ease and celerity ; work, too, that has a meaning and a purpose, — guiding legislators in their course, and enriching the historical literature of his country. In addition to his official and public labors this year (1868), he published a handsome volume of four hundred and sixty-seven pages, entitled " The History of the Reconstruction Measures of the Thirty-ninth and Fortieth Congresses, 1865–1868. By Henry Wilson." In this important work the author traces vividly the course of legislation during those eventful years which followed the collapse of the Rebellion, and the contest between Congress and the president on the various questions growing out of the reconstruction of the Confederate States. " My purpose in this work," the author says, " has been to narrate with brevity and impartiality this legislation of Congress, and to give the positions, opinions, and feelings of the actors in these great measures of legislation." In the treatment of his subject he brings forward in *propriâ personâ* the different speakers, — Sumner, Trumbull, Fessenden, Wilson, Davis, Hendricks, Howe, and others, — and presents them as they introduced, opposed, or advocated measures in the legislative chambers. The very words of the disputants are given, which imparts dramatic interest to the subject, and makes interesting what otherwise might, except to a statesman, prove dull reading. The combatants stand forth prominently on the canvas: the blow of every champion is made manifest. When the author himself speaks, the style is manly, clear, and forcible, — an evident advance upon his former record as a writer. To the student of our political history this book is invaluable, bringing the subject-matter on the great questions before the Thirty-ninth and Fortieth Congresses, which runs through several thousand pages of "The Congressional Globe," into the compass of a single portable volume. The reconstruction of the Confederate States demanded comprehensive views of the condition of the country, generous sympathies, and decisive action; and strong men who took the lead in legislation through the war came up with fearless front to resist the policy of the executive, and save the nation from the rule of rebels. As an impartial record of this struggle by one who himself bore no unimportant part in it, Mr. Wilson's book will doubtless ever hold a prominent place in legislative history.

The home of Mr. Wilson was enlivened on the 25th of December, 1868, by the marriage of Lieut. Alexander L. Smith, who was in Gen. Sherman's army when he made his grand march to the sea, and Miss Annette Howe, a daughter of one of Mrs. Wilson's brothers, and an estimable young lady.

During the Fortieth and Forty-first Congresses Mr.

Wilson was steadily engaged in framing and carrying important measures for the public good. Among them may be mentioned a bill to amend the elective franchise of the District of Columbia; a bill for the reduction of the army; a bill to equalize distribution of banking capital; a joint resolution as to the management of the Freedmen's Bureau, — of the Fortieth; and bills to establish a line of steamships; to appoint a commission to examine claims of loyal persons for supplies; to grant two million acres of land for education in the District of Columbia; to remove disabilities from persons engaged in the Rebellion; to grant increase of pensions to widows of officers; and joint resolutions granting Lincoln Hospital to Columbia Hospital for women, and respecting pay of enlisted men, — of the Forty-first Congress. On these and many other measures Mr. Wilson made remarks evincing great legislative experience and ability. The pages of " The Congressional Globe " bear constant testimony to his senatorial industry and efficiency. His eyes were ever open to watch, his tongue was ever ready to defend, the rights of the injured and oppressed. No senator ever framed and carried so many bills through the Senate of the United States as Mr. Wilson; and some of them are the most important ever enacted in this country. In his management of measures in the Senate he has shown the practical good sense of a sound and accomplished statesman. When he has found it impossible to carry a measure as first presented, he has been willing to accept such modification or substitute as might secure its passage; consenting willingly that another should receive the credit, if by any change or compromise the end could be obtained. His idea has been, that one step in advance

is better than no progress : so that, while others have in-
sisted on the whole or nothing, he has accepted the best he
could at the time secure ; and, gaining that, he has often
found himself in a position to gain the whole.   His bill
for the soldiers' bounties finally appeared in another form,
under another name, and for a lower sum than he proposed ; but he rejoiced that eighty millions were secured,
though his original measure was defeated.

His method is to throw himself out of the question,
and to support a measure on its own merits : and this, in
part, accounts for his success ; for a statesman attempting
to carry himself with his measures generally finds himself overborne by the burden.

CHAPTER XX.

DEATH OF MRS. WILSON. — VISIT TO EUROPE. —
WRITINGS. — NOMINATION. — ELECTION.

Mrs. Wilson's Death and Character. — Mrs. Ames's Opinion. — Visit to
Europe. — American Missionary Society. — Rise and Fall of the
Slave-Power. — Extract. — Nomination as Vice-President. — Letter
of Acceptance. — Address at Boston. — Regard for the Memory of
Mrs. Wilson. — Visit to North Carolina and Virginia. — Regret for
One Expression. — American Party and Crédit Mobilier. — Mr. Sum-
ner's Course regretted. — Election as Vice-President. — His Poverty.

IN May, 1870, Mr. Wilson was brought into profound
affliction by the decease of his beloved wife, who for
many months had been sinking under an incurable disease. At the close of the 28th she passed peacefully
away; and those who stood around her dying-bed then
realized the meaning of the words, "He giveth his
beloved sleep."

An address was made at her funeral in the church by
the Rev. Edmund Dowse; and her remains, in a casket
covered with flowers, and followed by a long concourse
of sincere mourners, were borne to the Dell-park Cemetery, where they repose beside those of her only son.

Mrs. Wilson was a woman of rare gentleness, earnest
in purpose, unassuming in manner, ever blessing those
around her by her words and deeds of love. Early in
life she became a Christian; and she united with the
Congregational church at Natick on the fifth day of
December, 1852. Whether moving in the fashionable

society at Washington, or in the quiet circle of her home, she was ever a bright ornament of the doctrines she professed. Her sufferings, though severe, she bore without a murmur or complaint, and shed the light of a sanctified and loving heart upon her friends and kindred to the last. In her elevation, she did not cast off, as many do, the companions of early days; and they will always bear among the richest treasures of the memory the smile and the tear of her sympathy and affection.

"Into the sacred privacy of that wifely devotion which she always manifested," says one who knew her excellence, "we may not intrude: but it can at least be said, that she was all that the heart could desire a Christian wife to be; and eternity alone can reveal how great was her influence upon the companion of her life, whose feet she, more than any other human instrumentality, led to the cross of Christ."

Another writer said of her, "For thirty years she has been of rare service to her husband in all sweet and wifely qualities. Of true instincts, unobtrusive piety, untiring benevolence, and equal temperament, ever a lover of justice, she was alike guide and inspirer to her husband, whose long, distinguished, and honorable career is, in no small degree, due to her discreet and loving co-operation."

Her character is thus portrayed by Mrs. Mary Clemmer Ames: —

"Within the last week, the body of one has been laid in her native earth whose lovely presence will long be missed in Washington. Mrs. Wilson, the wife of Senator Wilson, went out from among us in the fair May days; and the places which have known her here so long and so pleasantly, will know her, save in memory, no more for-

ever. She was a gentle, Christian woman. I have never
yet found words rich enough to tell *all* that such a woman
is. My pen lingers lovingly upon her name. I would
fain say something of her who now lives beyond the meed
of all human praise that would make her example more
beautiful and enduring to the living. For, in profounder
intellectual development resulting from wider culture and
larger opportunity, are we in no danger of losing sight of
those graces of the spirit, which, however exalted her fate,
must remain to the end the supreme charm of woman?
There is nothing in all the universe so sweet as a Christian woman; as she who has received into her heart, till
it shines forth in her character and life, the love of the
divine Master.

"Such a woman was Mrs. Wilson in this gay capital.
When great sorrow fell upon her, and ceaseless suffering,
the light from the heavenly places fell upon her face:
with an angel patience, and a childlike smile, and an unfaltering faith, she went down into the valley of shadows.
She possessed a keen and wide intelligence. She was
conversant with public questions, and interested in all
those movements of the day in which her husband takes
so prominent a part. Retiring by nature, she avoided
instinctively all ostentatious display; but, where help and
encouragement were needed by another, the latent power
of her character sprang into life, and then she proved
herself equal to great executive effort. No one can praise
her so eloquently as he who loved her and knew her best.
To hear Senator Wilson speak of his wife when he taught
her, a little girl in school; when he married her, 'the
loveliest girl in all the county;' when he received into
his heart the fragrance of her daily example; when he
watched over her dying, only to marvel at the endurance

and sweetness and sunshine of her patience,— is to learn what a force for spiritual development, what a ceaseless inspiration, was this wife to her husband. Precious to those who live is the legacy of such a life."

Mr. Wilson regarded his wife and always spoke of her with most affectionate tenderness. He fully appreciated and revered her excellences. To him her word and her wishes were sacred. Her departure filled his heart with unutterable grief; and the dark cloud of that bereavement still casts its shadow over his pathway. But he has the hope of the Christian, which alone can give the cloud a " silver lining."

In a letter in response to an invitation to the " Gathering of the Howe Family," held in Framingham, Aug. 31, 1871, he thus touchingly alludes to her : —

" I regret, and shall long continue to regret, that I was not permitted on that occasion to mingle with those who bear the name of one endeared to me by the holiest and tenderest ties of earth ; of one of the purest and loveliest spirits that ever blessed kindred and friends by her presence, or left, in passing through death to a higher life, more precious memories."

In the memorial of that meeting the author says, " Mrs. Wilson was a lady of unusual mental and personal attractions, blending grace with dignity in manner, and ornamenting, both in private and in public life, the doctrines of her Lord and Master."

None but him that has followed the light of the household to the silent grave can know the desolation of a deserted home. To relieve his mind from the sad memories which every object tended to awaken, Mr. Wilson decided to spend the summer of 1871 abroad. Leaving New York in " The Scotia " on the 7th of June, he had a prosperous voyage across the Atlantic, and was somewhat "lionized" by the passengers, as one of them has written, on the way. The writer adds, " He spoke to me with feeling of the virtues of one whom he had lost, of her sickness and her death; showed me the picture of her face; and expressed the hope that he should meet her in the skies."

Mr. Wilson did not visit Europe to study art, to gain receptions, or to hunt for kings. He was, however, kindly received by Mr. Gladstone, Thomas Hughes, and other eminent men. He had the pleasure of spending several days in the British Parliament, as well as in the French National Assembly, and of listening to the debates. The plain and sensible style of speaking of the former body he admired. With the exception of the strong and fervid Spurgeon, the English preachers did not please him, their manner being too monotonous and scholastic.

He travelled over six thousand miles in Europe, visiting Amsterdam, Berlin (where he was cordially received), Vienna, and many other cities; noticing the manners and customs of the people, and, as far as possible, the working of the different educational, religious, and political systems.

Never had the liberal institutions of America appeared more glorious to him than when, after this survey of foreign life, he breathed again the air of freedom. During his absence he wrote once a week to Mrs. Howe, the mother of his departed wife, who now, though over eighty years of age, presides over his household with dignity and grace.

This was the memorial-year of the American Missionary Association; and at the meeting in Hartford, Oct. 24, Mr.

Wilson made a brief and vigorous address, in which he presented his belief in our common brotherhood, and his view of the work to be done by the philanthropists of America : —

"God has given us the care of this magnificent continental empire, broad and grand. It is ours, — ours to develop and improve: the responsibility is with us, — with the people of these United States. These poor black men at the South need our prayers and our labor; they need education, moral culture, and elevation. And they are not the only ones who need it: there are thousands of others, who have been referred to in the admirable address to which we have just listened, — others coming from the Eastern world. Our gateways are open on the Atlantic and on the Pacific coast; and people will come here. I would bind my heart and hand, and what little I have of property, and the aspirations of my soul, to elevate humanity. Every human being who steps on the soil of the North-American republic, — no matter where he comes from, nor what blood runs in his veins, nor what language he speaks, — he is a man : God made him, and our Lord and Master Jesus Christ died for him as well as for us; and it is our duty to lift him up. It is our duty to elevate all classes and conditions of men who come to our shores. God knows to-night there is a mighty work to do. Look over the broad land to-day, and what do we see? It is not alone the poor negro, whose mind for long centuries has been closed against education and culture. Look at the poor white people of the South, who were trampled down when the black men were trampled down. Look at the master class; look at the Ku-Kluxes: they dishonor human nature to-night. I tell you, friends, we have a work to

34*

do in the South, not only for the black race, but for our own white race. Slavery is gone : but it has left passions, prejudice, and ignorance ; and it is for us to remove them.

"Look at our own country, — whole sections of it dishonored every day. Men abuse public stations, dishonor their names, and degrade their country. We have examples of this before us to-day that astonish the world. Education will not cure this entirely. We want, with our education, a great deal of moral culture. We want the heart cultivated as well as the head. This is the great want of the times.

"I would make this republic an honest example to all nations. To every philanthropist, to every humble Christian, — I would say to all such, that, among all the benevolent associations of our country, this is one of the best, and should have our contributions, our generous support, and our prayers in our closets on bended knees."

In the early part of this present year (1872) Mr. Wilson published the first volume, containing six hundred and seventy pages in royal octavo, of "The History of the Rise and Fall of the Slave-Power in America."

It is indeed refreshing, now that the clamor of war has subsided and the smoke of the battle-fields rolled away, to sit calmly down in the sunlight of peace, and trace the progress of that malignant power which grew with the nation's growth ; which fastened on the body politic, until it perished in the very wounds it had itself inflicted. Human servitude was the cause of our calamity as a nation ; and, in rising up from those calamities, we look back upon them as upon some fearful dream. With consummate ability, Mr. Wilson, in this portion of his work, presents the origin, progress, domination, of this power in America, up to its Texan victory in 1844; and in the two succeeding volumes, to be published in 1873–4, will describe its arrogant assumptions up to 1861, and then its mighty struggle for existence, till its final overthrow and extinction in the surrender of the rebel arms, and reconstruction of the rebel States. No man living has higher qualifications for such a work than Mr. Wilson. With accurate knowledge of our national history; with more than thirty years' experience as a legislator; with an intimate personal acquaintance with the prominent political leaders of that period; with views enlarged by years of meditation on the theme,— he brings to the execution of this great work accomplishments which must render it, when completed, one of the most valuable contributions to American history ever made. Through the first volume the hand of the master is visible on every page; and, although the master is of necessity a partisan, he has, in general, risen above the spirit of partisanship, and ascribed honor to whom honor is due.

"Of the living and of the dead," he says, "I have written as though I were to meet them in the presence of Him whose judgments are ever sure." To the Christian patriot the author's constant reference to the hand of God in the evolution of our national destiny is as satisfactory as it is in itself just and philosophical. This, he says, in closing his first volume, should be "a perpetual inspiration in the darkest hour, a perennial source of faith and hope, of consolation and of courage." "This work," says an able writer, "must take first rank among the historical productions of the nineteenth century; and it will give to the author an additional claim upon the consideration of his countrymen that he has written so well of that work in which he was one of the chief actors, thus winning for himself the position of the scholar and the historian, in addition to that of the politician and the statesman. He and others have done that which deserves to be well told ; and he has told it well. His words, like his works, will be immortal, — the just reward of the excellence of both."

As an example of the author's imaginative power, and vigor of his style, the closing page of his chapter on " The Amistad " captives may be cited. It will be remembered that in 1839 these Africans, fifty-two in number, rose upon the captain and the crew of " The Amistad," took the vessel, and then, through their ignorance of navigation, were landed and imprisoned at New London. The administration would have returned them to the hands of the slave-trader ; but, through the humane exertions of Mr. Lewis Tappan and his friends, the captives, after a sharp contest in the courts, were set free. After stating the whole case with perspicuity and force, the author says, —

" In all the acts of slavery's grim tragedy, there have been few scenes which presented more elements of interest than that of ' The Amistad ' captives. With two continents and the wide Atlantic for a theatre ; with the robber-chiefs of Africa, the slave-pirates of the ocean, the representatives of a European monarchy and an American republic, for actors, seemingly engaged in a common cause, and inspired by a common spirit, — it presented through the whole, with dramatic variety and force, the strangest contrasts and the most unlooked-for and contradictory combinations. It presented barbarism in its most repulsive and rudest aspect, and Christianity in its most attractive and lovely attitude. It began with the midnight hunt for captives in the wilds of Africa: it closed by Christian men and women sending and accompanying these captives back to Africa to plant churches and schools among their benighted countrymen. Through the whole, however, the one dark and hideous fact stands out, — that slavery is essentially the same, its adherents substantially alike. A system of violence impatient of all restraints, whether of reason or of conscience, humanity or religion, the laws of the heart or the laws of the State, it seems mainly intent on compassing its own ends by whatever means and at whatever hazards. It was the same in Africa and in America ; in the barracoon and in the middle passage ; under a monarchy or in a republic ; in a Pagan, Protestant, or Catholic country."

At the Republican Convention held in Philadelphia last June, Mr. Wilson received the nomination for vice-president of the United States. Mr. Colfax, who was a personal friend of Mr. Wilson, had, in a private letter, signified his intention of declining a renomination, when the latter allowed his name to be presented. The vote for these gentlemen in the convention was very close ; when Virginia changed twenty of her votes from John F. Lewis to Mr. Wilson, and made sure his nomination. On the reception of the despatch announcing it in the Senate, Mr. Colfax came forward and heartily congratulated his friend on the result. Among many congratulations, the following was received from Philadelphia, which doubtless is the general sentiment of the people of color, for whom Mr. Wilson has labored so long and effectually : —

PHILADELPHIA, June 6, 1872.

The colored working-men of the country send you their congratulations, and second your nomination ; and will march in solid columns to the polls in November, and cast their votes for the representative laboring-man of the American nation.

(Signed)　　ISAAC MYERS,
Pres. Colored National Labor Union.

Speaking of the nomination, "The New-York Tribune" said, —

"Henry Wilson is a working-man, and life-long Republican, who has passed through thirty years of political contests without a question of his devotion to principle, or a stain upon his integrity."

His letter of acceptance points briefly to the leading features of the past, present, and future policy of the Republican party.

HON. HENRY WILSON'S LETTER ACCEPTING THE NOMINATION.

WASHINGTON, June 13, 1872.

To the Hon. THOMAS SETTLE and others, President and Vice-Presidents of the National Republican Convention held at Philadelphia on the 5th and 6th of the present month.

Gentlemen, — Your note of the 10th instant, conveying to me the action of the convention in placing my name in nomination for the office of Vice-President of the United States, is before me. I need not give you the assurance of my grateful appreciation of the high honor conferred upon me by this action of the Fifth National Convention of the Republican party. Sixteen years ago, in the same city, was held the first meeting of the men who, amid the darkness and doubts of that hour of slaveholding ascendency and aggression, had assembled in a national convention to confer with each

other on the exigencies to which that fearful domination
had brought their country. After a full conference, the
highest point of resolve they could reach, the most they
dared to recommend, was the avowed purpose to prohibit the existence of slavery in the Territories. Last
week the same party met by its representatives from
thirty-seven States and ten Territories at the same great
centre of wealth, intelligence, and power, to review the
past, take note of the present, and indicate its line of
action for the future. As typical facts, headlands of the
nation's history, there sat on its platform, taking an honorable and prominent part in its proceedings, admitted
on terms of perfect equality to the leading hotels of the
city, not only the colored representative of the race
which were ten years before in abject slavery, but one of
the oldest and most prominent of the once despised abolitionists, to whom was accorded as to no other the
warmest demonstration of popular regard and esteem ; an
ovation not to him alone, but to the cause he had so ably
and so many years represented, and to men and women,
living and dead, who toiled through long years of obloquy
and self-sacrifice for the glorious fruition of that hour.
It hardly needed the brilliant summary of its platform to
set forth its illustrious achievements. The very presence
of those men was alone significant of the victories
achieved, the progress already made, and the great distance which the nation had travelled between the years
1856 and 1872. But, grand as has been its record, the
Republican party rests not on its past alone : it looks to
the future, and grapples with its problems of duty and
of danger. It proposes, as objects of its immediate
accomplishment, " complete liberty and exact equality for
all ; " the enforcement of the recent amendments to the

National Constitution ; the reform in the civil service ; the national domain to be set apart for homes for the people ; the adjustment of the duties on imports, so as to secure remunerative wages to labor ; the extension of bounties to all soldiers and sailors who in line of duty became disabled ; the continual and careful encouragement and protection of voluntary immigration, and guarding with a zealous care the rights of adopted citizens ; the abolition of the franking privilege, and the speedy reduction of the rates of postage ; the reduction of the national debt and rates of interest, and resumption of specie payment ; the encouragement of American commerce and of ship-building ; the suppression of violence, and the protection of the ballot-box. It also placed on record the opinions and purposes of the party in favor of amnesty ; against all forms of repudiation ; and indorsed the humane and peaceful policy of the administration in regard to the Indians. But, while clearly defining and distinctly announcing the policy of the Republican party on these questions of practical legislation and administration, the convention did not ignore the great social problems which are pressing their claims for solution, and which demand the most careful study and wise consideration. Foremost stands the labor question. Concerning the relations of capital and labor, the Republican party accepts the duty of so shaping legislation as to secure full protection and the amplest field for capital, and for labor, the creator of capital, the largest opportunities, and a just share of mutual profits of these two great servants of civilization. To woman too, and her new demands, it extends the hand of grateful recognition, and proffers it a most respectful inquiry. It recognizes her noble devotion to the country and freedom, welcomes her admission to wider fields of usefulness, and commends her demands for additional rights to the calm and careful consideration of the nation; to guard well what has already been secured, to work out faithfully and wisely what is now in hand, and to consider the questions which are looming up to view but a little way before us. The Republican party is to-day what it was in the gloomy years of slavery, rebellion, and reconstruction,— a national necessity. It appeals therefore, for support, to the patriotic and liberty-loving; to the just and humane; to all who dignify labor; to all who would educate, elevate, and lighten the burdens of the sons and daughters of toil. With its great record and the work still to be done under the great soldier whose historic renown and whose successful administration for the last three years begat such popular confidence, the Republican party may confidently, in the language of the convention you represent, start on a new march to victory. Having accepted thirty-six years ago the distinguished doctrines of the Republican party of to-day; having, during the years of that period, for their advancement, subordinated all other issues, acting in and co-operating with political organizations with whose leading doctrines I sometimes had neither sympathy nor belief; having labored incessantly for many years to found and build up the Republican party; and having, during its existence, taken a humble part in its grand work,— I gratefully accept the nomination thus tendered; and shall endeavor, if it shall be ratified by the people, faithfully to perform the duties it imposes.

Respectfully yours,

(Signed)   HENRY WILSON.

At a grand ratification meeting held in Faneuil Hall on the 22d of June, 1872, in which able speeches were made by Judge Hoar and Gen. Butler, Mr. Wilson, being presented amidst a storm of cheers and applause, in substance said, —

" Mr. Chairman and Fellow-Citizens, — I thank you for this kind welcome, and will not detain you at this late hour by any remarks of mine. I hardly know why I was invited here. The doctrines of your platform I have proclaimed to hundreds of thousands of men in nearly thirty States of the Union. I gave an unhesitating support to Gen. Grant during the war, and I have given an unhesitating support to his administration during the past three years (applause) ; and I assure you to-night, if you need the assurance, that I shall give an unhesitating support to his re-election to the presidency. (Applause.) As for myself, I leave it to my friends, personal and political, in Massachusetts and in the country ; and I am sure, whatever my friends may say, that those who do not agree with me politically will not accuse me of any want of fidelity to myself. I only say to you at this hour, that I trust you, men of Boston and of Massachusetts, will this year, and in the future, be as true as you have been for the past twelve years for the cause of the country and the cause of liberty. No matter who may be the candidate at Baltimore, — whether it be Horace Greeley or any other man, — you will meet in this canvass the Democratic party of the United States. You have met the party before ; you have defeated it before. You can, and I have no doubt whatever you will, defeat it in the coming election. Listen to no voice. You remember Republicans said a few years ago in Virginia, ' We will put up a Republican for governor, and we will have a Republican administration with the support of the Democratic party.' He went into power. The Republicans were defeated; and he became — what he knew he was before — the mere instrument of the Democratic party in Virginia. Republicans in Western Virginia joined the Democratic party; and to-day the question is submitted in a constitutional convention, whether the black men shall have the right to vote or not. Republicans joined Democrats, and restored the Democracy to power, in Tennessee; and the school system, under which there were a hundred and ninety thousand children in the schools in that State, was broken down. Republicans joined the Democrats in Missouri; and Frank Blair, who represents Democracy, sits in the Senate of the United States. The experiment made shows, that, when they join issue, the Republicans go to the Democratic party: that party would never come to them. Stand, then, I say, by the Republican platform, by the Republican candidates. (Applause.) Continue and hold and secure what we fought for in war; and, in addition to all, march with events, keep pace with human progress, bearing the flag of Republican civilization and improvement in our country, and our efforts will be blessed for the good of our country and the world." (Applause.)

Of his title to the suffrage of the colored people of America, Mr. Garrison thus, in a recent letter, speaks: —

" During thirty-six years of public life he has made the freedom of the race, so long peeled and trodden down, paramount to all other political considerations. Instead of persistently shunning antislavery meetings, he was a frequent attendant upon them, and freely participated in their proceedings. Now that he has been deservedly nominated by the Republican party for the vice-presidency of the United States, and, if elected, may possibly, in the turn of events, be the acting president, it should be a matter of pride and gratitude on the part of colored voters to give him their united suffrages."

When the news of his nomination to the vice-presidency was telegraphed to him by his friends in Natick, his touching reply was, "Place a bouquet of flowers on my wife's grave." She ever shone as a benignant star in his memory. In July he visited North Carolina and Virginia, and made effective speeches at Wilmington, Richmond, and other cities, aiming ever to conciliate the disaffected Republicans, to induce them to return to the ranks of the regular party, and to stand true to the principles for which they had so manfully contended on the field of battle. The meeting at Wilmington continued seven hours; and great enthusiasm was manifested by the white as well as colored citizens. He returned in excellent health, and with hopeful views of the condition of the States he had visited. He observed to a friend, on his return, that, during thirty-two years of political life, he had made about thirteen hundred speeches that had appeared in print; and that, so far as he could remember, he had uttered but one sentence that he regretted, and that because of misapprehension: it was in reply to Mr. Benjamin of Louisiana, when he charged him with treason to a country "which even secured freedom to the race that stoned the prophets, and crucified the Redeemer of the world."

In August following, he made a Western tour, and was everywhere received with great enthusiasm by the people.

At Richmond, Ind., he addressed an audience of ten thousand persons; and his earnest and eloquent appeals for the maintenance of the integrity of the Republican party met with hearty and prolonged responses from the vast multitude. Returning home (Aug. 13), he spoke to an enthusiastic meeting in Natick; and a banner bearing the names of Grant and Wilson was unfurled in the westerly part of the town, near the spot where he had arrived, penniless and unknown, in 1833, and where he commenced making "brogans" in the little shop of Mr. William P. Legro. He then, in September, visited several cities in Maine, where he met with a most cordial reception, and spoke with his wonted fire and wisdom before many enthusiastic audiences. As many as fifteen hundred people, for instance, received him in Columbia Hall, Bath; and hundreds were unable to gain admittance. Thus moving with untiring activity from State to State, and city to city, he conducted, as a veteran understanding well the strategy of the opposing forces, this exciting presidential campaign.

It was urged against him, that he had once belonged to the Native American party; and he, of course, admitted it. "But," said he, "in 1854, there were a million men in this movement. I, with the rest, went into it, as the people went into the Union leagues, to break up the old parties. The antislavery friends, then, out of this, formed the Republican party. In the National Convention at Philadelphia, I told them, that if they adopted that narrow, intolerant, bigoted platform, I would use my influence to crush it to atoms. They adopted it. I left it; and we crushed it to atoms." Attempts were also made to implicate him in the questionable transactions of the Crédit Mobilier, by which

35*

the fair fame of several congressmen was tarnished; but he most emphatically and truly denied that he ever received any of its bonds, shares, or stocks; and, though some property belonging to his wife had been therein invested, it was immediately withdrawn when it appeared that such investment might not be legal, just, and right.

Of the departure of his colleague, Mr. Sumner, from the ranks of the old Republicans, he spoke with unfeigned sorrow. " I have," said he to a friend, " most earnestly expostulated with him on his course. I believe that he is wrong: I have frankly told him so; but, without resenting my appeal to him, he stands immovable. I am sorry for him." Then, in reference to himself, Mr. Wilson said, " My own course has been as straight as that of a cannon-ball; and men will yet acknowledge it." It is worthy to be noted, and alike honorable to both, that political differences produced no personal animosity between these eminent statesmen. Though diametrically opposite in mental temperament and habits of thought, they well understood each other's worth and power, and had labored too long, shoulder to shoulder in the great struggle for human freedom, to allow any place for personal resentment. And so they continued to speak kindly to and of each other, the ties of friendship remaining bright, until severed by Mr. Sumner's death.

Though the most strenuous efforts were made by the opposition, so effective were the arguments of Mr. Wilson and his coadjutors, such were the memories and convictions of the soldiers who had imperilled their lives for the maintenance of the Union, and such were the popular traits and characteristics of the candidates, proclaimed by the press, the platform speakers, and set forth in the campaign melodies, such as

> " A song and a chant
> For Wilson and Grant,
> Who rose from the lowliest station;
> The tried and the true,
> Who whate'er they may do
> Will be done for the good of the nation.
> CHORUS: Then work for our leaders,
> All good men,
> For they are men of leather,
> And raise the chant
> For Wilson and Grant,
> And we'll vote them in together,"

and received with wild enthusiasm in the vast assemblies of the people, that the Grant and Wilson ticket became triumphant in November; and the "Natick cobbler" reached the second position in the government of the nation. Well, indeed, had he, by his long and faithful services, by his eminent abilities, and his life of immaculate integrity, earned this high distinction; yet his noble soul was not in anywise elated by the honor. He even expressed regret to his intimate friends at his elevation, inasmuch as it deprived him of the opportunity of discussing great national questions in the chamber of the Senate, where he had so long effectually served his country.

President Grant and Senator Wilson received on the popular vote a majority of 762,991 over Horace Greeley and B. Gratz Brown, and 300 to 66 electoral votes thrown for various candidates; and so on the 4th of March, 1873, Mr. Wilson took his seat as presiding officer of the United-States Senate, where he

had most manfully defended, for almost twenty years,
the principles of the Constitution and of civil freedom.
So poor was Mr. Wilson at the time of his inauguration,
that, on the evening previous to that ceremony, he
called, says Mr. F. B. Carpenter, on Mr. Sumner, and
said, —

"Sumner, can you lend me a hundred dollars? I
have not got money enough to be inaugurated on."
Mr. Sumner replied, "Certainly. If it had been a
large sum, I might not have been able to help you; but
I can always lend a friend a hundred dollars." He
then gave Mr. Wilson a check for the amount; and,
after the latter had retired, Mr. Sumner, turning to
Mr. Carpenter, remarked, "There is an incident worth
remembering, — such a one as could never have occurred
in any country but our own."

CHAPTER XXI.

MR. WILSON AS PRESIDENT OF THE SENATE. — HIS HEALTH DECLINING. — HIS SECOND VOLUME OF THE RISE AND FALL OF THE SLAVE-POWER. —HIS LAST SICKNESS.— HIS DEATH.

Mr. Wilson presiding over the Senate. — His Industry. — Declension of his Health. — His Retirement from Labor. — Visit to New Hampshire. — Letter to "The Springfield Republican." — The Bounty Bill. — Death of Charles Sumner. — Health Improving. — The Second Volume of "The Rise and Fall of the Slave-Power in America." — His Back Pay as Senator. — His Opinion of President Grant. — His Tour to the South-west.—Summer at Saratoga.—The Republican Convention at Worcester. — His Last Sickness and Death.—The Autopsy.

COMMANDING in person, quick in perception, and well versed in parliamentary practice, Mr. Wilson presided with dignity and great acceptance over the Senate ; and his decisions were respected by the members of both parties. His earnest desire, expressed on every suitable occasion, was conciliation between the factions in the Republican party, and the restoration of fraternity and friendliness between the North and South.

Although his elevation to the office of vice-president lessened his senatorial labors, he still allowed himself no rest. Every leisure moment was devoted to the composition of his great work on " The Rise and Fall of the Slave-Power in America," for which the consultation of numberless authorities, and an extensive correspondence, were demanded. His arduous labors were often extended late into the night; and he observed to a friend, at this period, that he seldom laid aside his pen until the clock struck two in the morning. " My mail comes in late," he said; " the journals must be read; my letters must be looked over, some of them answered; and so I am obliged to steal an hour or two from the coming day before retiring."

But though strictly temperate, and early inured to toil, his constitution was not adequate to the strain of such incessant industry. His health began to yield to this habitual transgression of hygienic law. His first fearful warning was a sudden, but only partial, paralysis of a facial nerve, in 1873, by which his countenance was slightly altered, and his utterance somewhat impaired. The usual remedies were prescribed; and, above all, the physicians imperatively enjoined repose from labor: but how could a mind of such intense activity obey the injunction? This very monition of the uncertainty of life incited the desire in the Vice-President to complete his book, which he considered the most valuable legacy he could leave to his countrymen. He, however, yielded somewhat to his medical advisers, and spent the summer, — some time at the house of his friend, ex-Gov. Claflin, some time at his home in Natick, some time in profound retirement, endeavoring to rest from labor, and to recuperate his health. On one occasion, a friend, calling at the house where the Vice-President was living very quietly, inquired of the servant for Mr. Wilson; when she replied to him, " There's no such person here: I never heard of such a man." On being further questioned, she responded, " Yes, sir, there is an invalid stopping here; but I don't know who he is, and he is out to-day." She reported this to her mistress, and was not a little surprised to learn from her, that, for several weeks, she had been waiting on the Vice-President of the United States.

In September, Mr. Wilson made a journey to the White Mountains, stopping, on the way, to visit the spot where he was born, near the Cocheco River, in Farmington; and, on returning, found his health improved, and thought, if the papers would but let him alone, he might hope for a complete recovery. In November, however, he excused himself from speaking at the Massachusetts Club, on account of illness; and although he repaired to Washington, and took his seat in the chair of the Senate at the opening of Congress, he was soon obliged to retire from it, and seek repose in his peaceful home at Natick.

Early in January, 1874, he greatly enjoyed a re-union at No. 13 Chestnut Street, Boston, with Ralph Waldo Emerson, Wendell Phillips, Charles Bradlaugh, and other celebrities; and, on the 16th of the same month, addressed a letter on the political situation to "The Springfield Republican," in which he hopefully says, "I believe the Republican party has it in its power to recover what is lost, and to elect the next President." And he also expresses his earnest desire for reconciliation between the conflicting elements in the party, and the return of those who had abandoned it. In another letter, written about this time, he assigns his reasons for voting for the Bounty Bill, very sensibly avowing that "the nation is bound in honor to be as liberal now towards the men who fought its battles as it pledged itself to be in the time of danger."

Mr. Wilson was profoundly affected at the death of Charles Sumner, who had fought with him so many hard battles in the senate-chamber; and shed over his grave at Mt. Auburn the tear of sad regret, observing, as he took his farewell look of the distinguished statesman, "I soon shall follow him."

In April ensuing, a passage was engaged for him for a second trip to Europe, under the hope that a change of scene, and foreign medical advice, might restore him to his wonted vigor; but, feeling soon that his health was gradually improving, he abandoned this design, and spent the summer in recreation at various watering-places along the shore, and in carrying through the press the second volume of his great work on "The Rise and Fall of the Slave-Power in America," which was published this year, in superior style, by James R. Osgood & Co., Boston. In it Mr. Wilson, with the hand of a master, analyzes and describes the leading national events through that stirring period extending from the admission of Florida to the election of Mr. Lincoln; and fully sustains the reputation for candor, for profound research, for classification of facts, for logical reasoning, and for force, clearness, and dignity of style, which the first instalment of this important contribution to our political history gained for him. His chapters on the origin of the Republican party, and the assault on Mr. Sumner, are most ably written; and the whole work, coming as it does from an actor in the events recorded, is worthy to be profoundly studied by the American people.

At the opening of the session of Congress at the close of the year, the Vice-President had so far regained his health as to be able to preside over the Senate with his usual ability. His back pay as a senator he nobly returned to the treasury; and, though differing in many points from the policy of the President, he lived on the most friendly terms with him, and entertained, as ever, a high opinion of his executive wisdom. To a friend he said, one day, "The third-term movement is all nonsense. President Grant is a singularly able man; and the country hardly knows any thing about him personally. He is immensely underrated. The President is reticent; but, in reference to the third term, I do not really think that he himself desires it." He also mentioned Mr. Blaine and Mr. Washburne as probable Republican candidates for the next presidential canvass.

In the spring of 1875, he made a tour in the South-western States, where he examined the condition of the schools, and spoke, in no less than twenty-nine public addresses, words of fraternity and encouragement to the people. He visited the graves of Jackson, Clay, Taylor, Polk, Crittenden, Bell, and Benton, for the latter of whom he ever entertained the most profound respect. In the streets of Memphis he spoke a moment with Mrs. Jefferson Davis. He saw with delight the loyal demonstrations of the people, and returned with renewed hope and vigor for the prosecution of his literary labors. After the centennial celebrations at Lexington and Boston, in which he took an active part, he repaired to Saratoga, where his physician gave him permission to spend the morning in writing on his book, on condition that he would rest for the remainder of the day. Here he made two effective addresses on behalf of temperance to large audiences, and re-affirmed the principles by which his whole life had been guided.

36

In September, he was called to preside over the Republican Convention at Worcester. His address on that occasion was strong, but conciliatory, advising union on the part of all Republicans, and predicting the triumph of their principles, and the election of Alexander II. Rice to the gubernatorial chair. To this, and to his letters written at this period, the success of the party at the last election is, no doubt, largely due. There is something of sublimity in the course of a man standing thus steadily to the principles of his party, which so many in times of trial had deserted, and, by his inflexible integrity and judicious counsel, rallying it again to victory.

But the days of this wise political guide were numbered. Dining at Young's Hotel a short time afterwards, he suddenly received another paralytic attack, and was immediately carried to the residence of his friend, Mr. Webster, where the usual restoratives were applied. His speech was again affected, and his face somewhat distorted. He then said to a friend beside him, " I have received my mortal blow ; but I greatly desire to remain a few years longer to finish up my work."

Convalescing rapidly, he repaired to Washington early in November, subjecting himself, on the way, to the same severe trial by fire which Mr. Sumner received from Dr. Brown-Séquard. He was, however, after taking a warm bath (Nov. 10), again prostrated by another and still more serious paralytic shock. The most effective remedies were prescribed ; and, though greatly suffering, such was the vigor of his constitution, that he rallied under their effect, and, on the 13th of November, was pronounced convalescent by his physi-

cian. " If I could arrange my death," said he to one
of his attendants, " I would die quietly in my home, and
have the privilege of saying good-by to my friends,
and be laid quietly away. But I have a premonition
that I shall die suddenly; be snuffed out like a candle,
without an opportunity to say good-by to any one."
These were prophetic words.

On the night of the 17th following, he slept so
soundly, and felt so well in the morning, that he desired
to leave his room at the Capitol, but was restrained by
his physician, who was constantly compelled to combat
the intense activity of his nature. In a conversation
with a friend on the day following, he said, " Everybody has been very kind to me during my illness. See
here," he continued, turning to a splendid basket of
flowers, — " see what the wife of the President has sent
me ! " And, pointing to a superb lily in the centre, he
remarked, " This is a fit emblem of the purity which sur-
rounds the world of immortality, which we all hope
some day to reach." He then added, " The doctors
think that I am getting better, and I believe so myself.
They say that I shall be able to go North on Monday:
we will see." In reference to politics, he said, " The
Democrats will have to improve a great deal before the
people will intrust them with the government; and they
will never put one into the presidential office, if he ever
had any connection with the Rebellion." On Sunday,
21st, he was not quite as well, but received a number
of visitors, among whom were Messrs. Burt and Cross-
man. So little apprehension was felt, that Dr. Baxter,
his physician, having given directions to his attendants,
Messrs. S. H. Boyden and F. A. Wood, to administer
his medicines, left him early in the evening with the

hope that he might be able to ride out the next day.
Soon afterwards Mr. Wilson said, " If the doctor were
here, I would have a blister put on the back of my
neck ; but it is not worth while to send for him ; " and,
after his limbs had been rubbed, observed that he felt
unusually well, and fell asleep. Awaking about midnight, he arose, walked around his room, and then, going
to his table, took up a little treasured volume of poems,
called " The Changed Cross," containing photographs of
his wife and son, whose memories he most tenderly
cherished, and read from it three stanzas, one of which
formed the burden of his daily prayer : —

> " Help us, O Lord, with patient love to bear
>   Each other's faults ; to suffer with true meekness:
> Help us each others' joys and griefs to share ;
>   But let us turn to thee alone in weakness.''

Having laid down the book, he spoke of the kindness
of his friends, and, returning in a pleasant mood to bed,
soon fell asleep. At three o'clock he again awoke, re-
quested Mr. Boyden to rub his breast; when he again
fell into a profound sleep, which continued until seven
o'clock in the morning. On awaking, he expressed
himself as feeling very well, and, on being informed of
the death of Senator Ferry, said, " Poor Ferry, he has
been a great sufferer: that makes eighty-three dead
with whom I have sat in the Senate. What a record !
If I live to the end of my present term, I shall be the
sixth in the history of the country who have served so
long a time." He then, referring cheerfully to his improved condition, drank some bitter water, turned over
on his left side, and in a few moments, without any
apparent pain or struggle, ceased to breathe.

" So fades a summer cloud away;
    So sinks the gale when storms are o'er;
So gently shuts the eye of day;
    So dies a wave along the shore.
Triumphant smiles the victor's brow,
    Fanned by some guardian angel's wing:
Where is, O Grave! thy victory now?
    And where, insidious Death, thy sting? "

Thus in his room at the Capitol, where he had spent so many years in the defence of civil liberty, with but

The Capitol at Washington.

one attendant at his bedside, the Vice-President of the United States departed, at twenty minutes past seven o'clock on the twenty-second day of November, 1875, in the sixty-fourth year of his age. Thus the brain that had devised so many measures for the good of his country ceased from its throbbings; thus the heart that had so magnanimously beaten for the sons of toil and suffering became cold and still; and, as Judge Hoar observed, no cleaner hands were ever folded on a truer breast.

An autopsy of the body of Mr. Wilson disclosed

black fluid blood in the sinuses of the brain, which weighed forty-nine ounces and a half, and thus made it manifest that the immediate cause of his death was apoplexy. His body was then embalmed, and laid out on Tuesday morning in the room where he expired, dressed in the black suit which he wore on state occasions, with a wreath of white flowers at his head and a floral cross at his feet. Rich bouquets of flowers, sent by Mrs. Grant and others, also decorated the apartment.

CHAPTER XXII.

THE NATIONAL BEREAVEMENT. — OBSEQUIES AT WASH-
INGTON AND OTHER CITIES. — BURIAL AT
NATICK. — MR. WILSON'S CHARACTER.

The National Grief at the Death of Mr. Wilson. — President Grant's Order.
— Honors paid to the Remains at Washington. — Dr. Rankin's Ad-
dress. — The Baltimore Fifth Regiment. — Honors at Philadelphia;
New York. — Announcement of Gov. Gaston. — Remarks of Mr.
Stebbins; of Judge Clark. — Reception of the News at Natick. —
Meeting in Faneuil Hall. — Address of Gen. Banks. — The Remains
in Doric Hall. — Memorial Services in the House of Representatives.
— Dr. Manning's Eulogy. — Services at Natick. — Address of the
Revs. E. Dowse and F. N. Peloubet. — The Burial at Dell Park Ceme-
tery. — Mr. Wilson's Will. — His Character.

THE intelligence of the death of the Vice-President
was received with profound emotion by the whole
country. Flags were displayed at half-mast; minute-
guns were fired; bells were tolled; the United-States
courts were adjourned; and men of all parties, from
Maine to Texas, united in expressions of sorrow. In
the afternoon of the day on which Mr. Wilson died,
President Grant called a meeting of his cabinet, and
issued the following order : —

EXECUTIVE MANSION,
WASHINGTON, Nov. 22, 1875.

It is with profound sorrow that the President has to
announce to the people of the United States the death
of the Vice-President, Henry Wilson, who died in the

Capitol of the nation this morning. The eminent station of the deceased, his high character, his long career in the service of his State and of the Union, his devotion to the cause of freedom, and the ability which he brought to the discharge of every duty, stand conspicuous, and are indelibly impressed on the hearts and affections of the American people. In testimony of respect for this distinguished citizen and faithful public servant, the various departments of the government will be closed on the day of the funeral; and the executive mansion, and all the executive departments in Washington, will be draped with badges of mourning for thirty days. The Secretary of War and Secretary of the Navy will issue orders that appropriate military and naval honors be rendered to the memory of one whose virtues and services will long be borne in recollection by a grateful nation.

U. S. GRANT.

By the President,

HAMILTON FISH, *Secretary of State.*

On Thursday, the body of Mr. Wilson in a costly casket, resting on the catafalque which bore the remains of President Lincoln, Chief Justice Chase, and Senator Sumner, lay in state in the Rotunda of the Capitol, and was visited by thousands, who bent over it with tearful emotion and profound respect. On the day following, the remains were removed to the senate-chamber, where at half-past ten, A.M., the nation, through its highest officers, performed the solemn obsequies in honor of the dead. The day was ushered in by the firing of cannon and the tolling of bells; and, though dark and rainy, every seat in the galleries was occupied long before the

services commenced. The senate-chamber draped in
mourning, the President and Cabinet, the Justices of
the Supreme Court in their black gowns, the members
of the diplomatic corps (at the head of which was Sir
Edward Thornton), the officers of the army and navy in
uniform, and the committee of arrangements with white
silk sashes, and black-and-white rosettes, presented a
most solemn and impressive scene. The chair of the
Vice-President was arrayed in crape, Senator Ferry
occupying another seat. When the casket, borne by
twelve soldiers, and followed by Mr. Colbath and wife,
with other relatives of the deceased, was brought into
the chamber, the entire audience arose; and Dr. Sunder-
land, chaplain of the Senate, pronounced the passage:
"Lord, make me to know mine end," &c., with great
solemnity and impressiveness. Dr. J. E. Rankin, whose
church the Vice-President attended, then delivered an
appropriate eulogy, in the course of which he made this
just distinction between the character of Mr. Wilson
and that of his co-worker in the Senate, Mr. Sumner:—

"It is beautiful to see how these two great men of
Massachusetts, born one year apart, starting so differently in life, educated so differently, supported and
complemented each other. The one, a man of books;
the other, a man of men: the one, a man of ideas; the
other, a man of facts: the one, a man of the few; the
other, a man of the many: the one sometimes almost
losing himself in his distance of advance before the
nation; the other always keeping step with the grand
movement of the people, going forward only so fast
as his true popular instinct taught him that people
were ready to follow. In these two men, so unlike,
and yet so representative of the extremes in American

society, was the New-England idea enshrined and represented on this floor."

At the conclusion of the services in the senate-chamber, the procession attended the funeral-car, drawn by six white horses caparisoned in black, with solemn dirges, and with cannon pealing, to the station of the Baltimore and Potomac Railroad, where Senator Thurman delivered the remains to the charge of Massachusetts Committee of Arrangements, which left for Baltimore early in the afternoon. The Fifth Regiment of that city, which Mr. Wilson had addressed, and which had received many courteous attentions on its late visit to Boston, tendered its services as an escort of the body to its final resting-place; but, inasmuch as many other military organizations had done the same, it was thought advisable to decline the offer. The rotunda of the new City Hall in Baltimore was draped in mourning for the reception of the remains; and demonstrations of sorrow everywhere prevailed. In Philadelphia, funeral-honors were imposingly rendered to the body of the beloved statesman in Independence Hall, on Saturday, where as many as ten thousand people passed in tearful silence by the beautiful casket. The hearse was drawn by ten black horses; the chime of St. Stephen's Church pealed forth the "Dead March;" and business was generally suspended along the streets through which the solemn cortège passed. The remains were escorted through the city of New York by a military force, consisting of several regiments, followed by representatives of the State and City authorities, the Board of Trade, the Republican Central Committee, and the New-England Society. Guns were fired, and expressions of public sorrow manifested in all sections of the city.

While the death of Mr. Wilson, who was perhaps personally known by more people than any other statesman of his time, produced a deep impression of sorrow through the entire country, which might be said to be all arrayed in mourning, it was in Boston and vicinity, where he had spent so many of his days, and where his sterling virtues were best understood, that the national loss was most profoundly felt, and the manifestation of grief the most prolonged and touching. On the reception of the sad intelligence of Mr. Wilson's death, Gov. Gaston made the announcement : —

COMMONWEALTH OF MASSACHUSETTS,
EXECUTIVE DEPARTMENT, BOSTON, NOV. 22, 1875.

It becomes my most painful duty to announce to the people of this Commonwealth the death of Vice-President Wilson, which occurred at the Capitol at Washington, this morning, at twenty minutes past seven o'clock.

The loss of this pure and distinguished statesman and honest man will be the cause of great mourning throughout the country, and especially in the State in which he resided, where he was best known, and therefore most highly honored.

WILLIAM GASTON.

A meeting of the Board of Aldermen was held; resolves were passed, and addresses made, in the course of which Mr. Stebbins said, —

"For a period of nearly forty years, his struggles, defeats, and labors, which were crowned in his later years with reward and honor, have closely identified the name of Henry Wilson with the history of Massachusetts and of our country. His life has ever been

an incentive to the common people in their aspirations
by honest personal labor to reach a higher level. His
death will teach the lesson and value of personal
integrity, which enabled him to withstand the temptations which ever surrounded his years of public service.
His labors in behalf of the oppressed will endear his
memory in their hearts ; and on the memorial which
will mark his last resting-place should be engraved,
'He served his imperilled country faithfully, withstood
temptations, and died an honest man."

> " The good and true never die, never die:
> They live in our hearts, ever nigh, ever nigh.' "

The United-States District Court was adjourned ; and,
in his address, Judge Clark appropriately said, —
"There is a beautiful prayer of Eastern poetry, 'May
you die among your kindred!' The Vice-President has
died, not among his kindred in the ordinary sense, nor
in the land of his nativity, but in the broader sense, —
among the American people, who were his kinsmen, at
the nation's capital, at the place of his highest usefulness, and the scene of his greatest activities. Fortunate
in his life, fortunate in his death. Eminently fit it
is that we pause, and recognize the solemnity of the
occasion. . . . When a public servant falls by death, it
is a public loss ; and the nation mourns. But when a
person so eminently active, wise, honest, and good, as
was Henry Wilson, dies, the public heart is well-nigh
crushed. The Court has no inclination to proceed with
the business of the day ; and sure it is that Massachusetts, called so lately to bury her illustrious senator,
will pause, and let fall bitter tears, as she receives to the
bosom of her soil the remains of the late Vice-President

to rest in fit companionship with him by whose side he struggled so heroically in the nation's peril.

"The Court will now adjourn until to-morrow."

On the reception of the mournful news at Natick, the bells were tolled, a public meeting was held, at which eulogistic speeches were made; and this among other resolutions was unanimously adopted: —

"*Resolved*, That, in the death of Henry Wilson, our town has lost a valued and beloved citizen; and as a people, without regard to sectarian or party lines, we unitedly mourn the loss of one whose character and career have reflected so much honor upon the town of his adoption."

A committee, consisting of Messrs. Dunn and Turner of the Executive Council, and Cols. Wyman and Campbell of Gov. Gaston's staff, were appointed to convey the remains of the Vice-President to Massachusetts; and on Saturday, Nov. 27, a large memorial meeting was held in Faneuil Hall, in which eloquent tributes of respect were paid to the dead by Mayor Cobb, Gov. William Gaston, Gen. N. P. Banks, Hon. E. R. Hoar, Hon. Charles F. Adams, and George L. Ruffin, Esq. The hall was festooned in black and white; and the white bust of Mr. Wilson stood upon the platform. In the course of his remarks, Gov. Gaston most truly said, —

"A statesman has gone to his rest, and a nation mourns. The benediction of a people grateful for his services will follow him to his grave. Such, under the providence of God, even in this world, are the final rewards of an honest and well-spent life. By his energy, his ability, and his merit, he trod the various paths of honor, until he reached almost the highest office in the gift of forty millions of people. From his example and

37

success, the humblest boy in the nation may learn that
in this republic there are no summits upon which his
eyes may not rest, or upon which his feet may not
stand."

In his eloquent eulogy, Gen. Banks paid this noble
tribute to his lamented friend : —

"It was the choice and the privilege of every man in
this country to fashion his own career. Mr. Wilson
made his choice, and worked out his own career. It
was a majestic, a multitudinous constituency, of which
he became at once the distinguished representative. It
was for the poor and the oppressed that he gave his life-
long services, in the same category with Messrs. Burlingame, Rantoul, Sumner, and others, among whom he was
entitled to a distinguished position. There may have
been momentary departures ; but he always returned to
duty with unfailing fidelity and with undaunted heroism. It was necessary for such men to work constantly
among the masses of the people, whom he represented.
As a practical man, he stood one of the first and foremost of the time. In all that information which was
more necessary for government than all the learning of
the schools, he was one of the leaders of the age.

" Added to this, he had an unceasing activity, an exu-
berance of strength, and a determination of personal
character, that enabled him fully to acquaint himself
with the wants and feelings of the people. He had left
behind him, through his energy, and his devotion to principle, a reputation second to none in our day, and which
entitled him to the respect, the love, the enduring remembrance, of all his fellow-men in this and in coming years."

The funeral train, draped in mourning, arrived in Boston at half-past ten o'clock on Sunday morning, Nov.

28, where it was awaited by a vast concourse of sincere mourners, who felt that they had lost a personal friend. Amid the tolling of bells and other signs of general lamentation, the casket was escorted by the Independent Cadets to the Doric Hall in the State House, where Col. Wyman, delivering it to Gov. Gaston, spoke as follows: —

" YOUR EXCELLENCY, — In obedience to your orders, we proceeded to Washington, where we received from the National Committee the remains of the late Vice-President; and we have escorted them to this place."

To which his Excellency replied : —

" Massachusetts receives from you her illustrious dead. She will see to it that he whose dead body you bear to us, but whose spirit has entered upon its higher service, shall receive honors befitting the great office which in life he held; and I need not assure you that her people, with hearts full of respect, of love, and of veneration, will not only guard and protect the body, the coffin, and the grave, but will also ever cherish his name and fame. Gentlemen, for the pious service which you have so kindly and tenderly rendered, accept the thanks of a grateful Commonwealth."

Doric Hall was heavily draped in black, the battle-flags being looped with crape, and covering the cannons; while Mr. Wilson's monogram rested on a black curtain at the head of the catafalque. A harp composed of white roses and other flowers rested on the casket; while a cross and crown of violets and roses, and of elegant design, stood at the head, and an anchor of funereal-flowers at the foot, of the casket. A single soldier, immovable as a statue, guarded the remains, as the vast throng, amounting, it might have been, to twenty thousand, filed in silence through the hall, and gazed for the last time on the pallid features of the beloved advocate of civil progress, freedom, and fraternity.

Eloquent memorial discourses were pronounced in many of the churches during the day; among which those of Dr. D. C. Eddy, Dr. George C. Lorimer, Dr. S. F. Upham of Lynn, of the Revs. M. J. Savage, J. B. Dunn, and Henry A. Cooke, evinced a just appreciation of the exalted worth of the deceased Vice-President.

On Monday, Nov. 29, the citizens of Massachusetts, through the State officers, performed the obsequies of the Vice-President in a style of grandeur and solemnity that evinced the depth of sorrow in the bosom of the Commonwealth. The public buildings generally were closed; flags were placed at half-mast; mourning-emblems were displayed on many private residences; and half-hour guns were fired. The Hall of Representatives was most elaborately decorated with festoons of smilax intwined with delicate white flowers. The speaker's desk, draped with black cloth, was almost covered with flowers; while on that of the clerk was placed a stately shaft composed of tuberoses, camellias, and white pinks, and resting on a base of ferns and other graceful leaves. The catafalque opposite the speaker's desk was decorated with tender vines and roses. The pall-bearers, ex-Govs. Boutwell, Banks, Gardner, Washburn, Bullock, Claflin, together with the Hon. A. H. Rice, the Hon. Carl Schurz, and Frederick Douglass, entered about twelve o'clock, followed by other dignitaries of the State, and friends of the deceased. The services were opened by the solemn strains of the anthem, "I heard a voice saying unto me, Write," from a quartet of Dr. Eben Tourjée. Dr. A. A. Miner then followed with an impressive prayer. Dr. W. F. Warren presented selections from the Scriptures. The Rev. Phillips Brooks read a chant, "Lord, let me know mine end, the number of my days," to which the choir responded; and Dr. J. M. Manning then delivered a discourse from the words, "Thy gentleness hath made me great," which was worthy of the man and of the occasion. Of the many eloquent passages we can cite only the following, the former referring to Mr. Wilson's almost superhuman labors in the Senate, and the latter to his departure from the scenes of earth: —

"At length the gathering cloud burst. It could not be averted: the storm must come. God foreknew this as we did not; and the men whom his gentleness had been lifting up were ready, each for his solemn part. To Henry Wilson fell the chairmanship of military affairs; and the prodigious capacity for work which he showed in that place is known to all who saw him there. What president or cabinet officer, what general in the field, what governor, or regiment, or patient in the hospital, or soldier's widow, ever had occasion to complain of him? The general-in-chief at the opening of the war said that his daily task was equal to the strength of ten men. Thus he toiled till the forces of the Rebellion were spent. And in the clear dawn of peace, during the weary efforts at reconstruction, which were finally successful, the problem of his life was solved. We all saw for what God had made and endowed him, in the light of the terrible exigency which had been his grand opportunity. . . .

" ' You will ride out to-day, Mr. Vice-President,' said his attendant, just as his last earthly dawn was fading into the everlasting morning. He did ride out, but not in any material vehicle. The chariot of God was in waiting for him. He rode out of death into life, out of the shadow into eternal sunlight, out of corruption into incorruption."

At the conclusion of the eulogy, the vast audience united in singing Mrs. Adams's beautiful hymn, —

" Nearer, my God, to thee."

Dr. R. H. Neale offered an appropriate prayer; the choir sang with touching effect, —

" Unveil thy bosom, faithful tomb; "

and the Rev. Phillips Brooks pronounced the benediction.

A procession, consisting of a long array of military forces, — among which was the Twenty-second Regiment, of which Mr. Wilson was the original commander, government officials, and civic organizations, — attended the remains, while guns were pealing, bells were tolling, and bands performing dirges, to the station at Cottage Farm, from which the casket was conveyed, under a special guard, to Natick for the final obsequies. Here it was received at Concert Hall, which was tastefully draped in funereal emblems, by Mr. C. H. Perry, on behalf of the mourning citizens, who came with tearful eyes to view the sacred dust of their distinguished and beloved townsman. On the day following, private funeral services were held at the house of the Vice-President, on Central Street, on account of the inability of Mrs. Howe,* his aged mother-in-law, to be present at the Hall. They were conducted by the Rev. A. E. Reynolds and the Rev. Edmund Dowse, the latter of whom, a long and intimate friend of the departed, said, in substance, —

" We are to-day gathered in the home of Henry Wilson. Here he lived for many years. Here he enjoyed the sweets of domestic life. Here he watched over a loving wife in sickness, and, when her spirit passed away, with loving hand bore her remains to a resting-place in yonder cemetery. Here he rested from his labors, and, could he have had his wish, he would have closed his eyes in this house upon the world and its cares, amidst friends and relations. But God decreed otherwise. We feel to-day that darkness is around and about us ; yet we have full faith in the saying, that light dwelleth with the righteous. Here in this house, though the former occupant sleeps in dust, is the holy Bible ; here is the family altar he created ; and from all these sources comes to us to-day comfort, preparing us to say, ' Even so, Father : thy will be done, not mine.' " The minister closed with a touching allusion to the great kindness manifested by Mr. Wilson to his aged mother-in-law.

The remains were then carried back to the Hall, from the ceiling of which was suspended a large black canopy having a beautiful wreath of flowers beneath,

---

* Mrs. Mary (Toombs) Howe, relict of Mr. Amasa Howe, is the daughter of Joseph and Mary (Homer) Toombs of Hopkinton. He was born in 1750, and was the son of Daniel Toombs, who married Mary Collen, Oct. 3, 1739. They were of Scotch-Irish descent, and among the early settlers of Hopkinton. Amasa Howe (son of Perley Howe, and his wife Anna Hill of Medway) was descended from Hezekiah Howe, who married Jane Jennison of Sudbury, Oct. 31, 1746.

that sent forth a white dove with unfolded wings, directly over the coffin, which was also covered with flowers. The services were opened by singing, —

"God is our strength;"

when the Rev. A. E. Reynolds offered a tender prayer; the Rev. J. S. Whedon read selections from the Scriptures; the response, "Abide with Me," was sung; and admirable addresses were made by the Rev. Edmund Dowse and the Rev. Francis N. Peloubet, pastor of the church of which Mr. Wilson was a member. In the course of his eulogy, Mr. Peloubet said, "He needs no monument to show where he died; for he built his own monument here, by which men shall remember where he lived. We are surrounded by his labors as by a great cloud of witnesses.

"Is there a work-bench that is not made more sacred and honorable and hopeful, because Henry Wilson for years worked at one, and while there gained his education, and grew into larger powers? Is there a young man whose heart does not expand, and hopes grow brighter, because Henry Wilson contended with the same difficulties, fought the same temptations, encountered the same trials, and came off conqueror?

"We look at our beautiful library, and remember that Henry Wilson was the first, or one of the first, subscribers to the fund from which the town library grew. We think of our schools, and remember that he was once a teacher in them; and more, under what hard schoolmasters, after what hard days' works, by what light of the kitchen-fire, he gained his education.

"We look at our thriving churches, and remember that he was a Christian, and took a deep interest in all that pertains to the kingdom of Christ. His voice was heard in the prayer-meeting. He helped found, and was one of the most liberal supporters of, the Young Men's Christian Association.

"Henry Wilson made many speeches; but the best speech was his life and character at home. He longed to finish the book he was writing; but Natick itself is his best book, known and read by all.

"To us, his fellow-townsmen, many lessons come from yonder coffin. His spirit seems to come back from the mansions of the blest, and, taking us each by the hand, points to the lessons he has lived, written in letters as bright as the light on the emblems of mourning. Let us read them: Religion, temperance, industry, patriotism, courage, principle, character. He shows how we may gain an education. He shows us the way to true success. He shows us the possibilities of good before us all, — what we can be, and what we can do, if we will trust God, and do the right; that the circumstances which would hinder us may be made stepping-stones of success; that the enemies which bar our way may be made soldiers to fight our battles for us; that the burdens which would crush us may become the eagle's wing to bear us upward."

At the close of Mr. Peloubet's address, the audience united in singing, —

"Nearer, my God, to thee;"

and the Rev. B. R. Gifford pronounced the benediction. At three o'clock, P.M., the long procession, in which were the officers of the Maryland Fifth Regiment, moved with slow and reverent step to the Dell Park Cemetery, a charming eminence that overlooks Cochituate Lake and the town of Natick; and there, in tearful silence were deposited, just as the sun was sinking in the west, the mortal remains of the illustrious dead in their final earthly home. The lot of Mr. Wilson, in the north-east corner of the burial-ground, is tastefully ornamented with shrubs and flowers, and contains a marble sarcoph-agus, surmounted by a hat, feather, sword, belt, and sash, and having the inscription given on p. 370 of this biography. At the right of this stands a well-wrought marble headstone, bearing these words : —

" Harriet M. Howe, born in Natick, Nov. 21, 1824; married to Henry Wilson Nov. 28, 1840; died May 28, 1870. She made home happy.

" But oh for the touch of a vanquished hand.
And the sound of a voice that is still!" *

Beside this grave the body of the late Vice-President reposes.

* A beautiful white lily chiselled on this monument, and intwined by an ivy planted by the bereaved husband, is noticed in these graceful lines, which appeared in the Traveller in September, 1872: —

A lily on the marble slept,
Emblem of one whom many wept,
Chiselled by the sculptor's care,
It lay in graceful beauty there,
While flowers blooming in the ground
Shed a sweet fragrance all around.
A little ivy planted there,
And fostered by a husband's care,
Had with its clinging tendrils sought
The flower on the marble wrought,
Then 'mid the lily's leaves so fair,
It wove its green ones closely there,
As to the emblem it would cling
And a rich, leafy tribute bring,
To show that love still fondly turned
To her whose form was there inurned. — E. W. S.

THE GRAVE OF HENRY WILSON AND FAMILY, DELL PARK CEMETERY, NATICK.

"No monument a broader base sustains
  Than thine must have, — on equal rights and laws:
No memory the continent retains
  Truer to God's will and manhood's holy cause."

At a little distance, in the same lot, stands the twin headstone of his father and mother. It is of beautiful design; and on it is inscribed: —

"Winthrop Colbath, born April 7, 1787; died Feb. 10, 1860; and Abigail Colbath, born March 21, 1785; died Aug. 8, 1866."

In his will, dated April 21, 1874, Mr. Wilson bequeathed all his property of whatever kind to his nephew, W. L. Coolidge, to be held in trust for the benefit of his venerable mother-in-law, Mrs. Mary Howe, for the support and education of his adopted daughter, Eva Wilson, an intelligent girl, now about ten years old, and under the charge of Mrs. Fifield; and for other minor purposes, leaving it all to the "friendship, discretion, and sense of right" of Mr. Coolidge, who is constituted the sole executor. The whole property will not exceed $10,000. The life of the testator was insured for $3,500. The third and last volume of Mr. Wilson's "Rise and Fall of the Slave-Power," of which about sixteen chapters are written, will, it is supposed, be completed by the Rev. Samuel Hunt, an intimate friend, and, for the last seven years, private secretary, of the Vice-President. Mr. Wilson left four brothers, all of whom are younger than himself; and all are married, and have had children. John Colbath, the oldest, is a farmer, living in Compton, Canada; Charles H., who married Eliza Newcomb, is a stone-cutter, residing in Hingham, Mass.; Samuel is a doorkeeper at the United-States Senate; and George Albert is an inspector at the Custom House in Boston.

In person, Mr. Wilson was robust and well proportioned. He was five feet, ten inches in height, and weighed about one hundred and eighty pounds. With a light complexion and a clear skin, his whole countenance glowed with health and vigor. His eyes were quick and clear: his forehead, broad and high. The portrait by Mr. Butré, from a photograph by Mr. Black, in this volume, presents his features with correctness; but the marble bust of the sculptor Milmore, introduced by a resolution of the General Court into the State Library in May, 1872, exhibits something more of the ideality and the lofty spirit by which his countenance was in his happiest hours irradiated. His frame was compact and solid, and, even to the last, bore little indication of the eventide of life. In dress and manner he was plain and unpretending, and, when at leisure, remarkably frank, open, and confiding in his conversation.

Note.—His family, as has been stated, belonged to that excellent stock, the Scotch-Irish, who emigrated to New England in the beginning of the last century. The earliest form in which his family name appears in this country is Colbreath; evidently the same as Calbreath, a name of respectability in Scotland. James Colbreath was baptized Sept. 19, 1725, at Newington, N.H.; and from him is descended, through Winthrop, and Winthrop, jun., the subject of this memoir. The children of James and Olive Colbreath were Leighton, Independence, Winthrop, Hunking, Benning, Keziah, Deborah, and Amy. His son Winthrop married Hannah Rollins of Newington, N.H., and they removed to Rochester, now Farmington, about 1783, or a little anterior to the birth of Winthrop, Mr. Wilson's father. The name Colbreath is among those Scottish emigrants who petitioned Gov. Shute for permission to settle in this State. They were largely from Argyleshire in Scotland. The coat-of-arms of the Colbreath family is, "Bendy of six argent and azure on a chief sable, three crosses pattée or."—Burke's Encyclopædia of Heraldry.

As an orator, Mr. Wilson was strong and vehement, rather than bland and graceful. He cared but little for the rules of the rhetorician, and seldom turned aside in search of ornament: still he studied the best English and American models, — Pitt, Burke, Sheridan, Adams, Wirt, Webster, — and used elevated, or what might be termed forensic diction. Grasping his subject firmly, he presented his propositions with distinctness, and defended them by a constant appeal to facts. His memory was an inexhaustible magazine of facts; and out they came as solid shot from a columbiad, to break up the intrenchment of his enemy.

His great speeches in reply to Mr. Hammond, in reply to Mr. Butler, as well as those on the Pacific Railroad, the Lecompton Constitution, and the Crittenden Compromise, consist mainly of statements, or citations of matters of fact. With some speakers, such a liberal use of facts would be intolerable; but with Mr. Wilson they were so pertinently selected, and so earnestly presented, that they, in general, commanded profound attention.

With kindly sympathies and an earnest purpose, with an open countenance, a clear, strong voice, and animated gestures, Mr. Wilson always secured the attention of a popular assembly; and his words, where more finished speakers failed, were greeted with applause. He found the way to the heart of the people; and that is something higher than any studied eloquence.

He made his loftiest record as a speaker in the senate-chamber. In most of the stirring debates that agitated the country during its most tremendous struggle, he took a leading part. He measured blades with most of the veteran champions of the South, — Toombs, Davis, Benton, Hammond, Butler, Breckenridge, — and often gained the mastery. Many of his brief speeches here are models of forensic eloquence; and parts of some of them have found their way into our reading-books. Of his speaking and his influence in the Senate, a letter-writer at Washington, March 16, 1867, said, —

"But yesterday he rose to speak in the middle of the protracted debate on the Supplementary Reconstruction Bill; and at once the great indifference disappeared. Senators on every side turned from their papers and letters to listen; and what Mr. Wilson had to say was attended to with a greater degree of interest and respect on the floor of the Senate than had been given to any thing which had fallen from the lips of. Mr. Sumner, Mr. Sherman, Mr. Fessenden, or, in fact, of anybody else, since I have been an observer in the galleries. Such a phenomenon must mean something; and, listening to the remarks of the Massachusetts senator myself, I found the explanation in the fact that he talked more directly to the matter in hand, with more of fact, and less of theory, more of substance, and less of ornament, than any other speaker who had taken part in the debate; and so I concluded that Congress, if not also the country, on this subject of reconstruction at any rate, has had enough of rhetoric, and enough of oratory, and has an appetite only for those plain facts of the need of the day, which Mr. Wilson so forcibly urged."

Had Mr. Wilson read more of the classic poets, his style might, indeed, have had more finish, but not, perhaps, more force. Great national crises demand of leaders, not smooth, rounded periods, and rhetorical flourishes, but substantial facts, strong argumentation, and honest purpose: these Mr. Wilson had, and hence the Senate and the people heard him gladly.

His reasoning was sustained by the grand argument of a consistent life: hence it came home to the conscience, and was fraught with power. No man of his time, perhaps, addressed so many people in America as Henry Wilson; and none, perhaps, spoke so few words that he, if living, would wish to have unsaid. On rising to speak before an audience, his manly form, his honest, open, florid face, and sympathetic voice, bespoke for him a generous reception. The people saw at once that "honesty, poverty, and politics had agreed with him, and that a congressman might ignore crime, keep a clean palm, hold his Maker in remembrance, and yet wear a rosy, unclouded face." Thus he moved the masses to accept his counsels, and translate them into practice; and, if this be not eloquence, it is something above eloquence: it is, in the words of Webster, "Action, — noble, sublime, Godlike action."

As a statesman, Mr. Wilson's views were broad and comprehensive, and at the same time eminently practical. The works of the immortal sages — Washington, Hamilton, Adams, Jefferson, Jay, Marshall, and others who laid the foundation of this government — were his life-long study: in their spirit and opinions, his political education was perfected. His inspiration came indeed from a still higher source, — the instructions of the Son of Mary. The great principles of equality, fraternity, civil and religious freedom, and social progress, formed the basis of his political system; and, having confidence in the stability of popular government so administered, he labored with invincible determination to defend those principles. Because he apprehended with such clearness the extent and bearing of a present exigency, so quickly saw the tendency and drift of things, some

thought that his political views were superficial rather
than profound ; but a rapid river may be also deep and
strong. Mr. Wilson was a thinker, grasping as easily the
broadest principle as the most restricted precept; and
he had the power to examine them either under the light
of past experience, of present utility, or of future good.
His view of the slavery-question from the outset, his
forecast of the final issue, his legislation for the conduct
of the war, and his conviction of the grand result, most
clearly manifest the scope, as well as the accuracy, of his
vision. While he was a sound, sagacious statesman, he
at the same time possessed great administrative ability.
He framed a bill with remarkable precision, and carried
it through its various stages up to its final passage with
surprising speed and skill. It has been said that more
than half the legislation in Congress during the civil
war was done by Massachusetts, and certainly enough
of that by the military senator to entitle him to a grand
historic position in the annals of the nation.

As a writer, Mr. Wilson's style is characterized by
perspicuity, force, and dignity. His figures, when they
do occur, are striking ; his quotations from the poets,
apt and pertinent ; his pictures, strongly drawn, and
sharp in outline. He had no turn for wit or humor:
indeed, the subjects on which he wrote do not demand
it. His periods are, in general, well rounded and harmonious. His last work is his best ; and this, in point
of diction, as well as in respect to accuracy of statement,
cogency of reasoning, scope of vision, and unity of construction, will rank with the writings of the best historians of America.

As a man, Mr. Wilson was intensely earnest and sincere. He had a wonderfully quick conception of what

was just and right: he dared to act on his convictions, and this was one secret of his power. He had no fear of his antagonist: he never cowered in front of danger. In every trying crisis of his life, he stood a hero, undaunted and unterrified. At the first National Republican Convention in Philadelphia, when an assault was anticipated, he came upon the "platform with a stout hickory cane in his hand, and, after the protracted applause which greeted him had subsided, commenced very deliberately and emphatically as follows: 'I learn that there is much apprehension existing here and at the North in regard to the peril which your senators and representatives are supposed to be in at the national capital, in consequence of their non-combative principles. Gentlemen, I beg you to dismiss your fears. Your public servants there have made up their minds, and know how to defend their persons, whenever, however, by whomsoever, attacked.' A storm of the wildest cheers told how accurately the senator had read the temper of the convention."

So when a musket-ball was fired into the assembly which he was addressing in New Orleans, and struck into the ceiling near his head, he manifested no emotion, but proceeded with his address as steadily as if nothing had occurred.

He was large-hearted, self-sacrificing, and liberal to a fault. He was a friend of the friendless, and a compassionate comforter of the poor and needy. Here is a single instance among thousands that could be cited. An Irish boy was killed by the cars, while his mother, for drunkenness, was an inmate of the House of Correction. She had an intense desire to see her son's remains; but no one could remove her. Mr. Wilson then

38*

went himself to Cambridge, gave bonds for her return, took her in the cars to Natick, gave her his arm, and escorted her to the house, and, when the funeral services were over, went back with her to the prison. Though having it in his power to hoard millions, he lived and died comparatively poor. He was ever in liveliest sympathy with the working-classes. From them he sprang; with them he fought the battle for free labor; and for their rights, their social, moral, and intellectual elevation, he spent with cheerful heart his time, his money, and his mental energies. He believed in human progress, and in the power of the people to perpetuate republican institutions. The means for doing this he clearly indicated, in an able article on " The New Departure of the Republican Party," in " The Atlantic Monthly," January, 1871, to be the education and unification of the people. He saw with hopeful eye the prospective grandeur of the United States, yet felt, that, to attain it, we must have a nobler educational system, a broader knowledge of the principles of our civil and political institutions, a better understanding, and a closer application of the teachings of Christianity to our public, social, and private life.

He was, therefore, the earnest friend of the public school, the university, the pulpit, and the press. Profoundly acquainted with the genius and the spirit of this nation, from the workshop to the halls of Congress, he labored wisely and persistently to make the nation what it is : hence his opinions are entitled to profound respect. Among the self-made men of the times, he stood pre-eminent as a man magnificently made. Though reared among the intemperate, his tongue was never contaminated by the touch of alcohol ·

though wielding immense patronage, his palm was never stained by bribery; though breathing for so many years the infected atmosphere of politics, his heart still beat fresh and free for human sorrow ; though rising by indomitable energy and integrity from a low position to the vice-presidency of the United States, his spirit remained subdued and humble. His life, so marked by manly struggle, earnest words, and noble deeds, is a model for the young men of America to hold before them for encouragement and imitation. It was developed and guided by the solid principles of a Book which he received in childhood, and which sustained him in his conflict with the world, and gave him full assurance, when the scenes of earth were fading, of a more resplendent life to come : hence above the statesman, patriot, and historian, he stood, and will ever stand, before the world, as the devoted and aspiring CHRISTIAN.

It is not by any means desired to present him as a perfect man, nor to claim for him any thing more than is justly due ; but so far as those grand elements which form true manhood go, so far as a living sympathy with man as man, so far as a life unselfishly devoted to the sons of toil and suffering, so far as the daily exemplification of the ennobling principles of Christianity, may be regarded, he made a record that will hold its brightness when the memories of men more brilliant in exterior graces shall have passed into oblivion. He was an intensely practical and earnest working-man; but work finds little room for outward graces: yet the times demanded working-men strong and fearless. He had the will to work ; and, as we said in the beginning, WORKERS WIN.

From boyhood, he sought wisdom as most men seek gain. He stood firm for human right in defiance of power. He bore an honorable part in guiding this nation through the perils of war, through the equal perils attending peace. He spent his life in giving liberty to the slave, and in opening this continent to free labor. He evinced an integrity which no temptation could corrupt, no threat intimidate, no danger shake; a confidence in God, which triumphed over death itself: and, having so lived and died, he deserves well of his country. His character, as a star of serene, benignant ray, will shine the brighter as men shall examine it the more.

www.ingramcontent.com/pod-product-compliance
Lightning Source LLC
Chambersburg PA
CBHW022024110726
47901CB00006B/1650